Also by Nalini Singh from Gollancz:

Archangel's Storm

Nalini Singh

First published in Great Britain in 2012 by
Gollancz
An imprint of the Orion Publishing Group
Orion House, 5 Upper St Martin's Lane, London
WC2H 9EA
An Hachette UK Company

1 3 5 7 9 10 8 6 4 2

A CIP catalogue record for this book is available
from the British Library

ISBN 978 0 575 11949 9

Printed in Great Britain by Clays Ltd, St Ives plc

The Orion Publishing Group's policy is to use papers
that are natural, renewable and recyclable products
and made from wood grown in sustainable forests.
The logging and manufacturing processes are expected
to conform to the environmental regulations of the

Hush

Jason didn't know how long he'd been hiding in the dark place in the ground where his mother had put him, telling him to "hush." He'd waited so long, hadn't even crawled out when his stomach hurt with hunger, but she hadn't returned as she'd promised, and his wings were cramped and hurting from the small space, his face wet with tears.

She knew he hated the dark. Why had she put him in the dark?

The sticky dampness that had dripped through the floor-boards above, it covered him, the taste of it thick and ripe in the air. The smell made him nauseous, and he knew he couldn't stay here any longer, even if his mother was disappointed by his disobedience. Stretching his stiff limbs as far as he was able in the confined space, his wings still crumpled, he pushed up on the trapdoor, but it wouldn't budge.

He didn't cry out, had learned to never ever cry out.

"You mustn't make a sound, Jason. Promise me."

Digging his feet into the earth, he pushed and pushed and pushed until a tiny crack of smudgy light appeared at the edge of the door, the handwoven mat above thin enough not to blot out the sunshine. Whatever was blocking the trapdoor was heavy, but he was able to wedge his fingers under the lip of the door, touch the mat he'd helped his mother weave after they'd collected the leaves from the flax bushes. It felt rough against his knuckles as he pushed his hand through to the wrist, and the trapdoor hurt when it came down on that wrist, but he knew his bones wouldn't break—his mother had told him he was a strong immortal, that he'd already grown deeper into his power than she had by the time of her hundredth birthday.

"So strong, my baby boy. The best of both of us."

He didn't know how long it took to wedge his other hand under the lip of the trapdoor, to twist his body around in the hole, the skin rubbing off his wrists, until he was holding the edge and pushing it up. He just knew he didn't stop until he shoved hard enough to slide off the blockage, the mat sliding away with it. The door came open with a dull thud, as if it had landed on something soft. Chest heaving and arms sore, he had to wait to attempt to climb out, and even then, his hands slipped, slick with the blood from his torn-up wrists.

Rubbing them on his pants, he gripped the edge again . . . and sunlight from the sky-window hit his hands.

He froze, remembering the dark and viscous liquid that had dripped onto him while he was trapped in the hole. Crusted and dried and flaky, it had turned into a kind of rust on his skin. Just rust, he tried to think, just rust, but he could no longer fool himself as he had in the dark. It was blood that covered his hands, his hair, his face, stiffened the black of his wings. It was blood that had seeped through the mat and the wooden slats below, to the special hidey-hole his mother had made for him. It was blood that clogged his nostrils with iron as he gasped in ragged breaths.

It was blood that had spilled like water after the screams went quiet.

"No matter what you hear, you mustn't make a sound. Promise me, Jason. Promise!"

Trembling, he forced himself to stop looking at the rust

that wasn't rust, and pulled himself out of the hole, closing the trapdoor with careful hands—and averted eyes—so it wouldn't make a noise. And then he stood staring at the wall. He didn't want to turn and see what lay on the other side, what he'd pushed off the top of the trapdoor. But the wall was splattered with the rust that wasn't rust, too. Tiny bits of it had begun to flake off, baked by the hot sun pouring in through the sky-window.

Stomach all twisted and his heart a lump, he looked away from the wall and to the floor, but it was streaked with pale brown, his feet having made small prints on the polished wood. The dirt inside the hole hadn't been wet. Not until after.

After the screams went quiet.

He closed his eyes, but he could still smell the rust that wasn't rust.

And he knew he had to turn around.

Had to see.

1

Standing on velvet green grass still sparkling with dew, Jason watched Dmitri cup the face of the hunter he had just made his wife, the dawn sunlight kissing her skin, lighting up eyes that saw only the man in front of her.

The grounds of the archangel Raphael's home, Jason thought, the Hudson rushing past beyond the cliffs and a mass of fragrant roses in full bloom climbing the walls of the house itself, had seen centuries pass, but a scene such as this, they had never witnessed and perhaps never would again. A scene in which one of the most powerful vampires in the world took a Guild hunter for his bride.

That Honor loved Dmitri was in no doubt. It didn't take a spymaster to read the incandescent joy in her every breath, her skin radiant with it. What startled Jason was the potent emotion he saw in the eyes of a vampire who had been a pitiless blade for all the centuries Jason had known him.

Cruelty came easily to Dmitri, maybe too easily in recent times. The vampire was near to a thousand years old and jaded with it, blood and death no longer enough to cause him to break his stride, much less shock. Jason had seen

Dmitri wield his scimitar on the field of battle to take off invaders' heads, glory in the spray of their dying blood, and he had seen Dmitri seduce women with sensual elegance and a cold heart simply to amuse himself.

Yet the man who touched Honor, who claimed her lips in a kiss of possession, had a tenderness about him that was as dangerous as it was gentle. And Jason comprehended that Dmitri would be a brutal weapon against anyone who dared harm his wife, that the darkness in him had not been tempered but merely leashed.

"He cannot deal with the Cadre if he is leashed," he said to the woman who stood next to him, a hunter with wings of midnight and dawn. Feathers of a rich, silken blue flowed from the pure black at the inner curve of her wings, to segue into a softer indigo and the ephemeral shades visible in the skies when day broke, before becoming a brilliant white-gold at the primaries.

Elena was Raphael's consort, and Raphael was Jason's liege. Perhaps that was why he felt an unexpected kind of ease with her. Or it might be that she was a stranger in the land of immortals, searching for a path that would take her into the centuries to come, as he once had. Or perhaps it was that, unbeknownst to Elena, they were linked by a far bleaker tie, a tie that spoke of mothers and blood.

Iron rich liquid matting his hair, soaking into his tunic, sticky on his arms.

Elena looked up, shook her head, the startling near-white of her hair pinned back in an elegant twist, her body clothed in a simple ankle-length gown of a blue the shade of a pristine high-mountain lake. Her only ornamentation came in the form of the small amber hoops she always wore as an outward sign of her commitment to Raphael. "Don't you see, Jason?" she said as the bridal couple broke a kiss that had more than one sigh rippling through the crisp morning air. "He is only this Dmitri for Honor." She joined in the clapping and cheering when Honor and Dmitri turned to the assembled guests, well-wishers moving forward to congratulate them.

Having spoken to Dmitri before the ceremony, Jason waited for the crowd to thin. Elena, too, held her place, giving others a chance to speak to the newly wedded couple. As he'd been with Dmitri before the ceremony—alongside Raphael, Illium, and Venom—Elena had been with Honor, the archangel and his consort having turned over a suite in their home to the bride's party. That party was composed of hunters, all certainly with a weapon or two hidden beneath the sleek, elegant clothes they wore for the wedding.

Blue flickered at the edges of his vision, and he turned to see Illium spread his wings for a hunter who had made the request. Clad in the same formal black worn by the groom as well as Raphael and the others of the Seven here today, he had a flirtatious smile on his face. The smile was real as far as it went, but then, it did not go far. Jason had seen Illium love until his heart broke, and he had seen the angel mourn until there was no light in those eyes of molten gold.

"I understand," he said to Elena when she glanced back at him, reminded once again of the capacity others had for endless nuances of emotion. Jason had watched mortals and immortals alike for centuries, was able to glean even the most subtle changes in their emotional equilibrium, for no man could be a spymaster without that capability. Yet, through all that time, he had never been able to feel as they did. It was as if life skimmed across the surface of him, leaving his heart and his soul untouched.

"You are the perfect spymaster. An intelligent, gifted phantom unaffected by anything he sees."

It was Lijuan who had said those words to him, four hundred years ago. The oldest of the archangels had also made him an offer—riches and women trained in the sensual arts, men if that was what he desired—if he would change his allegiance, put himself in her service. Except Jason had already earned and created enough wealth for a hundred immortal lifetimes. As for the other—when Jason wanted a woman, he had a woman. He had no need for anyone to act his procurer.

Elena's wing shimmered lightly over his as she stretched

a little, and he didn't shift away to break the fleeting contact. In many ways, he was the opposite of Aodhan, the angel so broken, he couldn't bear the slightest touch. Jason, by contrast, sometimes only felt real and not the phantom Lijuan had named him if he had the pressure of another's skin, another's wing against his own. It was as if all those years, *decades*, when he hadn't felt the touch of another sentient being had created a thirst in him that could never be assuaged.

A sybarite drunk on sensation, that was what he might have become, but for the fact that those years of excruciating, endless aloneness had left him with other scars—scars that led him to embrace the very shadows he'd hated as a child, scars that meant he meted out trust with a careful hand. Regardless of his need, Jason allowed very few people to touch him outside of the bedroom; for the touch of a friend, it was a far different thing than the caress of a lover taken in the dark of night and left behind when morning broke.

"It was a beautiful wedding, wasn't it?" Elena said, her eyes soft in the way women's often were at such things.

"Do you wish for one?" Marriage was thought of as a mortal thing, but as today showed, some immortals continued to embrace it—Dmitri had been most insistent on the ceremony.

Startled laughter from Elena. "Raphael and I married above the wreckage of New York, when he fell with me in his arms."

Raphael, too, Jason thought, was a different man with his consort, this mortal woman become an angel. Such a weak angel in terms of power, her immortality a flickering flame, and yet she had a strength that spoke to the survivor in him. So he'd taught her how to remain unseen in the sky, watched her push her body to merciless extremes in an effort to achieve a vertical takeoff so soon after her becoming, and listened for threats to her life.

For Elena was Raphael's biggest weakness.

A tiny giggle, a mischief-eyed little girl running to Elena on wobbling legs, curls of bronze-threaded black captured at the sides of her head with ribbons of summer orange. Smiling in unhidden delight, Elena bent to pick up the child in her arms. "Hello, Zoe, Warrior Goddess in Training." A kiss on one plump cheek, Zoe's flower girl dress a confection of lace over Elena's arm. "Did you give your mom the slip?"

Jason met the child's direct gaze as she nodded, saw that she held a silver-edged feather of distinctive blue in a careful fist. The daughter of the Guild Director stared at his wings for a moment before whispering something in Elena's ear. Jason heard what she said, understood none of it, her language that of very small children.

Clearly not at the same disadvantage, Elena glanced at him, silver-gray eyes shining with laughter. "The imp's coveting more of your feathers for her collection, Jason. I'd be careful." She was distracted a second later by a tall man with long black hair tied neatly at the nape of his neck, his cheekbones sharp against copper-gold skin.

Ransom Winterwolf.

Hunter.

It was strange to see so many of the Guild on the grounds of Raphael's home. Located in the Angel Enclave, on the other side of the river from the gleaming glass and metal of Manhattan, it was undoubtedly elegant, but Jason knew the Sire had offered Dmitri far more stunning locations in which to make Honor his bride. However, the leader of the Seven had been adamant.

"Daybreak," he'd said a bare three hours before sunrise. "We marry at daybreak."

In those three hours, Elena and the Guild Director had managed to alert every hunter in the New York area who wasn't on assignment and was within traveling distance, while Jason, Illium, and Venom stood for the rest of the Seven. Naasir, Galen, and Aodhan had been told, had all three spoken with Dmitri before the wedding.

United in their loyalty to Raphael—and to each other— the Seven had forged bonds that were unbreakable, but even had there been more time, it was impossible for all of them to ever be in one place at one time. To keep the balance of power in the world, Raphael needed to maintain a presence in the Refuge and in New York, and now, in the lost city of Amanat, home to the Ancient who was Raphael's mother.

That three of them stood here to witness Dmitri's wedding, it was an unexpected gift. There were other invited guests of course—the proud staff who ran Raphael's home; a number of men and women who worked directly under Dmitri at the Tower, and whose loyalty belonged as much to the vampire as it did to Raphael; two mortal policemen who were considered part of the Guild family. The well-respected man who'd officiated the ceremony belonged to that family, too, having headed the Guild before passing on the mantle.

Raphael himself had stood at Dmitri's side during the ceremony, the friendship between the two men old enough, deep enough, that it was the archangel who had played the second this day. Jason didn't know of any other such friendships among those who served the Cadre of Ten, the archangels who ruled the world, but he knew this one had endured centuries, through anger and war and even a short defection by Dmitri to Neha's territory. That hadn't lasted long, and now Dmitri's lips curved at something Raphael said.

While the vampire was dressed in a crisp black-on-black suit, his bride wore a gown of deep, vibrant green that caressed and embraced her curves before rippling in a liquid waterfall to the dew-laden grass, the fabric arranged cleverly at her left hip to give the illusion of waves. When her gaze landed on Jason, she smiled and came toward him, halting at the border of the invisible space that separated him from the world, one hand holding the wildflower bouquet Elena had created using the blooms in her greenhouse.

"Thank you," she said, her happiness so luminous, it outshone the diamonds at her throat, diamonds Jason had seen Dmitri buy as rough stones three centuries ago.

It had taken the vampire another hundred years to get them finely cut and set into a necklace of exquisite beauty, until the stones appeared to be droplets of captured starfire.

"Who will you gift it to?" Jason had asked at the time.

Dmitri's response had been a sardonic twist of his mouth, the hardness in his eyes akin to the gems he held. "A woman whose spirit dazzles brighter than these stones."

The necklace had graced none but the honey-skinned neck it now encircled.

"For this amazing dream of a dress," Honor continued, stroking her hand down the fabric. "I don't know how you found it so early in the morning. It fits like it was made for me."

"No thanks are necessary." So much of life he spent on the sidelines—many times out of choice, sometimes because he didn't know how to belong—but he'd needed to be a part of this day when a man he respected, and who was as close a friend as he was capable of having, claimed this woman for his own.

"Jason can find anything," Dmitri said, walking over to slide his arm around Honor's waist. "The winds talk to him, tell him where to go."

Honor laughed, husky and warm, and then she was being embraced by Elena, the hunter's wings iridescent in the white light of morning. Stepping a little to the right, Jason met Dmitri's gaze. The vampire shrugged, the words unspoken but not unheard.

No one will ever believe it.

No, Jason thought, no one would. Even he had thought himself mad when he was a boy on the verge of adulthood. It had taken reading Jessamy's history books once he arrived at the angelic stronghold that was the Refuge to understand he'd inherited his mother's "ear," her ability to sense things happening hundreds of miles away, across oceans and beyond mountains. It was how she'd always had stories to tell him about people in the Refuge, though they lived on an isolated atoll surrounded by the shimmering blue of the Pacific.

"I will write this story down for you, Jason. You must practice your reading."

He had. Over and over, until the parchment disintegrated,

he'd read those stories and the others in the books in the house. Then he'd copied the words out on wood, on flax, in the sand, forcing himself to remember that he was a person, that he should know how to read. It had worked . . . for a while.

"I'm happy for you, Dmitri," he said now, allowing the ghosts of the past to fade into the background. "This is my gift to you and your bride."

As Dmitri glanced down at the small note card Jason passed across, Honor's second—a long-legged hunter who had unique gifts of her own—came to join Elena and Honor, and the women laughed and began to talk all at once.

"A safe place," Jason said when Dmitri looked up from reading the address on the card, the sun glinting off the simple gold band he wore on the ring finger of his left hand. "Where no one will find you."

Understanding whispered across the sensual lines of Dmitri's face. Moving a small distance away from the women, he said, "I shouldn't be surprised at what you know, and yet I am." He slid the card away. "How certain are you of the security?"

"The house is mine, and no one has found it in two hundred years." Hidden in the dense forests of an otherwise uninhabited mountain, it could only be reached via a very specific route that he now shared with Dmitri, mind to mind. *Even aerial entry is impossible unless the angel in question knows how to find a particular small clearing.* He gave Dmitri the coordinates. *Without that, severe damage to the wings as a result of the thick canopy—and the safeguards hidden within—is a distinct possibility.*

Dmitri's eyes gleamed. *Good.* His next words were spoken aloud. "I didn't know you had another home in this country."

"I don't." He had houses he used when needed, but home was a concept that had no meaning to him, though Dmitri likely assumed he considered his apartment at New York's Archangel Tower home. "You'll be safe there, and you can be private." Honor's transformation from human to vampire would take time, and while Jason knew Dmitri would ensure she navigated it in a deep sleep, safe from any suffering, he also knew the other man would not leave her side during the process. "There is no need to take a guard unit."

"I wouldn't trust those words coming from anyone's mouth but yours," Dmitri said, his face angled toward Honor. "I don't know when we'll use your gift. I have her promise . . . but I will not rush her on this."

"You want to."

"Yes." Unvarnished ruthlessness. "But you see, Jason, it appears I have a fatal weakness when it comes to Honor—even should she change her mind and decide to remain mortal, I can't force her and still live with myself."

Jason said nothing as Dmitri walked back to his wife, who looked up to offer him a smile Jason had seen her share with no other. Her friends moved away to give husband and wife a moment of privacy, but everyone continued to linger on the luxuriant green of the lawn, the birdsong a delicate accompaniment to the murmur of conversation. Champagne was sipped, greetings exchanged, friendships renewed in the glow of the joy that came off Honor and Dmitri.

Unlike the others, Jason felt exposed out here in the sunlight, the unrelieved black of his wings a target, but he didn't give in to the compulsion to fly up high above the cloud layer, where no one could see him. A minute later, when the winds began to whisper, he listened.

A single word. A name.

Eris.

The only significant Eris that Jason knew of was husband to Neha, the three-thousand-year-old archangel, the sole member of the Cadre who had chosen to follow the mortal ceremony of binding. Eris was also her consort, but he hadn't been seen in public for some three hundred years. Many believed him dead; however, Jason knew the male lived, imprisoned in a palace inside Neha's sprawling fort. Except for when he'd attempted to escape early on in his captivity, he had not been physically harmed.

Neha loved Eris too much to hurt him.

It was also why she hated him so violently for his betrayal. *Eris.*

Sliding into the shadows of the trees that edged Raphael's property, a welcome respite from the light, Jason took out his cell phone. In earlier centuries, even with his considerable mental abilities, it had taken him days to communicate with his men and women, weeks to gather a single piece of information. Technology made it so much simpler—unlike some angels of old, and though his chosen weapon remained a sword, Jason did not abhor the modern world.

Now, he saw that he had a number of missed calls that must've come in during the ceremony, while his phone had been in silent mode. All were from Samira—she was a servant with clearance to work in Neha's private quarters and technically his highest-ranking spy in the other archangel's court, though Jason had his doubts about her continued efficacy. "Samira," he said when the call was answered. "What has happened?"

"Eris is dead." A hushed whisper. "Murdered inside his palace."

"When?"

"I don't know, but he was found an hour ago. Neha has not left the body. Mahiya is by her side."

Jason had never spoken to Mahiya, but having done a subtle investigation when Neha first adopted her just over three centuries ago, he knew the princess was of Neha's bloodline. That relationship was accepted knowledge, but the facts behind it had long been buried. Many in Neha's own court *chose* not to remember, not to see the truth—that Mahiya had been born of Nivriti, sister to Neha and dead as long as her child had been alive.

No terrible secret that . . . except if you knew the name of Mahiya's father.

Eris.

2

Though Mahiya was the fruit of Eris and Nivriti's forbidden relationship, she was, to all outward appearances, treated as a beloved princess by her aunt, the title a courtesy to elucidate her status as kin to Neha. "Is there anything else?"

Samira's breathing went very quiet for a minute, and Jason waited without interruptions or demands, knowing she had to be concerned about being overheard. "Neha is half insane," she said at last. "I'm worried she'll release her power."

Knowing as he did the depth of the archangel's emotions where her husband was concerned—she'd neither been able to forgive him his infidelity, nor set him free after centuries of confinement—Jason shared Samira's concern. And Neha was a being of immense power. If she gave voice to her agony, she could lay waste to cities, and it was near certain she would aim her rage toward those she held responsible for another terrible pain—the execution of her daughter, Anoushka.

Raphael had delivered the final blow that reduced Neha's daughter to dust.

"Tell me the instant she makes a move."

Hanging up, he looked out over the grounds to see the bridal party and guests walking inside for the no doubt exquisite breakfast prepared by the proud household staff, under the butler Montgomery's dignified guidance. Raphael's wings glittered in the sunlight, the gold filaments striking against the white. *Sire.*

Raphael didn't pause, his expression giving nothing away. *What is it, Jason?*

Eris is dead. Murdered. He knew Raphael had seen Eris court Neha, win her, and Raphael understood the twisted emotions that had tied the two together.

The archangel's reply was swift. *Meet me in the study.*

Two minutes later, when Jason slipped into the study through the French doors that opened out onto the lawn, he did so with a stealth that meant no one would've seen him, though the sun rose higher on the horizon with every breath. That was as it should be—it was his job to be unseen, unheard, a shadow among shadows. After six centuries, his status as Raphael's spymaster was no secret when it came to the oldest immortals, though that knowledge gained them nothing and had even less impact on Jason's activities. While people focused on him, his operatives quietly found places in courts and towers across the world.

Raphael entered the room at that moment, closing the door behind him. "Neha was already on the edge of madness after Anoushka's execution." The archangel's tone was unforgiving in its honesty. "This may well push her over."

Jason had seen other archangels lose fatal control, had walked through devastated cities full of rotting corpses, watched an entire country fall into a dark age in which all hope was extinguished, children's eyes dull with despair. Even if Neha chose a target outside Raphael's territory, the world could not suffer such devastation so soon after the destruction of Beijing without breaking—and regardless, the ensuing archangelic war would engulf them all.

His phone purred discreetly at that instant. Answering it, he heard Samira say, "She's left the body—her eyes are of madness."

"Get her to the room where she has her communications suite."

"Jason, she won't see reason."

"You must find a way." Every one of his operatives was of cutting intelligence, able to think on his or her feet. "Then get out of the fort and Neha's territory."

Samira took a deep breath. "I might be able to do it if I stretch the truth and say the Cadre wishes to speak to her."

"Do not linger, Samira." In this mood, Neha *would* kill her.

"I'll leave as soon as the words are spoken."

Hanging up, he looked at Raphael. "If we make the call now, we have a chance of catching her before she can no longer see or hear through the rage."

"I can divert her," Raphael responded, "but it could involve your presence in her territory."

"I'll go." While the risk to Samira was now too high, Jason was far stronger, knew he garnered a certain respect from Neha.

Raphael nodded and waited for Jason to retreat out of view before he input the call on the large screen in one corner of the study, for Raphael, too, understood the value of technology. The answer took so long in coming, Jason thought Samira must've failed in her task. But the screen cleared at long last to show Neha as he'd never before seen her.

The Archangel of India was always elegant, always graceful.

Now, her black hair hung matted and snarled around her face, as if she'd been pulling at it; streaks of blood slashed across her skin and soaked into the marigold yellow of her silk sari. "Raphael," she said, her voice so calm it was lethal. "You circle like a vulture even as Eris's lifeblood stains my hands."

Raphael's response was gentle. "I have never been that, Neha."

A faint smile that was of the reptile that gave Neha her name as the Queen of Snakes. "No, perhaps not. So, do you offer your commiseration?" An almost bored statement, her lashes lowered to shield the wild rage that boiled within.

"I offer my help."

Neha raised a single regal eyebrow. "Unless you have been keeping secrets, I think bringing Eris back to life is beyond your capability. Lijuan herself could not achieve that."

Jason wondered if Neha had considered consigning her once-husband to the horror of being one of Lijuan's "reborn," a shambling, mindless monster fed of human flesh, and couldn't immediately discount the idea. That only added to the urgency of the situation, because if Neha and Lijuan joined forces, the world would drown in blood and death and screaming terror.

"No," Raphael said in response to Neha's taunt. "Eris was murdered inside your fort, thus, you cannot trust anyone within. I have someone with the skill to unearth the murderer for you."

The pause was longer this time, the insanity in Neha's eyes replaced in slow degrees by cold, hard reason. "That black shadow of yours? The rescued pup?"

Jason felt no insult, though the latter description was inaccurate. No one had rescued him.

Raphael's response, too, was unruffled, the flawless blue of his eyes calm as a glacial lake. "Jason's skill is beyond dispute."

"He is also your spymaster." Raising a bloody hand, she stared at it, her voice altering without warning to a shaken whisper. "Eris bled so much—I did not know he had that much in him."

"I sorrow for you, Neha. He was your husband and your consort." It was a solemn statement, one archangel to another.

"Yes." The madness returned, swirling and clawing. "He was also father to the child you helped murder," she hissed, her eyes changing in a way that was too quick for Jason to truly see before they returned to normal, but that put him in mind of her serpents once more.

Raphael didn't back down under the venomous attack, didn't remind Neha that Anoushka had signed her death warrant when she harmed a child in the quest for power. "You wish to do violence, that much is clear," he said, "but rather than lashing out indiscriminately, would it not be more satisfying to torture the one responsible?"

Neha turned away from the camera to pick up what appeared to be a juvenile python, settle it around her neck. Stroking the creature like it was a cat, she seated herself in a chair of a pale wood carved with infinite patience, polished and varnished until it gleamed like a jewel. "You think me mad," she said as the snake raised its head, tasted the air with its tongue.

"I think you are grieving. And I think this was a cowardly act."

A lazy blink, fingers pausing on the python's sleek body. "Do you?"

"Eris was not powerful. Beautiful in a way men are rarely beautiful but with little personal strength. This was done to hurt and spite you."

"My poor Eris." Another lingering caress. "You are right. I cannot trust anyone within the fort until I know the identity of the assassin . . . but if your spymaster is to enter it, he must bind himself to me."

"That," Raphael said with a gentleness that took the sting out of the refusal, "I cannot allow, not even for you. He is one of my Seven."

"Would you protect him at the cost of thousands of lives?" Ice-cold and rational and manipulative, she was the Archangel of India in that moment.

"Loyalty is not so easily discarded a coat."

For some reason, that made Neha's lips curve in what seemed a near-genuine smile. "So attached to your men. Never have I been able to fault your fidelity." Her smile changed, became inscrutable. "Very well then, it must be Mahiya."

This time, it was Raphael who paused.

Eris's child with Nivriti, Jason reminded the archangel, for it wasn't a topic they'd had much cause to discuss. *She is now just over three hundred years old.*

"You think to compare so young an angel to Jason?" Raphael said.

"No, indeed. Mahiya is a court trinket, nothing more." The archangel allowed the python to flick out its tongue at her bloody fingers. "But as I'm sure the pup has informed you, her lineage is of my family. A blood vow to her will suffice."

Raphael held Neha's gaze. "I will speak to him."

Neha inclined her head in regal acquiescence before ending the call.

Turning to Jason, his wings folded neatly to his back, Raphael said, "She's stable for the time being, but it's a temporary reprieve. The more she stews on the murder, the more dangerous she'll become."

"I'm willing to take the blood vow." It was an ancient custom, one rarely practiced by even the oldest of angelkind—in swearing a blood vow to Mahiya, Jason would become family in a sense and thus bound to protect that family's interests. The reason the custom had fallen out of favor was that it skated too close to crossing the line into forced intimacy—for in the distant past, the blood vow had been used to seal the most private of relationships.

However, like all angelic laws and customs, the blood vow was a creation far more subtle than it appeared at first glance. While the ceremonial tie would stop no one with treacherous intentions, in *making* the invitation, Neha acknowledged the honor of Raphael and his Seven. If Jason then used his entrée into her court to seek and exploit any flaws in her defenses, it would be considered a declaration of war. And once the knowledge of his faithlessness spread, Jason would lose every bit of respect he had earned from the most powerful immortals.

That was no small thing, especially for a spymaster. Much of his information came to him via those immortals.

Worse, his people would be in far more danger—though they were the best, it was inevitable that some were unearthed during the course of their duties. Where once they might've been forgiven on the strength of the older angels' respect for Jason, they would now be executed as a sign of those very angels' displeasure at the breach of the blood vow.

Raphael's wings rustled as he resettled them, the only sign of his surprise at Jason's agreement with the archaic custom. "You do not need to," the archangel said. "The Cadre may be able to control her now that I have time enough to warn the others. And a blood vow places you at risk—should Neha judge that you have broken it, she can ask for an execution." He shook his head. "You know she agreed too readily to your presence in her territory. She wants you in her power, plans to use you in vengeance against me."

"Yes." Jason had seen the calculation in Neha's gaze, knew the Archangel of India understood what Raphael's Seven meant to him—if Neha could not reach Elena, could not harm Raphael's heart, she was fully capable of going after the next best thing. "But," he added, "while Neha may be driven by the need for retribution, she's also a creature of pride. For her to break the promise of safe passage implied by the blood vow stains her own honor—and notwithstanding what she says, that honor matters to her." It was all she had left.

"Are you willing to stake your life on that?"

"Yes." Jason had watched Neha for centuries, as he watched every member of the Cadre, so he knew that she wasn't an archangel who used a heavy hand when more subtle methods would suffice. "Neha is more apt to attempt to turn me against you or to entice me to change camps."

Raphael met his gaze. "It will be a dangerous game of patience and power."

"A short one." Jason already had his ideas about Eris's death. "We state the vow is to be considered fulfilled the instant I unearth the murderer." Neha would expect the stipulation. "There's nothing in the custom that bars me from continuing with my other duties, so long as I don't betray Neha for the duration."

Eyes inscrutable, Raphael said, "It remains a bad bargain . . . unless you want to get inside Neha's court for reasons of your own."

"There is something happening within," he acknowledged. "Samira was unable to get close to it—I'm near certain Neha knew she was one of mine." Permitting a certain level of spying, mostly so they could seed false information, was an amusing diversion to some of the archangels.

"The vow," he continued, "will get me deep inside the fort, and as I wish only to observe, not interfere in this other matter, I do not risk a breach of the vow." He wouldn't be able to use any of what he discovered, not unless he could verify the same information through another source, but it would at least confirm that he was on the right trail.

"A fine line."

"I can walk it."

Raphael's next words were pragmatic. "She will not give you free reign. This Mahiya is apt to be your shadow."

"It matters little." Jason was skilled at disappearing in the midst of a crowd, at remaining unseen even when he stood right in front of a person. "She's comparatively young, and to my knowledge, has never been beyond the borders of Neha's palaces." Surely schooled in the art of court intrigues, there was a high chance she was no "trinket"—but she couldn't hope to match a man who'd spent a lifetime learning how to become kin to the dark, until the night was his natural home.

"I've never tied your hands," Raphael said, "and I won't do so now. It's your choice." He frowned. "As for Mahiya—I recall you had doubts about the rumors of her paternity since the whispers of Eris's infidelity were never proven. Nivriti was also apparently executed for another crime months before the newborn child appeared at Neha's court. Why are you now so certain she is Eris's get?"

"She wears her lineage on her face." It was Mahiya's

highly distinctive eyes that gave away her parentage to anyone not blinded by fear of an archangel's wrath. "I've also
heard enough fragments from my spies over the centuries
to confirm the evidence of my sight."

Raphael's nod was thoughtful. "Neha has a reputation for
not harming children, mortal or immortal, so I can see her
adopting the child even in this circumstance." Glancing up,
he said, "I leave the choice to you, Jason. And who knows?
Perhaps this Mahiya will prove to be your downfall—they
say the intimacy of a blood vow is powerful indeed."

Jason said nothing, but they both knew it to be an impossible thing. Jason had never loved anyone after he dug a
grave under a tropical sun, no longer understood the emotion; the boy he'd once been was a faraway mirage in his
mind. The closest he came was in his loyalty to Raphael,
but he knew from watching Dmitri with his wife, Raphael
with Elena, Galen with Jessamy, and long ago, Illium with
his mortal, that it was not the same thing at all. "I'll leave
within the hour."

"Remember," Raphael said in a quiet tone that cut
through the air like a blade, "she is not only the Queen of
Snakes, but the Queen of Poisons."

And Jason was about to walk into her lair.

3

She wears my ring.

Dmitri watched Honor's face light up as she laughed at something her clever friend Ashwini had whispered to her. With her sly wit and eyes that saw too much, the other hunter had been a good friend to Honor, and so Dmitri would've been inclined to like her, even if she hadn't provided him with a source of amusement—the game of cat and mouse she and Janvier had played for over two years was as inexplicable as it was fascinating.

Honor's eyes turned in his direction, her face holding an unasked question.

"I'm looking at my wife," he murmured for her ears only, running his fingers over her nape as he told himself he really should behave since they were in public. "My beautiful wife, whom I'd like to peel out of her dress and set naked on my lap so I can do debauched things to her sexy body." He never had been much good at behaving.

A faint shiver. "You shouldn't be let out to torment women."

Smiling with a slow deliberation that brought slumberous

heat into those eyes of haunting green, he leaned in close, his next words a purr against the shell of her ear. "I only plan to torment one woman for the rest of eternity."

Her pulse thudded in her throat, the call of her blood an erotic siren song. He drew in a deep breath, took her scent within, but he wasn't about to rush. Not today. "Shall I tell you what I intend to do to you for your wedding night gift?" He wrapped her up in tendrils of chocolate and a sensual promise rich and decadent.

"No." It was a laughing refusal, her husky voice entangling him in chains he had no intention of ever breaking. "Or I'll tell you what I'm wearing under this dress."

He felt like stretching in pleasure, as if he were a great cat that had been stroked, her laughter as precious to him as the rarest of gemstones. About to respond, he caught something out of the corner of his eye, shifted to see Jason walk into the room. "I think Jason has come to say his good-byes."

He rose to his feet. "You're leaving?" he said aloud as the black-winged angel stopped by the table. *What has happened?*

"Yes, I'm afraid I can stay no longer." *Eris is dead. I must head to Neha's territory.*

When Jason lifted his forearm, Dmitri clasped it in the way of the warriors they had been in battle together. "I'll see you when you return." *I will remain in contact.*

Jason's hand tightened on his arm before falling away. "Enjoy your time away." *I have it under control, and you have a wife who will not be pleased by a husband tied forever to his work.*

Dmitri glanced at Honor, his lips shaping into a faint smile. *My wife is a hunter and far more likely to join me in riding to your rescue should you need it.* Pausing, he added a personal message for Neha, for before Anoushka, she had been a great lady, an archangel he was not ashamed to have once served.

I'll ensure she receives it. Jason inclined his head toward Honor. "I take my leave."

"I'm so glad you were able to attend." Honor's smile dazzled. "I'll see you again when we return to the city."

Jason left in a sweep of black wings seconds later, and Dmitri retook his seat by his wife . . . who leaned into him not long afterward, her voice a hushed whisper as she asked, "Are you going to tell me what's going on?"

Arm around her, he rubbed his thumb over the sensitive arch of her collarbone. "When we are alone," he murmured, body hardening at the idea of her warm and naked in his arms in their bed. "Come for a walk."

Honor gave him a narrow-eyed look. "So you can talk me into your Ferrari?"

"I like what you do to me in my Ferrari." Sultry and hotly feminine, she'd made him her slave the day she'd taken him with such lush confidence.

A slow, slow smile from the woman who owned him body and soul. "Maybe we should make a detour on our way back to the Tower after the reception."

He knew his eyes were gleaming, but he didn't care. Leaning forward, he captured her lips in a kiss that made the guests around them cheer. "A long detour." It was a promise.

4

Over fourteen hours of intense flight later, Jason used the night clouds to his advantage as he circled the stone and marble of the magnificent fortress perched on a high ridgeline. It was known simply as Archangel Fort, for it was where Neha made her home. Bathed in the light of a full moon that hadn't yet begun to wane, though morning lay only a few hours away, its defensive walls glowed not the amber gold they were under the sun's rays, but a pale, haunting silver.

Having stashed his small bag for later retrieval, he'd earlier flown down toward the dark mirror of a lake at the base of the fort, done a sweep over the slumbering city beyond. From the lower vantage point, the fort had appeared a mirage, a fantasy imagined.

A fitting throne for the archangel who was queen of this land.

Flaring out wings of ebony that absorbed the moonlight as they absorbed sunlight, he came to a silent, invisible landing in the shadows cast by one of the great gates that protected the fort, a gate big enough to dwarf an entire cavalry unit. Each gate was hidden from the previous and the next by the angles at which the fort had been built, cutting the sightline and providing no straight runs on which to build up speed that could be used to ram the next gate. As a defensive measure against a mounted attack, it was magnificent.

Flying enemies required further countermeasures, including the squadron of angels in the sky and the vampires armed with land-to-air weaponry on the ramparts. None of them had seen Jason. That was not to say they were useless—it was the rare guard who ever spotted a man who'd been designed to blend into the night. Jason was fairly certain he'd avoided detection by the satellite surveillance system, too, his ability turning him into an indistinct shadow dismissed by man and machine alike.

Rather than walking through the gate, he watched in motionless silence until he could predict the watch route and timing of the vampiric guards, then—taking advantage of a fleeting blind spot—flew up and over the gate to land on the edge of the geometrically patterned gardens on the third-level courtyard.

The fountain in the center sparkled in the moonlight that lit up the courtyard to luminous brightness. Neha's private palace, he knew, was to the left of his landing position, its marble walls inlaid with ancient motifs created from semiprecious stones. But that was not its most stunning feature—thousands of diamonds had been embedded into the walls, intertwined into the design, until the palace could glitter as hard as the stone itself . . . or shimmer with a fiery heart that awoke wonder in young and old.

"Of all the buildings I have seen in my lifetime, it is the Hira Mahal that steals my breath."

It had been Titus who'd said those words, and the warrior archangel was not a man given to poetry. Jason could understand the urge, for the Hira Mahal or Diamond Palace—also often referred to as the Palace of Jewels—was a work of art unlike any other. Now, rising from his low, crouched position, he once again timed his movements to avoid the guards and reached the glittering door of the palace without being seen.

The guard who opened it in response to his knock hissed in surprise and went for a weapon.

"I assume that is the spymaster," said a feminine voice from within, the language the principal dialect in this region. "Do come in, Jason."

Keeping the guard in his line of sight, Jason walked into the glimmering illusion of the palace to see the Queen of Poisons, of Snakes. Unlike when she'd spoken with Raphael, Neha was now the picture of grace where she sat on a thronelike chair, her body clothed in a sari of palest green rather than the stark white of mourning. She, like the rest of the room, shimmered with the candlelight bouncing off the endless cascade of faceted gemstones.

"Lady Neha." He swept down into a respectful bow that nonetheless made it clear he was no sycophant and never would be. He'd learned the elegant movement from Illium, and it was useful on the rare occasion when he had to make a public appearance in front of one of the Cadre.

"You surprise me."

Greeting complete, he met the penetrating brown of her gaze, conscious of the fine emerald-hued snake she wore as a living bracelet. "Did you expect a savage?" he asked in the same dialect, having long ago learned the dominant languages of the world—including variations used in the home territories of the Cadre. Secrets, after all, had no one language.

Lips painted a sedate blush curved. "You do give that impression." Rising from her heavily carved chair of black marble, the carvings inlaid with gold, she came down the three steps to a floor covered by a hand-knotted silk carpet the shade of sapphires under sunlight.

When he didn't offer her his arm, she raised an imperious eyebrow.

"I need both arms free to fight."

Neha's laugh was delicate . . . hiding a shrill note beneath. "So honest, but then that is a clever lie, is it not? A spymaster can never give everything away."

Jason said nothing, having no interest in playing this particular game.

"Come," she said with a gleaming smile that held the appreciation of an immortal who rarely lost a battle of wits and who had only shot her first volley, "it's time to meet the one to whom you will swear fealty in blood. All is in readiness for the ceremony."

Jason laid out his single condition as they walked. To his surprise, Neha not only made no demur to his stipulation as to the duration of the vow, she welcomed it.

"You are too dangerous a creature for Mahiya." An unreadable darkness in the archangel's tone. "The poor child will likely die of fright unless she knows she'll soon be free of the chains that bind her to you." She paid no heed to a large owl flying silent as a ghost just beyond the open outdoor passageway where they walked. "Mahiya is not capable of handling such a burden for long."

Again, Jason kept his silence. The princess had never struck him as weak, but he'd only ever caught the most fleeting glimpses of her, for she was no power in the court, not at the center of any intrigues, and thus of little interest to a spymaster. Yet he knew it could all be a clever subterfuge, Mahiya a well-hidden blade. It made little sense to charge a fragile "trinket" with keeping watch on the movements of an enemy spymaster.

On the other hand, Mahiya might have been the only available choice, the sole known direct descendant of the same ancient bloodline as Neha who was both alive and not bonded to a lover.

Even as he went over everything he knew of the princess, he took in the liveried and armed guards hidden behind fluted columns of red stone; the way modern lighting had been integrated to appear a seamless part of the centuries-old structure; the lithe loveliness of the ladies-in-waiting out for a night stroll who bowed as Neha led him not across the gardens, but up a level and into the fourth-level courtyard.

As the exquisite palace on the highest level was used only to house guests the caliber of the Cadre, and otherwise left empty but for the watch rotation, this was effectively the most remote section of the fort, the walls falling off steeply on either side. However, parts of it were newer than the rest of the structure, this level having been altered from its original design roughly three hundred years ago.

A pavilion, delicate columns holding up the roof, sat in the center of the courtyard. That much was unchanged, but gardens had been added around it in the shape of a single stylized flower, each of the "petals" planted with different blooms. A fountain created gentle music somewhere, but he couldn't immediately see it—then he realized the water was cascading down the raised sides of the pavilion to run into fine channels that kept the gardens healthy in spite of the desert climate in this part of Neha's territory.

Where once the entire courtyard had been surrounded by interconnected apartments, there were now two separate palaces—one on the side that faced the jagged terrain of the mountains and one that overlooked the city. The remaining two sides appeared to have been part of the older architecture. However, both sets of buildings now stood apart from the palaces, the apartments no longer interlinked.

The entire section was under heavy guard.

Those guards didn't bow as Neha passed, their absolute attention on their task. Sari whispering in the wind as she walked, Neha kept her wings scrupulously off the clean stone of the pathway that led to the lamp-lit pavilion, the otherwise open sides curtained with gauzy silks currently tied back to columns that reminded Jason of elongated vases, the arches above finely scalloped. A woman stood at the center of the pavilion, and she wore a sari that may have been palest pink, but appeared a creamy white in the soft light—as if she mourned where Neha didn't.

Jason already knew that her face was small and pointed, her body softly curved and of a height that would barely reach his breastbone, her eyes a light tawny brown so vivid against her honey-colored skin and black hair that they were the first things anyone noticed about her. The eyes of a lynx or a puma. Eris's eyes had been blue, but Eris's father possessed the same distinctive irises that marked Princess Mahiya as illegitimate.

However, no one in the world had Mahiya's wings—deep emerald and vivid cobalt with splashes of rich black, the wild spray akin to a peacock's fan. Except that somehow, Mahiya had managed to remain out of the limelight, until no one mentioned the princess with wings to rival a bird famed for its beauty when they spoke of the most stunning wings in the world.

She went into a graceful curtsy as Neha approached, bowing her neck to reveal the vulnerable nakedness of her nape, her hair parted down the centre and gathered into a simple knot at the back of her head. "My lady."

"Do try not to frighten her too much, Jason," Neha murmured, the fine filaments of cobalt in the primaries of her otherwise snow-white wings whispering of their blood tie. "She is rather . . . useful on occasion."

Jason nodded in greeting toward the woman who made broken razors slash through Neha's tone, received a curtsy as elegant, though not as deep as the one she'd given the archangel. However, she maintained her silence as Neha lifted a single finger and a turbaned vampire wearing the uniform of the guard appeared from behind one of the columns, a velvet-lined tray in his arms. The crimson fabric was home to a ceremonial knife, its hilt embedded with yellow sapphires.

Neha picked it up with long fingers clearly at home with the blade. "It's time."

The ceremony was an ancient one, the words Neha asked him to speak to Mahiya, and Mahiya to him, unchanged for millennia. Stripped of its ritual robes, the core of it was a promise of loyalty that did not challenge his deeper oath to Raphael, yet that bound him to keep faith with Mahiya and her blood for the duration of his task.

"I hold your vow," Mahiya said, speaking the closing words for this part of the rite. "Until the name of the traitor is known. It is done."

Neha smiled into the thick silence after Mahiya accepted their bargain. "Your neck, Jason."

"I think not," he said without blinking, and turned his arm to reveal his wrist. "Blood is blood."

"You do not trust me?" A silken question that dripped menace.

"I trust no one at my neck." He was powerful enough that he'd most likely survive a beheading, but that didn't mean he wanted to chance it.

The head falling from his blood-slick hands to thud onto the floor. "I'm sorry . . ."

When Neha's eyes remained ice-cold, he expected her to bleed him far more than necessary, but she made only the shallowest nick on his wrist, right above his pulse. As a droplet of blood welled onto his skin, she ordered Mahiya to angle her neck and made another cut above the beat of the other angel's pulse.

This last act was the final, and for many, the repugnant reason why the ceremony was no longer in favor. "Princess Mahiya," he said, stepping close enough to see the taut line of her jaw, her spine as rigid as the tendons in her neck.

A slight nod, permission for him to seal the vow with the most basic of acts.

Dipping his head, he flicked his tongue over the ruby red droplet that shivered against her dusky skin, the warm iron of it metallic against his tongue. He stepped back, held up his wrist.

Mahiya placed both of her hands under his wrist and lifted it to her lips. The touch of her lips on his skin, light as butterfly's wings. Lifting her head, she said, "The blood vow is sealed," her expression unreadable in its very lack of deep emotion. Except for that single betrayal of distaste during the sealing of the vow, it was as if they stood at a cocktail party, exchanging pleasantries, the effect was so curiously shallow.

Perhaps that was all there was to the princess, but Jason's every instinct whispered otherwise.

He turned to Neha, never losing his awareness of the enigmatic Mahiya. "Eris?"

Clapping her hands, she laughed. "Oh, what a thing to say directly after a primal act of blood." A reminder that in times lost to the mists of history such vows had been spoken between lovers, the blood exchanged an erotic kiss. "You truly are cold, Jason."

He'd been called that many times in his life, and it was a fact he didn't dispute, though deep within him burned a cauldron of black fire. "It's why I am here."

"Of course. Come."

When Mahiya went to drop behind him, Jason shook his head. "I will not have you at my back." She was an unknown, her threat level as yet a mystery. "Walk ahead of or beside me."

A flash of startling tawny brown, but she fell into step at his side . . . a fine, fine hum of tension across her shoulders. It was so subtly camouflaged, even Jason might not have caught it if he hadn't already been on alert for any sign of the woman behind the mask. Mahiya, it seemed, did not like having anyone at her back either. Unusual for a court "trinket," even more so for a princess who should've been used to a retinue.

Neha said nothing further until they reached the palace that overlooked the city, its wide doors guarded by two angels armed with swords and guns both. "Treat this investigation with the respect my consort deserves."

Understanding the archangel had no intention of accompanying them, Jason waited for her to take her leave before he entered the palace through the doors the guards pulled open, their eyes flat with suspicion. The scent of putrefaction hit him the instant he walked in, and he knew at once that Eris still lay within, in spite of the time it had taken Jason to reach the fort.

Neha's love for Eris had been such that she would never offer up his violated body as a spectacle, so this must've been a rational choice to preserve the scene. He hadn't expected it of her after the madness he'd seen in her eyes when she spoke to Raphael, and he should have—Neha was strong, not simply in power, but in mind, regardless of her recent losses. He would not forget that again.

Holding his wings tightly to his back in order to avoid any inadvertent contact with objects inside the palace, he said, "Where is Eris?" He could have followed the scent of decay to the body easily enough, but he needed to open a line of communication with the woman who stood silent by his side.

Mahiya was a mystery, and Jason did not like mysteries.

So he would solve her.

5

"This way." Mahiya began to walk, every cell in her body conscious of the black-winged, black-garbed angel keeping pace beside her . . . an angel who fascinated her. The same way a child might be fascinated by the gleaming edge of a blade, wanting to run a fingertip over the metal to see if it really was that sharp.

Such fascination always ended in blood.

Yet she couldn't stifle her reaction, for he was unlike anyone she had ever before met, a man who wore his sleek midnight hair in a neat queue and was unafraid of an archangel's anger. If the latter were not intriguing enough, he sported an intricate tribal tattoo on the left side of his face, the ink a rich black against the warm brown of his skin, the swirling curves of it telling a story she wanted to understand but knew instinctively he would not share.

That face itself was a mix of cultures, the Pacific and Europe entangled to create a masculine beauty that was as harsh as it was compelling.

Raphael's spymaster.

It was what Neha called him. As a description, it was

succinct, but it hid as much as it divulged. He was so silent that had she not been able to see him from the corner of her eye, she'd have thought herself alone—a man gifted at becoming a shadow, was Jason, able to navigate the dark secrets of the Cadre unseen and undetected.

However, he was nothing so simple as a spy who saw and reported. He was one of Raphael's Seven, that tight-knit band of angels and vampires Mahiya little understood. All she knew was that the seven incredibly strong men had *chosen* to put themselves in service to an archangel—and that their loyalty was reflected in Raphael's own.

"Such a power is Jason."

Neha had murmured those words after Jason agreed to come to the fort, agreed to swear a blood vow to Mahiya. It wasn't the only thing the archangel had said, her lips twisted into a smile that dripped poison.

"Raphael's Tower will be crippled when the spymaster changes his allegiance. And he will . . . for I can offer Jason something Raphael will never be able to match."

Mahiya didn't care about Neha's vengeful game playing. She cared only about the cold, practical contract that underlay the ceremony of the vow Jason had spoken, her bones filled with a chill determination to complete this task without dropping the mask of inoffensive grace that was her most powerful weapon. No one considered her a threat. Neither would this spymaster.

Reaching the gauzy curtains of amber and gold that fluttered in the archway leading into the high central core of the palace, she took the time to tie them to the sides before waving her hand inward.

Jason remained in place.

"I will not have you at my back."

Ignoring the prickling at her nape that warned her of lethal danger, she preceded him into the echoing central chamber that rose all the way to the roof. Her stomach threatened to revolt against the stink, but she brought her gag reflex under control through sheer grim determination and practice—Neha had left Mahiya in the palace to "keep Eris company" for hours after his murder.

"He was your father, after all. I give you time to say your farewells."

For once, Mahiya did not think it had been a conscious cruelty—Neha herself had returned to sit with the body until an hour prior to Jason's arrival, her fingers stroking Eris's hair, the deep mahogany streaked with lighter strands as a result of all the time Neha had recently allowed him to spend in the searing sunshine of the courtyard.

"He is a creature of the sun, born on a clifftop overlooking the Mediterranean."

However, this windowless, sunless room with its marble floor overlaid by a thick carpet in swirls of gold and amber had been the place where Eris spent most of his time. The chandelier overhead was a masterwork that glittered light across the entire expanse, made the carnelian in the walls glow with inner fire . . . and the crystallized blood on the floor sparkle with stomach-churning beauty.

That blood had dripped from a wide divan where Eris had so often mockingly "held court" when Mahiya came to him with a message. A glass of red wine spilled an ugly stain onto the swirling colors of the carpet, while a plate of fruit—exotic peaches and dark cherries from far off lands of cold and ice, figs and apricots from Neha's own plantations—sat half eaten.

Flies buzzed over the silver plate, but they weren't truly interested.

No, their attention was taken up by the rotting carcass of the man who lay broken half on, half off the divan, his wings spread out in a final dramatic display and his chest cracked open to exhibit a hollow body cavity. While the blood outside his body had crystallized into a brittle substance akin to shimmering pink rock salt, inside that hollow, it had hardened to the same dark, dark red as the cherries, evidence of the fact his body had attempted to repair itself and failed.

Death rubies.

The idea of wearing jewelry created from the blood of a dead angel revolted Mahiya, but it had been an accepted practice in times past, the gems worn as memento mori by the lovers of those angels who died in circumstances that led to the creation of the death rubies. Fitting that Eris should be beautiful in this way even in death—for in life he had been a man who was the embodiment of physical perfection, his skin shimmering gold, his eyes lapis lazuli blue.

Jason displayed no distaste at the sight of Eris's mutilated body, his breathing even as he examined the remains of her "father."

"Did I have the chance to strangle you in your crib, I would have done so in a heartbeat. Without you, she would've forgiven my transgression long ago." A wineglass smashing onto marble. *"Be careful when you sleep, girl. I have friends who may yet snap your neck for me."*

It was her most vivid memory of the man who had contributed his seed to her creation.

Ignoring the flies that buzzed around what remained of a man who had once been the toast of courts from ancient Greece to the Forbidden City, Jason leaned in close, making certain of his first impression that Eris's heart had been removed, as had all his other internal organs. He could see a pile of indeterminate decomposing material to the right, guessed they might be the hacked-up remains of the organs.

That his head was still attached to his neck was a surprise—though Eris was universally considered too weak to have been consort to an archangel, that weakness had stemmed from his character, rather than the raw power contained within his body. He was more than old and strong enough to have risen by now were his brain intact.

Jason examined what appeared to be dried blood under one of Eris's nostrils, the color near black, the substance clotted rather than crystalline. "Was a long needle found with the body?"

Mahiya shook her head, her expression devoid of the

sorrow and distress he might've expected from a woman standing by the body of her dead father. "Nothing has been taken from this palace since Neha discovered his body." A pause. "Do you wish me to search this room?"

"Yes." Bending as she began to do so, he put his hand under Eris's head and lifted, knocked on the bone with the knuckles of his free hand.

Mahiya paused in her search. "It sounds . . . hollow."

"His brain's been removed."

Sari held neatly off the blood-matted carpet, the princess returned needleless from her search and spoke words he most assuredly had not expected to hear from a woman dressed in softest pink, her every move speaking of elegant femininity. "How?" Determined curiosity leaked through her facade of distant politeness. "His head is unmolested."

Jason's interest in Mahiya grew deeper, more intense. "A hooked needle thrust into the brain through the nose," he said, describing a method used by the people of ancient Egypt as part of the mummification process. "That needle is then moved around until the brain is in a state that it can be extracted via the same route."

From the thick area of dried material directly below the head, the brain might well have been turned into soup, allowed to drip out of Eris's nose before he was turned back over and posed as he was now.

A small silence, and he wondered if he'd misjudged the internal strength of this princess raised in the hothouse that was the fort, but who watched him out of those eyes bright as a cat's with a steely intelligence that fit neither her quiet acquiescence to Neha's demands, nor the way she'd followed his own commands without argument.

Then she spoke, and he knew his instincts hadn't steered him wrong. Mahiya might not be an opponent strong enough to concern him, but she was no pampered princess he could ignore. "So"—a considering look—"whoever did this came well prepared, not only with the blade he or she used to carve up Eris, but with the hook, perhaps other tools as well."

"Including a garrote." Jason pointed out the mark on Eris's necrotic flesh, his sun golden skin now a home for creatures who fed on death. "It may have been the first attack." Enough to disable the angel, allow time for the murderer to inflict more debilitating injuries. Because though humans termed angelkind immortal, there was perhaps one *true* immortal in the world—Lijuan. The rest of them were simply harder to kill.

"He was tied up," Mahiya said, indicating the still-visible marks on Eris's wrists, the decay of his flesh having exposed bone. "For the skin to decay that fast—"

"Means the bindings had to have cut through to bone." It also explained the splatters of crystalline blood below where his wrists hung. "He was powerful enough to have snapped ordinary rope—this must've been infused with metal of some kind."

"Or maybe the killer used extra garrotes as ties?" Mahiya offered, a sudden hesitancy to her.

Jason wondered exactly what kind of life the princess had lived that she'd made the same dark intuitive leap he had even as he finished speaking. "Yes. Could Neha have untied him, gotten rid of the evidence?" The act of a woman who did not want her lover found bound and helpless.

But Mahiya shook her head. "No, she only entered the room half a minute ahead of me."

Which meant Eris had been left this way on purpose—displayed like a trophy, or a warning. But who would dare play such a game with Neha? Another of the Cadre? It was something to consider. As was the fact that Eris hadn't simply been killed; he'd been tortured. Again, his suffering could've been intended to hurt Neha, but there seemed something deeply personal about this.

Everything was close contact, from the strangulation to the way the man's other organs had been removed—by a small blunt knife, if Jason was reading the marks on the bone correctly. He was gut-certain the brain had been left for last, so there was a high chance Eris had remained conscious as the killer hacked out pieces of his body. He'd have drowned in pain and terror . . . which explained the raw flesh around his mouth, the cuts on his tongue and lips.

A gag of some kind to muffle his screams.

Rising, he took in Eris's silken pants and vest embroidered with traditional designs that would've exposed his muscled chest. "Did he dress like this normally?"

"Yes—he was never untidy, never ungroomed, but he had long forgone the formality of court."

And instead, Jason thought, chosen to embrace the languid sensuality that would appeal to his wife. A wife who had not forgiven him in three hundred long years. Looking around the room, Jason saw a clean floor beneath the recent bloodshed, polished statuettes, and gleaming walls. Clearly, servants had entrée into the palace.

So, he recalled, did others.

Kallistos, the vampire who'd sought to kill Dmitri, had known the location of Eris's home in the United States, though it was a place many had forgotten. There was a good chance the vampire had received the information directly from Eris, either in return for some favor or by putting together discrete pieces of information Eris had let drop. Thus access to this palace was not an impossible thing.

"I've seen enough." He headed toward the archway through which they'd entered, waiting so Mahiya wouldn't fall behind, though he'd had time enough to assess her level of threat and decide she posed no danger at his back—she might move as quiet as the wind, but she wasn't quiet enough. More, she had no heavy weapons on her body, her sari falling flawlessly around her form, the curve of her waist naked beneath the drape.

Her walk was too fluid for her to have a knife in a thigh sheath, and her bangles too thin to conceal a garrote. However . . . the pins in her hair were very, very sharp. Used the right way, they could blind a man, cut his carotid, even stop his heart. They were the weapons of a woman who wasn't a trained fighter, but who did not intend to be a victim waiting to happen.

Jason felt a curl of unexpected fascination awaken within him. *What other secrets do you hide, princess?*

Stairs wide enough for a being with wings greeted him to the right of the doorway, the fading moonlight falling onto the higher steps colored in the reds, yellows, and blues of a stained glass window that was maybe two handspans across but at least three feet long. Walking up, he ignored the hallway that led to the rooms on this level, and turned right instead—to go through a pair of doors set beside another long window of stained glass.

They opened onto a wide balcony enclosed on all sides by stone carved into delicate filigree that would've allowed Eris to look out into the yard but would've hidden him from the view of those below. Exquisite in its workmanship, it wasn't an unfamiliar form of ancient architecture, though in most cases, it had been used by males to hide their lovers and concubines from the view of those who might covet them.

Stepping to the stone filigree, he found himself looking out over the city beyond the lake at the foot of the fort—the steep drop that led to it would've been a quiet torture to a winged being forbidden to ride the winds. "I heard a rumor that Neha clipped Eris's wings in truth." Despite the violation of the rest of Eris's body, the wings Jason had just seen had been whole.

"I was too young at the time to remember it myself," Mahiya said from where she stood with one hand on the doorjamb, "but I've heard it whispered of by others. However, she didn't repeat the punishment once his wings grew back . . . and I think she regretted ever having done it."

Love, Jason thought, could be the most debilitating of weaknesses.

"Jason, I'm sorry I scared you, son. I did not mean to rage."

Walking further down the balcony, he took in the windows along the inner wall, each created with ten red and green pieces of stained glass. The individual pieces were squares roughly the size of his palm, the effect delicate against the stone of the palace. The glass was echoed in the doors that stood open to reveal a bedroom that appeared to occupy most of the second level, its inner walls gently curved to embrace the central core of the palace.

A magnificent chandelier poured muted, flickering light from the ceiling. Its crystal sconces cradled a thousand candles, many of which had burned down, else the light would've been sharper, brighter. "Eris didn't care for modern things?" he asked the woman who'd entered the bedroom from the corridor.

"No, he just preferred candlelight in his private chambers."

Which meant the room downstairs had acted as his receiving area. "How many guests was he permitted?"

"It depended on Neha's mood." An answer that said much about Eris's existence. "Never any women aside from Neha and myself. Even the servants who worked in this palace were all male."

For a man who had been a favorite of women, it would've been akin to having a limb amputated. "Do you think the rule was observed?"

"I think Eris did not have any wish to anger Neha further."

That didn't answer the question, and the way Mahiya had subtly angled her face away from the light as she spoke told him she knew more than she was saying.

The stealthy hunter in Jason rose to full wakefulness.

6

"A leopard, as they say," he murmured, his mind working at the question of Mahiya's true loyalties, at whose secrets she kept, "does not change its spots." Eris had never been good at self-denial where women and sex were concerned.

An adoring conquest looking up into the face of the golden god who was Neha's consort, her eyes blazing with shy desire.

Jason had witnessed that particular scene approximately a century and a half after Neha's marriage, during a ball given by the archangel Uram. At the time, he'd put Eris's responding smile of sensual invitation down to male vanity, never considering the other man might ever actually *accept* such an invitation.

Yet Eris had needed to have his ego stroked enough that he'd fathered a child upon the sister of the woman he'd sworn to honor. Jason didn't fool himself that Eris had loved Nivriti—the man had been a narcissist, had cared about no one but himself. *And* in spite of his trespass, he had survived. What was there to stop such a man from taking another risk and seducing a lover within the walls of his luxurious prison?

"Tell me," he said, pinning Mahiya with his gaze, "Did Eris have a lover?"

Mahiya had avoided his earlier question, having realized far too late that she'd betrayed a knowledge and a curiosity beyond the woman she was meant to be. Her only defense for the unprecedented failure was surprise—it had been so very startling to speak to someone who watched her without judgment or pity, and who did not divine a lack of understanding simply because she chose to keep her silence . . . but of course he wouldn't. Jason was a man who guarded his words, yet she had not a single doubt that his intelligence was a piercing arrow.

Now, looking into eyes a deep, impenetrable brown that stripped her to the bone, she realized it was too late to put the mask back on.

Jason had already seen her.

There was a strange exhilaration in showing her true face. "I have no proof of a new infidelity," she said, "but there were times of late that I caught a certain musk in the air." A woman should not know such things about her father, but Eris's only claim to paternity had been through their shared blood.

"You didn't tell Neha." It wasn't a question.

Mahiya held that dark blade of a gaze. "I would not be the messenger who bears such tidings." Neha would've struck her down, ended her for it. "You're welcome to attempt it."

His response to the challenge was a calm "Let us see if it proves necessary."

The exhilaration in her bloodstream slowly turned to ice as she watched him explore every inch of the palace that had been Eris's home. She knew his reputation, but it was only now, after witnessing his thorough, meticulous search, that she realized the exact level of Jason's skill, his dedication . . . and understood that none of her plans would come to fruition should he decide to pledge his skills in service to Neha.

Gritting her teeth to fight a shiver, she realized the sands had just begun to fall with increased speed through the hourglass. The Seven were meant to be an impregnable unit, immune to enticement from others in the Cadre, but Neha had had a glint in her eye that said she held an ace. If she did . . . Mahiya and her traitorous intent had to be long gone before Jason accepted the archangel's offer.

Heart thudding hard enough to bruise against her ribs, she shut the door on those thoughts lest they betray her, and followed Jason into a large bathing chamber below the level that held the receiving area. Curls of steam rose from the clear water. "This was meant to be turned off," she said, sensing the fine tendrils of hair at her nape beginning to curl from the humidity. "I'll take care of it after we leave."

Not responding, Jason began to walk the edges of a bathing pool so large, it could've easily accommodated five adult angels. Ancient by design, the chamber had been put in when the palace was constructed for Eris's incarceration, and he'd made good use of it. Many a time when she'd been sent by Neha to see if he needed anything, it had been to find him lounging in the bath.

"Has Neha not slit your throat yet?" A bored sigh, his wings spread as he leaned against the edge, arms lying on the painted tiles carried from Italy by angelic couriers. "A pity."

The stab of memory wasn't enough to distract her from catching the subtle twist of Jason's hand as he slipped something into his pocket. "What's that?"

No surprise or guilt on his face. "I assume this is Eris's?" he said, retrieving the object.

Walking to stand nearer to him than she had till then, she examined the thick gold ring set with tanzanite, dangerously conscious of the penetrating intensity of the spymaster's eyes. "Yes." Only centuries of practice kept her voice from cracking under the silent, inexorable pressure. "Not a favorite, so he may well have forgotten it here."

Jason placed it in her hand. "I would not want to be accused of stealing."

Mahiya felt color tinge her cheeks at the gentle, lethal words. "My apologies. I didn't mean to imply anything of the kind." What she'd meant to imply was that he was hiding something from her. That, she couldn't permit.

"Look at her, Eris. She has your father's eyes—they are so unique."

Words Neha had spoken in a venomous murmur when Eris angered her a century ago. By that time, Mahiya had already been well aware of the single reason for her continued existence. However, Eris was now a corpse who could no longer be tortured with the serrated knife that was the presence of his illegitimate child, and Nivriti lay dead in some forgotten grave, her flesh rotted to dust and her bones bleached white.

The only one left who'd be pained by the mere sight of Mahiya . . . was Neha.

Mahiya had to keep the archangel from remembering that as long as possible. She was almost ready to escape the fort. *Almost.* But almost wasn't good enough when an archangel hated you with a spite that had survived three centuries, a spite that was a caustic flame dipped in poison. The only purpose she currently served was in keeping watch on Jason. The instant she failed in that task, she'd join her mother below the earth, the maggots feasting on her flesh.

Jason said nothing to her apology, shifting to walk back out and upstairs to the main door. He didn't shorten his stride to accommodate her, and she found herself almost running to keep up, the neat folds of her sari flaring out in front of her. Breathless, she wondered if he sought to humiliate her before the guards. If he did, he'd be in for a long wait—the guards had seen her in far more humiliating positions.

The crack of a whip.

Fire on her back, sticky liquid trailing down her broken flesh.

Jason came to a sudden stop ahead of the still-closed

doors, his voice shattering the memory of the punishment meted out to her in Neha's inner courtyard, the whip wielded by the Master of the Guard.

"My rooms?" he asked, his voice so pure, she found herself wondering, not for the first time, if he ever lifted it in song.

"In the palace across the courtyard," she said, barely managing to keep her wing from sliding across his as she halted her own forward momentum.

Jason was not a man any woman would touch without invitation.

Now, reaching out, he opened the door and waited for her to exit. Courtesy, she thought—he'd given her his back earlier, had clearly written her off as a threat. She was too practical to be insulted. If Jason wanted to hurt her, she could do nothing to stop him. Hundreds of warriors, angelic and vampiric, might live in the fort, but the only offensive or defensive training Mahiya had came from what she'd been able to glean by covert study of their training sessions.

And no one, not even a woman determined to protect herself in any way she could, could learn to be a master fighter simply by watching, then attempting to copy those movements in the privacy of her bedroom or up in the isolation of the mountains. However, to ask for help would be to pay a price she couldn't ask anyone to pay.

Her first fledgling friendship as an adult—two hundred years ago—had resulted in the angel in question having both his arms and his wings excised for an outwardly unrelated offense. Mahiya would never forget the way his blood had coated the stone of the warriors' courtyard, darkening the granite to near-black even as his screams echoed off the walls of the surrounding barracks.

Mahiya had understood the brutal lesson, had never again attempted to build bonds with those in the fort, until many believed her a creature of conceit. Better that than to have their screams ringing in her ears as that young angel's did to this day, though he was long healed.

"No one ever sees Jason coming. No one."

The overheard words reverberating in her mind as she reached the courtyard, she heard him say something to the two angels at the door before he reappeared at her side. She glanced at his wings as they crossed over to the mountainside palace, expecting to see them silvered by the waning moon as were the black filaments in her own wings, but there was only darkness at Jason's back—if she hadn't known him for an angel, she'd have thought the spymaster a vampire.

Blinking, she stared, though it was a rudeness. "How do you do that?"

He didn't ask her to explain what she meant. "A natural gift honed by time."

Conscious that this predator—fascinating and darkly intriguing—was deadlier than any other she'd faced save Neha, she walked up the steps of the palace where Jason would stay for the duration. Though it wasn't overtly guarded, only a fool would assume it wasn't under constant watch.

When she walked through the open doors and turned to welcome Jason inside, he paused. "You live here."

"Yes." And had done so since she returned from the Refuge school, but it wasn't home and never would be.

Soon, she promised herself, *soon I will have a home where I will be safe, free from Neha's bitter hate and the shadow of a father who didn't know the meaning of fidelity.*

Lowering her head in an apparent gesture of subservience lest Jason see too much, she said, "I'll show you to your room."

He followed her upstairs and into the sprawling room that overlooked the courtyard. Once, that had been the room she'd shared with Arav, believing herself loved. Desperate for happiness, she hadn't wanted to see the truth until it slapped her in the face.

"You have been a most amusing diversion." A laughing, condescending pat on the cheek at her bewildered

*expression. "And rather delightful. But Neha has approved
my territorial proposal, and I'm afraid I must return to my
lands and cease partaking of your pleasures."*

That heartbreakingly young, naïve girl was long gone,
but Mahiya refused to allow the poison of Neha's hatred to
infect her—she knew full well Arav had only used her as
he had because he'd divined her pain would please the archangel. That was a stain against his honor and said nothing
of Mahiya's own. She *would* love again, and she would love
with all her heart, living her life in a brilliance of hope
and joy.

"Will you be needing anything?" she asked the spymaster, who, feminine instinct whispered, was far more dangerous to her than Arav had ever been.

"No."

Stepping back, she pulled the wooden doors shut and
walked quickly to her own room, situated right next to his.
However, she knew she'd be too late and she was. By the
time she opened the doors to their shared balcony, Raphael's
spymaster had disappeared into the gray twilight that was
the first harbinger of night's fading kiss.

Gliding on the cool winds of the hour before dawn, Jason
came to an easy landing on one of the walls of the heavily
fortified Guardian Fort. It overlooked Archangel Fort and
was considered an extension of it, a place where a considerable number of Neha's angelic guard made their homes.
Seen from its strong walls, Archangel Fort was a great lady
yet asleep, though the scattering of lights burning in the
windows told him the place never truly closed its eyes. As
it should be. The Tower in New York never slept, either.

He saw an angel come in to land at the lower fort at that
instant. From the way he brought himself to a harsh stop with
two simple backbeats, Jason pegged the flyer as one of the
warrior guards. Those guards were not exclusively angelic—
Neha had her share of vampires in all positions, displaying
no bias that could be utilized as a vulnerability.

If the archangel had had vulnerabilities, they'd been named Anoushka and Eris.

Reaching into his pocket, he retrieved the small object he'd secreted away even as he passed Mahiya the heavy gold ring. He'd taken the masculine ring exactly for that purpose but hadn't actually expected her to catch the movement. Something else to add to his growing mental file on the princess who watched him with eyes that saw far too much for a woman who'd been cloistered within sumptuous palace walls her entire adult existence. Now, he used his extraordinary night vision to examine the find he hadn't returned.

7

The ring was a woman's from the look of it: fine strands of gold woven around an opal at the center. Quite aside from the feminine quality of the design, the ring was too small to have fit even the little finger of Eris's hand. And, Neha was known to dislike opals, considering them a bad omen, so it couldn't be hers.

Mahiya's ring finger . . . yes, it would fit. However, he had the niggling feeling that opals were not the princess's chosen gemstone. Clearly, he'd seen something his conscious mind couldn't articulate, but that made him certain that should Mahiya be free to exercise her will, she would wear bright, cheerful jewels like citrine and peridot, aquamarine and canary diamonds.

"Amesyst. Is that how you say it?"

"Almost. Here, listen to me say it again. Amethyst."

Lashes lowering, rising again at the fragment of memory, he focused on the piece of jewelry once more. It was the sort of quiet, pretty ring a woman might wear constantly, an everyday item, perhaps something with sentimental value.

Modest, but with a fine color to the opal and a touch to the design that spoke of a master jeweler Jason knew in Jaipur, it was unlikely to belong to a servant, even had maids been permitted within Eris's palace.

And, given Eris's proclivities, an innocent explanation for the presence of the ring was so unlikely as to be an impossibility. However, if another woman—a lover—had indeed been permitted within the walls of Eris's luxurious prison, it could not have been done without the goodwill and silence of at least one pair of guards.

"A silver tongue, he has ever had it."

Add wealth to Eris's gift of charm, plus perhaps a certain history with the guards, for many in the elite unit had served centuries, and it may have been enough to induce them to forget who it was they served. Neha had always draped her consort in the most expensive furs and silks, the most dazzling jewels—if he had "lost" a piece or two, the archangel wasn't even likely to notice, much less care.

Even without the inducement of money, it might be that the men had felt sympathy for the husband who had strayed. In most angelic unions, it would've meant the end of the relationship, not a lifetime of confinement, the sky forever out of reach. Yes, Jason could see how the guards could've been persuaded to look the other way while Eris entertained.

As for the initial contact, a still-loyal servant could've carried the messages after Eris caught a glimpse of the object of his attentions through the stone lace of the smaller balcony that faced the courtyard.

Having memorized the pattern of the ring and ascertained that it carried no engraving on the inside, he slipped it away. He didn't yet have enough information to uncover the name of the woman who'd worn it, but he knew where to look. Not in the inner court . . . or not in the center of the inner court. She'd be on the edges, a beautiful woman who felt she hadn't received her due. Someone who'd both be flattered at Eris's attentions and full of enough pride that she sought to cuckold an archangel.

After all, she'd been audacious enough to wear an opal in Neha's court.

It was a game no one of age and honed intelligence would dare play, so she had to be young and impressionable enough to fall for Eris's blandishments. To strip the veil off her identity would mean entering the battlefield of court, which Jason had no intention of doing. It was Mahiya of the cat-bright eyes, and silence as haunting as a wolf's midnight song, who had the necessary skills to navigate that particular terrain.

"Or maybe the killer used extra garrotes as ties?"

Not much fascinated Jason after a lifetime spent unearthing secrets and listening to the darkest truths, but he found himself returning again and again to the problematic Princess Mahiya, a woman who didn't fit her environment and who had secrets in her gaze older than they should be.

It mattered little. She was an intellectual curiosity, one that would lose its luster once he knew every facet of her. Of that he was certain. Nothing and no one had managed to get under his skin since the day he dug a deep hole under the shade cast by happy yellow hibiscus flowers, the seagulls cawing and fighting overhead.

Stretching out his wings with that truth in mind, he flew off Guardian Fort and along the ridgeline before winging his way high into the dark gray skies, the clouds yet heavy enough to conceal him from detection. It was here, far above land, that he felt more at home than anywhere else in the world.

"Slower, Jason!" A hand gripping firmly at his ankle as he tangled his wings and threatened to plummet.

"Father!"

"I have you, son. Spread out your wings slowly . . . yes, like that."

Catching his other ankle, his father pulled him farther into the sky. "I'm going to release you again. Ready?"

Taking a deep breath, Jason said, "Yes," and felt his stomach tumble as his father opened his fingers.

He was falling!

Except this time, instead of fighting the wind, he turned into it, allowing it to sweep him out over the sparkling waters that surrounded their home, a shimmering blue green so clear he could see the darting orange and red stripes of the fish swimming through the coral reef.

Above him, he heard his father's joyful exclamation, and he laughed.

It wasn't that Jason couldn't fly. He'd just never had need to practice the more advanced techniques, to go any farther than the roof of their home or up over the trees. However, if he wanted to accompany his father to the small uninhabited island he could just see in the distance—where his father harvested fruits his mother particularly liked—he would have to learn to ride the currents and conserve his energy.

"Father!" It was a delighted cry this time. "I'm doing it! Can you see me?"

"I knew you could do it, son! Well done!" His father swept out in front of him on wings of pure black but for the deep brown at the tips of his primaries, angled against the wind for a second before sliding into another updraft and circling back to their atoll.

Copying him, Jason found that it wasn't hard at all if he did what his father had taught him and thought first.

"Efficient flight is as much about intelligent choices as brute strength."

Now Jason made a conscious decision to change his angle when he realized his father's greater size gave him an advantage . . . and it worked! Until he felt like he was being carried on the winds. He couldn't wait to show his mother, and when he saw the pale purple of her tunic in the distance as she flew up to join them, he pushed himself to go even faster, his wings shining blue black in the sunlight. His father said Jason was meant to be a night scout, like he had been in his youth, before he decided to pursue his passion for music and the instruments that created it.

Jason wondered when he'd be allowed to fly alone during the night. He thought he might like chasing the stars, but it would get lonely after a while. Cold and lonely.

8

Standing on the railingless balcony outside his Tower office, Raphael considered the report he'd just had from Naasir. The vampire was currently stationed in the formerly lost city of Amanat, risen to new life in a mountainous region of Japan, a city controlled by Raphael's mother, an archangel so old, she was a true Ancient.

The reawakening of Amanat has gathered speed, he said to the woman with hair so pale it was white-gold, the strands catching the light from the surrounding skyscrapers as she flew in a zigzag pattern a short distance from the Tower.

We expected as much. Elena dipped left. *Gimme a second. Ransom asked me to help him trail a troublesome vam—gotcha!*

His vision acute as a raptor's, he watched as she spoke into a cell phone, caught the wave of her exultation when the hunter on the ground made the capture. Angelic consorts were a rare breed. Other than Elena, only Elijah's Hannah could truly carry that title. Even before Eris's death and though it was polite to refer to him as such, the position occupied by Neha's husband had been nothing akin to that of either of the women. That wasn't to say Hannah and Elena were cut from the same cloth. No, they were as distant in their temperaments and views on the world as fire and ice.

Of the two, it was Raphael's consort who was considered a peculiar creature indeed.

"Why does she continue to work for the Guild?" Favashi had asked the last time they met, genuine puzzlement in her tone. "Does she not understand the honor of her position?"

Favashi believes you should give up your penchant for chasing vampires and sit by my side as a proper consort.

No offense to Favashi—who seems decent enough in comparison to Lijuan the zombie maker—but she knows jack about how we work.

Raphael's lips curved. "Yes." He caught his consort around the waist as she came in for a high-speed landing. "You would surely have 'brained' yourself, as you put it, at that velocity."

"I only flew in so fast because I knew you'd catch me."

He was a being of immense power, had lived a millennium and a half, and yet she had the ability to stagger him with such simple words, her trust a jewel multifaceted and brilliant. Raising his hand, he ran it over the arch of her left wing, the area exquisitely sensitive. Her shiver was delicate, the pale gray of her eyes going smoky, the developing rim of pure silver around her irises vivid in the night.

"So," she said, leaning into him with a sigh of bone-deep pleasure, "what do you think your mother will do next?"

"I do not yet know." Caliane was a wild card no one had expected to have to deal with—least of all the son she'd left bloody and broken on a field far from civilization. "When she woke, she had no inclination to rule anything other than Amanat, but she is healing into her strength, and there is an open spot in the Cadre."

The Cadre of Ten had been so called for as long as angelkind had had written history. Even when there was an absence of a hundred or two hundred years while a new archangel came to power, and only nine ruled, the name did not change. Such gaps were unremarkable in the life of an immortal. The empty chair this time around had been so for less than a fragment of a second, Uram's execution not yet two years past.

"Caliane's return threatens to unbalance the power structure of the world." While there had been times when archangelic numbers had fallen as low as seven, they had never gone *above* ten, a natural balance that ensured large enough buffer zones between the biggest predators on the planet. "There is one who is on the brink of ascending to archangel status—"

"By brink, you mean . . ." Elena asked, and he was reminded of the mortality so dangerously close to her skin, for immortality was a gift that took time to grow, to settle.

"A decade, a century." He angled her face to check a bruise she'd sustained during their earlier sparring session. "It's unpredictable at this level of power."

"So we have time to figure out a solution." Sliding her arms around his body, she turned her gaze toward her beloved Manhattan. "And fact is, it's not like anyone could stop Caliane if she wanted to rule again."

No. His mother was too powerful. She'd also been insane when she decided on her centuries-long Sleep. Now she told him she was sane, and her actions seemed to bear that out—but Raphael knew madness in the old ones could be an insidious thing. Lijuan was the perfect example.

Jason is worried Lijuan may be creating further reborn. The report had come in an hour ago, his spymaster continuing to control his network of informants even as he hunted Eris's murderer.

"What!" Elena shook her head. "That makes no sense—those creatures are so infectious they'd become a plague across her lands as well as the lands of others in the Cadre, and she saw how they could turn against her." *Even she's not that batshit crazy.*

I'm not sure I agree. "She is old, and the old do not always think as they should."

Elena took time to reply, her gaze tracking a small troop

of angels coming in to land on the balcony below. "She might have figured out a way to control the rate of infection, some way to make certain of their loyalty."

"If she has, she'll be unstoppable." The last time Lijuan had risen, the rest of the Cadre had banded together to execute her, only to inadvertently help her in her strange evolution—now, she was no longer wholly corporeal. "I must find some way to strengthen my new ability." The sheer life of it, born of his tie to his consort with her mortal heart, was inimical to the death that was Lijuan's touch.

"Too bad we no longer have the element of surprise there."

Running his hand down the silken tail of her hair, he smiled. "You will always provide surprises, Elena. You are my secret weapon."

She laughed, eyes dancing. "Did Jason say anything about Neha when he contacted you?"

"The blood vow means he cannot speak of that which happens in the fort, unless the information becomes public." *It is a matter of honor.*

I understand. "I just hope he's safe." Worry was a shadow across the dark gold of her skin. "The way Neha looked the last time I saw her . . ." A violent shiver.

"Jason is a survivor." Raphael didn't know everything of what had happened to Jason as a child, but he'd put together enough pieces to understand the other angel had lived through things no child should ever have to experience.

Elena glanced up, as if she'd heard something he wasn't aware of betraying. "You're still worried about him."

"Unlike Dmitri," he said, releasing her to walk to the very edge of the balcony, his mind filled with images of a young angel with wings of lush black who had barely spoken when Raphael first met him, "Jason has never been in danger of becoming jaded."

Having come to stand beside him, her wing brushing his in an intimacy he'd accept from no other, Elena said, "You think that's changing?"

"On the contrary. The reason Dmitri became so jaded

was that he tasted every sin, drowned himself in sensation." The endless round of pleasure and pain had been an effort to escape a loss that had brutalized the other man, but the end result was a kind of emotional numbness Raphael had thought nothing would ever break, much less a mortal with a fractured spirit.

"Jason by contrast," he continued, "immerses himself in nothing." Raphael had known him too long not to realize that even the lovers Jason took touched nothing of him beyond his skin.

Elena blew out a quiet breath. "He's like that all the time, isn't he? Part of the world . . . but apart. A shadow who never becomes too involved."

Raphael had no need to voice agreement, because it was the truth. His spymaster might not be jaded, but he was numb in a far deeper sense. "To survive eternity," he murmured, "Jason needs to find some reason to exist beyond duty and loyalty."

He cupped the face of the woman who was his own reason for being, who made immortality seem an iridescent promise rather than an endless road. "Such things are powerful and not to be dismissed lightly . . . but they are not enough to thaw a heart that has been encased in ice for near to seven hundred years."

9

Jason looked out through a window of the palace that was his residence for the time being, his attention on the small enclosed garden on the mountain side of Mahiya's palace. It was a spot he'd had to cross the center of the house to see, and one the princess had made no effort to point out to him when she'd shown him to his suite. He could see why.

Unlike the structured courtyard behind him, this hidden area, tucked between the palace and the high defensive wall that protected the fort, appeared to have been set up as a pleasure garden long ago, complete with irrigation channels that kept the wildly blooming plants luxuriant in spite of the desert sun, then forgotten, allowed to run wild.

The exquisite tiles visible on the winding pathways between the garden beds told him it had been designed by someone who expected to spend a great deal of time within its environs . . . or perhaps expected someone else to do so, someone about whom they cared enough to create a concealed paradise.

Eris.

His mind made the connection it had been seeking—the

tiles echoed those he'd seen on the steps of Eris's palace. So perhaps this palace had originally been meant to be Eris's prison, the garden his private area. Except Eris had attempted to use his time outdoors to escape, quite possibly from this very garden, thus losing even that modicum of freedom.

He made a mental note to follow up his theory with the woman who walked the pathways of the wild garden now. She looked up at that moment, and though he was cloaked in the shadows, a faint tension invaded her spine beneath the ice green of her tunic.

The hemline of the fitted garment reached an inch above the knee, the splits to mid-thigh on both sides allowing freedom of movement but remaining modest, as the tunic was worn over tapered pants of a fine cotton that hugged her legs. Dark blue, the pants echoed the thick blue border on the ends of her elbow-length sleeves and along the bottom of the tunic.

Though styles varied, the pants sometimes loose and sometimes tight; the tunics high-necked or scooped, flaring out in a full skirt or cut neatly to the body; and most often worn with a long, gauzy scarf, it was attire he'd seen many a time in this land, as common on laborers and servants as it was on courtiers. The difference was in the fabrics, the cut, and the depth of embellishment. It wasn't unusual to see one of the court butterflies in a piece hand beaded with tiny pearls or where the embroidery had been created using fine threads of pure silver and gold.

Mahiya wore lightweight silk, but though the tunic followed the shape of her body, it bore no sparkle, no embroidery. The neck was a shallow scoop that offered a bare glimpse of her shoulder bones, her golden brown skin glowing in the morning sunlight, her hair glinting with hidden strands of red where it hung in a simple, loose braid that reached the center of her back.

Armor, he thought, Mahiya used formal clothing as armor, and he'd found her stripped of it. Taking advantage, he made certain he was waiting for her on the lower level when she reentered the palace.

"Have you broken your fast?" he asked, caught by the way a ray of sunlight lit up the tawny brown of her eyes to even more startling intensity.

"No." She betrayed no surprise or hesitation at his presence, as if she'd realized his purpose and used the time between his sighting of her and their meeting to put on her emotional armor, if not the clothing that served the same function. "One does not leave a guest to dine alone . . . my lord."

Pretty words that meant nothing. "My name is Jason," he said. "I have never been a lord nor do I wish to be one in any sense."

A blink. "I cannot use your given name."

Jason considered the cultural mores of the land where he stood, layered them over the short period of his association with Mahiya, her status as a princess, as well as the unspoken rules of Neha's court, and understood that for her to use his name in public would breach a barrier, leading others to believe the ritual of the blood vow had segued into a far more intimate relationship. "In private, then, I am Jason."

An incline of her head, followed by a graceful wave as she led him into a sunny room that overlooked the main courtyard. The polished wooden table within, of a size meant to accommodate six, was already set with breakfast— the places situated across from one another. "There are no servants in this palace except for those who come in once a week to clean," she said, picking up the elegant silver teapot to pour him a cup after they'd both taken their seats. "However, I can have someone assigned to you should you wish it."

"No." He took a sip of the sweet tea rich with milk and spices, and returned the cup to the table, intending to pour himself a glass of water.

Mahiya's eyes flicked up from where she'd been putting food on a plate. "It is not to your liking?" Before he could answer, she rose and disappeared through a small door, to return with another pot only minutes later. "Perhaps you'll prefer this."

The pure taste of fine black tea touched his mouth when he lifted the cup to his lips, the leaves no doubt sourced from the plantations in Neha's territory. "Thank you." He didn't tell Mahiya not to serve him, because it told him something else about her that she put down the plate she'd been making to create another one—one much more suited to his tastes, her decision based on nothing but his preference when it came to tea.

A smart woman with many facets . . . who preferred to give an impression otherwise.

Serving herself after passing across his plate, she said, "You wake early." A penetrating look. "Or you do not sleep. Did you, perhaps, fly all the hours before dawn?"

"I'm not mortal." Angels weren't immune to the need for sleep, but the older they became, the less they needed. Jason slept perhaps two nights out of a month, and it was enough to maintain his strength. "However, you need more sleep than you've been getting." Faint bruises marred the skin under her eyes, bruises that couldn't be accounted for by a single night without sleep.

A genuinely startled look before her lashes veiled her expression. "I wake when you wake, my lord."

"Jason."

"Jason."

It was no victory, he thought, the capitulation as meaningless as any of the other pretty words she said to him. This was not the woman who had talked of garrotes and offered to search a room for a hooked needle, shields of polite courteousness having risen to hide the truth of her in the hours since he'd flown into the vanishing night. "Tell me," he said, deciding to use not brute force to get past those shields, but rather a subtle enticement to the inquisitive nature she'd earlier betrayed, "about Eris's guards."

Putting down her tea, she began to speak, her tone one that said she'd expected the question—which meant she had also worked out why he might need the information. It turned out there were twelve guards in total, a unit whose sole task it was to "protect" Eris by keeping him in his palace. "The unit is composed of highly trained angels, no vampires."

A winged guard made sense for a prisoner capable of taking flight. "Who do you believe killed Eris?"

Another flash of surprise. This one, she made no attempt to hide, and he understood something else about the princess—she was unused to having her opinions solicited, much less listened to with the respect they no doubt deserved. No one saw more than a person others dismissed as beneath their notice. It was why Jason placed so many of his spies among servants.

However, Mahiya was not a servant, and he didn't know her well enough to judge whether or not she played a very clever game with him, her "true" face as false as the obvious facade. Only one thing was for certain: Princess Mahiya, with the blade-pins even now hidden in her hair, had just become an even more fascinating creature to his spymaster's mind.

"It isn't my place to say" was her smiling response to his question now, the self-deprecation in her tone so natural, most would have accepted it at face value. "I have none of your experience."

Jason was used to waiting hours, days, weeks if he had to, to unearth a single truth. "I would see the rest of the fort," he said, permitting her to believe he'd accepted her carefully calculated nonanswer.

"Of course." Breakfast finished, she quickly cleared the table, then led him outside. "The fort is too big to walk—I can give you an overview as we fly, then—"

"No, show me directly to the area utilized for the formal court." He would not make himself a target against the painful blue of the sky. Neha had no reason to shoot him out of it, but Neha was also an archangel. The only one of the Cadre Jason trusted was Raphael.

Mahiya hesitated. "If you will give me a moment, I must return to my rooms. My lady will be displeased to see me thus in the main court."

When Jason nodded, Mahiya knew she was trapped. She'd have to leave the spymaster on his own while she changed, giving him a chance to throw her off once more—but going as she was, was not an option. Neha would deem it an insult, and attracting the archangel's attention would be a very stupid move on her part at this stage of the plan. No matter what it cost her, she must swallow her pride, bite her tongue, bow her head, whatever it took to survive just awhile longer.

Thanking Jason for his forbearance, she walked upstairs and quickly undid the small row of hooks at her ankles that fastened the tapered cotton of her pants. Many of the younger generation in the city preferred to wear tight jeans below the tunics, but Neha was an archangel of old, preferred an adherence to tradition within the fort.

The buttons that closed the wing slits gave her a frustrating moment when they refused to open, but she managed to get them undone and shrugged the tunic to the floor. That done, she picked up not a sari, but another tunic set. Jason was apt to take to the skies at some point, and much as Mahiya appreciated the grace a sari bestowed a woman, it didn't make for the most appropriate flight wear.

Of a soft yellow fabric heavily embroidered with white flowers set with tiny mirrors in their centers, the tunic was formal without breaching the mourning etiquette in force since Anoushka's death. The fine cotton pants that hugged her legs were a contrasting white, as was the long scarf she folded lengthwise and placed over her left shoulder, attaching it to the tunic with a brooch from the jewels available for her to use but that belonged to the fort Treasury.

Her hair was easy enough—she pulled it back into a neat knot at the nape of her neck, anchoring it with the high-quality blade-pins she'd managed to buy from a traveling tinker without anyone being the wiser, bartering a richly embellished sari in exchange. The tinker believed he'd gotten the better of their bargain, but the pins had given Mahiya a priceless sense of safety in the darkness, a constant reminder that she wasn't a broken, crushed creature, but a woman willing to fight for her right to live, to exist.

Her face, she left untouched. Her eyes already attracted too much attention—she wanted no more.

"Such pretty eyes you have."

A half-grown child, Mahiya didn't know why the words made her sick to her stomach. "Thank you."

A slow smile from the archangel who she'd been told was her aunt. "They are your grandfather's eyes. The line, it seems, breeds true."

Shrugging off the chill of the memory, she slid her feet into flat slippers, her toes fitting perfectly into the crystal-studded leather, the strap around her ankle similarly bejeweled. No one could ever say Neha didn't give the child she'd "adopted" every luxury.

Less than seven minutes after she'd come upstairs, she ran back down—to find Jason standing in front of the courtyard pavilion, his hands behind his back and his attention on the palace that had been Eris's prison. Relief had her releasing the breath she hadn't been aware of holding.

He didn't fit here, she thought, caught by the starkly masculine beauty of him as she walked to the pavilion. He was too untamed a thing for the polished elegance and polite rules of Neha's kingdom. From the wildness of the tattoo that covered the left side of his face, to the implacable black of his wings and the clean lines of his clothing—simple black pants, a shirt in the same dark shade, black boots, no jewelry—everything about Jason screamed that he was a man, an angel, who made his own way, forged his own path.

He might offer Neha his respect, but he would never worship her as a demigoddess, Mahiya thought, her eyes going to the hair in its neat queue at the nape of his neck . . . which was when she noticed he wore a sword in a black sheath along the centerline of his spine, the straps merging into the black of his shirt. "Neha does not allow weapons in her formal court but for the guard."

Jason's eyes locked with her own, and though she knew it for an illusion, it felt as if he was stripping her down to the soul, seeing things she'd never shared with another living being. "Neha," he said, "understands how I work."

Mahiya doubted very much if anyone understood the spymaster in truth, but she gave a small nod, taking the opportunity to end the disturbing eye contact. "Shall we go?"

Jason said nothing as they left the courtyard, his silence so profound she knew it must be a part of him, not something created to unsettle her. Strangely enough, she didn't find it disquieting in the least—Jason's silence was an honest thing, unlike the lies that came out of so many other mouths. "We'll find my lady in the public audience chamber."

Neha was always available on this day to those of her land who would speak directly to her, a paradoxically fair queen whether the constituent was an aristocrat or a farmer. "It's early enough that we may be able to see her unhindered," she added as they walked through an intricately painted gate large enough for several elephants to pass through side by side.

The fort was alive and awake, and Mahiya nodded hello to any number of people. The women were all dressed in soft shades rather than the intense reds, yellows, and blues normally favored in this region, but styles varied dramatically. A number wore day gowns, several vampires neat suits that said they had business outside the fort, while still others wore plain work saris. Then there were those dressed in the uniform of the guard, complete with weapons—Neha did not discriminate when it came to skill and ability.

Everyone looked to Jason for an introduction, but Mahiya ignored the unspoken requests and continued on her way, well aware he wasn't a man who would play the polite games of court. She was glad to get out of the thoroughfare when they reached the public audience hall, which was in actuality a large stone pavilion open on three sides. Six rows of seven columns marched across the floor, holding up the curved roof and, above it, a large terrace.

Neha usually addressed her supplicants from the high throne already set in place, but it stood empty at present. Instead of petitioning the guard standing in front of the door Mahiya knew opened into a staircase that led up to the terrace, she stepped out and flew upward, her wings aching under the strain of the vertical takeoff. Jason, of course, had no such trouble and landed on the terrace before her.

Her instinct proved right—Neha stood at the edge where the original lattice wall had been removed to provide an uninterrupted view. Her eyes were on the mountains, the hills a golden brown in the early morning light, the greenery sparse.

"His funeral pyre blazes tomorrow," she said as Mahiya reached her. "You will not wear white. No one will wear white."

It was no loss to Mahiya not to wear the color of mourning—Eris had been less a father to her than a tomcat was to his kittens. As for Neha's own motivations, the archangel alone knew the truth, but Mahiya had seen her beside Eris's butchered body, heard her distraught keening. No matter what she tried to portray in her pride, the same pride that meant Eris spent three centuries as a prisoner, Neha mourned.

"My lady," she said, a sympathy within her that she didn't attempt to crush out of existence. Her continued ability to feel for the hurt suffered by another being—*especially* when that being was the archangel who saw in her only an endless vengeance—was part of who she was, a tenderness of heart she'd nurtured with fierce devotion even when it would've been easier to have acquired a carapace of hardness nothing could penetrate.

Neha turned to face Jason, dismissing Mahiya as another person might an insect. "What have you discovered, Spymaster?"

10

"Eris's palace might have been well guarded," Jason said, "but it wasn't impregnable."

Neha's lips curved in a humorless smile. "Only those without care for their lives would've broken the rules. Do you tell me there was more than one?"

"I can tell you nothing yet." Jason held Neha's gaze in a way Mahiya had seen no one in the court dare, not even the archangel's most trusted advisors.

Her stomach tensed at the risk he was taking. Though he was a stranger with no call on her loyalty, Mahiya found she did not want Jason bloodied. It would be a desecration of a beautiful, wild creature who should never be caged or broken.

However, Neha laughed, an appreciative glint in her eye. "All seven of you, so arrogant."

Sensing that she was missing something important, but unable to work out what, Mahiya fell into step behind Neha and Jason as they walked. Neha's almost wholly ice white wings were a stark contrast to Jason's black, as was the shimmering coral of the archangel's simple but exquisitely cut gown.

"How is Dmitri?" Neha now asked, the edge in her voice sharp as a scalpel.

Jason's reply was unexpected. "Have you still not forgiven him for returning to Raphael?"

Neha laughed again, the gleaming blade transmuted into the first real amusement Mahiya had heard from her since Anoushka's execution. "I thought the two feral pups deserved one another, and I was right, was I not?" Not waiting for an answer, she added, "He should, however, have invited me to his wedding," the words holding a dangerous politeness.

"Yes, he should have, but a vampire from your court did attempt to kill him only days past."

Neha raised her head, her smile as cold as the blood of the cobra curled up in a basket in one corner of the terrace. "Does he believe I would hide behind one such as Kallistos?"

"The fact is," Jason said, "Dmitri has always liked you better than most of the rest of the Cadre—but, and regardless of the brief truce born of my presence here, you and Raphael are not the best of friends at present."

"Playing politics, Jason?"

"I'm very good at it."

A small silence. "Of course you are." The anger was replaced by cool approval. "A spymaster who could not understand the nuances would be useless."

Jason didn't say anything in response to that self-evident truth. What he did say was, "When Dmitri discovered why I came to your territory, he asked me to convey his sympathy. He says he will always remember Eris as a swordsman who was a welcome sparring opponent."

Mahiya had seen Eris dance with a blade within the confines of his palace, the grace of it dazzling. Once, she had even seen Neha and Eris together in the courtyard, their swords and bodies moving with a harmony that—for a single piercing moment—made it painfully clear how the two could've fallen in love.

"I had forgotten," Neha murmured, "that Dmitri and Eris

had that in common. Two such different men connected by the blade."

"He also charged me to ask if you would welcome him and his bride once you are receiving guests again."

"If he spoke so prettily, I would be most astonished," Neha said, but Mahiya could tell she was pleased by the request, for the leader of the Seven was meant to be a cynical, hard-hearted bastard who trusted no one. Yet he respected Neha's honor enough to bring into her territory the woman he'd made his wife.

"Tell him," the archangel said, "that I will not be displeased if he and his wife should pay their respects. My quarrel is with Raphael, not Dmitri."

Jason nodded. "I will pass on the message. Do I keep you from your people?"

"No." Neha shook her head and stepped a wing-length away. "I have postponed the public audience. You will escort me to Guardian where I plan to remain overnight with Eris."

Wings spread, she executed a flawless vertical takeoff, Jason rising at her side. Mahiya was slower, found herself lagging behind, but she made no effort to catch up, her stomach lurching at the thought of being at Guardian. Instead, she let her eyes linger on the gentle bustle of the city below. It had had another name once, but after so many centuries in the shadow of Archangel Fort, it had become Archangel City.

Not surprisingly, the city reflected Neha's tastes. Though—aside from the residences of powerful vampires or angels who lived outside the fort—the buildings were mostly small and single leveled; they were graceful structures of stone that had withstood the march of time. Like any city, Archangel had narrow alleys as well as wider thoroughfares, but nothing was broken or ugly, dirty or derelict, the water in the lake running clear and so fresh it was drinkable.

On Mahiya's other side, hugging a natural ridgeline, sprawled the fort, and it too bore the stamp of its mistress. Guardian Fort was modest in comparison. It was also connected to the main fort by subterranean passages men had apparently died to keep secret—Mahiya only knew about them because Eris had let something slip on one of the rare occasions when he'd drowned his rage in a bottle.

"Instead of attempting flight, I should have waited for my opportunity and used the tunnels!"

"Tunnels?"

"To Guardian, you stupid girl!"

Eris had refused to say anything further on the topic, but she'd managed to get Vanhi to confirm the existence of the tunnels. However, the vampire, with her maternal ways, had known of only one entrance—*inside* the Palace of Jewels, a location that might as well be on the moon.

In front of Mahiya, Neha and Jason circled the higher fort, and she was struck by the span of Jason's wings, by the clean efficiency of his flight technique, not a motion wasted. He wasn't a man she ever wanted after her in the sky—escape would be impossible.

Putting on a burst of speed, she came in below them to land in Neha's private courtyard within the fort that made a chill bead of sweat roll down her spine even now. However, that wasn't the reason for her descent: It would not do for her to rise higher than the archangel—that lesson she'd learned on the fateful day a hundred years after her birth, when she'd officially crossed the line into adulthood and lost the protection afforded by Neha's unwillingness to harm the young.

The lesson had been a brutal one, the Master of the Guard instructed to strip her back of skin. Mahiya had long understood she lived on Neha's sufferance, having learned the truth from a nanny who thought she should know her place in the scheme of things, the gift of knowledge a rough kindness.

"Never forget that nothing you do will ever please her. To her, you are not a child to be protected, but a constant reminder of a betrayal that humiliated an archangel. Focus on survival."

As she'd hung from the whipping post, blood trickling

down her back, Mahiya had understood something else. That Neha wanted to break her until she was a living warning on the price of disloyalty. Enough people knew the unspoken secret of Mahiya's heritage that the warning would be understood.

I will survive and I will survive whole.

The vow was one she'd made even as the whip fell again and again. And it was one she had kept, refusing to let Neha twist her into an ugly mirror of Neha's own hatred. Allowing the archangel to believe she'd succeeded in cowing Mahiya was a strategic move on the chessboard that cost her nothing but pride . . . and pride was a useless tool in the fight for her very existence.

Jason landed after Neha, but that was to be expected—he was clearly acting as her guard in this moment. He ignored Mahiya's presence, sparing her not so much as a glance.

Something foul bubbled in her stomach, and she knew herself for the most pathetic kind of fool. What had she expected? That he'd continue to treat her with that inexplicable, alluring respect after it became clear exactly how little she mattered to Neha?

"Jason." Neha inclined her head in regal acknowledgment before entering the palace she used while at Guardian, ready to begin her vigil by Eris's lifeless body.

Swallowing the anger within her that could ruin everything, Mahiya said, "Do you wish to return to Archangel Fort?"

A nod, and he rose again, in a burst of blinding speed.

Her heart leaped into her throat. *He was faster than Neha.* Her own rise felt childish and painful by comparison, but she got airborne and made her way to the fort through the crystalline blue skies while Jason went so high he wasn't even a dot in the distance, reappearing at the last minute to arrow down to a clean landing in front of her—their—palace. The area appeared deserted, the guards having decamped after removing Eris's body.

Jason folded back his wings, waited for her to do the same. Then he turned to her. "Do you not," he said in a tone calm and measured, "have enough respect for yourself to not allow Neha to treat you like something scraped off the bottom of her shoe?"

The shock of the unexpected blow was so absolute, it felt as if he'd punched a fist into her rib cage, crumpling her bones inward where they ripped and tore and made her bleed.

Jason realized he'd made a mistake the instant after he spoke, as Mahiya's face paled to a sickening shade, her breath jagged. It had been a long time since he'd spoken without thought, and he knew he'd allowed his anger at Mahiya's acceptance of the treatment meted out to her by Neha to color his thinking.

Shifting a fraction closer, he spread his wings as if stretching them. "We are watched." He made his tone a whip. "Do *not* break."

She blinked at the harsh order, and then it was as if a rod of steel had been thrust through her spine, her tawny eyes wild with fury. "A test, spymaster? If so, I failed."

So at last, I see you again, Mahiya. "I could have spoken with more care, but that would not change the heart of my question."

Her fury now tightly controlled, she walked not into the privacy of the palace, but through the delineated pathways of the courtyard garden, the area bright with lush blooms that mocked the desert climate, the water running down the sides of the pavilion offering a cooling wash of air. "Am I meant to thank you for calling me a spineless coward?"

"No," he said, his own anger far more tempered but no less dangerous. "But you must know that weakness, real or feigned, only incites predators." And the archangels were the alpha predators on the planet. "Neha appreciates those who stand up to her—you have the strength to do so." She was no more spineless than he was stupid. "You have no reason to play dead."

A wash of dark red across her cheekbones, her hands

fisting. "Don't think to know me or my life on the basis of
a day's enforced intimacy, my lord." Turning away from the
garden with those cold words, she led him through a doorway into the cool rooms within the fort, heading downward
until he thought they must be on the level that housed the
Palace of Jewels.

They exchanged no further words until she halted by a
set of doors decorated with the familiar motif of slender
vases, the carvings inset with agate and what looked to be
green tourmaline. The doors stood ajar, but the angle meant
he and Mahiya were yet concealed from the view of the
people within. He took advantage of that to study the room
and its inhabitants.

Spacious and relatively free of furniture, the room opened
out onto a wide balcony, sunlight slanting in through there
as well as through the tiny squares of the lattice window to
the right. The illumination was bright but not hard, gilding
the angels and vampires who stood talking and laughing in
pairs or small groupings, all dressed in rich fabrics that
sparkled and glittered, diamonds like drops of ice in their
hair and their ears.

"Courtiers," Mahiya said, her tone frigid. "A private
brunch where they can display their finery without offence
to Neha. I can make the introductions."

Refusing the offer with a shake of his head, he walked a
few feet to the right—to a door that, as he'd hoped, led
directly to a balcony that paralleled the room of courtiers.
Even better for his purpose, it was small, unconnected to
the wider balcony he'd observed at the end of the room.
Walking out, he leaned against the sun-warmed stone beside
the lattice window and settled in to listen, darkly conscious
of Mahiya's silent presence by his side.

As she'd been silent in Neha's presence.

His renewed anger at her behavior was visceral, a raw,
bubbling thing. After near to seven hundred years of living
with memories that had never faded, he knew the cause of
his turbulent response, knew his fury was fed by the memory

of another woman who hadn't fought the violence meted out to her.

"He cannot help it, Jason. A terrible darkness has taken hold of his heart . . . but we can bring him back. We just have to love him."

Neha's treatment of Mahiya was nothing so obvious as a physical blow, but it was as effective a weapon in erasing her personality.

". . . rumors he had a lover."

Clamping down on his anger, Jason focused on the voices.

"Ridiculous. Who would chance execution for something as tawdry as sex?"

"Komal might. You know how angry she has been since Neha banished that vampire she intended to bed."

"Komal is a silly girl, but she isn't suicidal."

Jason listened for almost an hour, but heard nothing else as explosive as that short conversation. "Who is Komal?" he asked Mahiya once they were well away from the room.

"A vampire who has been part of the inner court for half a century. Her beauty is considerable, and she's adept at using it to manipulate men. I think she doesn't quite understand that Neha is not as susceptible." A glance that wasn't as circumspect as he'd come to expect from her, the frost yet present in the tawny brown depths. "I'll take you to her if you wish."

"Yes." Jason felt his own simmering anger spark in response, knew she'd sensed it when she jerked away her head and strode the corridor, her demure demeanor forgotten. Though she could not have meant it to do so, the show of temper soothed his own.

"There she is." Mahiya indicated a woman walking along one of the open hallways that overlooked the cityscape.

Komal proved to be exactly as described—a sensual invitation with her raven hair and red lips, honey gold skin and dangerous curves. A woman on whom vampirism had bestowed its exotic kiss, and one who was spoiled to the extent that she pouted when Jason didn't immediately fall at her feet. "We both know the mouse isn't going to satisfy you," she purred with venomous sweetness. "I promise to show you pleasures you've never tasted."

Jason stared at the hand she'd raised as if to touch him until she paled, dropped it, before shifting his gaze to lush brown eyes that had no doubt led many a man to hell. "Were you happy to oblige Eris, too?"

11

Pure, unmitigated panic. "Who has started that rumor?" It was a whispered hiss as she looked around for anyone who might overhear. "Neha will execute me if it reaches her ears. God, she'll probably torture me first, keep me alive for years."

Jason said nothing, watched her turn to Mahiya, her fangs flashing. "Tell me, or I'll have you whipped again."

"If I were you, Komal," Mahiya said in a tone cool with warning, "I'd forget about making trouble and stay out of sight for the time being."

Paling even further, the vampire turned and ran off inside, her figure-hugging gown dragging along the gray stone used in this part of the fort. Jason let her go, certain she had neither been, nor had any knowledge of, Eris's illicit lover. Her shaken response to the accusation and nasty nature aside, Komal wasn't smart enough to have pulled off such an intrigue. She'd have boasted to someone, been caught long ago.

"Why were you whipped?" he asked the far more complex, intelligent woman by his side.

No hitch in Mahiya's stride. "Which time?"

His nails dug into his palm. "The last time."

"I was disrespectful to a high-level courtier."

"Was he worth respect?"

Unsurprised at the question from this male who didn't follow any of the rules of accepted behavior and who'd incited a rage in her that had made her forget herself to a dangerous extent, Mahiya said, "No." Pointless to lie to him now.

"Then the whipping was worth it."

It was a strange sensation, being totally liberated of the need to conceal her true thoughts. As if she were drunk. "No," she said, her fury still cold enough to burn, "because after I was beaten and weak, he received what he wanted." Mahiya had had to prostrate herself at his feet, beg for forgiveness for the slight she'd done him. Only her stubborn refusal to become anything like Neha had kept her from stewing in the bitterness and hate that had sought to bloom in her that day. "I learned to choose my battles."

Jason's eyes, so very dark—like the finest chocolate, rich and decadent—lingered on her for a long, endless moment before he gave a small nod. "So long as you continue to fight."

Anger surged through her veins once more, until it took everything she had to bite out an outwardly civil response. "Yes, my lord."

A motionless pause that reminded her she was taunting a man so lethal, he met the eyes of an archangel without flinching. Then he said, "I apologize. I do not know anything of the battles you've already fought or the choices you've had to make to survive."

No man had ever apologized to her, and hearing it from *this* man shook her enough that she didn't say a word when he turned and began to walk the pathways of the fort, leading rather than being led. She knew he heard more than she did, saw more than she did, though she walked beside him.

He was beyond fascinating.

Dangerous and unpredictable and frighteningly

intelligent. A threat. And yet she wanted to run her finger over the blade of him even if it made her bleed, wanted to dance too close to the flame, wanted to take a risk that could destroy her.

Her gaze went to the pitch-black of his wings, her fingers aching to explore, as if her silent admission of just how much he drew her had opened a doorway she hadn't been aware of locking. Except—

Her eyes skated past him, though she knew he was *right* there.

Snapping back to full alertness, she realized most of the guards didn't even notice his presence, though they all greeted her with curt nods. Watching him with a focus that caused a dull headache to throb behind her eyes, she saw the outline of him, but an instant later, he stepped into a shadow created by a spray of flowers high up on a wall and was gone.

Unthinking, she reached out, her fingers brushing the edge of his wing, the feathers sleek and warm under her fingertips.

He froze, every muscle tense.

Heat flooded her cheeks, and she dropped her hand as she realized the altogether unacceptable nature of her behavior. "I'm sorry . . . but I couldn't see you."

"I'm very good at remaining unseen." His voice held none of the displeasure she would have expected after witnessing the way he'd warned Komal off from laying a finger on him. "I've had hundreds of years of practice."

She didn't believe him, but it didn't take a genius intellect to realize the spymaster would not tell her his secrets. "Again, I apologize." Her fingers continued to tingle from the fleeting contact. "I had no right."

"Actually, you did," he said to her surprise, his tattoo a tactile temptation in the sunlight. "I swore a blood vow to you. Skin and feathers are far closer to the surface than blood."

"I would never take advantage of the vow in such a fashion." Fisting her hand in resistance against the compulsion to commit an even worse breach by tracing the wild beauty of his facial markings, she turned her gaze forward and continued to walk. Her skin burned then went icy cold, her heart stuttered . . . and she realized that in spite of her deepening fascination with Raphael's spymaster, she was afraid.

Jason, with his quiet voice and watchful eyes, was infinitely more dangerous to her than Neha had ever been. He *listened* when she spoke, had already learned things about her no one else knew. Such a man wouldn't use his physical strength to overpower her, nor lies to trick her. He'd just know her so well that he'd get her to contribute to her own downfall.

Sweat dampening her palms, she realized too late they were headed for a part of the complex Neha would not want him in under any circumstance. "We can go no further in this direction."

"Why?"

"This area is for Neha's private use, off-limits except by her invitation."

"Very well." Flaring out his wings with that suspiciously quick agreement, he made a vertical takeoff so fast that she had no hope of catching him.

Compelling . . . and deadly.

It was a truth she could not permit herself to forget, no matter the temptation to touch the blade. Too much was at risk—her entire existence, her very life. Jason was a dream she'd have to save for another life . . . but first, she had to make it out of this one alive.

Losing him above the puffy white clouds that had crept across the sky, she returned her gaze to the pathway of red stone and to the small palace she'd warned Jason not to enter. Neha was secluded at Guardian, would not return till morning. Jason had left Mahiya alone. She'd have no better chance to grab the brass ring.

The trickle of sweat down her spine a chilled bead, she stepped forward.

None of the guards attempted to stop her—Neha often called her in when she wanted something done. But then, Mahiya only ever entered the front rooms. Today, taking advantage of the fact that no guards were permitted within, she continued down the corridor and toward the room at the very center of the palace, a room within which she could sense things that made her hindbrain skitter in warning, jibbering at her to *run!*

Mahiya wrenched the primal urge under control. This wasn't her first foray into the forbidden section. The last time had been in the depths of the night, while Neha was actually inside the room at the center. It had taken gut-clenching courage and grim determination, her heart pulsing in her mouth with every jagged breath. What she'd seen that night had been disturbing, but the discovery hadn't been enough to complete her plan.

Today, the smooth marble walls weren't encrusted with ice, her breath didn't fog the air, and her bones didn't hurt with the pain of extreme cold. Touching her fingers to the marble, she walked quickly and silently down the long final corridor, the door to the room within sight. It had been so hardened with ice the previous time, she hadn't been able to glean the handle.

Now, the knob shone bright gold. Mahiya went to put her hand on it, hesitated at the last instant. This was far too easy. Forcing patience, she hid herself in a small alcove while she considered the situation from every angle—to discover what Neha was up to, she had to get inside that room, but getting inside that room might well mean her death. Because Neha was an archangel, with abilities both secret and overt.

Her most overt one was the way she could control and manipulate reptilian creatures of every kind. Like the golden vine snake wrapped around the doorknob. Mahiya's heart punched against her ribs as the creature flicked out its red tongue and she realized what she'd taken for an ornate design was a living being.

A poisonous living being.

Because one of her more covert abilities was the fact that Neha could create poison glands in nonvenomous species. Touching that knob would have meant a bite that left Mahiya paralyzed and helpless for hours.

However, that was unlikely to be the only security feature, because while Neha was an angel of old, she was in no way blind to the benefits of modern technology. Now that Mahiya was thinking properly instead of being driven to act by the knowledge of how quickly her time was running out, she realized that even were the door unlocked, Neha would have set it with a silent alarm that alerted her to any trespass.

Once inside, would an intruder find the room unoccupied . . . or herself surrounded by hundreds of snakes irritated to hissing anger at being disturbed?

A hint of noise, a whisper.

Freezing, she hoped whoever it was—a maid?—had only entered to take care of something in the front rooms.

"So," said a tempered, familiar voice from the left of the alcove, "you seek to unearth Neha's secrets."

A bolt of terror hitting her bloodstream, she shifted into the light to face Jason. "I came to get something I'd forgotten," she said, then considered her empty hands. "I didn't find it."

Near-black eyes watched her without blinking. "You're very good at lying, but I'm even better at detecting it." Turning his attention to the closed door guarded by the vine snake, he looked at it for several careful seconds before shifting on his heel and saying, "We need to talk in privacy."

It wasn't an invitation.

Mahiya would've liked nothing better than to refuse the order, but if he mentioned this to Neha, she'd be dead and nothing else would matter. Frustration, fear, and anger boiling a caustic brew in her veins, she followed him out into the light, blinking against the brightness . . . to find that he was no longer beside her.

"It wouldn't do for Neha to learn that I'd been in there," he said several minutes later, having rejoined her once she reached a more public area.

"How did you get in?" Even as she spoke, she remembered all those guards simply *not seeing* him.

His only answer was to glance at her wings, ask, "Can you do another vertical takeoff?"

"Yes." She was slow, not weak. "Where are we going?"

"Follow me." Rising into the sky, he held his position until she joined him, then swept out across the city, farther, until they were flying over villages where excited children ran and waved at them, and stacks of blue pottery sat ready to be decorated, while sleepy cattle dozed in a rare green pasture fed by a stream nearly concealed by tall grasses.

I will miss this.

It was a thought that made her heart ache with sorrow. This land of desert and color and hidden oases was all she'd ever known. She couldn't imagine living in a place without rolling sand dunes, the sight of camels with their swaying walk as familiar as those of the regal elephants. Animals were treated with affection and care under rules Neha had set in place long ago, and many roamed over land set aside for them, as with the herd of camels below, their necks bent as they grazed.

A lone herder, her long skirt and hip-length tunic a sun bright yellow, looked up, raising her hand in a wave. Mahiya waved back, struck once more by Neha's many—sometimes violently opposed—aspects. She was a queen, could be cruel, but she was also beloved by her people for her generosity and fairness, the angels from her court welcome wherever they went.

Should Mahiya land in the village below, she would be received with warmth, given tea hot from the pot and savories fresh from the oven. There was fear in the populace, of course, but it wasn't crippling, simply a quiet acknowledgement that the immortals were stronger and more dangerous, that it was better to live peacefully with them, to serve when called than to rebel.

However, it wasn't to one of those villages that Jason took her, but to a small, deserted field. Landing under the branches of a tree whose roots went deep enough that it thrived even when there were no rains, its light green leaves lacey and delicate, he folded back his wings, watched her come down. She felt graceless in comparison to his shadow silent descent, her wings rustling, her feet too heavy.

"Now," Jason said when she'd settled, "we will talk."

The desolate vista in front of her, the land lying fallow, was nonetheless home, and it gave her courage. "What would you have me say?"

Jason looked into Mahiya's eyes and saw a steely determination. She wasn't a woman who would easily break . . . and he was not a man who would ever shatter a woman's spirit. However, there were other ways of getting what he wanted—and he didn't have time to play games. "We both know I hold the cards here."

"You swore a blood vow to me," she pointed out, though her skin had paled under the soft shade created by the fine leaves of the tree under which they stood. "You cannot cause me harm."

"Remember the words we spoke," he said, crushing his primal response to her refusal to surrender. "I am charged only with unearthing Eris's murderer and protecting your family's interests as I do so. And it appears you have traitorous intent."

She clenched her jaw. "What will you tell her?"

"It depends on whether or not we can come to an accommodation." So long as he completed his task and discovered the identity of the killer, he was not bound to report everything he found to Neha.

A hardened jaw, flinty eyes. "And what is your price, my lord?"

The last two words may as well have been an insult. "Tell me about that room," he said, his gaze dropping to lips thin with anger, "about what goes on within."

"I don't know," she grit out. "I've never been able to get inside."

True enough, he thought, watching a face that was incredibly expressive if you took the time to learn the subtle movements that betrayed her every thought. And Jason had taken the time. "But you've seen something."

Her wings rustling restlessly, she blew out a deep, shuddering breath. "Ice. It coated the walls, covered the door. My breath frosted, and I could feel my blood beginning to freeze." She shivered. "My veins . . . they stood out against my skin, and when I pressed down, they felt hard."

Angels were built for flight, and as such, did not feel the cold as mortals did. And what Mahiya was describing was a cold so terrible, it was an impossibility in this particular region. Yet, as far as he knew, Neha's archangelic abilities did not include the capacity to manipulate the elements.

"Was Neha alone in the room?"

The tiniest hesitation.

12

"I've never seen her enter with anyone."

Very cleverly put, but Jason had been playing this game
centuries longer than Mahiya. "Have you heard her speaking
to anyone while she's within?"

"If I tell you everything," she said in a tone so resolute,
it was granite, "it won't matter if you betray me to Neha.
The end result will be the same."

Jason considered why a princess might need to hoard
dangerous knowledge. "You need a bargaining chip," he
guessed. "For what?"

"Why are you doing this?" A hunted look in her eyes,
the pupils vivid black against cat-bright irises. "Stripping
me bare?"

That look, it hit the part of him he preferred to pretend
didn't exist, but he didn't back off, didn't soften. He needed
to know who Mahiya had heard in that room with Neha,
because if what he suspected was true, the world might yet
drown in horror such as no one could imagine.

The princess twisted away to give him her back, her
wings sweeping in graceful arches to the dusty earth, in

direct contrast to the rigid stiffness of her spine. "I'm going to die soon if I don't find a way out." The words were as stark as the land that surrounded them. "Neha will never voluntarily set me free to live my own life, and she no longer has any reason to keep me alive—I was only ever useful as a means to torment Eris."

"And as a surrogate to punish," Jason said, all of the pieces he'd glimpsed coming together to form an ugly, twisted whole. "Where do you plan to go?"

She turned on her heel, showed him two empty palms. "Where can I go?" Rippling anger in every word. "I want only a life away from this prison of hate, be it in a hovel, but only another archangel can stand against Neha, so it *must* be one of the Cadre."

"Lijuan is the closest."

Blind terror racking her frame, so vicious and deep that he made the rarest of moves and reached out to touch her, squeezing her upper arm. "Mahiya."

"Not Lijuan." Her voice was hoarse, as if she'd been screaming.

"You've attempted it before," he guessed, the warmth of her skin lingering on his palm though the contact had been fleeting. "What happened?" There were a thousand horrors in Lijuan's court, a thousand nightmares given flesh and blood form.

Mahiya leaned back against the tree, her profile limned by the light that caught hints of sunset in her hair. "It's difficult to have a conversation with a man who sees everything."

"You mean it's difficult to manipulate me into seeing what you want me to see." The truth was, his strength came not from how well he could read her, but from his acceptance of how much he might *miss*. Even when he'd known someone for centuries, he was always conscious he'd caught but a glimpse of the complex tapestry that was their inner life.

The woman in front of him had an intricate pattern to her heart and emotions he might never fathom, didn't have the ability to fathom. All he could do was watch for cues others took for granted, put those cues together to form a picture of her emotions. He knew that wasn't how the rest of the world did it, knew his inability to connect to those around him on that level was a lack in him.

It troubled him enough that he'd spoken to Jessamy about it a century ago. The gentle teacher of angelic young had taken time to consider his question. "I think," she'd said at long last, "you have the capacity to feel with the same depth as any other immortal. Perhaps more.

"You have a heart so powerful, it scares me at times. And the way you keep your emotions under lock and key . . ." An intent look. "The storm *will* break one day, of that I'm certain. You've never had reason to take the risk yet." She'd given him a rueful smile. "I know something about avoiding pain, so trust me when I say that."

Jason had the utmost respect for Jessamy, knew her words were no lie. Born with a malformed wing that meant solo flight was out of her grasp, she'd suffered anguish such as Jason couldn't imagine. He would never discount it, never consider it less important than the forces that had shaped him, but he knew the way they had grown and developed was fundamentally different.

As he couldn't imagine what it was not to be able to touch the sky at will, Jessamy couldn't imagine what it was to be alone. Utterly, absolutely alone. Not for an hour, not for a day, not for a year. For decades.

Until he had forgotten how to speak, how to be a person.

That endless aloneness had withered something within him when he'd still been a boy with wings too heavy for his body, and unlike Jessamy, he believed it to be a permanent loss. As irrevocable as the fact that the atoll where he'd been born, where his mother had been buried, was gone, crushed by a massive quake caused by an underwater volcanic eruption. It was as if his parents had never existed, as if he'd *always* carried this aloneness inside him.

"Obviously," Mahiya said into the silence, "I'm outclassed," having utilized the pause to paint on the mask of a woman who had grown up in a court—where venom was most often delivered with a honey-sweet smile.

"Enough games." Though the survivor in him admired her fierce will, he couldn't allow that to give her the upper hand. "Make your decision and make it quickly."

A fine tremor silvered over her skin, and he knew that beneath her stubborn refusal to give in, she was afraid. Jason didn't like inciting fear in a woman. It brought back too many memories that would not fade no matter how many years passed, his hands tingling as if he'd been pounding on a locked bedroom door in a futile attempt to get out, to stop what was happening beyond.

"No, you are mist—"

"Don't lie! I saw the way you looked at him!"

The roar echoed through time, but haunted as he was, Jason had long learned to dance with his demons. He held his silence even when the quiet grew jagged with the sharp bite of Mahiya's fear, even when his every instinct snarled at him to destroy the thing that made her afraid.

"You need to give me something in return." Lines forming around soft lips, shoulders squared. "I can't surrender the most valuable piece of information I have without gaining something equally valuable in return."

It was then that Jason understood this princess with her quiet grace had learned to use fear to strengthen herself rather than allowing it to crush her. Some unknown, hidden part of him felt a searing joy, the emotion raw and unexpected and so extreme, he had to use conscious effort to wrench it under control. Even then, it burned, the midnight flames licking at his veins.

"If your information is good," he said, thinking through his violent response to judge that she was willing to risk death to hold on to this final piece of information, "I'll speak to Raphael."

Hope shot golden light across her face. "Will he—"

Jason would not bargain with lies and half-truths. "No archangel will start a war over you," he said bluntly. "It doesn't matter what secrets you possess."

Mahiya could feel herself beginning to fracture from the inside out. With a few words, Jason had just destroyed the single precious drop of hope she'd cultivated through humiliation and hurt and a lifetime of knowing she lived on borrowed time. The worst thing was, he betrayed no emotion about any of it—as if her life meant *nothing*. And this was the man she'd wanted to touch, wanted to learn?

"Then," she said, clawing her way out of the abyss on a tower built of rage and pride and an agonizing sense of loss for something she had never possessed, "what use is your promise?"

"A direct defection isn't the only way to get what you want." Jason's tone was harsher than she'd ever heard it, his eyes so dark they were ebony. "You grew up in a court. Think about it."

Mahiya blinked at his anger, her own emotions skewing sideways.

"The information," Jason demanded before she could unravel the tangled skein of her thoughts.

In the end, it wasn't a difficult choice. Because the cold, hard fact was that Jason was right—it didn't matter that she'd done nothing to warrant incarceration in this gilded prison. Neha was the ruler of this territory, had absolute authority over her citizens. If she wanted to torture Mahiya for an eon, that was her right.

As Jason had pointed out, no other archangel would step in and risk inciting a war for the knowledge Mahiya currently held. Therefore, it must be Jason. At least, he hadn't lied to her. Rather, he had a way of being too honest, stripping away illusion and hope. So she would throw the dice and hope he kept his end of the bargain.

"Lijuan," she said, her chest aching at the remembered sensation of the bone-chilling cold in the corridor that night. "No one saw her arrive, and no one saw her leave, but as she's no longer fully corporeal, that means nothing. I heard her speaking with Neha inside the room guarded by the vine snake—and yes, I am certain. Her voice is distinctive." Screams, that was what lived in Lijuan's voice.

Jason was silent for a long, long time, the swirling curves and fine dots of the tattoo on his face stark in the sunlight. When he did speak, it was to say, "I need you to find out if any of the women in the court—high or low—have gone missing. Focus on the ones who aren't at the center but at the edges."

Startled by the abrupt change of subject, she answered instinctively, "That should be easy enough to discover. The population inside the fort is tightly controlled."

Jason spread his wings, the darkness spilling off them, and she knew it for a sign of dismissal.

"That's it?" she asked, wanting to grab hold of him, shake him, shatter the obsidian walls that kept him remote from the world. "That's all you have to say?" So easily, he'd destroyed then forgotten her.

"For now." He rose into the air.

Teeth gritted, she pushed herself into a vertical takeoff, knowing the conversation was over. She could never catch him in the sky. Not only that, he was a spymaster. If he wanted to vanish, Mahiya was ill-equipped to keep track of him . . . and Neha had to know that. "A game," she said through a throat raw with such rage that it threatened to blind. "It was a game from the start." Neha had set Mahiya up to fail, set her up to die.

13

Dmitri braced himself on one elbow and leaned down to kiss awake the woman in his bed, her silky skin warm. The fathomless green was yet hazy with sleep when her eyes fluttered open. "Is it morning already?" Fingers threading through his hair, she claimed a deeper kiss that reminded him he belonged to her, should he have forgotten. "Good morning, husband."

"Good morning, wife." He would never tire of saying that. "Are you hungry?"

Honor's response was a husky laugh that wrapped around his heart. "I do think you have an ulterior motive for that question."

Since he'd already tugged down the sheet to display the lush mounds of her breasts, that was a moot question. He caressed her with teasing strokes, in the mood to play with his wife, and when she kicked off the sheets in unhidden frustration, he moved in to settle between her legs.

Where he teased her some more.

With his fingers.

With his body.

With his mouth.

Honor arched under him on a soft gasp, her hands clenching in his hair hard enough that it hurt a little. It was an exquisite pain that could grow into an addiction—the pain of her pleasure. Smiling, he rubbed his unshaven jaw against the soft skin of her inner thigh, alert for even the tiniest indication of distress, before prowling up a feminine form rippling with aftershocks of erotic ecstasy.

"Open your eyes." Only when she obeyed the quiet order did he push into her. Always, *always* he made certain she was with him every step of the way. Because Honor had been brutalized, and those scars wouldn't magically disappear in a week or even a year. They were an indelible part of her, but there was no need to make the damage any worse, something he'd once done and would never again so much as chance—he'd carve out his own heart first.

"Dmitri." A throaty whisper, her lips on his neck, her fingers on his nape, caressing him, kissing him, just the way he liked.

It wasn't the same as before, when he'd been with Ingrede, and he didn't mourn that. No, he felt like the luckiest bastard on the planet. Because as Ingrede had loved the Dmitri he'd been, Honor loved the Dmitri he'd become. There was no horror or distaste in her at the darkness he carried within, nothing but an acceptance that told him he was home after centuries in the most barren wasteland.

"Stop," he warned when she used her body to caress his cock, internal muscles utilized to painfully pleasurable effect. "I'm not ready to finish yet."

"I love that tone in your voice." Biting gently at his jaw, she fell back on the bed and interlocked her wrists above her head. "Here I am. With what new torment do you plan to torture me?"

She was teasing him, the wench, her body a molten fist that squeezed and tempted. Another day, he might have played an erotic game with her, but having kept his wife awake to near dawn, he was feeling as satisfied as a well-fed cat this morning. "A long, slow ride for you I think." He placed a hand on her breast. "Very slow."

"Not that." Again, that playful light in her eyes. "Anything but."

Kissing the smile from her lips and feeling the warmth of it travel through his own veins, he moved his body in a steady, deep rhythm that drew another shuddering wave of pleasure from Honor. Even as she cried out, her body locked possessively around him, he gave in to his own need and pierced the pulse in her neck for the merest taste.

"Dmitri." A sigh of sensual delight, and then they were both tumbling into sensation lush and languid, limbs entangled and hearts fused.

Afterward, he soaped her body in the shower and helped her dry her hair. It wasn't the kind of tenderness he'd have shown any other woman, had long believed he'd lost the capacity for it—but it made his bones hum in masculine satisfaction that she let him do what he would, her trust blinding. Kisses on his naked chest, her legs twining around his jean-clad ones as she sat on the counter bundled in a fluffy pink robe, she also made every attempt to distract him, and he laughed, threatened to punish her.

"Promises, promises."

Ten minutes later, they sat across from one another at the little round breakfast table in the villa on the outskirts of Tuscany that Raphael had gifted them on their wedding. With Michaela in accord with Raphael for the moment, and no one aware of where Dmitri and Honor planned to honeymoon, it was a safe enough location.

"Dmitri?"

Catching the solemn note in her voice, he glanced up from where he was scanning through messages on his phone. "What is it?" Tower business could wait. Everything could wait. Honor came first.

She rose, walked around to lean against the table by his side, her fingers playing with strands of his damp hair. "You haven't brought up the change . . . to becoming a vampire."

Nudging aside the part in her robe, he placed his hand on the warmth of her thigh. "There's no rush." He'd once thought to do exactly that, to push her into immortality before she could change her mind, but with the dawn had come the realization he could no more force this on Honor than he could hurt her.

"I made my choice." Her tone reminded him she was a hunter, blooded and honed.

"It was a choice made in the aftermath of glory," he said, the emotions from that night vivid in his mind. "I won't ever try to talk you out of it"—he wanted a thousand lifetimes with her—"but I find I have just enough of a scrap of goodness inside me to not railroad you."

She smiled, his wife with her heart that belonged to him, a gift beyond price. "I still can't believe you're here, that we're here." Sliding into his lap, she laid her head against the bare skin of his shoulder. "I keep expecting it all to disappear."

"It won't." That was a promise he'd spill blood to keep. "Eternity or a single mortal lifetime, we'll walk the road together."

14

Having spent the remainder of the day listening unseen to courtiers and soldiers, mortals and vampires, angels young and old, Jason used the cloak of night to conceal himself as he flew over the fort. He was near certain of the identity of the person who had murdered Eris. However, he needed two further pieces of information—Mahiya was currently attempting to gather one of those pieces in the trenches of Neha's court.

Sweeping down to land near the exquisite courtyard garden where the beautiful had gathered tonight ostensibly to share their sorrow, he allowed the pool of darkness he'd chosen as his landing place to seep into him. Regardless of what some whispered, Jason couldn't create shadows from thin air, but he could extend and amplify the smallest tendrils of the dark until he simply didn't register in most people's vision, or if he did, it was as a ghost image caught out of the corner of the eye.

He hadn't always been so at home in the shadows.

"How can I be a night scout if I'm afraid of the dark?" His lower lip quivered as he walked beside his mother,

helping her collect shellfish from the beach half a morning's flight from their home.

"Everyone's scared of the dark when they're young." Tugging him to a shallow rock pool, she showed him a hermit crab crawling around with its home on its back. "You love the dark sometimes—like on the night flight you took with your father."

"There were stars then." They had reminded him of the sparkly jewels his mother used to wear when the visitors came. No one had visited for a long time, probably because his father was always so angry. "It wasn't really dark."

His mother's amethyst dress floated in the breeze. "You already see better in the dark than I do—you helped me find my lost earring two nights ago, remember?"

Jason nodded. "It wasn't hard." The black pearl with the pretty blue shimmer had kind of twinkled at him in the dark.

"Not for you, my smart boy." Laughing in that way that made him laugh, too, she said, "One day, you'll see so well at night, it will be as if you walk in daylight. You'll never again be scared of the dark."

His mother had been right. By the time he was a hundred and fifty, his night vision had developed to the point where he had the sight of a nocturnal predator. The dark was home to him, and now he wrapped it around himself as he stood watch.

The open space was lit only by the flickering light from hundreds of candles, many cradled protectively in colored glass holders that turned the marble of the buildings around the courtyard into a dreamscape. As for those who stood within—laughter was muted, the hues less vibrant than might be expected in an archangel's court, but that was the only bow to Eris's death.

No one would guess that his funeral pyre blazed tomorrow.

Yet regardless of the many painted butterflies who held glasses of champagne and spoke with elegant gestures while subtly jockeying for position, he had no difficulty pinpointing Mahiya. Dressed in a silk sari of blue green embellished with a thin gold border, she moved through the crowd with the ease of someone on familiar ground.

Right then, she halted, angling her head in his direction, her gaze so intent he imagined he could glimpse the brilliant tawny brown even from this distance. There was no way she could've sensed him, but he was certain she had. When she moved again, it was with a fine layer of tension across her shoulders. An enigma was Mahiya, with the manners of the court elite and the instincts of a hunter.

Looking away to sweep the crowd with his gaze, he confirmed that Neha remained with Eris's body. Jason had had confirmation that she'd granted Eris's family permission to attend the dawn funeral ceremony, but no one else. Some whispered the archangel was jealous of her consort even in death, but Jason believed Neha mourned too deeply to share her grief.

Returning his attention to Mahiya, he saw that she was drifting away from the group. He scanned the guests who remained once more before making his way to the palace he shared with Mahiya, catching a glimpse of blue green silk whispering past the doorway.

Entering behind her, he locked the main doors and made his way upstairs to find her on their shared balcony, her gaze on the courtyard lit only by four quiet lamps. She didn't startle when he came to stand beside her. A single wide, shallow step separated his balcony area from hers, and where he had columns holding up the roof, the edge open for easy flight, she had a railing, which she now gripped.

"Her name was Audrey." Quiet words, no apparent residue of her earlier anger. "Tall, curvaceous blonde vampire. She'd been part of Neha's circle for two decades but hadn't made it into the inner court."

"How long ago did she disappear?"

"The same day as Eris's murder, though no one else has yet put the two events together. Those who've noticed Audrey's absence believe it's a simple case of conflicting schedules. No one has bothered to try to contact her—she wasn't one of the favorites, and the friendships she made were shallow at best." Hands clenching on the railing, she continued to stare out into the night. "Do you believe she killed Eris?"

Look at me, princess. "It's one conclusion."

Her fingers flexed on the railing. "Do I matter?" It was a question with so many nuances, he knew he caught but the bluntest edge. "In the grand scheme of your existence, does my life matter to you on any level?"

He was a man used to keeping secrets, but he knew at that instant that he had to answer this, or he risked losing something he wasn't even aware he searched for. "Yes. You matter."

A tremor quaked Mahiya's frame . . . and at last, she turned those bright eyes his way. "Then you will uphold our bargain?"

"Yes." Bargain or not, Jason had no intention of leaving her to Neha's mercies, but he would make her no promises until he knew they would not be broken.

When he stepped to the edge of his side of the balcony in preparation for taking flight, Mahiya said, "She isn't in her chambers. I checked earlier."

Jason wasn't used to explaining himself to anyone. Even Raphael gave him free rein, but Mahiya's statement held a brittle pride that said this woman, this survivor, had been pushed to the brink. "Good." He turned, held her gaze to show that he wasn't ignoring her. "I have another idea I wish to explore."

A pause, then a small nod, her voice no longer cool when she said, "I'll wait for your return."

Strange what those simple words did to him as he flew off the balcony and up into the diamond-studded jet of the night sky. There, he hovered invisible against the stars and *listened*. His gift wasn't one he could call up on command, but he could put himself into the optimum frame of mind to trigger it. Now, he did just that, the capricious winds whipping strands of hair from his queue and pasting the thin linen of his shirt against his body.

Whispers began to filter through to his mind minutes later, a thousand small fragments that meant nothing. Patient, he allowed the river of sensory input to flow around him. Then he caught a single whisper that wasn't a word so much as a *sense*. Shifting into the wind, he flew over the ridges and valleys of the mountains, following an instinct honed to a keen edge by near to seven hundred years of life.

Nothing stood out about the valley where the trail stopped cold, but he came down under the moonlight nonetheless, careful to land with a stealth that was as innate as breathing. Swathed in shadows, the land betrayed none of its secrets . . . until the wind shifted.

Dusty decay, but no scent of rot.

Catching the line of the breeze, he traced it back to a tumble of gray stone, some of the rough chunks the size of small cars. The sheer rock face above told him their origin, though enough time had passed that the hardy grasses evolved to survive this harsh climate had grown to above his knee around the rocks.

It was, he thought, sheer luck that the body had fallen into a crevice when it had been dropped. Or the remnants of it in any case. The long skirt set with hundreds of tiny mirrors would otherwise have been a beacon in the sunlight. As it was, that girlish skirt was shaded by the rocks, the majority of the body caught in a fissure created by two adjoining hunks of stone.

The blood had dried and flaked over the time she'd lain here alone and forgotten, her long blonde hair dry but paradoxically shiny, her face unrecognizable. However, the shade between the rocks had preserved enough tissue on her face and body that he could speculate as to the fact she'd been severely bruised. The rocks could be responsible for the damage, but Jason would bet she'd suffered the abuse prior to death. Because this killing, like Eris's, had been about fury, about rage.

The viciousness of it was such that even the decay and the foraging of small animals and birds couldn't hide the fact that she'd been stabbed over and over. Where the skeletal structure of her body lay exposed to the elements, he could see the notches the blade had cut into her bones, marks of an ugly violence that would last long after the maggots had cleaned up what remained of her flesh.

Audrey had clearly not been the strongest of vampires, because while her heart was gone—ripped out by a brutal hand if her splintered rib cage was any indication—her head was still attached to her body. That head had been cracked and damaged, the skin of her neck shriveled to mummylike dryness where it wasn't missing, but from what Jason could see, the damage had been caused by birds and rodents eating at her flesh, not by an attempt at decapitation.

Her hands were bone now, no way to tell if she'd worn a ring on a particular finger, but he could as easily glean that from a photograph now that he knew her name. Walking the area around the body, he saw nothing else of note. It went against his every belief to leave her here, but he could not risk bringing her to the fort as yet. Neha's response was unpredictable—things could get deadly very quickly unless he did this exactly right.

And Audrey was long past being hurt. He had to consider other lives now.

"Whatever happens, I'll make sure you get home," he promised, before shifting back to a more open part of the valley and rising into the night sky.

Mahiya's balcony doors were open as if in invitation, and when he entered, it was to find her seated on a cushion on the living room floor. She'd changed from the sari into a tunic of vivid aquamarine teamed with slim cotton pants in plain black, her hair gathered in its familiar knot at the nape of her graceful neck.

In front of her sat a low table carved of dark wood and inlaid with the merest glimmer of fine gold around the edges, on top of which stood a pot of tea alongside a tray of mixed savories and sweets, and two cups. He halted, disappointment curling through his body. "You're expecting someone."

Mahiya's laugh was warm. "I am expecting you."

He hadn't been caught off guard for a long, long time. "How did you know when I would return?" Swirls of steam rose from the fine black tea she'd begun to pour.

"A good host learns her guest's rhythms." She waved a slender hand bare of rings but circled by two glass bangles the same shade as the tunic, toward the flat cushion on the other side of the table "Please, sit."

He wondered if she sought to seduce him, decided it unlikely—her tunic was too modest, the mandarin collar high, her sleeves elbow length, and her face scrubbed clean. Thrown a little off-balance by the fact she'd gone to all this trouble, he nudged aside the cushion and took a seat directly on the floor, his wings draping over the smaller jewel-toned cushions thrown around, the fabric soft against the bottom of his wings. "You must have a sensory gift of some kind to have anticipated my arrival with such accuracy."

"What? No." Her startled look transformed with the second word into an honesty so rueful that he knew she would've preferred to claim a gift. "I was watching the skies for you. So you see, there is no mystery after all."

Except that she had seen him. No one saw Jason when he didn't want to be seen, and he hadn't wanted to be spotted coming in to the fort. Which meant Mahiya did have a gift. "When did you spot me?" he asked in a casual tone, wanting to gauge the extent of her abilities. "When I dropped out of the clouds?"

"I assume so—I saw you on the horizon just past Guardian."

He'd been *high, high* in the sky at that point, a black dot against black. The fact Mahiya had developed what appeared to be an acute visual sense at such a young age told him she had the potential to grow into a power among angelkind. He'd erred, he admitted, lulled into complacency by the gentleness of her strength, akin to the quiet but persistent fall of water against stone rather than a violent quake, forgetting the fact she'd been born of two powerful immortals.

"Your tea."

"Thank you," he said in the same language she'd spoken, received a smile in return.

When she nudged over the plate of savories, he ate over half of them before halting—he'd missed dinner, was hungrier than he'd realized. All the while, Mahiya watched him with those cat-bright eyes of hers, and he searched for the poisonous hatred that should've infected her . . . only to find an incisive intelligence and a sweetness of spirit she couldn't hide, no matter how good she was at court masks.

Fascination entangled with a pride he had never expected to feel for the Princess Mahiya, for she had to have the will of a lioness to have managed to hold that poison at bay, though it dripped on her each and every day.

"Did you find Audrey?"

Jason considered the question, decided to trust her with the truth, measure her response. "Yes."

"She's dead, isn't she? And she was most likely the woman warming my father's bed."

The speed and accuracy of her conclusion made Jason still. "You know who killed Eris," he said slowly, realizing he'd erred in more than one way. "You've always known." She was far too smart, far too good at listening to what was unspoken, not to have put the pieces together.

In the process of placing her teacup on the table, she jerked, had to act quickly to stop the fine porcelain from tipping over. "What?"

Setting his own cup on the table, he reached for the pot and poured her more tea. "Drink."

Fingers trembling, she didn't dispute the order. By the time she put the cup back down, her expression was acute with determination. "You first."

15

Jason saw no reason not to acquiesce when they both carried the same knowledge. "Perhaps others could've bribed their way in, but we both know only one person could have walked *out* of Eris's palace soaked in blood and not been stopped by a single guard." Guards who professed not to remember a single unusual detail from that murderous night—and who Neha hadn't executed, though they had permitted the death of her consort.

Mahiya picked up a sweet that was a combination of sugar and milk spiced with cloves and topped with slivers of almond, ate it with great deliberation. "Yes," she said at last, her tone rough silk, "that was my first thought."

"You've changed your mind?"

"Why would . . . Your presence, it makes no sense."

Yes, Jason thought, why would Neha invite him to solve a murder she herself had committed and for which no one would ever hold her to account? That was a far more power-ful mystery than why Eris had died. It was either madness or fatal arrogance that had led the male angel to believe his wife wouldn't discover his affair with Audrey. Or perhaps

Eris had sought death after three hundred years of imprisonment.

Jason discarded that thought as soon as it arose. Eris had been too self-centered, too much a man of ego to have ever chosen suicide, especially by such a convoluted method and in a way that left him violated and stripped of pride and beauty.

Porcelain clinked on porcelain as Mahiya put her cup on the saucer. "Neha would subvert you from Raphael. Perhaps that is the reason why."

"No." Not when Neha had met him soon after he arrived at the Refuge. "She must surely know I will never serve a woman who did such to the one she claimed to love."

Mahiya's gaze grew piercing, as if she'd heard the history that drove his declaration.

"And she is too proud to lie and claim you broke the vow in order to have you executed. Which does not leave us with any answers." Reaching forward, she topped off his tea. "What will you do?"

He considered each of the facts he currently had, both together and as separate pieces. It wasn't the murder that was the most important. That Neha and Lijuan were involved was problematic, but the two were neighbors—a friendship between them was not incomprehensible. Without further details, he remained in the dark as to the nature of their secret meetings.

And . . . he hadn't yet worked out how to gain Mahiya her freedom. "I'm not ready to leave."

Mahiya nudged forward the savories again. "Do you expect me to lie to her when she asks what you have discovered?"

He ate two more of the baked pastries filled with a sweet and spicy vegetable mix. "She won't listen to the truth from you," Jason spoke the merciless words knowing Mahiya had already come to the same conclusion. "Rather, she'll use it as an excuse to kill you."

Mahiya ate another sweet, her expression unruffled. "She doesn't need an excuse."

"I'm not so certain." In killing Mahiya, Neha would be killing a child she'd helped raise, and angelkind revered the bond a child had with his or her parent or guardian. For a guardian to kill that child . . . it would break a taboo so deep, it was a racial imperative.

Jason, more than anyone, understood that such taboos could be broken, but doing so came at a price. "Executing you without due cause, and while she is clearly sane, would make her a pariah among our kind." And Neha was a social creature, one who valued her connections around the world.

Sipping at tea that must be tepid by now, Mahiya met his gaze. "I'll keep my silence, but your reputation precedes you. As the days continue to pass with no result from you, she'll become suspicious."

As it turned out, coming up with a way to allay Neha's distrust was the one thing Jason didn't have to worry about—because the crimson of blood violently spilled hadn't yet stopped flowing.

Shock and sorrow both colored Neha's eyes when she joined Jason beside the crumpled body discovered on a rooftop terrace on the other side of the courtyard from the Palace of Jewels. The weak postdawn sunlight washed everything in soft gold, made it appear a macabre painting. In the center of the painting lay a vampire dressed in a pair of black silk pajamas, the straps of her camisole ripped to expose heavy breasts, her skin gray with death.

Her legs were twisted and broken, as if she'd fallen or been dropped from a height. However, the position of her body made it impossible to confirm whether she'd begun her descent from the sky or from one of the small ground-to-air defense towers mounted around the fort—the nearest one was at the right distance. Jason would speak to the guard who'd been on duty in the predawn hours, but instinct said the victim had never been in the tower, her fall arranged by an angel.

In spite of her exposed breasts, the attack didn't appear

to have been sexual. The damage to her clothing had most likely occurred during the struggle. Unlike Audrey, this victim's head wasn't attached to her body; it had rolled to settle against one of the latticework barriers where he'd seen several exquisitely dressed women leaning and laughing yesterday as they looked out over the edge into the courtyard below. Today, the only sound he could hear was that of a woman's jagged sobs, while in his line of sight lay splatters of congealed rust red where the head had bounced and rolled after being dropped.

She was looking at him from the other side of the room, her pretty dark brown eyes filmed over with a whiteness that was wrong. The stump of her neck was crusted with blood where it sat on the table in the corner, as if placed there for just this purpose.

Unsurprised by the echoes of horror that resonated through time, Jason locked the memory shut behind shields he'd had a lifetime to build, and continued to look at the body that lay in front of him, not one long gone from this earth.

This woman's chest had been left unmolested, her heart still within her flesh, but in one thing, this body and Audrey's were identical. Though the crush injuries caused by the fall obscured most of the bruises, Jason could tell the victim had been beaten with pitiless brutality before death. When he turned her over to look at her back, he saw that her spine had been ripped out to lie broken against blood-encrusted skin. He eased her back down with gentle hands, certain she'd been conscious for the beating, the torture, paralyzed and helpless as a babe.

Rage and violence, the killer's fingerprint was unmistakable. "Do you recognize her?" he asked Neha, aware she had only just returned to Archangel Fort after Eris's mountaintop funeral. From the heavily damp hair scraped into a knot at her nape and her simple tunic of pale blue paired with white pants, she'd been bathing afterward as was custom, when she received word of this death.

"Her name was Shabnam." The archangel's tone held raw

grief. "She was one of my longest-serving ladies-in-waiting."
Crouching down beside the vampire's head with its ravaged
skin, uncaring that her wings scraped the cool marble and
the blood that stained it, she reached out to close Shabnam's
eyelids over hazel eyes dulled in death, using a dot of power
to make sure they remained so. "I scattered Eris's ashes less
than an hour ago while his mother sobbed, and now I must
inform Shabnam's people of her murder."

Jason heard the anger beneath the grief, and it was
another puzzle. "Will you tell me about her?"

"She was a butterfly," Neha said, rising to her feet, her
movements heavy, as if she was weighted down with sadness. "A pretty ornament who cared for glitter and sparkles.
She was not dark of heart or wise of politics. The only reason
she made it so high in my court was that I enjoyed her sense
of innocence." A twist of her lips. "Of all the women who
serve me, she was the most harmless."

Yet she had been killed with terrible cruelty. Jason wasn't
arrogant enough to think he could read all of Neha's moods,
but her sorrow appeared genuine. And while he could see
her murdering Eris in a jealous rage, it beggared belief that
she'd spill innocent blood while preparing to say her final
farewell to her consort. Even if she had done so in a grief
or guilt-fueled madness, she had no need to pretend. Brutal
as it was to say, Shabnam had been Neha's to kill.

"Do you believe it to be the same person who murdered
Eris?" Neha asked, the cold blade of an archangel's anger a
faint nimbus of light burning off her wings.

"Perhaps." Jason rose from his crouched position beside
the body. "Or it could be an attempt to use Eris's murder to
cover an unrelated crime." Shabnam had surely been a stunning woman in life. "Did she have a lover?"

"Yes. But Tarun is gone to Europe on a task for me—he
could not have done this."

Jason made a note to confirm Tarun's whereabouts himself. It might be a truism, but the lover was most often the
one responsible for the murder of a woman, mortal or

immortal. Some darkness knew no boundaries. "Anyone else who might hold a grudge against her?"

Neha walked to the part of the terrace that flowed down a wide step to a covered pathway that, if followed, led to another, lower terrace. "She was a lady-in-waiting, Jason. I know little of her life."

Of course.

Unlike the Seven, Neha's ladies-in-waiting were there to entertain, amuse, and otherwise see to Neha's comfort, dismissed from the archangel's mind the instant they were out of sight. "May I have access to the others who serve you?" He would also contact Samira, gain her impressions of Shabnam and Tarun.

"Yes." Neha flared out her wings. "Mahiya will know where to find them." With that, she rose off the terrace, an angel of grace, power, and . . . centuries of blood that stained her hands to ruby blackness.

Jason found Mahiya in the courtyard below the terrace, and though he'd given her no instructions, she said, "Most of the ladies-in-waiting are even now gathering in their private garden. I would, however, recommend you speak to them one at a time."

"Agreed. However, seeing how they act as a group may prove helpful."

"This way." She turned left, her mint green tunic crisp against her skin. "Word travels fast in the small city that is the fort," she said, answering the question he hadn't asked. "I knew about the discovery of Shabnam's body perhaps five minutes after the guard made it." Fixing the pin that held her long white scarf neatly over her left shoulder, she shot him an assessing look. "He says you arrived seconds later. Dropped out of the sky like a black arrow."

"Do you think I killed Shabnam?" He knew he was capable of murder should he ever have anyone of his own to protect. But that, of course, was an academic consideration.

"No." An answer far more resolute than he'd expected. "However, everyone wonders how you knew."

The winds had whispered a name, tugged him in a certain direction, but that wasn't a secret he could tell this princess who saw things no one should be able to see . . . and who made him think impossible thoughts about always being welcomed home as he'd been last night. "I was flying above the fort, saw the guard running in a panic. It wasn't difficult to sweep down, find out why."

Mahiya raised a single eyebrow but kept her silence, and a minute later, they walked through one of the cool passages inside the fort to exit a few feet from gardens clothed in a profusion of fragrant blooms. Five women stood in a knot in one corner, blooms of another kind. When Mahiya would've moved out from the passageway, Jason stopped her with a hand on the silken warmth of her arm, the scent of her a caress to the senses. "Wait."

"The body language is interesting, is it not?" Mahiya's quiet comment echoed his own thoughts, her wing brushing his as she leaned in so he could hear her.

He didn't move away. "Very."

The tallest lady, an angel, had positioned herself so she didn't fully face any of the others. Another angel, her wings the dusty brown of a sparrow's, was holding on to a sylph of a vampire with the broken desperation of someone who isn't sure her legs will support her, while a dark-eyed angel and a vampire with pale skin wiped at their eyes with what appeared to be lace handkerchiefs.

"The sparrow," he murmured, "she actually grieves." The rest indulged in theatre.

"Yes." Sympathy in the single soft word. "Shabnam and she were both inducted into their positions at the same time, and rather than competing for Neha's attention, they became friends who helped each other navigate the politics."

"Why should there be politics? They occupy the same rarefied position."

Mahiya shot him a frowning look. "Are you making fun?"

Jason hadn't ever been accused of that, even by the

irrepressible Illium. "Strange as it may seem," he said, "I have never had reason to know about the inner workings of a group of ladies-in-waiting." He had operatives who were far more capable in that arena and who kept him apprised of any necessary information from such quarters.

"A lady-in-waiting has certain access to Neha." Mahiya appeared to have decided to take him at his word, though the suspicion in her eyes didn't totally dissipate—and for some reason, that made a quiet amusement warm his blood. "None of them would be stupid enough to risk their position by actually asking for anything, but occasionally, if a lady is particularly favored, Neha will grant her a boon."

Even a small boon from an archangel, Jason understood, could change the balance of power in a given situation. "Do they represent different groups in the court?" He looked at the women with new eyes, seeing iron butterflies, their wings edged with razors of ambition and greed.

"Not simply the court, but the territory."

Thus, they all had puppet masters at their back, tugging strings, situating each for maximum gain . . . doing the dirty work.

"Lisbeth holds the most power at present." She indicated the dark-eyed angel. "She's very intelligent. They all are."

He nodded in acknowledgment of the warning. "I take care to never underestimate an opponent, but I may have in this case." Like the others around her, Lisbeth looked . . . frothy. Clothes of a gauzy fabric that caught the wind and glossy brown hair done up in an intricate mass of curls, jeweled combs in the strands, features painted with an artful delicacy that highlighted her ebony-skinned beauty. "I've seen enough."

"Do you wish for me to organize interviews for you with the ladies?" Mahiya asked once they were back in the corridor.

"No." He'd find them on their own when they didn't expect to be questioned. Right now, he wanted the answer to a different kind of question. "You've become cooperative beyond the call of duty."

A shallow court smile—one he realized he despised after having glimpsed a real one last night when she admitted to watching for him. "You," she murmured, "are my best hope of escaping this hell."

It made him wonder just how far she'd go.

16

"Tell me who gains from Shabnam's death."

Mahiya felt a sudden, frustrated urge to scream when Jason used the haunting clarity of his voice to speak those words. She'd deliberately baited him with her sweetly poisonous reply, wanting to incite a response, to shatter the obsidian ice that surrounded him until it felt as if she spoke to a black mirror.

"Is there a lady who waits to take her position?" he clarified when she remained silent.

"There are always those who wait." She wrenched the strange madness under control, for what did it matter to her if Jason preferred to live a step distant from the world? "But Neha chooses who she will—an aspirant could kill off the entire group and fail to gain a place." Her scarf lifted on the wind as they walked upstairs to take the high terrace path, flicked over Jason's arm, his chest, before falling back neatly by her side.

I am jealous of a piece of fabric. Foolish when he does not even see me. "Sorry." Last night on the balcony, when

this deadly shadow of a man had made the clear effort not
to hurt her feelings, her fascination with him had altered
into something both tender and far more dangerous. The
way he'd looked at her after his return, she'd hoped . . . but
clearly, his actions had been nothing more than a quiet
kindness.

The realization made her heart ache.

"You cannot leash the wind," he said, his gaze an impenetrable depth she couldn't fathom.

"No, I suppose not." She broke the eye contact that was
too much, too strong, too visceral. "It would've been better
had Shabnam disappeared if this action was politically motivated," she said, forcing herself to concentrate. "Her killing
may well make Neha sympathize with her intimates and
choose the next lady from within their ranks."

"Might they gain an extra boon?" Jason's wing was so
close, she could see the fine black filaments that made up
each midnight feather.

Her fingers curled into her palms. "No." Though she was
in no doubt that were such a thing a possibility, Shabnam's
"family" might well have sacrificed her with cold-blooded
calculation. "Shabnam was worth more alive—she'd been
with Neha a long time, had her trust and liking."

"Your wings are dragging."

"What? Oh." Cheeks heating at the reminder one might
give to a child, she raised her wings so that the edges no
longer trailed on the red sandstone of the terrace.

Then he spoke again, and her embarrasment transformed
into the most bittersweet of emotions. "You need to work
on strengthening your wings in every detail. If Neha's temper turns, it may come down to a race to a safe hiding place
until I can work out a political solution to your freedom."

"I am just over three hundred years old, Jason," she said,
using his name of her own volition for the first time, the
small intimacy filling her mind with all the other fragile
moments she'd dreamed of experiencing with the nameless,
faceless lover she'd imagined in her darkest hours. One with

whom she'd fly, see the world, build a life, build a *home*, fill it with laughter and love and happiness such as she'd never known.

"Even were I to have trained for endurance flying every day of my existence," she said, holding onto that dream with every ounce of her strength in the face of harsh reality, "I couldn't outfly Neha, even for the shortest flicker of time." Neha was an archangel who had lived millennia, her power vast. She'd crush Mahiya like an insect and never notice.

"And a hiding place?" Mahiya shook her head. "I won't let her bury me again. Better I die fighting for my freedom than to turn into Eris, dead in chains." It was a fierce vow. "I will not allow her to pin my wings to the wall as Lijuan does to the butterflies she collects."

Jason felt a dark wildness come to life within him at Mahiya's impassioned declaration, but the response that came out of his mouth was almost icily calm, the words he'd wanted to speak hidden deep inside the silence that had been his existence for so long. "Lijuan would like to add me to her collection."

Mahiya stumbled on a rough part of the terrace, would have fallen if he hadn't shot out a hand and gripped her upper arm. Ignoring his hold, she stared at him. "Did she say that to your face?"

"Such unique wings you have, Jason. A pity if you should die in battle, those midnight wings destroyed. A quiet, measured death in the arms of a lovely girl ripe with her womanhood would be so much easier, do you not think?"

"She offered me a peaceful death." He forced himself to release Mahiya, his need for touch a clawing thing inside him. "She's been much more vocal about Illium."

"Blue tipped with silver, yes, his wings are stunning," Mahiya murmured. "I saw him once when he accompanied Raphael on a visit."

Jason glanced down into eyes bright even in the shadows of an archway, and had the sudden realization the brilliance was an indication of emerging power. One no one had noticed because the change, like every aspect of Mahiya's power, had to have been incremental. "Your own wings are just as unique."

"No, they're not." Mahiya's tone went flat. "My mother had the same."

He hadn't known that, and if wings of such beauty had been forgotten, it meant someone had buried the information. Neha, it seemed, had wiped her sister out of existence as well as out of life. Now she attempted to do the same to the child who bore wings the exquisite sapphires and emerald greens of a peacock's spray.

"Did you . . . Have you seen Lijuan's Collection Room?"

Jason halted, watched Mahiya rub her hands up and down her arms, as if they did not stand in sunlight thick as syrup. "Yes," he said, "I have." The Collection Room was located within the stronghold where Lijuan had first created her reborn, and kept permanently cold to preserve the bodies that hung on the walls, their wings spread out in magnificent display.

Some, Jason knew, had died in circumstances where their wings had remained undamaged, but others . . . others had simply vanished from the world. "If you saw that room," he said, driven to touch a single finger to Mahiya's cheek, "you're lucky to be alive."

She didn't shrug away the touch. Flattening her hand over her belly, she said, "I thought I could bargain service for sanctuary. I convinced myself it would be akin to being a servant, that I'd be free aside from my duties." A shiver wracked her frame. "I think the only reason Lijuan returned me to Neha rather than keeping me as a trophy was that she was deeply offended by the fact I would dare run from the archangel to whom I 'owed duty.'"

"Were you a cat," he murmured, his mind on the massive cold-storage room behind the Collection Room, filled with drawers big enough to hold angelic bodies, "I would say you are now poorer by at least seven of your nine lives."

"What do you know?" It was a whisper dancing over his skin.

"Many things I cannot unsee."

Jason's words continuing to circle in her mind, heavy with a lingering darkness that tugged at the vulnerable core of her in spite of her conclusion that he felt no such need in return, Mahiya parted from him several minutes later. "I must attend to Neha," she said. "I am meant to be spying on you after all."

Jason's response was as unexpected as the fleeting touch that had anchored her to the here and now when the nightmare of Lijuan's stronghold threatened to suck her under. "You're not hard enough for such a task"—almost gentle words—"and I honor the strength it must've taken to fight the bitterness, to refuse to allow your heart to petrify to pitiless stone."

No one else had *ever* understood that truth, understood the conscious will it had taken to remain untainted and unbroken. Shaken at the way he could reach her so deeply when he remained so distant, she said, "I must go," and turned to walk away.

When she looked over her shoulder seconds later, he was gone, the sky showing no sign of the spymaster who threatened to strip her to the soul. "Who are you, Jason?"

The wind held no answers for her.

Lowering her gaze from the sky, she took a deep breath and replaced the emotional armor Jason had disassembled with nothing but a touch, a few words. She could not go to Neha vulnerable and exposed.

Ten minutes later, when she located the archangel, it wasn't within the cool confines of her private palace, but walking the ramparts, looking down at the city that was her own. Keeping her wings neatly to her back, her emotions under rigid control, Mahiya watched the archangel nod to the visitors walking or riding up the steep, curving path to the fort. Neha didn't allow modern vehicles on the pathway or within the fort itself, but elephants, camels, and horses were considered acceptable means of transport.

"Have you forgotten who it is you come to speak to?" It was a silken question.

"I apologize if I have misstepped, my lady." Once, the words would've been knife shards in her throat. Now, they were nothing but tools she used to distract the archangel while she worked to break out of this prison.

Silence. Neha's wings a sweep of cool white scattered with a rare few jewel blue filaments that echoed Mahiya's own feathers. The familial connection showed itself in other ways, too, but only to someone who knew what it was they searched for, and those old enough to deduce the truth also knew never to speak of it.

To everyone else, Mahiya was a distant descendant of Neha's the archangel had taken in out of kindness after the death of her unnamed parents. That the newborn child had appeared eight months after Eris's incarceration and Nivriti's assumed execution had further distanced any connection that might've been made by most. Few could imagine that Neha had been cruel enough to have kept her sister chained through the months of her pregnancy, but Mahiya had heard the story from Neha's own lips.

"A gift on your hundredth birthday." The archangel's smile caused a chill along Mahiya's spine. "The history of your becoming."

Angels didn't easily die, but a female angel was most vulnerable after childbirth, especially a childbirth where her womb had been cut open with a rusty blade, her baby literally torn out of her by uncaring hands, her internal organs left to spill to the floor. Add in a lack of food and water, and the thin, thin air at the top of the distant mountain fort where her mother had apparently been held, and Nivriti had stood no chance.

Even then, powerful as she'd been, it must've taken her years of agony to starve to total death.

"You give offense by existing," Neha said at last, and it was an almost absent comment. "Tell me about Jason."

Mahiya did, and it was the truth . . . what she spoke of it in any case. As Jason had pointed out, she could hardly accuse Neha of murder and hope to live. "He appears to be upholding the vow," she concluded, "and working to unearth the identity of the murderer or murderers."

Neha's eyes focused on some distant aspect Mahiya couldn't see, the silk sari Neha wore now a cool champagne bordered in bronze, the folds pinned with neat precision on her shoulder by an antique brooch. Her blouse was a bronze that echoed the border, the cut perfect, the intricate back work necessary to accommodate wings done with such precision that the fit remained flawless.

No one, Mahiya thought, could say the Archangel of India was not the most elegant of creatures, but Mahiya alone understood the vindictive depth of hatred that had driven Neha for so long. It hadn't surprised her in the least when Anoushka was found guilty of crimes against a child—the angel had watched her own mother raise a child for the sole purpose of vengeance after all. Kindness to a thousand other children could not eradicate the evil taint of that single heinous act.

"Do you mourn your father?" Neha asked into the silence.

"I mourn who he could've been." There had been promise in Eris, and perhaps if he'd had better guidance as a youth, as a husband, he might have fulfilled it. That was as much forgiveness as she could give him, because he'd been an adult, too, had made his own choices.

"In that we are in agreement, child of my blood's blood."

Mahiya went motionless—it never augured anything but ill for her when Neha referred to the ties that connected them. However, today, the archangel simply tilted her face to the burning heat of the sun, allowing it to wash over the golden brown of her skin, imbuing it with warmth. At that moment, Mahiya could imagine why her people saw her as a benevolent goddess.

"I first met him when I was an angel of a thousand." The words were soft, her gaze on a past long gone. "At four hundred, he was barely an adult to my mind, and I treated him as such. Irresponsible, I thought, but beautiful and with such masculine charm. Our paths did not cross again until I had become an archangel, and Eris a man elegant and confident."

A hot desert wind waved over them a second later, breaking Neha's reverie. "Have you ever loved, Mahiya?"

Knowing what was coming, she steeled her spine. "No."

"Not even Arav?"

There it was, the blow that reminded her of a humiliation that had crushed her young heart, threatened to fracture her fledgling spirit. "I was a child then. What did I know of love?" However, she'd learned that pretty words were not to be trusted—and that she had a strength she'd never before understood.

"My daughter is dead," Neha said, in an apparent non sequitur, "and so is my husband and consort. Some would say I am being punished for what I did to you and your mother." Dark eyes on Mahiya's face. "Do you think I am being punished, Mahiya?"

If you believe so. For your karma is of your own making.

"It is not my place to think such things, my lady." Mahiya used every ounce of skill she'd picked up from her years in the court to hide her thoughts, keep her voice expressionless. "I am only grateful for your kindness in giving me a home."

Neha's lips curved, but the ice in her gaze remained frigid. "A pretty speech. Perhaps you will prove interesting, after all." A slight motion of a slender hand, and Mahiya knew she'd been dismissed.

Walking the wide pathway along the ramparts until she came to steps that led down into the sprawling main courtyard—built at a time when ground armies were mounted on elephants—she made her way down with slow grace, though she wanted nothing more than to spread her wings and fly off into the mountains. That deadly chance was one she'd save for last, when she had no other hope.

"Yes. You matter."

Hugging Jason's quiet words to her heart, her faith in his integrity an instinct she had no will to fight, Mahiya crossed the stone of the courtyard with measured steps. Open as it was, with only a few miniature trees in large planters on the edges, she could feel a hundred eyes on her—guards, courtiers, servants.

She acknowledged those who acknowledged her, but stopped for no one . . . until a tall, handsome angel with skin of darkest brown and eyes of smoky gray walked into her path, his wings a mottled brown two shades paler than his skin. And she understood why Neha had spoken of the man who had taught Mahiya her first and most lasting lesson about love.

17

"Mahiya, my sweet." Arav went as if to take her hand in preparation for lifting it to his mouth, but she halted that by the polite expedient of a small bow, hands clasped together in greeting in front of her.

"Sir," she said, and in her mind, it was an insult. "I did not know you visited my lady."

"Of course I visit Neha." A charming smile he'd once convinced Mahiya was for her alone.

Now she trusted no man's smile . . . and was starting to trust a man who smiled not at all. It was an impossible thing, but there it was. She had more trust in an enemy spymaster than she had in any other person in this fort—Jason's truths might be dark and often brutal, but they were never lies wrapped in acidic sweetness that could corrode.

"She and I are friends of an age." Arav's gaze lifted to where Neha stood on the ramparts, her gaze cityward. "And of course, I have not seen you, my favorite lover, for many a year."

"I am no longer your lover and have not been for centuries." She felt defiled by the memory of how she'd allowed him to take her innocence with a satisfaction she'd then mistaken for care. "I wish you a good visit, but I must be on my way."

Arav blocked her when she would've walked around him. To insist would be to cause a scene, and while Mahiya had no compunction against slapping Arav if need be, giving in to the urge while Neha stood so close could be dangerous. Because in one thing Arav did not lie—he and Neha did have a friendship.

To this day, she didn't know if Arav had been acting under orders when he seduced then threw Mahiya away like trash, or if it had been simple chance, the male in front of her taking advantage of an untutored girl who did not enjoy her archangel's favor and thus had no one from whom Arav might fear reprisal.

"I hear you share rooms with one who has sworn a blood vow." Arav's eyes glittered. "Raphael's pet mute."

Mute? It was an insult so incomprehensible as to have no impact. Jason didn't chatter, but he wasn't a wholly silent creature—he simply chose not to speak until he had something to say. "Neha," she said, with glacial politeness, "appears to hold him in high esteem."

His lips twisted in a reflection of the putrid inner self she hadn't seen until it was too late. "She is grieving."

Ah. "Is that why you're here? To offer solace?"

"It is a friend's prerogative."

"A friend who wishes to take Eris's place."

"I am stronger than he ever was." Arrogance backed by fact; Arav was one of Neha's generals. "When I am consort," he said, gripping her jaw between thumb and forefinger before she could flinch away, "I will ask Neha to give you to me as my special pet."

Fool. Mahiya twisted out of his grip, heedless of whether it might attract Neha's attention. Because if there was one thing the archangel had never done, it was to overlook the mistreatment of women in her court. Any man found to have forced, beaten, or coerced a woman was summarily punished by having parts of his body amputated—the worse the assault, the more he lost, until some didn't survive to regenerate.

It did not matter if the woman was in favor or not, rich or poor, peasant or courtier. The rule was absolute and part of what made Neha such a beloved queen. But that Neha, Mahiya thought suddenly, a prickling of cold along her spine, might not be the one who ruled now . . . at least not where Mahiya was concerned.

"Some would say I am being punished for what I did to you and your mother."

Stifling the chilling realization, she favored Arav with a scalpel-sharp smile. "Neha values loyalty in a man above all else. If she ever thinks you have plans to touch another while bound to her, Eris's torture and disemboweling will seem a gentle punishment in comparison."

Paling until the loss of blood was obvious even under the darkness of his skin, Arav took two quick steps away from her. Mahiya was already gone, having used his momentary shock to skirt past and down the pathway toward the stables—petting the horses she so loved would go some way toward calming her. She felt Arav's eyes boring between her shoulder blades until she disappeared around the corner, and knew that where he had previously seen her as a toy, he now saw her as something he wanted to break. She'd made an enemy this day.

Three hours after the discovery of Shabnam's body, and having completed a number of other crucial inquiries, Jason had intended to interview the ladies-in-waiting, but found he had need to speak to Neha. "Venom asks permission to enter your territory."

Neha's lips kicked up a notch where she walked beside a large outdoor mural of a lissome maiden carrying a water pot on her head. "So, the prodigal returns," she said, the grief and anger in her voice leavened by warmth. "Is he on his way to the Refuge?"

"He says he would not dare pass by without paying his respects."

Neha's laugh echoed off the marble around them. "Though he did dare run off to Raphael as soon as his Contract was complete."

"I think you would've been disappointed had he not shown spine enough to forge his own path." Though she would not be pleased to know exactly how powerful the vampire had become in the years since.

Smile deepening, Neha said, "I assent to his visit, so long as he accepts the vow that binds you also includes him while he is here. Let us hope he has brought a gift that will soften my anger at his defection."

What Venom brought was nothing expected. No exotic snake or a necklet in the shape of a cobra, no jeweled comb or rare wine.

"Explain this," Neha said in a cool tone when he unveiled the mechanical monkey that beat drums and crashed cymbals with manic glee as it walked in circles on the sapphire-hued silk carpet in front of Neha's throne.

Venom turned off the toy. "It is a smile, my lady." Glancing up from his crouching position, he allowed the sunlight pouring in through the windows to hit the shocking green of eyes that were not human in any sense, the slits contracting against the brightness. "I thought you needed one more than jewels. Especially on this day."

Neha said nothing for a long minute before she sighed and gestured for him to rise. "Put that in my private chambers," she said to the servant who stood discreetly to the side, and Jason knew the danger had passed, Venom's gamble at referring to Eris's funeral paying off.

"Tell me," she said once the servant had departed, "of what you have been doing in Raphael's Tower."

It was a loaded question, one that asked Venom to divide his loyalties, but the vampire fielded it without lying—and without betraying any secrets. "Learning to be stronger, better. Now I go to work under Galen."

"Yes, that one is a man who understands patience, as you have never done."

"It's in my nature." Venom shrugged, and Jason knew he referred to the impulses that had been seeded in him by the Queen of Snakes, of Poisons.

A faint smile curved Neha's lips, the calculated gleam of her earlier question replaced by amused affection. "When does that barbarian weapons master expect you?"

"I am early. If I may beg your indulgence, I would stay and talk with friends I have not seen for many a year."

Neha's eyes *shifted* in that quicksilver way, now brown, now a jagged, slitted green, the speed such that Jason could almost believe he'd imagined it. "So, Raphael thinks to plant a second spy in my court?"

"You insult Jason, my lady." Disarming charm. "I would be a great thumping elephant to his sleek cobra."

An exasperated shake of Neha's head, the archangel appearing more indulgent than Jason had seen her with anyone but Eris and Anoushka. "Stay, play your games, but, Venom? Do not forget who I am."

Venom bowed over her hand, pressing his lips to her knuckles. "My lady, never will I forget who you are—you did not Make a fool."

Later, when Venom and Jason walked up onto the wall above one of the magnificent fort gates, Jason saw the vampire sigh as he looked out over the city below, the homes hugging the earth for the most part, but even the smallest with a door painted in a bright shade, or shutters of red, a roof of blue. "You miss this place."

"At times," Venom said, his hair lifting in the breeze that tugged at Jason's queue. "This land is where I was born, this fort where I was Made. It'll always have a claim on my heart, though it is Raphael who has a claim on my loyalty."

Jason thought of the palm-edged sands of the Pacific, of the remote island that was his own, where he went when he wanted to disappear from the world. Though it wasn't the place where he'd been born, it was close enough that it made his heart ache. "I understand."

"Raphael thought you might appreciate a familiar face, someone you can trust to watch your back."

"I'm glad you're here," he said, thinking of a woman who lived in a fort surrounded by hundreds of others, but who was and had always been alone, without anyone of her own.

Even he had memories of love to keep him going. Mahiya had nothing. And still she had hope in her heart, the capacity for tenderness of the soul. Strong, she was so strong, stronger than him, for where he'd had to shut down to survive, she'd managed to do so intact.

"So," Venom said, "tell me what has happened—I won't betray your vow, and Raphael won't expect it of me."

Jason had never believed otherwise. "There is something wrong here." He told Venom of the triple murders, of the details that didn't quite fit. "You still know many people in this court intimately." Friends the vampire had stayed in touch with, some out of true affection, others because they were useful—Venom could be coldly practical beneath his charm. "Find the connection if you can."

The murders bore too familiar an emotional fingerprint to be the work of disparate entities, and yet Neha had no need or apparent motive to murder her lady-in-waiting in such a violent fashion. Regardless of all else, he simply could not see her breaking her vigil beside Eris's body in order to commit the act, not when those were the final hours she'd ever spend with him.

Venom gave a thoughtful nod, sliding his mirrored shades back over his eyes. "I'll do everything I can, but I'll have to leave in three days at the most. Neha will not give me her indulgence beyond that."

"You're a better judge of her mood than I—go when you need to." Getting Venom's nod, he asked the vampire a question that had nothing to do with his task at the fort. "How is Sorrow?" The girl had survived an attack from a mad archangel, come out of it infected by a toxin that had changed her from mortal to something other, her abilities erratic.

Venom's jaw went taut, tendons pushing against the skin of his neck. "Janvier has taken over her vampiric training for the time being," he said, referring to the vampire who had worked directly under Dmitri on any number of operations and whose loyalty to the Tower was unquestioned— though until now, it had been more useful to have him out in the world as an apparent free agent.

"You know how good Janvier is," Venom added, "but I'll have to return periodically to do the speed dances with her."

Venom could move with snake quickness, a skill Sorrow shared, though hers came from a different source. "Can she call it up on command?"

"No. And if she doesn't learn to do that, she'll die." Unforgiving words. "But Honor's right—she needs to get the basics down first before I start pushing her again, or she'll make stupid mistakes speed alone can't cure."

"Who's undertaking her physical training with Honor out of the city?"

"Ashwini." Venom's face thawed, his lips twitching a fraction. "You know what she did to Janvier the last time they met?"

"Honey was involved." Jason had watched the hunter and the vampire spar since their first meeting, never quite understanding their relationship—they were adversaries one minute, determined to run each other to the ground, and allies the next. It was Janvier Ashwini had taken with her when she'd needed to work in Nazarach's dangerous territory, and it was Janvier whose sapphire pendant the hunter wore around her neck. Yet, as far as he knew, they had never been bedmates.

"Why don't they just sleep with one another?" he asked Venom, wondering if he'd missed a subtle nuance in their relationship.

Venom's chuckle was quiet, his eyes eerie in the sunshine as he pushed his sunglasses to the top of his head. "That is an enduring mystery." He cocked his head. "Who is that very pretty woman coming this way?"

Jason didn't need to follow Venom's gaze—he could feel

Mahiya's presence as a gentle heat against his wings. "The Princess Mahiya, and she is mine." He had no right to make such a claim, but Venom had a way of charming women when he was in the mood, and Jason discovered he did not wish Mahiya to be charmed.

"Ah." The vampire turned and jumped off the gate with an insouciant carelessness that had Mahiya's hand slapping over her heart.

But Venom came to a crouching landing on his toes, lithe as a cat. Landing beside him, Jason watched Mahiya rather than Venom as the vampire rose and bent over her hand. "Impossible as it seems, I do not believe we have ever met."

Mahiya's fascinated gaze lingered on Venom's eyes as he lifted his head and released her hand. "No . . . but I have heard of the vampire with the viper's eyes. You were based at the Delhi court in the main."

"I was," Venom agreed, "but I visited here more than once. You must've been studying at the Refuge."

"Yes. I believe you had sworn allegiance to Raphael by the time I returned to the fort."

Jason caught the fine tremor that rippled over Mahiya's skin as she spoke of a homecoming that must have been a terrifying experience for a young girl, and spread his wing just enough that it brushed over her own. It was an intimacy, and one she had not offered, one he'd never have initiated had he stopped to think about it, yet instead of flinching, she relaxed.

"It's good to finally make your acquaintance," she said to Venom, genuine warmth in her tone. "Neha has always said you were one of her proudest Makings."

Venom's grin was sharp, his next words directed at Jason. "Shall we meet over dinner?"

"Come to Mahiya's palace."

"Until then." He kissed Mahiya's hand again before departing.

Jason traced Mahiya's profile with his gaze as she watched the vampire leave. "You had no hesitation in allowing him to touch you."

"I think it was the shock first of all—those eyes . . ." She shook her head. "And then I saw he was your friend."

A fine crack, something fundamental breaking inside him.

Mahiya continued to speak when he didn't reply. "Neha has tried to recreate the effect you know, and some of her Made have the slightest sense of it, but never has she succeeded as she did with Venom."

"He will be pleased to know he is unique," Jason said, examining the fissure she'd created in his shields, the damage deep, repair no simple matter.

Mahiya's bright eyes smiled at him. "You go to speak to the ladies-in-waiting?"

He took so long in replying her smiled faded, her expression intent. And he knew that he would touch her again should she give the slightest encouragement, his body hungry not just for sensation, but for the mystery and—when her guard dropped—the inexplicable sweetness that was Mahiya.

18

Mahiya watched after Jason's black-winged form as he rose up into the sky, the tiny hairs on her arms still standing up in reaction at the look she'd caught in his eyes. The primal response wasn't fed by alarm or fear, but a passion that was no simple physical craving. Jason fascinated her on many levels. He was a rough-edged carving, a beautiful man she had the sense no woman had ever come close to taming.

It would be a shame were that ever to happen. His wildness was an integral part of him—perhaps others would not deem it so, not given the cool distance with which he viewed the world, but Mahiya understood . . . she carried the same wildness within. Just because it had been imprisoned and confined and controlled didn't mean it wasn't there. Jason wore his nature in his skin, in the curving lines of a tattoo she wanted to trace with her fingertips . . . her lips.

It was a dangerous admission, but lying to herself served no purpose. Better she accept she had a vulnerability where the inscrutable spymaster was concerned, so she could guard against the weakness. The only problem was, Mahiya wasn't certain she *wanted* to turn away from the shimmering dark of the nascent flame between them.

Jason landed behind Lisbeth where she sat on a marble bench in a small enclosed terrace garden off the palace that housed the ladies-in-waiting. Men were strictly forbidden in this area except if sent on business by Neha herself, all of the guards—angelic and vampiric—female.

The tiny woman jumped to her feet with a gasp. "Sir, I realize you are my lady's guest, but you cannot be here."

"Neha will not be displeased with you." She might be with Jason, but since she hadn't specifically barred him from talking to the ladies-in-waiting in their private quarters, he broke no rules. "I wish to speak to you about Shabnam."

A change on her face, a quickness of thought. "We are distraught." Her eyes watered, the deep brown turning into shimmering topaz, her beauty luminous. Lifting a delicate lace handkerchief to her face, she dabbed at the crystalline purity of her tears.

"I am sorry to cause you further sorrow." He pitched his tone to soothe.

While he couldn't mimic emotion anywhere near as well as Lisbeth, he was proficient at using his voice as a weapon. Once, he'd used it in song, but the songs in his heart had gone silent long ago, and he knew that one day so would his voice. A man who had nothing inside him eventually had nothing to say.

Wings of midnight blue and vivid green, a smile that saw too much, stirred things that had not been touched in an eon.

Lisbeth's voice tangled with the unexpected images whispering through his mind. "It is all right." Sniffing with a delicacy that did nothing to mar her beauty, she said, "You ask for help to seek Shabnam's murderer?"

He inclined his head. "Do you know of anything that may shed light on the matter?"

A calculated hesitation before she shook her head. "I'm sure I couldn't say."

"She is dead." Jason added gentle, warm notes to his voice. "What you say cannot hurt her."

Swallowing, Lisbeth wrapped her arms around herself as if cold. "It is not done to speak ill of the dead, but . . . Shabnam was not faithful to her lover." The words were shaped with utmost sincerity, yet Jason knew them for a lie. Still, he allowed her to continue, wanting to see how black she would paint the victim. "She was generous with her favors . . . particularly when it came to the guards—I believe she thought to ease her way into places we are not meant to go."

An adroit accusation of spying, perhaps even treason. "Do you believe one of the guards may have become jealous?" he asked, acting obtuse on purpose.

The faintest hint of impatience flittered across her face, fracturing the thus far flawless illusion of beautiful sorrow. "I'm sure for all her airs, Shabnam was nothing but a diversion for them. But her family, they're proud. They may have considered her actions shameful." A demure downsweep of curling black lashes. "I'm not accusing them of anything, and I'm sure they would never . . . but you asked. And I just wanted— Oh, forget I said anything."

"I appreciate your trust. Thank you."

"Of course." She could not quite keep her smug satisfaction out of her voice. "I only hope I helped."

"Yes, very much." Excusing himself, Jason rose into the air. It didn't take him long to track down the rest of the ladies-in-waiting. They were creatures who did not like to go too far from their habitat, fearing another would take their place or gain some favor from which they were excluded.

Everyone but for Shabnam's sparrow-winged friend, Tanuja, attempted to malign the victim. One even insinuated that she'd seduced Eris. However, Tanuja was adamant that Shabnam had been a faithful lover and no spy.

"She was a *nice* person," Tanuja sobbed, skin of soft brown blotchy from her distress. "Too nice for this pit of vipers, and the fact that she was a favorite with Neha only made the others act uglier toward her. She used to laugh and say they were jealous witches, but now she's dead." A hard stare out of red-rimmed eyes. "Lisbeth may not like getting her hands dirty, but she comes from a family that doesn't mind blood."

The sky was the lush gray of a balmy evening when he came in to land on the balcony outside his suite. Ignoring his own doors, he knocked on Mahiya's. She opened the left side a fraction, her wary expression changing the instant she saw him. "Oh, it's you!" Smile reaching her eyes to light them to tawny brightness, she pulled the doors fully open.

At that instant, Jason felt something slam into him, a powerful, amorphous realization that he tried to capture, to examine, but it was so much smoke, wisping out of his hand yet leaving an imprint behind. "Why were you worried?" he asked, feeling as if he'd been marked in some immutable way.

"I—" Mahiya shook her head. "Come in first. The food is hot."

Walking inside when she turned away, he shut the doors at his back. She didn't startle at the act, the silverwork on the pale pink of her fitted tunic and on the ankle cuffs of her white harem-style pants catching the light from the tiny crystal chandelier above. The comb in her neatly bound hair was intricately worked silver set with diamonds, the gauzy white scarf thrown over her shoulders from her front embellished with threads of the same metallic shade at the ends. "You dress formally."

Taking a graceful seat on the flat cushion in front of the low table, her wings spread out behind her in a glory of emerald and peacock blue with splashes of jet, she picked up the water jug. "You'll need to dress, too. Neha has summoned us to a formal dinner. But we have time enough to eat and drink."

He took his place opposite her, noticing the color on her

lips, the skillful use of other cosmetics to highlight her cheek-bones while playing down her eyes. This, too, he thought, was a subtle mask. "The food at dinner will not be agreeable?"

"The food will be exquisite, but the conversation will curdle my stomach. And you will be too busy watching and listening to everyone to eat more than a bite or two."

He thought perhaps the strange sensation in his chest might be amusement. Illium occasionally incited the same response in him, but this was somehow gentler, more tender. "In that case, I thank you for your thoughtfulness."

She gave him a sharp look, eyes narrowed. "Be careful or I'll stop feeding you."

"A great punishment indeed." And it would be; this fragile ritual of homecoming was important to him in a way she could not comprehend. "May I have some water?" he said, absently noticing a little bag of carrots set on a small table that held an unlit lamp, as if Mahiya had put the bag down, then forgotten about it.

"Since you asked so nicely." Lips twitching, she poured it for him, then removed the lids off the trays that sat between them. "I was in the mood to cook, so you have several choices. Do you want to try a little of each?"

"Yes." He knew he should protest the way she served him, but she seemed to take pleasure from it . . . and so did he. So he stayed silent, took the plate she made up for him. As they ate, his mind cascaded with memories of how he'd tried to cook after he was alone, how he'd burned everything, lived on fruits and raw cassava root for a time until his stomach rebelled.

Later, when he'd arrived at the Refuge, he'd demanded to be treated as an adult regardless of his chronological age, and no one had argued. Until Mahiya, he wouldn't have said he'd missed such a quiet indication of care as someone bothering to notice whether he ate or not.

"Now," he said, after they'd cleared away the plates and she'd poured them both mint tea, refreshing and strong, "tell me if the reason your stomach will curdle is the same one that made you afraid to open the door."

Mahiya looked at him over the top of her teacup, tendrils of steam caressing her lips. "Are you always this persistent?"

He raised an eyebrow, and her lips parted in a quiet laugh. "Of course you are. How else would you have become the best spymaster in the Cadre?" Cupping her hands around the tea, she said, "Arav . . . a man with whom I had a relationship when I was little more than a girl"—the laughter leaching out of her eyes—"is in the fort, and he's being persistent, too, in an unwelcome way."

Black fire, cold and deadly, formed in his bloodstream. "Did he touch you?"

"Only my hand." Putting down her cup, she rubbed at that hand. "He caught me in the courtyard an hour ago when he had no reason to be on this level of the fort. I know he did it to remind me of his presence, to intimidate—I walked away from him earlier, and no one does that."

Jason listened as she told him of her morning encounter with the angel, the black fire within tempered a fraction when she added, "It may not have been the smartest move to deliberately antagonize him, but it was satisfying, and I'm not sorry." She set her jaw, as if expecting censure.

"When I was a hundred and twenty-three," Jason said, making a note to pay Arav a visit in the darkest hour of night, remind the other man of the acrid taste of fear, "I asked Michaela to dance." It wasn't because he'd been drunk on her beauty—he'd always seen the truth of her selfish heart—but because he'd wanted to experience that drunkenness, wanted to feel more than the remote distance that was his normal mode of existence. "She wasn't an archangel then, but still a queen, her power immense."

Eyes huge, Mahiya leaned forward. "Well?" she demanded with unhidden impatience. "What *happened*?"

"She was so astonished at my gall she said yes." And he'd had his question answered; whatever it was that was broken in him, even the proximity of the most beautiful woman in the world couldn't fix it. "Afterward, Raphael told me she could just as well have taken offense and killed me on the spot . . . but I wasn't sorry, either."

Mahiya laughed again, the vivid clarity of her eyes sparking with flecks of gold that captivated him, because he'd never before glimpsed those flickers of shimmering metal. And he thought that perhaps the young man he'd been might have been wrong, that perhaps even a frozen heart might one day be awakened.

"Surely," she said when she caught her breath, "you were legend among your peers."

Jason hadn't had many friends back then, but he'd had Dmitri and Raphael. "Raphael poured me a glass of a thousand-year-old Scotch then, together with Dmitri, toasted me on my balls." It had been another link in his relationship with the two men, a link that had been further strengthened over the years, each of the others in the Seven adding their own pieces to create a chain that held him to the world, to life.

"I do not think Neha has ever been so informal with any of her court," Mahiya said. "Though I didn't know her when she was as young as Raphael must've been at your first meeting."

"I'll ask Lijuan the next time we cross paths."

Mahiya's eyes flicked up, widened, then sparkled once again. "You do know how to laugh!" She lifted a single finger to lips curved in mischief. "I promise I won't tell a soul."

"No one will believe you in any case."

Mahiya put down her cup, the tea almost spilling. "I can't believe you made me *giggle*," she accused between gulps of air.

He couldn't move his eyes away from the luminous joy of her, his fingers itching to grip her chin, tug her across the table so he could taste lips shiny wet from her last sip of tea. "Who else will be at this dinner?" he asked, as her smile faded to be replaced by a hectic flush of color on her cheekbones.

Swallowing, she dipped her head in the guise of pouring more tea, but he saw her fingers tremble, his every hunting instinct roaring to the surface. "It'll be a small group, I think." She went through a concise list of possible guests, while he struggled to contain the primal urge to shove the table aside and quench the thirst he had for this princess with her stubborn hope and her heart untainted by poison and her way of looking at him that said she might just accede to his every demand.

"Whether she wears mourning white or not," Mahiya added without meeting his gaze, "Neha grieves for Eris— even as she continues to hate him. So it will be a solemn affair."

"I'm so sorry. Forgive me."

The centuries-old echo was a chilling reminder that love and hate were often intimately intertwined—in a way that might be incomprehensible to a child, but that the man understood too well. As that man understood the embers of need in his gut would not go cold until he'd gorged himself on the soft skin and pleasure-riven cries of the Princess Mahiya.

"Mahiya."

Fingers tucking back a tendril of hair. "Yes?"

"I think," he said, reaching across to cup her chin, brush his thumb across her lower lip, "you must decide something tonight."

19

Mahiya tidied away the tea things after Jason left to change, carrying them down to her small private kitchen. Where she poured herself a glass of ice-cold water. "Dear God."

Jason was . . .

Shuddering, she rolled the cold glass over her neck. But, in spite of the sexual fire that smoldered between them, threatening to turn her bones molten, she had no rose-colored lenses clouding her eyes and her judgment, understood that Jason was a top-of-the-food-chain predator with loyalty to a rival archangel. More, he was a spymaster with centuries of experience at intrigue, could well be playing her for reasons of his own.

But . . . he made her no promises, and thus, he would not break them. He listened to her. Treated her as someone with *worth*. And if that worth was only in the information she could give him, he was truthful about that, too. She took it as no insult, for Jason was in the business of information.

As for the lack of love words and pretty courtship? Mahiya shook her head. She would far rather be with a man who was honest in his desire than with one who brutalized her with the sweet lies of seduction. Jason had more honor in a single bone of his body than Arav would know in a lifetime.

Heading back upstairs, she refreshed her makeup before pressing a sparkling silver teardrop to her forehead, centering it between her eyebrows. "Yes," she whispered to her reflection. "The answer is yes."

The single knock came just then, as if he'd heard her. Slipping her feet into flat silver sandals, she took a deep breath and walked out of the bedroom and across the living area to open the door—to reveal Jason's harsh masculine beauty showcased in a flawlessly fitted black suit worn with a steel gray shirt.

"You look wonderful." *Beautiful*, his hair in that neat queue she felt a sudden urge to undo. "Neha will be pleased." Jason's expression didn't change, and yet she knew—"You care nothing of what Neha thinks."

"On the contrary," he said, letting her precede him down the stairs.

Her nape prickled, not in warning, but with the awareness that he was watching her body move. It made her breath catch, her skin stretch taut over her flesh.

"It's never a smart idea to enrage an archangel," he continued, "but while she may demand it, Neha will never admire subservience."

Mahiya shook her head as they exited the palace. "Your opinion is colored by your strength." A strength she knew he'd had from a very young age. "You can afford to rouse her anger, for she sees you, if not as an equal, then as someone intriguing enough not to summarily kill. You do not know what it is to fear."

"I wasn't always the man I am now," Jason said, a door unlocking inside his mind, spilling a cold shadow across his soul.

She looked at him from the other side of the room, her pretty dark brown eyes filmed over with a whiteness that was wrong. The stump of her neck was crusted with blood where it sat on the table in the corner, as if placed there for just this purpose.

He didn't scream. He knew never to scream. Instead, he looked at the chunk of meat that had been blocking the trapdoor. It wore a silk sheath of brilliant amethyst.

Amethyst. That's what his mother always called her favorite color. Amethyst.

It had taken him a long time to say it right, and she'd always laughed in delight when he used the word, her shining black hair dancing in the sunshine.

"Jason." A softly feminine face lit to glowing warmth by the lamps along the pathway, concern in every line. "You . . . weren't here. Where did you go?"

Brilliant white sands beneath his small feet, burning hot. The wind waving through the palm trees, sending a coconut plummeting to the sand with a dull thud. The gulls gossiping up and down the wet sand, leaving three-clawed footprints the sea erased with its next crashing arrival.

"Jason! Come in and eat your lunch before it gets cold."

"A place that no longer exists," he said gently, and removed the hand she'd placed on his chest . . . to resettle it around his upper left arm, where it wouldn't get in the way if he had to reach for his sword. "About Arav," he said, while they were still private, "you have no cause to fear him."

"He's very strong." The concern in her eyes lingered, grew. "Don't underestimate him."

"I know exactly how strong he is." Though they'd never met, the fact the man was one of Neha's generals meant Jason had made it a point to learn about him—and, in spite of his arrogance and posturing, Arav was no peer of Jason's. "He is like a peacock, spreading his feathers and squawking loudly to distract you from the fact his body is but weak."

A stifled laugh, genuine delight that was a kind of music. "I propose a rooster would be the better analogy," she whispered, "strutting and pecking anyone who gets in his way." Releasing his arm, she lowered her voice even further as they entered corridors peopled by servants and courtiers both. "He is merely the first. Many will come, hoping to take Eris's place, or at least the place he would've had but for his inability to keep his lusts in control."

He saw the speculative glances they attracted, made no move to widen the distance between them, the occasional brush of her wing against his a welcome caress. "Did you ever consider Eris your father in truth?"

"Not after I realized he wanted me dead." A false smile for the benefit of those who watched, but the woman with mischief in her voice was gone, washed away on the waves of memory and the cruel reality of life. "I was a child. It broke my heart to realize the handsome man Neha took me to meet every week hated the sight of me. I didn't understand then that she was using me as a weapon."

Jason had always dealt in information, until gathering it was part of his very nature, but he wished he'd remained silent this night and allowed Mahiya's eyes to laugh awhile longer.

"Are you close to your father?" she asked, rifling the pages of his own memory.

"Here, son. You use the string to pull it forward so. Do you see?"

"I was." Before his father had been eaten away from the inside out, the progression of what Jason thought of as a disease so slow and stealthy that no one who had seen him had realized the true depth of the demons he fought. "He's dead."

"I'm sorry." Her fingers alighted for a fleeting instant on his forearm, and he felt the touch all the way to his bones.

"It was a long time ago." He'd learned to live with the ghosts. "Tell me about Anoushka," he said, closing the door on the memories. "Of her relationship with Eris."

"I think they may have been close when she was young," Mahiya said slowly, the scent of her a subtle blend of exotic flowers and some bright spice that fascinated. "But when I knew her, she held him in contempt, considering him weak and spineless. I never saw her betray that to Neha, however."

No, Jason thought, Anoushka had been too smart to alienate her mother that way.

"We're here." Mahiya halted before the Palace of Jewels.

What appeared to be a thousand candles flickered along the outer wall, in alcoves and on special stands, each flame refracted by the diamonds that studded the palace, until the entire building was ablaze, an astonishing work of art. "This," he said with utmost honesty, "is stunning." No wonder Neha preferred it over larger, more ornate palaces.

"Yes." Mahiya's reply was soft. "It fascinated me as a child."

Something there, a hitch in her voice. But he had no chance to follow up on it, because they'd been seen by the guards. Opening the doors, the two vampires bowed deeply as they passed. Jason was unused to such subservience—Raphael's Tower functioned in a far different fashion—but he was no longer the uneducated boy-man who'd made his way to the Refuge by shadowing other angels.

His father had chosen an island out of the way of angelic sky roads by design, and so it was the rare angel indeed who had passed over Jason after he was alone. He'd tried to hail them, but he'd been too small and weak to fly up high enough to catch their attention before they were out of range. So he'd survived, grown stronger . . . and after a while, he'd stopped his attempts to alert others to his existence, and simply waited—until he knew he was strong enough to fly for a full day and night without failing, should there be no islands where he could rest.

In the interim, he'd lived in silence.

"It's a shame the boy's a mute. The instruments he makes are things of such virtuosity, you'd think he'd learned from Yaviel himself."

Jason had never been mute. He'd just needed to remember how to speak. And he'd done that by watching and listening. Those skills would hold him in good stead tonight. The room in front of him was warm with candlelight, a table of honey-colored wood polished to such a high sheen that it glowed like amber set upon the carpet, the seat cushions of the matching chairs a rich claret. It was a contrast to the pale colors chosen by the guests, the conversation muted, for no one was yet ready to dance on Eris's grave.

Save perhaps a man Jason identified as Arav from the way he'd made a place for himself at Neha's side, a charming, elegant companion as the archangel played gracious hostess. Jason knew she hid a terrible sadness behind that persona, but in itself, it was no lie.

"I have never been to a court as gracious as the one Neha keeps." Dmitri played a knife through his fingers, one of three he'd brought back from Neha's territory. "She truly believes in giving honor to a visitor." He threw the knife at Jason.

He threw it back as Venom added, "Though she might have that guest neatly executed while the court sleeps."

Venom's response was as accurate as Dmitri's—Neha was no two-dimensional caricature. No archangel was, and to believe otherwise was to set yourself up for a nasty surprise. Jason had no intention of falling prey to such blindness. Some mortals might seek to see divinity in the archangels, but Jason saw them for what they were— creatures of violent power who'd had millennia to hone their every lethal edge.

Right then, the Queen of Snakes, of Poisons, turned, met his gaze.

Jason inclined his head but didn't move toward her, and she returned the greeting before shifting her attention to the guest who stood in front of her.

"The vampire heading this way," Mahiya said sotto voce after the silent exchange, "is Rhys, one of Neha's trusted inner council."

"I've met him in the Refuge." However, he didn't know anyone in the room as well as Mahiya did, intended to ask her for her opinions after this was done.

"Jason." A polite nod before Rhys turned his attention to Mahiya. "You are looking lovely, Princess."

Mahiya's response was warm enough that he realized she liked Rhys. "Thank you, sir. Is Brigitte well?"

"She is, indeed, though you know her." A smile shared between the two. "I'm afraid my beloved is not a court creature," he said to Jason. "However, she is so good at her job as a cryptographer that Neha forgives her the eccentricity."

"I know of her work." Everyone in Jason's profession knew her name. "I've even attempted to lure her away a time or two."

The other man laughed, his eyes twinkling. "Ah, I must admit, I was aware of that. She was very flattered, but we are loyal."

While the spymaster in him was disappointed in that fact, the Jason who was one of the Seven understood the decision.

"Now Neha tries to lure you away." Rhys's tone was warm, but the icy calculation in his eyes made it clear he considered Jason a threat to the security of the fort.

Jason said nothing to that—silence was often a better weapon than words. Instead, he chose to direct Rhys's attention to another threat. "The fort hosts a visitor who wants to be consort, it seems."

Rhys didn't turn to look at Arav. "There are always pretenders." A hardness in his tone betrayed the blooded general beneath the mask of courtesy, before he excused himself to talk with a female angel Jason knew to be another one of Neha's inner council.

"Tell me about him," Jason said to Mahiya.

Mahiya's response was quiet, with an undertone of steel. "I have come to realize exactly how much you like to give orders."

Jason considered her words as he watched the intriguing flow and interplay of the people in the room. "You aren't my equal," he said, and it was a test.

She fisted, then flexed the hand he could see. "I carry the information you need about the people here." The smile she sent him was a creation of such feminine complexity he knew he was seeing and understanding only half of it. "At least for this moment"—a shadow flitting over her eyes—"I hold the cards."

Jason had no reference point for how to behave with a woman who was not his lover and yet already knew him better than any lover ever had. Such intimacy, he thought, was a thing of give and take and constant balance.

"Dance with me."

"I'm making breakfast. Yavi!"

His father with his arms around his mother's waist, twirling her around the kitchen, their wings sweeping out to send Jason's hair back from his face as he sat playing with his blocks on the floor.

"Put me down!" A laughing command. "Yavi! The pancakes are burning."

Bending her over his arm, his father claimed a smiling kiss. "Say please."

"Tell me about him . . . please," he said to this woman with whom he might never dance, but who had a claim on his loyalty nonetheless.

Shooting him another impenetrable look, she turned her face forward, and he thought he'd missed something, a moment, an emotion slipping through the cracks, water through his fingers . . . as his mother's severed head had once slipped from his hands to hit the floor.

"I'm sorry, Mama."

"For the most part, Rhys is what he appears." Mahiya's voice cut over the dull thud of sound that had followed him through time. "He has been with Neha for over six centuries and is not ambitious—except if anyone dares threaten his position at her side.

"Eris as consort-in-name posed no such threat," she added as the same thought passed through his mind. "Rhys knew that when it came time to discuss politics and war, power and strategy, Neha would seek his own counsel. Arav, however, is a very able general himself, has led Neha's troops in battle. More, he is as efficient at dealing with angelic politics as Rhys."

The other man looked up at that instant, as did Neha. This time, the archangel flowed toward Jason. "I have never seen you dressed thus," she said, her approval patent. "All of Raphael's Seven do clean up well, even that barbarian general of his."

"I will tell Galen you said as much," Jason said, knowing the weapons master didn't give a damn about what any woman but one thought of him.

Gaze shifting to Mahiya, Neha said, "You do not greet Arav," in a tone rimmed with frost.

20

"We met in the courtyard." Mahiya kept her voice even, refusing to give Arav the satisfaction of seeing her stumble. Maybe her courage came from having Jason's dark strength beside her—but she didn't think so. Arav was the one individual who could make her forget reason and step perilously close to insult.

"Insult to a guest is an insult to me."

Something Neha had said long ago to the child Mahiya had been when she'd returned to the fort for a visit during a break in her schooling. She'd never liked those visits, her time at the school with Jessamy the happiest of her life. The censure that particular day hadn't been personal, and yet the way the archangel had looked at her had made the tiny hairs on the back of her neck prickle in warning.

The instant Neha had left, she'd run back to the nanny who looked after her when she was at the fort, the same one who'd later told her nothing she'd ever do would please Neha.

"Why doesn't the lady like me?"

Her nanny's stern face set into a frown before she gave

a curt nod. "You're old enough to know. Though you must never repeat this in public, your father is Eris, Neha's consort. Your mother was Neha's sister, Nivriti."

She was small, didn't immediately understand. "They shared a consort?"

Horror filled her nanny's expression. "Never speak such filth, child." Putting away the tunic she'd been folding, she shut the dresser. "Your mother seduced a man who was not her own, and she bore the fruit of their ugliness."

Me, Mahiya thought, the fruit is me. "I'm ugly?"

A sigh, a softening in her nanny's face. "You are not ugly, child, but you remind my lady of that ugliness. It is a testament to her kind nature that you are given all the rights and privileges of a princess."

The latter, of course, was a lie. But even Mahiya would concede that Neha's treatment of her while she'd been a minor had been scrupulous. Perhaps there'd been no warmth, but there'd been no abuse, either. She'd attended the Refuge school, studied in its libraries—and there, she'd had access to Jessamy's kindness and guidance, felt what it was to be loved, for the Teacher loved all her students.

Then she'd come "home," turned a hundred . . . and learned that Neha's cruelty had simply been saved for the adult that hopeful, innocent child had become. The man who stood beside Neha was proof enough of that cruelty— even if the archangel hadn't ordered the seduction, she hadn't warned Mahiya about Arav's duplicitous courtship, either, making certain that Mahiya's first taste of romantic love would be a bitter one.

"You didn't tell me you had spoken with Mahiya." Neha's voice was silk over steel.

Arav's cheeks creased in a smile that glowed with charm. "We passed as I was on my way to speak to you." He favored Mahiya with a condescending look of approval. "I did not say how glad I am to see you looking so well." Raising his glass, he took a sip of wine, the square ring on his index finger flashing vivid blue in the candlelight, the stone a rare form of tourmaline.

"He is like a peacock, spreading his feathers and squawking loudly . . ."

"Thank you," she said with a smile so dazzling, it took Arav visibly aback.

Small crystalline sounds silvered through the air as the glass bangles on Neha's wrist moved against one another. "Come. Let us be seated." Her gaze landed on Jason. "As guest at the fort, you sit on my left. Arav can entertain Mahiya—they are great friends."

Mahiya felt an ineffable tension radiating off the man next to her, though his expression remained opaque, and she knew it was because of her. She also knew she couldn't allow him to make an enemy of an archangel in an effort to spare her from Arav's attentions. "Actually," she said with a quick smile, "I see scholar Quinn across the room. I've just read his newest treatise, and I promised him I would talk with him about it."

Neha didn't bristle—the vampire was one of her favorites. That mattered less than the fact that Jason was no longer a blade about to be unsheathed.

"All in all," Mahiya said to Jason after the tea had been served and they were readying themselves to return to their palace, "it was not so terrible a dinner party." Quinn had been a lovely companion, and Neha had been so engrossed in conversation with Rhys and Jason that she'd ignored Arav most of the night. "Arav has no idea who he's dealing with— Neha's playing with him as a cat does with a mouse."

Jason's response to her murmured supposition was silence. She didn't read anything into it. He was, she thought as they walked out and began to cross the courtyard, thinking about the subject before he replied. "Temperature's dipped." Still, the night air was relatively balmy—though when she glanced up, it was to see the stars hidden by fat clouds that threatened rain.

When something fell from that sky, she thought it must

be a bird, it was such a tiny thing. But then it grew bigger
and bigger and—"Jason!"

However, Jason had already seen. Instead of running
toward the body that had just crashed to the earth in a splatter of blood and bone that sprayed guests closer to the impact
site, he shot straight up into the air, chasing the one responsible for the carnage.

Mouth dry, Mahiya watched him go, a black arrow soon
invisible against the night, then made her way to the body,
taking care not to step in the gore. She shut out the sound
of a woman screaming about the blood on her face, the
deeper voices of the men who called out to one another in
a panic, the snap of the wind as others took off in pursuit,
and swallowing her gorge, she focused only on the identity
of the body.

That square ring of rare blue tourmaline, those mottled
brown wings . . .

For a second, her brain couldn't quite process what it was
she was seeing, and then all her synapses fired, connections
made, and she realized the angel without a head and likely
without internal organs, was . . . "Arav."

Jason was fast, an ace at vertical takeoffs, but his prey had
disappeared by the time he breached the heavy layer of
dense waterlogged clouds. Given the limited time frame and
Jason's speed, he guessed the killer had flown just out of
visual range, then dropped in a steep dive to slip into a hiding place.

Cocking his ear to the wind, he listened to where it had
been interrupted, used it to track as one of the hunter born
might use a scent. The ephemeral trace ended abruptly in
the mountains just beyond the fort. Conscious his quarry
had had enough time to take a low flight path, backtracking
while Jason was above the cloud layer, he nonetheless landed
and began to scan the rocky ground around him. There was
no overt sign that anyone had landed, nothing but darkness—

Shimmering blue green caught by a ray of silver before the moon was hidden behind a cloud again.

Sliding the feather into his pocket for later examination, he flew up and back to Mahiya, confident that no matter her shock, she would not have broken.

She hadn't.

Rather, she'd nudged one of the senior guard into organizing a perimeter around the splatter, though Jason expected the guard thought it all his own idea. "Good girl," he murmured, and was almost expecting the raised eyebrow.

Then she shook her head, and he thought perhaps they'd just had a conversation.

Storing the moment to reflect on later, he sent two of the guards to find either high-powered portable lamps or torches. While they did that, he took in the bloody ruin of Arav's body, weighed it against the wider situation. Shabnam's murder could perhaps be put down to a smart copycat using Eris's death as cover, but Arav's?

It stretched the bounds of coincidence that a second hunter had been waiting to take advantage of the circumstances. There had to be a hidden connection between the victims he wasn't yet seeing. Also, given how determined Arav had been to act Neha's port in a storm, it must've been a strong temptation indeed that had drawn him up into the skies, away from those who might oppose his bid to be Neha's next consort.

Jason considered the way Arav had looked at Mahiya when he'd thought himself safe from other eyes toward the end of the dinner, his mask slipping to reveal an ugly possessiveness that said he saw Mahiya as nothing but a trophy, a *thing* to be taken and used.

As Jason had already decided to teach the other angel a lesson in fear he'd never forget, he wasn't particularly motivated to discover Arav's killer. However, Shabnam had done nothing to deserve the death meted out to her, and so it was for her that he began to consider the hows and whys of this crime.

A man such as Arav might well find himself unable to control the impulse to take what he wanted should the chance arise. Yet in spite of the feather Jason had found—been meant to find?—Mahiya had never left Jason's sight, couldn't have lured Arav into the skies.

Another woman?

Arav wouldn't be so stupid, not now.

That left politics. It was a surety that Arav had had a spy of his own in the court. Again, however, the timing didn't make sense—why would the angel choose to meet his spy now? Yes, he'd disappeared outside for a cigar, but it had been clear to Jason that the other man was merely passing time until Neha finished speaking to her guests.

With Rhys having left earlier, Arav had had a clear run at lingering to be the last remaining guest. He would never have chanced missing that opportunity and the associated privacy to advance his embryonic courtship, regardless of any temptations of the flesh.

Rhys?

It had surprised Jason when Neha's senior general had taken his leave while Arav was still buzzing around the archangel, but the move would make perfect sense had Rhys planned an ambush. Rhys wouldn't even have to worry about skirting the attention of the guards. He was a general known to hold the loyalty of his men—because he did not mind getting blood on his own hands.

"Were you here when Arav stepped outside?" he asked the closest guard, an angel who stood stiff backed and at attention, facing outward from the body.

"No, sir. I was flying past when he plummeted, came to see if I could help." A small pause as he glanced around at the other guards present. "I think Ishya and Gregor—who went to get a lantern—would've been on the doors at the time."

Jason spoke to the petite, competent Ishya next, was told that yes, she and Gregor had seen Arav walk outside for a cigar. "However," the vampire said, "he didn't remain by the palace. I heard him comment to another guest that he'd

walk off the dinner while he waited to speak to Lady Neha."
Ishya nodded at the courtyard garden, left in heavy darkness
as a frame for the glittering Palace of Jewels. "As our task
was to monitor the door, we didn't follow his path. Jian was
on the other side of the courtyard, may have seen more."

"I saw the glow of his cigar in the dark," Jian confirmed,
his uptilted eyes speaking of the edges of Neha's territory,
where it brushed up against Lijuan's, his wings a dusty white
speckled with amber at the edges. "Once I recognized him
as an invited guest, I continued on in my perimeter check.
He'd vanished by the time of my next pass."

Gregor returned with the portable outdoor lamps then,
and Jason waited until the strong light sources were set up
to talk to the vampire. He supported Ishya's story but added,
"I did see someone fly down toward Arav as he disappeared
out of view, but he didn't raise an alarm so I thought it must
be a friend." When asked for specifics about the second
angel, all he could say was, "A woman . . . maybe. Or a
slender man."

"Thank you." Leaving the mangled remains lit to garish
brightness, raw red and wet pink over broken feathers of
mottled brown, he nodded at Mahiya to make certain no
one disturbed the scene, and walked inside the Palace of
Jewels. Neha paced within, her anger so frigid it had frosted
the mirrors.

So.

"Games," she hissed. "Someone is playing games in my
court."

Yes. It was only the pattern that was proving elusive. Eris
had been Neha's consort, Audrey the woman who'd thought
to cuckold an archangel, Shabnam a lady-in-waiting Neha
had mourned with genuine sorrow, and Arav a suitor the
archangel had been playing on a leash for her own
amusement.

Jason accepted his initial conclusion had been false; Neha
was innocent of the murders of Eris and Audrey. Rather,
she'd been framed with a cunning that had fooled him and
Mahiya both. A smart opponent, then, and one with enough

skill and power to evade elite guards and lure both a lady and an experienced general to their deaths.

"A woman . . . maybe. Or a slender man."

It could still be either. The lure didn't have to be sexual, not when immortals played games of power.

"You will find the person responsible," Neha ordered, her breath white in the chilled air. "You have the resources of the fort at your command."

He understood he was being given freedom beyond that which he'd first been offered. "Are you aware of any reason why Arav might have been a target?"

"He was not even meant to be here," Neha said, wings sweeping across the frost-lined floor, the tips glittering with broken-off flecks of ice. "He came to pay his respects after hearing of Eris's death, stayed to press his suit." She shook her head, her voice becoming strangely quiet. "He must've believed me cold of heart indeed, to think I would welcome a courtship when I stood vigil over my husband's funeral pyre only this morn."

Arav's murder had been a chance opportunity, then, no finely tuned plan. "This will take longer than I initially estimated," he said. "I may have to leave your territory for a period to take care of certain other matters."

Neha's eyes hit him full force, her skin incandescent with the lethal power that made her one of the Cadre.

21

"Do not break your word and my faith, Jason."

"I have never lied to you," he said, noting the ice that had begun to crawl up the walls, just as Mahiya had described. Mastery over the elements had never before been part of Neha's repertoire.

It seemed many archangels were evolving.

"No," she said at long last, the chill in the room retreating a fraction. "Unexpected for a spymaster, but you have honor. It is why I accepted your blood vow." At that instant, she was the Neha of old, before Eris, before Anoushka. A deadly immortal, but one with a mind unclouded by bitterness or rage. "If you do need to be absent, make it fast."

"I'll attempt to negate the need." Already working out how that could be done, he took his leave and exited to find that Rhys had arrived, along with a forensic team that was as modern as the fort was not.

He would've preferred his own team, but his instincts argued against Rhys's involvement in the murders. Jason had studied the man, understood he was an angel from another time. Though he was imminently capable of killing

Shabnam, he wouldn't have left her with her breasts exposed. "Any signs of life?" Arav was a very powerful immortal—he could conceivably regenerate his head, missing arm, and torn-off wing.

Rhys shook his head. "We'll give it the night, but his blood's begun to crystallize. He's not rising from this."

Jason sensed the same. The insult from the high-velocity fall had obliterated the other damage, but he had the feeling Arav's internal organs had been ripped out, along with his spinal cord. Jason could survive such an insult to his body, was certain Rhys could, too, but Arav hadn't been in that league. "Did the same forensic team cover Shabnam's death?"

"Yes—the report would've been ready tonight but for this," Rhys answered. "However, Neha allowed no one to touch Eris. He was cremated without any kind of a forensic examination."

Before, when all signs had seemed to point to Neha, that oversight hadn't mattered. Now . . . "I need them to retrieve another body," he said, making the decision to risk trusting the other man, "and I need everyone to stay silent on it."

Rhys's eyes darkened. "My lady—"

"Cannot know." Jason told Rhys what he suspected about the woman whose crumpled body had lain exposed to the elements for far too long.

Rhys thrust a shaking hand through his hair. "The *fools!*" It was a judgment spit out in a low tone that wouldn't reach beyond Jason. "Audrey was a woman of little wit, but to attempt to make a laughingstock of an archangel? Had she found out, Neha would have—" He bit off his words, suddenly the grim-faced general whose loyalty was to Neha.

"This"—Jason nodded at Arav's body—"changes things. I do not believe her involved in any of the murders."

A shuddering exhalation that sounded like relief. Jason didn't understand the reaction, not when Neha was an archangel, violence part of her nature, until Rhys said, "No matter her rage, if she had murdered Eris, it would've eventually driven her mad. My lady loved true."

Jason had seen the madness of love firsthand, scrubbed

its rust red imprint from the walls, smelled the smoky remnants of the inferno, knew the damage it could do. It was the most dangerous, most destructive emotion of them all.

"The world," Rhys added, "cannot afford a second insane archangel."

Lijuan, Jason completed silently, was more than enough.

Having left her watch over the body once Jason arrived, Mahiya returned to her rooms, her skin sticky with the scent of death. It took twenty minutes under the pulsing spray of near-scalding water before she finally felt clean. Dressed in a simple black tunic with tapered pants of a deep blue that echoed part of her wings, she dried and loosely pinned up her hair before going out onto the balcony.

It was impossible to think about anything other than the carnage that had turned the fort into an abattoir, images of Shabnam's violated flesh and Arav's crushed and savaged body burned onto her irises. Without the evidence of what remained of Arav's wings, as well as the heavy ring that had survived on a miraculously unshattered finger, she'd never have known it was him.

A quiet footfall.

Leaning over, she saw a servant passing along the softly lit pathway below, called out for him to halt. When she went down to join him, asking whether the servants had heard anything regarding Arav, his face closed up, his expression formal. "It was with great sorrow that we learned of General Arav's death."

"No one will punish you for speaking ill of him," she said, "least of all I." Everyone knew of her humiliation— she'd worn her heart on her sleeve during her involvement with Arav. "The lady's fort is being painted bloodred and she wants answers." Mahiya didn't mourn Eris or Arav, and Audrey had made her own bed, but Shabnam had been an innocent. "Did Arav cause insult?"

It was clear the servant was torn between obeying the dictates of the archangel who was his liege and self-protective distance. The former won. "He was heard speaking to one who is loyal to Rhys, offering the man a position he did not yet have the ability to provide on the condition the other switch loyalties."

"When I am consort . . ."

"How was he overheard?" Arav wouldn't have broached the subject of such treachery in public.

Lashes coming down, head bowed, the servant backed away into the dark. At first, she thought he was refusing to answer, then she realized it *was* his answer. No, Arav hadn't been stupid, but he'd been arrogant, an angel of nine hundred who considered weaker beings beneath his notice. "I see," she said as the servant reappeared from the shadows. "Was Rhys aware of Arav's attempts to subvert his people?"

Another falling of shutters. "I do not know."

Yes, Rhys knew. He knows everything that happens in this fort.

"But," she said to Jason when he returned much later, "Rhys has always been far more elegant in eliminating his enemies." Stepping out onto her half of the balcony where Jason waited, she handed him the cognac she'd poured from the bottle kept for guests.

"I think I'm beyond tea tonight."

The words had felt inexplicably intimate.

"I eliminated Rhys as a suspect before I knew this piece of information, but even with it, I still do not believe him to be the killer." He sipped at the dark amber liquid, his throat muscles working. "The way Shabnam was exposed—Rhys, I think, is not capable of such a thing."

"Yes. He'd never treat a woman with such disrespect, even in death."

Taking another sip, Jason reached back to put the glass on the window ledge behind them, before turning to lean his bare forearms on the balcony railing. He'd showered and changed, too, wore a plain black T-shirt and jeans, his feet bare. Behind him, his wings fell gracefully to the floor, shadows kin to the night. She'd never seen him this . . . relaxed, as if he'd taken off part of his armor.

Her eyes went to the tie at his nape, the brown skin beneath colorless in the night, and she remembered the brush of his thumb across her lower lip.

"I think, you must decide something tonight."

Her womb clenched. She hadn't trusted her body to a man in an eternity, and Jason . . . he had never lied to her.

"May I undo the tie on your hair?"

He went motionless at her soft request, until he could have been the most beautiful gargoyle ever created, his wings of jet. Heart thudding in her throat, she waited . . . until at last he inclined his head in a small nod.

Her fingers trembled as she reached out. Taking care not to touch his nape, not to assume a deeper intimacy, she undid the tie and slid it away. A silken black waterfall spilled across his shoulders, the strands cool but no longer damp, the night air just warm enough to have sucked the moisture away. Unable to resist, she ran her fingertips lightly over the strands before dropping her hand to her side.

"How far would you go?"

Startled at the murmured question, she jumped. "What?"

"As you said, I am your only way out—so, how far would you go?"

Her skin flushed hot then cold. "I was baiting you," she admitted. "Even to attain my freedom, I would never barter away the one thing that has always been *mine*." Her body, her desire.

"Good. You've made your decision?"

"Yes." Breath tight in her chest, she raised her hand, hesitated.

"Touch me, Mahiya."

It was all she needed. Giving in to the need, she ran her fingers through his hair. It felt akin to petting a tiger that had, for quixotic reasons of his own, decided not to bite her hand off. She made no mistake that this showed a crack in the obsidian shields around Jason's heart, indulged in no daydreams of a deeper relationship.

Still . . . it felt good to be close to a man who had never once treated her as disposable. Even at the very start, he'd given her a formal kind of respect. Now, she saw true respect in those eyes of dark, luxuriant brown. It saddened her deep within that the fragile bond between them would break when this task was done.

Jason, she knew without asking, wasn't a man who allowed anyone as close as a familiar lover would become. Her chest ached at the knowledge of the hurt that must have shaped him to such endless aloneness, but she also knew she must be so, *so* careful not to fall for him, not to seek more than the dark sexuality that swirled between them, hot and beautifully violent as a desert storm.

Jason knew he was walking a dangerous edge with Mahiya, but he also knew he craved her touch too much to turn back. Clenching his jaw to control his shudder as her fingers touched his scalp, stroked down, he forced himself to remain motionless when all he wanted to do was turn, pin her to the wall, and thrust into the lush heat of her body.

He heard the bones in his jaw grind against one another as she stroked again, and suddenly, her touch was gone. "I'm distressing you. I'm sorry." An edge of horror in her tone. "I would've never—"

Pushing off the railing, he halted her apology by the simple expedient of taking her delicately lovely face in his hands. "Stop."

Her breath rasped in her throat as she sucked in air, her eyes huge. But instead of flinching at the rough speed of his touch or pushing him away, she fisted one hand in the soft cotton of his T-shirt . . . and rose up on tiptoe.

It took every ounce of control he had not to accept the silent invitation at once. "You must understand," he said, and his voice was a harsh scrape, "this won't make me stay with you, won't make me commit. I don't have that ability." To bond, to open his heart, to trust that the one he gave it to wouldn't savage it.

Mahiya's breath whispered over his lips as she maintained her position. "I know." Soft words. "I also know that

I'd like to share myself with a strong man who doesn't court me with lies, is honest in his desire."

He saw her swallow, knew she wasn't as confident as she was attempting to appear. "Be certain. You'll never be able to take this back." And he would not taint an innocent with his darkness, would not turn her bitter because of the lack in him.

Her lips brushed his.

Thrusting both hands into her hair, the strands beginning to unravel, he slanted his mouth over her own, intent on devouring . . . when he felt her spine go taut.

Slow Jason. Slow. She is not a bedmate who is accustomed to seeking pleasure.

It took gut-deep self-control, but he gentled the kiss, suckling her upper lip into his mouth and releasing it, only to court her with sipping kisses that enticed rather than demanded.

Her fingers flexed on his waist, her muscles losing their tautness. Having gone down flat on her feet, she now rose up toward him again, her wings beginning to open. Coaxing her with another petting kiss, he nudged her into her living room, the area lit only by the glow from a single table lamp. He'd used his abilities to cloak them from curious eyes thus far, but the ability required focus, and all of his was now on Mahiya.

Breaking the kiss once they were inside, he murmured, "The front door."

Pulse a stutter in her throat, she gave a jerky nod and walked to lock the doors into her suite as he shut and locked the ones to the balcony. "I've—" Her words ended in a gasp, his chest pressed to her back, his head bent over the curve of her neck.

22

Placing his hands on her hips, he held her in position as he tasted her skin, as he drowned in the sense of connection, of being *real*, if only for the fleeting slice of night he'd spend with the woman in his arms. Her scent, that wild spice, it made him drunk, her skin so soft and warm, her body all graceful curves. He wished she wore a sari so he'd have only to stroke up his hands to caress the naked skin of her waist.

Her wings, trapped between them, shifted in tiny, restless movements as he reached up to remove the remainder of the pins she'd used to hold her hair in place. It tumbled over his hands in a cascade of unexpected curls, lush and thick and satiny soft. Fisting one hand in the strands, he tugged back her head, arching her neck for his mouth.

A tremor quaked her frame, her fingers splaying against the wood of the doors.

The flick of his tongue, the intoxicating taste of her.

Her pulse thudded a rapid staccato, her wings moving in as erratic a rhythm. Lifting his free hand from her hip, he closed it firmly over the edge of her left wing and stroked down.

A choked-off sound, her pupils hugely dilated when her lashes flicked up. "Jason."

Halting the intimate touch before it became too much, he spread his hand flat on her stomach. "How do I get you out of this?"

"The buttons that hold the wing slits closed." Husky words. "There's also a hidden zip at the side."

Wanting her skin against his own, he took a single step away and swept her hair off her back and over her shoulder. The buttons were faceted black crystals, shimmering in the soft light. Slipping out the top buttons without touching the sensitive arch of her wings, he reached down and found the matching buttons at the bottom of her wings.

The center panel at the back fell down, over her lower curves and he watched as she tugged the front section off her arms, holding the crumpled fabric to her chest with a modesty that paradoxically made him burn. Using her free hand, she reached up to her side and pushed down a concealed zipper that went from her ribs to the slit at the bottom of her tunic.

Heat met his knuckles as he brushed them down the centerline of her back, fine tremors traveling over her skin. Were he a better man, he would stop this—Mahiya didn't respond like a woman who'd had lovers enough to lose her shyness.

"*. . . who doesn't court me with lies, is honest in his desire.*"

His desire held no deceit, was a fist in his gut.

Not forcing her to release the front of the tunic, he put his hands on the curve of her hips and pressed up against her again, his wings spread wide behind them. She shuddered at the intimate contact, because while she'd been busy with her tunic, he'd peeled off his T-shirt.

The softness of her feathers against his naked skin rushed sensory information through his mind, a molten river that held him captive. Bending to the sleek slope of her neck once more, he used a finger to brush aside an errant strand of hair, felt her responding shiver through the place where their bodies connected. Even as he pressed his lips to her sensitive skin, he stroked one hand down her arm to close his fingers over the ones she had fisted on her front, holding the tunic in place.

He didn't force, just gave a gentle tug.

The tiniest hesitation before she uncurled her fingers and allowed him to take one hand, stretch it out to press against the door. When he traced his return journey down the slender warmth of her arm, she kept her hand where he'd put it. Switching sides, he swept her hair over to the other side with luxuriant slowness . . . because now that he was touching her, the fever in him had transformed into a dark sexual patience that promised crushing pleasure.

She knew what was coming this time when he stroked down her arm to her remaining fist, her breathing fast, shallow. Leaving his fingers over her own, he smoothed his free hand over the curve of her waist as he laved her neck with his lips before kissing the slope of one graceful shoulder, his face brushing the upper arch of her wings.

Trembling, she uncurled her fingers from her tunic and allowed him to ease that hand to press flat on the door, too. He caressed his way back down her arm just as slowly, kissing the temptation of her skin the entire time. Then he put both hands to where the tunic bunched at her hips and tugged.

It slipped down to pool at her feet. She stepped out of the fabric, let him kick it away. "The pants have"—a swallow, as if her throat was dry—"hooks at the ankles."

"They'll keep," he said, rising to take in the picture she made, her wings slightly spread, her body naked to the waist, the lush curls of her hair falling over one shoulder. "No need to rush." Reaching out, he ran his knuckles down the naked center of her back again, this time with deeper pressure, her soft cry a fist around his cock. "Close your wings."

The second she did, he pressed close and shifted his hand around the waistband of her tapered cotton pants to undo the string-tie that held them up. Only allowing the garment to slide down to her hips, he redid the tie. Her abdomen quivered against the hand he spread on her satiny skin, his ring finger brushing the top edge of her pants . . . which just barely concealed the slick tightness of her.

His body pulsed, thick and hot.

Sensing it, she shivered but didn't attempt to pull away as he slid his free hand up from her hip to just below her breasts. He didn't cup the small, ripe mounds, just brushed his fingers along the underside before plucking at one taut nipple.

The sweet need in her responding cry whispered over his skin like a tactile caress. Rewarding her with another teasing brush, another tug that made her tremble, he insinuated his other hand just under the top of her waistband. Her navel tensed, relaxed with a shudder as he caressed her breasts once more.

Kissing her neck, so very sensitive, he moved his hand lower, under the silky roughness of fine lace to touch the delicate curls between her thighs, the damp heat of her the most exquisite temptation.

"Jason." Dropping one hand from the door, she reached behind her to touch his hair. "Kiss me." It was a whispered request.

He halted his erotic exploration and spun her around, her wings spread out in magnificent display behind her as she faced him, a woman with a blush of red over her cheekbones and taut breasts topped with dark nipples he knew he'd soon taste.

"You," he murmured, closing his fingers over one breast, "are lovely." Bracing his free arm beside her head, while her own arms wrapped around him as she rose on tiptoe again, he gave her the kiss she'd asked for. It was a naked, wet melding of mouths that had her rubbing against him, her abdomen sliding over his cock.

His hold on the reins slipped.

Reaching between them, he undid the tie on her pants, broke the kiss and her grasp to push them down. Her navel was a lure he couldn't resist, the kiss he pressed there making her fingers fist in his hair before he ran his thumbs over her hipbones and pulled away. "Don't move," he murmured, pressing a kiss to the inside of one satiny thigh.

Mahiya sucked in desperate gulps of air, the cadence of her desire music in his blood. It urged him to rip off her pants, but he grit his teeth and took the time to undo the hooks, forcing himself to go slow, to not overwhelm his lover with her sweet passion and willingness to trust him to lead the dance.

Finally the pants were off. He ran his hands slowly up her calves, her thighs, the white lace that was all that covered her now. By the time he rose to his full height, the scent of her musk perfumed the air. "Take them off." He wanted to see her slick and ready, to taste her in the most erotic of kisses, but first he would have this indication that she remained a willing participant.

Her breath hitched . . . but she ducked her head and hooked her thumbs into the sides of the scrap of lace. He stepped back to watch her push that scrap down and off, because the visual sensation was a feast—though nothing could ever triumph touch for him, tactile pleasure his one true addiction.

Heat blazing over every inch of her skin, she pushed the crumpled lace aside with a slender foot, her lashes hiding her gaze. He reached out, ran the back of one finger over a pebbled nipple. She jerked. Unable to resist, he dipped his head, took part of her breast into his mouth, sucked.

Her knees buckled. "Jason, oh please . . ."

Holding her up as he released her sensitive flesh, he soothed her with a languid kiss that poured fuel on the black storm of his own passion. "Like that," he murmured against kiss-swollen lips as he continued to seduce her with his mouth, "just like that." Cock painfully hard, he slid one hand between her thighs and stroked lightly down the centerline of her sex with a single finger.

Over and over . . . and over again.

Her breath turned into jagged gasps, the tip of his finger slick with her need, her hands gripping at his arms. Dazed eyes locked with his own as he broke the kiss, and he knew the pleasure was building in her, a slow crescendo.

"Fly." It was rough encouragement as he demanded another kiss, craving the contact. "I have you." He continued with his slow, relentless caress, touching the glistening nub at the apex of her thighs with each stroke now that she'd spread her thighs farther in an effort to deepen the intimate contact.

Her fingernails dug into his arms, her neck arched.

Bending her over his arm, he took part of her neglected breast into his mouth, ran his teeth over the taut flesh as he released it . . . at the same time that he captured the sensitive nub between her thighs in his fingertips and pressed hard.

"Jason!"

Raising his head, he removed his hand before the pleasure racking her body became painful. "I have you," he repeated, nuzzling his face against the side of hers. "I have you."

Only when she stopped trembling did he shift his hold to her hips and raise her until she could wrap her legs around his waist. Her eyes were lazy, sated, her kiss languid. Arms twining around his neck, she opened for him with a sensual generosity that made him want to devour, her fingers weaving through his hair. He reached between them to undo his jeans, grip his cock, and position himself at her entrance.

A soft gasp into his mouth as the head of his cock rubbed against her passion-swollen flesh and then he was pushing into the silken welcome of her sheath.

"Oh!" Mahiya gripped him tighter with every part of her body, her internal muscles continuing to ripple with trailing waves of her pleasure.

Shuddering, he dropped his forehead onto her own as he fought the urge to shove. Her body was telling him it hadn't been used in such a way for a long time, her muscles struggling to stretch around him.

"It's all right, Jason." Fingers on his cheek, kisses gentle and tender and unexpected. "I want you so much."

He drew in a ragged breath, pushed a fraction deeper. A

bit more. Scalding heat, feminine muscles pulsing on his rigid flesh. The pleasure was almost pain, the bite exquisite. Turning his mouth to brush against her own, he continued to work his cock into her, slow and relentless.

"Jason."

Flexing his hips at the whimper of sound, he forced himself to halt. "Does it hurt?" he asked bluntly.

A dazed look. "It burns and yet it feels good. I want you in me."

That was all he needed to hear.

Sliding his hands under her thighs, he lifted her legs off his hips and pushed her knees up and wide, his strength more than enough to keep her pinned as he thrust into her to the feel of her nails digging into his back as her body spasmed around him, bathing his cock in molten desire.

Then he began to move.

23

Honor sat in sunlight rich as honey and as languorous, a glass of orange juice in hand and Dmitri's white shirt loose and comfortable around her, watching her husband pace back and forth across the sprawling gardens that surrounded their private villa. He held a phone to his ear, gave clipped orders in a tone that said he expected to be obeyed.

He'd asked her if she wanted to explore the countryside, but all she wanted was to be with Dmitri. They made love in the sunshine and in the dark, played bedroom games that caused her to blush, and fed each other treats they had delivered from a discreet grocer in the nearby village. It was a lazy, hazy existence, and she was glad for it after the horror of what had gone before.

Of course, Dmitri couldn't disconnect completely from the Tower that had been his responsibility for centuries, nor had she expected it of him. What mattered was that the instant she looked at him in a way that said she needed his attention, the phone went off. There was no doubt in her mind that she was the most important part of her husband's life . . . important enough that he would give up immortality should she choose a mortal existence. Because that was something else she understood; her Dmitri would not choose to go on after she died. He'd survived once, wouldn't again.

Striding back to her, he placed his cell phone on the wrought iron table that held a plate filled with slices of fruit she'd cut for them to share. "What are you thinking?" He leaned down, hands on the arms of her chair. "You're tense."

And he'd figured that out from meters away, while she'd believed him engrossed in his conversation. "I almost wish," she said, putting down her juice and tucking her feet up in the chair, "you hadn't given me time to rethink my choice."

His head dropped, and it was instinct to stroke her fingers through his hair. "I'm a bastard, Honor." Fierce voice, his eyes locking with her own. "We both know that." When she would've spoken, he shook his head and continued. "I damn well rigged your original decision—maybe I thought I was giving you a choice, but by asking you when I did, I made sure that choice was the one *I* wanted."

Trailing her fingers down his neck and over the faded gray of his T-shirt, she said, "Was that meant to shock me? Hmm?"

His lips, so sexy and tempting, curved. "You realize most people are intimidated by me."

"Really?" It was a blatant tease. "How strange."

He laughed, her Dmitri who had never laughed like this when they'd first met, with the light in his eyes. "You are definitely not Ingrede."

She'd wondered if he truly understood that when they married, understood that while she carried the soul and the memories of the woman he'd danced with on a field of wildflowers, she'd been shaped by the winds of another life. Now she saw the knowledge in his eyes, saw, too, the heart-piercing love he had for the woman she was in this lifetime, a hunter scarred but no longer broken. "Oh?" she said with a smile she could feel in every cell of her body. "I don't seem to recall your first wife accepting your every word as law."

"I do believe your memory must be faulty." Eliminating the inches that separated them, he claimed an unashamedly

sexual kiss that melted her bones. When he trailed his lips
over her jaw and down to the pulse in her neck, she fisted
her hand in his hair.

"Take me." It was an offer she'd make only Dmitri. "You
haven't fed today."

But instead of sinking his fangs into her willing flesh, he
lifted his head, frowned. "I don't want to weaken you. I can
have some blood packs delivered—"

"No. You feed from *me*." He was hers to care for, hers to
adore.

"Honor."

"I'm on a high-calorie, high-iron, high-fluid, high-
everything diet for a reason." She'd had a long conversation
with a Guild physician before they left for Italy. The elderly
and somewhat cantankerous man was used to dealing with
vampiric-human pairings and had given her guidelines to
follow if she intended to be one of those "possessive
females." "If you tell me you prefer a bag of old blood to
my neck," she muttered, "I'll bite you myself."

He didn't soften at the joke, continuing to lean dark and
dangerous and a bit pissed off above her. "I'll get the packs
delivered."

"Dmitri—"

"I'll let you have your way in every other thing you want,
but I won't compromise your health." His voice was steel.
"I'll allow myself to feed from you once a week."

Honor narrowed her eyes. "Every second day."

"This is not a negotiation."

"Yes, it is. It's a marriage. So negotiate."

His arm muscles turned rigid where he held on to the
chair. "Twice a week," he gritted out, "and you'll take an
iron test every five days."

Tapping her finger on his wrist, she saw the implacable
resolve in his expression, knew the negotiation was at an
end. It had gone better than she'd hoped—after all, Dmitri
was near to a thousand years old and arrogant with it. "Fine,"
she said with a pretend scowl, "but if you ever stop giving

me the little bites when we make love, I'm filing for divorce."
The erotic blood kisses were all about sex, not feeding.

This time, his smile was of the *very* bad man she had in
her bed three times a day at the very least. "Oh, I'll never
stop doing that. If you ask nicely, I might even bite you on
that spot on the inside of your thigh that you like so much."

Honor shivered. Once, the idea of a bite on her thigh
would've made her throw up, and even Dmitri could only
do it if she was in a certain position, where she could kick
him away if need be . . . but when it went right, when the
horrible memories of what had been done to her didn't overwhelm her . . . oh wow. "You are a menace."

His eyes gleamed. "Let's go inside so I can corrupt you
some more."

Impossible, but he gets sexier with every passing minute.

Tugging him down, she kissed those sensual lips,
received a loving that made her breasts swell, her nipples
tighten. "Come sit with me," she said before she forgot her
intent, "so we can talk about my decision."

Sprawling into the chair on the other side of the table, he
reached for a slice of sweet white peach with a desultory
hand. "Don't ask me to talk you out of vampirism. I'm only
being this good because I don't want you to hate me."

She nibbled on a piece of apricot. "Noted." Twisting
around, she put her feet on his lap, her toes—currently
painted a vivid blue green—shimmering in the sunlight.

His hand stroked over her in an absent caress. "You won't
ever be like the monsters," he said quietly, speaking to her
deepest fear. "Never, Honor. That's not in you."

It choked her with blind terror that she might become
like the soulless creatures who'd caused her such heart-
breaking harm not in one lifetime, but in two. But then she
looked across at the man who had loved her both those
lifetimes, and she saw not simply the darkness he wore so
close to his skin, but also the truth that he'd maintained a
claw hold on honor even as he sank into sin and depravity.
Dmitri had never brutalized a woman, and he'd never hurt

a child . . . not after he'd had to break their son's neck to save Misha from unimaginable horror.

Unlike Dmitri, she wouldn't be going into this new life through an ugly act of coercion, broken and twisted and tortured. She'd be ushered into it by a man who adored her, would spend eternity discovering every changing facet of him. Never would they become jaded with one another—*never*. It was a quiet truth deep within her, born of a love that had survived death and time itself.

"Dmitri," she said into the sunlit silence. "Where is your heart?"

Her question could've been taken many ways, but her husband knew what she meant. "In your hands, where it's always been."

Luminous joy in her every breath, a sense of peace in her soul. "And you hold mine. So you see, I only have to worry about your heart, not my own." As his heart was her most precious treasure, hers was his. He would love and care for that heart with every bit of his dangerous strength, would never permit her to lose the compassion and humanity he cherished in her. "Let's go home," she said, "begin the process."

Dmitri's hands tightened on her legs. "This is it, Honor. No more chances."

"No, Dmitri. Now we'll have an eternity of chances."

24

Mahiya felt bruised in places she hadn't known it was possible to have bruises, muscles sore in a way they'd never before been sore. Jason was . . . a storm.

Slow.

Relentless.

Inexorable.

She'd thought he'd be satisfied after that shockingly carnal union against the door, but he'd brought her back to her bed, allowed her only a small respite before he took her again.

Mahiya wasn't complaining. Never would, not so long as he came to her bed.

"*. . . this won't make me stay with you, won't make me commit.*"

A twinge in her heart as she opened the bedroom window to the bright morning sunshine, that of a woman who wasn't only in sensual thrall to Jason, but who was fascinated by the glimpses she'd had of the man behind the spymaster . . . and that man, he was a dangerous, complex, fractured creature she hungered to know. But it wasn't an opportunity she'd ever have, wasn't an opportunity Jason would give her. She wasn't even certain if he'd return to her bed.

"Goodnight, Mahiya." Watchful eyes.

She wanted only to sleep wrapped around the strength and heat of him, but she satisfied herself with a final caress of her fingers over his cheek, having the haunting sense of setting a wild creature free. "I'll see you in the morning."

"In the morning."

A rustle at the door shattered the whisper of memory. Then Vanhi was bustling in through to the bedroom, her rich ebony hair tamed in a severe knot at the back of her head, her body clothed in a sari of black dotted crimson. Only she could get away with such bold shades while the rest of the fort wore the faded colors of semi-mourning. Because only Vanhi had been alive since before Neha.

The vampire with her green eyes and skin of deep bronze had the appearance of a stunning woman in her thirties, but the manner and ways of a grandmother. She'd rocked Neha and Nivriti in the nursery as she'd later rocked Anoushka, then Mahiya. She was the only being Mahiya had dared love after the brutalization of the single friend she'd made as an adult.

Crimson on the stones, slick and thick, blood-drenched wings lying lifeless beside the unconscious form of a man whose only real crime had been kindness.

Even the beloved mare Mahiya had helped raise from a foal had been given away—to Arav's new lover, the cruelty a conscious one. However, Vanhi held Neha's affection and thus was safe to love, though even the vampire wasn't permitted to spend too much time with Mahiya without finding herself sent on holiday to another part of the territory.

"So," Vanhi now said, "that spawn of a she-goat is dead then."

Mahiya was unsurprised at the judgment. "I won't be mourning Arav, but the way he died . . . I would not have wished that on him."

Vanhi snorted. "He should've been castrated for the advantage he took of a young girl barely fledged."

"I allowed him to take that advantage," Mahiya replied, the argument an old one. "I was a fool." Willing to accept dross for gold. "I won't be one again."

"Oh yes?" Vanhi raised an eyebrow as she picked up a jet-black feather from the carpet. "Yet Raphael's spymaster is welcome in your bedroom?"

"He tells me no lies."

The quiet statement made Vanhi still in her energetic movements around the room as she settled this, straightened that. A heavy sadness in her expression, she laid a soft palm against Mahiya's face. "I wish you would expect more, Mahiya child."

"One day," Mahiya promised, "I'll have the chance to dream bigger dreams. Until then, I must work with what I have." False hope could be more devastating than unvarnished pragmatism—she'd learned that during her attempt to find sanctuary with Lijuan years prior to the archangel's "evolution."

"Silly girl." Lijuan's dove gray wings swept the floor as she waved her hand, dismissing the guard who'd escorted an exhausted Mahiya into a cavernous room that echoed with sound. "You ask me to make a ruin of my friendship with Neha for you?"

"No. I ask only sanctuary."

Eerie eyes of a strange pearlescent gray, staring at her out of a face with skin so pale, she imagined she could see the skeletal structure beneath. "Either you are feeble-minded," Lijuan said, "or you are being disingenuous."

Mahiya fought the ice invading her bloodstream to say, "You are far more powerful than Neha. She would not put your relationship in jeopardy for so insignificant a thing as I."

"It follows that I have no need of you. You offer me nothing." A smile that made Mahiya's stomach clench, her bones rattle. "Your wings . . . hmm, perhaps I will keep you after all."

That was when Lijuan had "invited" Mahiya to view her Collection Room, watching with that same inhuman smile as Mahiya bent over and threw up what little food there was in her stomach.

"Ju will clean that up." The man who shuffled out of the darkness was . . . wrong. Jerking up, Mahiya ran the back of her hand over her mouth as Ju produced a mop and wiped away all evidence of her lack of control, his eyes black and dull, his movements that of a marionette.

"He was a strong man once, but I broke him. Still, I cannot let him go." Lijuan reached out to stroke Mahiya's wing.

Twisting away, she waited to be reduced to ash for her insolence, but Lijuan smiled. "A pity I cannot take you for my collection. Better I think, to return you to Neha. I will be patient, and ask her to give you to me when you are dead. I would not want such beauty lost to rot."

One night and one day.

That was how long Mahiya had spent in Lijuan's stronghold, a nightmare span of hours it chilled her to the bone to think of even now. "Vanhi," she said, forcing her mind back to the present, "what are your thoughts on Arav's death?"

"That piece of elephant dung may have insulted someone, or he may simply have been in the wrong place at the wrong time." Vanhi shrugged, picking up a sari Mahiya had left out to air.

Walking to take the other end of the slippery fabric, Mahiya worked with Vanhi to fold it. "I don't know. It all seems calculated somehow."

"I tell you one thing, Mahiya child." A solemn tone. "Games are one thing, but to play them against Neha?" Shaking her head, Vanhi used her fingers to draw an ancient sign meant to ward off evil. "Only bad things will come of this."

Yes.

Exiting the palace half an hour after Vanhi's departure, Mahiya found an unexpected visitor about to take the steps to her door. "Venom."

A smile lazy with charm, his eyes hidden from view by mirrored sunglasses that reflected her own face back at her. Dressed in black pants and a white shirt, his damp hair combed neatly, he appeared one of the more dangerous courtiers—the ones who had the brains to scheme and collude.

"Lady Mahiya."

"Just Mahiya," she said, soaking in the morning sunshine cascading from such a pure blue sky, it seemed obscene it might yet bear witness to further carnage. "If you're searching for Jason, he is elsewhere." As Neha had expanded his mandate, Mahiya was no longer expected to act the spy and report back on his activities.

"Jason." She stepped out onto the balcony, fighting herself not to touch him now that the night had passed, not to attempt to claim rights of possession—it would be as foolish as attempting to own a storm. "Will you have breakfast before you go?"

"No, I have a meeting I must make." He spread his wings, paused. "I will see you when I return."

Perhaps it was a silly thing, but it meant a great deal to her that he'd knocked on her door instead of simply vanishing into the dawn, her spymaster who always walked alone.

"I should've called ahead," Venom said, his voice fracturing the memory, his smile that of a man who knew how to coax and beguile women. "May I offer you an escort to your next destination?"

The playful flirtation made her smile. "I go to Neha."

"The private audience hall?"

"No." Mahiya frowned. "The message asked me to meet her near Guardian." Looking up, she sought out the more spartan fort that overlooked Archangel Fort. It was isolated, with no one within hearing distance but Neha's troops—who'd see nothing and do nothing should the archangel decide to eliminate the annoyance of her consort's illegitimate child.

In truth, it would be no different than being at this fort. Except . . . Jason was here.

No, she told herself sternly, do not spin hopes out of air and a dark sensuality that had marked her deep within. Jason had promised to help her escape, but she had no further claim on his protection. "So you see," she said to Venom, "I must leave you here."

The vampire frowned. "Are you certain the message was from Neha? I saw her flying down toward the city not long ago."

"Yes. We are to meet at the ruined temple just outside the walls of the fort." Still, uneasy with the unexpected choice of venue, she reached into a hidden pocket in her tunic to retrieve the small card. "It is her hand."

Taking the card, Venom rubbed his thumb over the script. "Yes, you're right. But her writing's not so ornate as to be impossible to forge. I don't like the feel of this."

All at once, she knew why Venom had come to the palace, and her heart twisted. "Jason told you to watch over me." It did something to her to know that Jason cared enough about her to have asked another of the Seven to keep her in his sights. No one had watched over her since she left the Refuge and the protection of those who undertook the welfare of angelic young. She was not so proud as to refute the emotions his care engendered in her.

Venom gave her a faint smile in answer. "It says you have fifteen minutes till your meeting."

"I thought to arrive early." *Give myself room to settle so that nothing Neha does will goad me into a fatal mistake.*

"Indulge me," Venom said, "and arrive exactly on time."

Glancing up, she raised a hand and plucked his sunglasses off his face before he realized her intent. The way he moved away from her was a sinuous, beautiful, *fast* thing, but she held her position. "You had only to ask," he said, pushing back disordered strands of hair as he rose from his combat-ready crouch, his green eyes vivid and hypnotic against the desert brown of his skin, warm and of this land.

"I thought to read your eyes." Mahiya handed back his sunglasses, a faint niggling at the back of her mind. "But that was foolish," she said, the odd sense that she was missing something gone before she could pursue it. "I do not know anyone who might read such eyes."

Sliding the shades back on, Venom began to walk away from her. "Remember, arrive exactly on time." Then he picked up his pace and was gone in a quicksilver snap of movement that was nothing human.

Yet no matter how fast he was, he could not make it to Guardian before she did. Even so, she flew up to the palace roof to wait, having decided to give him the time he'd asked for, her sense of "wrongness" amplifying the more she thought about the situation. But not attending the meet wasn't an option, not when it *had* most likely been Neha who'd sent the note—the archangel knew Mahiya had a sickening fear of Guardian . . . and she knew why.

Please no! Please!

It was the only time she had ever begged. It was also the only time she'd seen an expression of horror on Neha's face, as if she could not believe her own actions. It hadn't stopped her though . . . and Anoushka had been standing beside her all the while, her mother's cold-eyed shadow.

Only two minutes to go till the meeting.

Spreading out her wings, she swept off the roof and up into the clouds, angling toward the ruined temple. In this, Neha had erred. Though Guardian made Mahiya's skin sticky with fear sweat, the temple held only happy memories.

Those memories a talisman, she swept over Guardian and its sentries. Some distance from the fort's protective walls to the south lay the crumbling ruins of a temple that had been built long ago to honor the archangel who had ruled here before Neha. Neha wasn't responsible for the destruction. It had simply fallen out of use some years after the archangel in question had been killed in a battle against another of the Cadre.

While one entire side had collapsed, the roof having crashed onto the paving stones below, the other half was

more or less upright. Ten sturdy columns held up the remainder of the roof, the holes in it scattering sunshine over the
floor below to create a mosaic of light and shadow.

Landing outside the temple, Mahiya took a deep breath
of the thinner mountain air and folded her wings . . . just as
a step sounded behind her. She twisted on her feet to find
herself face-to-face with a Venom whose skin gleamed with
sweat, his formerly pristine white shirt now damp and mold-
ing itself to sleek muscle, his unshielded eyes narrowed
against the sunlight.

Astonished, she stared. "No one's that fast."

A flash of fang as he grinned. "I beg to disagree."

Brain kicking into gear, she looked beyond him to the
flat walls of the fort, snapped her head back. "You know the
tunnels." From what little information she'd been able to
scrape up, the subterranean passages that connected the two
forts had been built up over millennia, had to be a maze.

"Maybe." Brushing past her with a speed that was in no
way human, he ran up the temple steps.

"Venom!" She stepped into the dappled light of the temple on his heels . . . and was overwhelmed by a sense of
peace. This had been her favorite playground when she'd
been a child angel on visits home from the Refuge. She'd
had a thousand adventures within its broken, tumbled-down
walls, written her name with a charcoal stick on one of the
columns before guilt made her return to rub it out.

The memory had her lips kicking up at the corners even
as she searched for any sign of Neha and found none. However, Venom stood not far in front of her, checking a shadowed alcove. "You have to step out before you make yourself
a target." Neha would not tolerate the fact that Mahiya was
being escorted by a vampire who remained something of a
favorite, regardless of his choice to serve Raphael. "You can
easily keep watch from a concealed position." His help
would be welcome should her sense of wrongness not be
her imagination running riot.

"Hmm? No, I don't think so."

"I'll drag you out if I have to." He was Jason's friend, and Jason, she knew instinctively, was a man with few friends. Venom couldn't be allowed to throw his life away.

Venom's response was low voiced. "Come look at this, Mahiya."

25

Caught by the odd tone of his voice, she crossed through a beam of sunlight and came to a dead halt. Within the alcove in front of Venom sat a box wrapped in sparkling gold paper tied with a silver bow. When the vampire gingerly slid out the card tucked in under the silver ribbon, it proved to contain nothing but her name in the same script as that on the note commanding her to be here at this time.

"I may not be a spymaster like our Jason," Venom mused, "but I would hazard Neha did not send that note."

Mahiya had to agree, her mind trying to make sense of the bizarre circumstances and failing. "Let's take the box outside before we open it."

"You shouldn't open it at all until Jason and I have a chance to—"

"As a strong vampire, your hearing is acute," she interrupted. "Do you hear ticking? Anything to indicate it may contain an incendiary device?" If an explosion hit either of them right, it could decapitate and kill.

Venom angled his head, finally gave a reluctant shake. "No. But—"

"And, there is a high chance you have an excellent sense of smell." She'd seen him "taste" the air with his tongue. "Smell anything suspicious?" The fact was, she knew if she walked away now, either Venom or Jason would take the risk. And that, she refused to allow. "Chemicals, anything?"

Gritted teeth. "No."

"I don't, either, and if this is the murderer," she said reasonably, "he or she has no reason to play such games." An angel strong enough to annihilate Arav could break her in half. "Someone else could have stumbled upon this—a guard on a break, a curious child—and none of the murders so far appear to have been random." The latter was arguable, but her gut said there *was* a connection between the four victims, and she knew Jason agreed.

The slitted black pupils of Venom's eyes narrowed as he considered her. "I thought you were a princess."

"You should know that an archangel's court is far more dangerous than the streets of New York." She picked up the box before he could and took it, very carefully, into the sunshine. Making her way around to the side totally hidden from Guardian, she placed the box on a clear patch of grass a good fifty feet from the temple, on the theory that she didn't want the walls collapsing on top of her. "Go stand in the distance."

A raised eyebrow. "I think not."

"Don't be foolish," she said, deciding she liked Venom not only because he was Jason's friend, but because he looked at her as if *she* were the dangerous creature. "If something does happen to me, you'll be unaffected and able to summon help. Or would you rather be injured at the same time?"

His lips curved. "That logic holds if I'm the one to open the box."

"True—but I have a higher chance of survival."

"I doubt it." He folded his arms. "You might be an angel, but I'm stronger than you are. And Jason is stronger than both of us."

Yes, and I will not have him hurt, no matter if that is a silly emotional decision. "So you'd wait for him?" When he didn't reply, she said, "Yes, that's what I thought. This box was meant for me, Venom. I'll allow no one else to open it"—to be hurt—"and you can't follow me in to the sky should I take off with it. Wouldn't you rather I stay here?"

Another hard stare. "Obviously, I need to study princesses further." With that, he turned on his heel and jogged to crouch behind a large rock.

Going to her knees, she undid the ribbon after examining it for hidden wires, realizing as she did so that the box wasn't wrapped in gold foil—the cardboard was actually painted the metallic shade, so once she had the ribbon off, all she had to do was lift the lid. "Venom! Do you see any branches nearby?" There was a tree not far from him.

"Wait." A minute later, he threw over a sturdy branch at least four feet long. "I'm happy to know you're not suicidal."

No, I plan to live, to love, to fly . . . and if he'll let me, dance again with a spymaster with wings of jet. "Here I go." Flattening her body to the ground to ameliorate the impact of any blast, she reached out with the stick and flicked the lid off.

Nothing happened.

Blowing out a trembling breath, she got up and padded closer, aware of Venom jogging across to join her. Both of them stared at what lay within the box before Venom crouched down. "Nothing smells off." He held up a hand when she would've reached for the object. "Wait, let me make sure it's not sitting on something."

Mahiya waited, patient, until he nodded at her to go ahead.

"Seems you have a secret admirer," he murmured as she examined the fluffy pink teddy bear with white paws and face. "Maybe I scared him off."

"Perhaps." She searched the whole toy, but could find no hidden compartment. "I admit this is so strange a thing I have no idea what to make of it. Maybe Jason will."

"If I might suggest that I carry it down."

"Yes, it's better if I'm not seen with it. If you are, it'll be assumed you're courting a lover."

"I have a reputation, it seems." A statement smooth as silk, but for the bite of it.

"I'd have to be blind not to notice your sensuality." Dangerous and languid at the same time. "I'm fairly certain you don't ever have to go to an empty bed unless you choose it." Regardless of the eerie "otherness" of his eyes.

"Careful"—taking the box and its cargo, he rose, the movement liquid with grace—"you'll make Jason jealous."

"Do not let this crush you, but you aren't my type." Though she framed it as a joke, the fact was, she saw Neha too deeply in Venom. His eyes were of her creatures, his movements the same—and that was why she said what she did next, for she refused to allow Neha to spoil the friendships she might make. "I do think we'll be wonderful friends."

A single raised eyebrow, sophisticated cool in his next words. "We will?"

"Of course. Admit it, you already rather like me even if I did win our argument."

A faint twitch of Venom's lips. "When I first met you, I couldn't understand the attraction, but I do believe Jason has met his match."

It took effort to keep her tone steady. "I'm going into the city for a short time. I'll see you when I return to the fort." It was a fuzzy memory at best, from over two years ago, but if she was right, there was a slim chance it might provide them with an answer of some kind.

Venom scowled. "Jason gave me strict orders to keep you safe."

Her heart hitched at the direct confirmation of her guess. Some women might have chafed at the protectiveness, but for Mahiya, who had never mattered much to anyone, such a thing was no unwanted chain, but a welcome indication of care. That didn't mean she intended to stop thinking for herself. "It's daylight," she said, "I don't plan to linger in any dark alleys and will in fact be in a busy market district."

"Some princess," Venom muttered, but dug in his pocket to retrieve a cell phone. "This is a spare. I'm inputting my number and Jason's. Call if you have any problems."

A few minutes later, she swept down over the city. Her target was a sunny yellow building with an old but gleaming treadle sewing machine in the window and a dusty child in short pants playing on the doorstep.

His eyes widened at the sight of Mahiya. He was off like a shot the next instant, running into the house yelling, "Ma! Ma!"

Making no effort to hide her smile, Mahiya waited politely on the street, aware of other shopkeepers poking their heads out of small storefronts and/or workshops, and of customers congregating on doorsteps across the narrow lane. Six or seven shops down, a camel chewed cud, while his owner fiddled with a saddle that bore little silver bells and pretended not to watch Mahiya.

Angels filled the skies of this city, but an angel in this street of the market district was a rare thing. It wasn't snobbery that kept her kind away, for angels were as curious as mortals when it came to exploring a city's hidden byways. It was because the shops here were tiny, with no room for wings. The only reason Mahiya even knew about this particular one was that the owner had been invited to showcase her goods at the fort in a trade exhibition.

Now, the young mortal appeared in the doorway. Of course, Mahiya thought, youth was a relative thing. This woman who had lived but twenty-seven, perhaps twenty-eight years, was old enough to have a little boy hiding behind her skirts. At the same age, Mahiya had been a babe not much bigger than the boy.

"My lady." The toymaker bowed, her hands fisting in her apron. "I would welcome you inside but . . ."

"The intent is enough," Mahiya said with utmost

gentleness in the informal local dialect. "I will not disturb you long."

"Please, let me bring you a cup of tea at least." Entreaty in eyes of melted chocolate. "I cannot send an angel from my doorstep without courtesy."

"Thank you. Tea would be welcome."

A shaky smile lit up the woman's face. "I have a pot on the stove. A minute, no more." As she turned to go, the little boy found the courage to stay behind, eyes of the same melted chocolate as his mother gazing at Mahiya in wonder.

"Hello," Mahiya said, and since he didn't bolt, asked, "Why are you not at school?"

His eyes became even rounder, and he sucked his thumb into his mouth. When she didn't say anything further, he withdrew that thumb with slow carefulness, as if not trusting her silence. "I'm not as big as Nishi yet." A pause, then he added, "Nishi goes to school," as if to make sure she understood.

"Ah," she said. "Will you be old enough soon?"

Lines on his forehead. "Not too soon. Maybe almost soon."

Biting back her smile at his flawless childish logic, she saw his eyes go to her wings. "You may come closer if you wish."

Thumb in his mouth again, he padded out to stand only inches from her, examining her feathers with the frankness of the very young. When his mother appeared in the doorway, cup in hand, she went to call him back, but Mahiya shook her head. Accepting the tea, she said, "He is smart and brave both."

"Yes." The proud woman beamed, her thin face beautiful. "Takes after his father."

Only then did Mahiya ask her question. "I saw someone with a toy bear—pink and white, with an embroidered collar—"

"Of white daisies." Quickening excitement.

"Yes, exactly. I thought it may have been your work."

Hand sewn and embroidered, the eyes a lovely blue crystal, and the stitch work exquisite.

"Do you remember if it had a tiny yellow star on the left foot?"

Mahiya thought back. "Yes."

"Then it is mine for certain. But I'm sorry, my lady, I don't have another."

"Oh, that's a pity. Do you keep many?"

"No, only one of each kind." The woman smoothed her hands down her apron. "I sold Daisy a week ago. Oh, let me take your cup."

"Thank you. The tea was delicious." Rich, milky, flavored with cardamom and sweetened with honey. "Do you remember to whom you sold Daisy? I may see if they are willing to sell it to me."

"A vampire. Unfamiliar, perhaps a guest at the fort." The woman bit her lip, shook her head. "He gave no name, but his hair was scarlet, his skin like fine bone china."

"A difficult man to miss." Yet she knew of no vampire with such hair and skin in the vicinity.

Another mystery.

Jason had spent the morning collecting information from quarters closed to others, and now landed in a farmer's fallow field, heading to the shade cast by a hut likely used as a resting place during the planting season. He needed the whispering silence to think, to put all the pieces together.

The fact was, though he'd said nothing to either Venom or Mahiya, he had the amorphous feeling that Mahiya was the key. But while she'd had relationships of some kind with both Eris and Arav, nothing significant connected her to either Audrey or Shabnam. Yet, his instincts persisted—as if he'd seen or heard something he hadn't consciously understood.

Frustrated, he took out his phone, deciding to pursue the answer to another question.

"Jason." The warmth of Jessamy's smile traveled through even the tiny screen. "It's good to see you."

"And you." It was Jessamy who had first helped him remember what it was to be a person again.

Standing outside the place where he'd watched the baby angels go to learn things, he waited for the last lingering student to disappear before he slipped inside.

The woman within looked up, her eyes gentle with a kindness that wasn't pity. "I have something for you," she said, as if she'd been waiting for him, as if she knew he'd been listening to her lessons from the shadows for many days.

Walking over, she handed him a set of hard books with big letters on the pages. "To help you remember."

He touched the cover, turned the pages.

He'd once had books like this, had read them over and over even after he was alone, but then they'd crumbled, and after a while, he'd forgotten he was supposed to know how to read. Until today, when Jessamy's newest lesson had turned a key in his mind, unlocking the sound of his mother's voice as she taught him his letters.

Taking the books, he left without a word.

It had taken him months to break his silence, but Jessamy, with her wise eyes and kind heart, had never pushed, always left him room to breathe. Now, he said, "I have a question for you."

A tilt of her head.

"You know Lijuan has evolved, and Raphael has gained a new ability. There are now signs that something may be happening to Titus, though I cannot yet say what." The warrior archangel's people were fiercely loyal, and Jason's spies had only been able to ascertain that Titus was battling an illness. As archangels did not get sick, Titus must be undergoing a transformation of some kind.

Neha's ability to wield ice wasn't public knowledge, thus he couldn't speak of it without breaking the blood vow, but he had further evidence of a Cadre-wide phenomenon. "You remember Astaad's erratic behavior." The archangel had beaten one of his beloved concubines to a pulp, when he was known to be indulgent with his women to the point of spoiling them. "What I'm hearing is that he's stabilized and may have gained nascent abilities over sea creatures."

Jessamy's expression was thoughtful. "At the time, his behavior was explained by the disruption caused by Caliane's awakening."

"The awakening of an Ancient is nothing to ignore," Jason said, thinking of the lost city of Amanat risen in a place far from its origin. "But could Caliane's awakening have been *triggered* by a more dominant force?" Lijuan's dark evolution had predated Caliane's waking by mere months, both events shifting the course of the world's history.

"There's no—" Jessamy went silent. "Wait."

When she returned, it was with an old bound book she held with such care, it was clear it was fragile. "This history mentions an event called the 'Cascade' and states: 'And the archangels were not who they should be, and bodies rotted in the streets, and blood rained from the skies as empires burned.'"

Expression solemn, Jessamy glanced up. "This Cascade was over twenty-five thousand years ago. I'll begin to search the archives for further information, but though her exact age is disputed, I believe there is one archangel awake who would've experienced it firsthand."

Caliane.

Ending the call soon afterward to make another, he rose on a flight path toward the fort, aiming for the office Rhys kept near the barracks that housed most of the guard. The other man was overseeing a training exercise from his balcony, but he had the forensic reports.

"Nothing we didn't already know," he said to Jason. "There was no finesse, no attempt to hide anything. Audrey appears to have had her organs removed, while Shabnam's head was torn off. Arav, too, was ripped apart—tendons sheared, muscles snapped."

Jason scanned the reports, saw the note about Shabnam's head, read that Arav had indeed been ripped apart—by bare hands. Not a single mark that could be attributed to a weapon had been found on his body. That told Jason something important. Very, very few angels had the strength to physically rip out another angel's spine, much less wrench off his head.

And to do that in flight against a general of Arav's abilities? It would require near-archangel level strength or an unknown new ability. He needed to have his people begin to covertly check the power status of certain angels, get an indication if they, too, were being impacted by this strange evolution that seemed to be affecting the Cadre.

Flipping back, he rechecked the report on Shabnam. Though the pathologist had been unable to confirm, given the nature of her injuries, it was his considered opinion that her face had been raked with claws of some kind. Jason had witnessed Neha's fingernails elongate into claws, but it wasn't an ability limited to her alone. Still, it was another piece of the puzzle.

"Yes," he said, retaining his copy of the forensic findings. "There's nothing important here." Rhys might be Neha's man, but he wasn't Jason's.

26

Raphael considered the discussion he'd just had with Jason, and made the decision to put through a call to Caliane. His mother had initially been resistant to utilizing any kind of modern communications equipment, but after he'd refused to communicate with her using raw power, she had finally acquiesced to a small suite Naasir and Isabel had put in place.

Now, Raphael waited as the angel on duty went to retrieve Caliane.

"Raphael." Eyes shining with love, she reached out toward the screen as she always did, as if she would touch him. "My son."

"Mother." So long had he thought her forever lost that each time he spoke to her, it was a kick to the gut, an ache in his heart. "I would ask you a question."

"First, you must answer one of mine." The order of an archangel who had been alive for an eon before her Sleep. "When can I next expect my son's presence?" She waved her hand. "And I do not mean through this device."

"I cannot leave the Tower until one of the senior Seven return."

"The beautiful blue one. He is certainly not weak."

No, Illium was in no way weak, but his power had been growing in unpredictable jolts; enough that he didn't quite have a handle on his new strength. "Mother," he said gently, for he would give her honor until and unless her terrible madness returned, "I am your son, but I am also Cadre. Do not attempt to run my Tower, and I will not attempt to run your city."

Caliane's gaze burned a dramatic blue flame, the glow deadly. "And should I decide to visit you, what then?"

"I and my consort would welcome you."

"So you intend to continue the liaison? I could break her in a finger snap."

"Then I would have to kill you—as I will do if I ever consider you a threat to Elena." His mother was an Ancient, used to getting her way and to seeing him as a child. She needed to remember that the boy she'd left bleeding and broken and heartsick on a green field far from civilization was long gone. "I am not who I once was."

The glow dimmed, melancholy in every line of her face, and he knew she relived the same memories. "Ask your question, Raphael."

He spoke to her of the "Cascade," saw immediate comprehension. "So"—a whisper that held the weight of too much knowledge—"it's true. I'd begun to sense the signs but had hoped I was wrong." Hair the shade she'd bequeathed him tumbled over her shoulders as she shook her head.

"Will you tell me about it?"

"It is exactly what the Refuge Historian believes it to be—a confluence of time and certain critical events that has ignited a power surge in the Cadre. Some will gain strength, while others will be reborn with new abilities. There is no way to predict the outcome, and many of these abilities will be erratic at best, have catastrophic effects at worst."

"The Cadre may be able to weather the change successfully now that we have this knowledge."

Caliane's expression was suddenly old, so very old that he could believe Lijuan was right, that his mother had lived two hundred and fifty thousand years. "Yes, but you see, it was during the last Cascade that I believe I first became touched with madness, though I did not know it then, for it was an insidious intruder hiding within. There is no way to protect against such a change."

27

Venom, his legs hanging over the side and his mirrored sunglasses in place, was sitting on the part of the balcony outside Jason's room when Jason returned to the palace. A steaming cup of coffee sat next to his left hand.

"I had to beg," the vampire said when he saw the direction of Jason's gaze. "Your princess considers coffee an insult to the taste buds." He raised his face to the sky, drinking in the sun with sinuous pleasure. "Did I ever tell you I hate the cold?"

"Every winter." Jason passed Venom the forensic reports. "What do you see?"

"Archangel strength or near to it . . . or maybe an ability of some kind," Venom said, because he'd been trained by Jason to see such things. "Puts a whole new spin on recent events. Lijuan?"

"She could've done it and been gone before we ever knew she was here." The Archangel of China had the ability to dematerialize her body, though as Raphael had shown in the battle above Amanat, she wasn't as omnipotent as she went to great lengths to make everyone believe.

"Yes," Venom said, "but she's always had a cordial enough relationship with Neha. And to kill Eris in that way? I've seen the sick things Lijuan has done, but this was personal."

"Yes." Catching a whisper of some unknown flower intermingled with spices bright and opulent, he turned to see Mahiya step out of her suite. Part of him went motionless, waiting to see if she'd come to regret the passion they'd shared in the hours before dawn.

Her smile lit up her eyes. "I heard your voice."

It took intense concentration not to reach out, part her soft lips with his own, taste a smile that was a kiss against his senses. "What did you discover today?"

Venom rolled up to his feet before Mahiya could reply. "Let's talk inside."

It seemed natural to follow Mahiya into the cool comfort of her living quarters, the low table on the floor set with food. "I thought you might be hungry since it's after lunch," she said, but Jason's attention was riveted by the pink teddy bear sitting beside the lamp.

"Ah." Venom closed the doors and said, "I have a story about that."

Jason stayed silent as Venom relayed the strange tale. "A scarlet-haired vampire?" he asked Mahiya once she'd added her findings. As for her taking the risk that she had with the box, they'd discuss that in private.

"Yes." A fiery glint in her eye. "Unfortunately, I couldn't ask anyone else in the area if they'd seen the man—it would've caused too many ripples."

Jason looked at Venom.

Sipping at his coffee, the vampire gave him a lazy grin. "Yes, I went down to the city, made some enquiries." Leaning back against the wall, he said, "Our buyer doesn't sound like he'd blend into the general populace, yet no one has any knowledge of him. Then again, my contacts are—relatively speaking—on the younger side. Might be he's an old one who's just come out of seclusion."

Angels Slept when immortality became too heavy

a burden. While vampires lacked that ability to put their bodies in a state akin to suspended animation, they could and did sometimes retreat into isolation accompanied only by their "cattle." It was what the old ones called the humans who were addicted to a vampire's kiss and remained with them as a ready source of food.

For the older vampires, the term was one of affection, the donors treated with the same respect one might show a beloved pet. Those cattle quite often recruited replacements as the decades passed—Jason had known one vampire to remain in seclusion for three hundred years and counting.

"He might be from outside the region," Mahiya said.

"He sent you what could be a courting gift. That argues otherwise." According to everything she'd told him, her trip to Lijuan's stronghold had been her only foray beyond the borders of Neha's territory since her return from the Refuge. "Did you see anyone who might fit the description while you were in China?"

A tiny shiver rippled across her shoulders. "No. Red wings, yes, red hair, no. No one with that skin tone, either."

"Refuge?" Venom asked. "Could be he saw you when you were younger."

Mahiya shook her head.

"Any visitors to Neha's court who've paid you undue attention of late?" Hair color could be altered.

"The usual meaningless court flattery. Nothing that would lead to such a convoluted scheme to pass on a gift."

And the gift itself, Jason thought, was unusual for an immortal, most of whom would woo a woman with jewels or unusual treasures. As for this particular woman, he found the idea of another man courting her incited in him a dark violence he'd spent a lifetime learning to contain.

"Don't lie to me, Nene!"

"I'm not! Why won't you listen? He's a friend—"

"Is that why you disappeared with him for an hour?"

"I was showing him the atoll while you spoke with his father!" A sobbing sound of frustration. *"I hate this ugly jealousy of yours, Yavi. It's killing us."*

His mother's prophetic words ringing through his mind, Jason turned to Venom. "See if you can dig deeper without it reaching the wrong ears."

Venom bent to put his empty cup on the table before flowing to his feet with a supple grace that was a thing of beauty to some, an indication of danger to others. "I think I'll jump off the balcony, scare the guards hiding outside." With that, he was gone.

Jason stepped closer to Mahiya. "You should not have taken that risk."

"It was a considered one." Her tone was resolute. "I would do it again in a heartbeat. I will not barter for my life with yours or Venom's."

Gripping her chin, Jason looked into an unflinching gaze bright as a jungle cat's. "I do not wish to scrape up the remains of your broken, violated body." It was a confession from a part of his self that hadn't seen the light in an eon. "So you must allow me to keep you safe."

Mahiya had been ready to fight arrogance, found herself bewildered by the quiet request so potent with emotions unspoken. "I won't take any unnecessary risks," she said, closing her fingers over the bones of his wrist, his skin hot under her touch. "I promise."

"You are the weakest one of us, Mahiya."

"But," she whispered, asking him to understand, "I am not *weak*. I cannot be that and survive."

Her black-winged lover said nothing for a long, motionless moment before releasing his hold on her. She forced herself to let go of him, feeling bereft. "Come," she said. "Eat with me before the food goes cold."

Jason caught her wrist when she would've moved to the table. "You don't treat food as other immortals do." His thumb moved over her knuckles. "Tell me why."

Snakes hissing all around her, fangs sinking into her skin, poison in her bloodstream.

Mahiya's fingers curled into her fist, but she held her ground. "No, Jason. I will not allow you to steal all my secrets while you hoard your own." He knew so much about her, while she did not even know where he made his home.

His fingers flexed, and he tugged her closer, until they stood toe to toe. "Do you know the story of Yaviel and Aurelani?"

It was the most startling of questions. "Of course." Theirs was one of the great angelic romances. "They were born of warring families from different sides of the world. Yaviel was a singer turned artisan, Aurelani a scholar gaining renown." Both families had been painfully proud of their children, but when the two fell in love, centuries-old hate had overwhelmed the tenderness of their devotion, and they'd been torn apart.

"It is said Yaviel survived torture to break into Aurelani's home to steal her away and that they disappeared to build a life together, far from the vicious power of their families." The romance of it had made her girlish heart sigh. Even now, as an adult, her soul ached at the idea of being loved with such devotion. "Yaviel's musical instruments continued to appear in the Refuge, so there were some who knew where the lovers lived, but it was a secret never betrayed."

Jason's voice was rough as he said, "He called her Nene, and she called him Yavi."

A chill over her skin, a vision of suffocating darkness.

"Nene couldn't abide the cold, and Yavi loved her so that he found them an uninhabited atoll in the warm waters of the Pacific, far, *far* from any sky roads to civilization." His fingers tightened on her wrist, but she didn't move, didn't dare breathe. "Trusted friends came and took Yavi's creations to the Refuge, where they sold for amounts that meant he could buy his Nene whatever she wanted. She loved amethysts, and he showered her with them . . . but what Nene loved most was her Yavi."

A tear trickled down her cheek though he'd said nothing awful, yet the sadness in him, it was a heavy weight she thought might crush a lesser man. "She must have loved you, too," she whispered, seeing in his face the history of two different clans who had eventually ended one another in a rage of violence.

"Yes." Haunted eyes meeting hers. "I was well loved by my parents."

Mahiya wanted to ask him why he used only the past tense, why he carried such black sorrow within, what had happened to Nene if Yavi was dead, but she couldn't hurt him when he was already so terribly hurt deep inside. "I never ignore food, because I know what it is to starve."

The profound sadness in Jason changed, became a black blade licked with flame. It took a great deal for an older angel to starve, but an angel of Mahiya's age remained vulnerable. "When?"

Mahiya swallowed, her fingers curling on his chest. "After Lijuan had me escorted back from her territory. Neha threw me into a windowless cell up at Guardian, and then she locked the door."

The fear that emanated from her was too violent a thing for the slow pain of starvation. And Jason knew. "You weren't alone in the room, were you?"

Tears welling in her eyes, teeth sunk into her lower lip, she shook her head. Releasing her wrist, he locked his arms around her. But she didn't sob, the princess he held. Breath ragged, she said, "There were so many of them. Pit vipers and spitting cobras, rattlesnakes and taipan."

Venomous snakes.

Their poison couldn't kill an adult angel her age, but it could cause excruciating pain, convulsions, even temporary blindness and paralysis. "Tell me one thing." He cupped the back of her head, pressed his cheek to her temple.

"Yes?"

"If you could kill Neha, would you?" A spymaster knew a great deal, such as when an archangel might be most vulnerable to attack by her enemies.

Mahiya shook her head. "No." Shifting so they were eye to eye, she whispered, "In making that my goal, I'd become just like her, a woman driven by hate until there's this knot of bitterness inside her that infects everything she touches."

Anoushka, Jason thought, hadn't become who she was in isolation.

"I'll find my vengeance in living a life overflowing with happiness," Mahiya vowed. "In drowning myself in love, not hatred."

In that instant, her eyes incandescent against the golden brown of her skin, she was the most beautiful woman he had ever seen, and he knew that she was too fine a thing for him, that the black emptiness within him would ruin her. And still he said, "The skies will be clear tonight. Will you fly with me?"

Her smile glowed, the horror erased by a fearless joy.

The hours passed with a leaden slowness. Jason retraced his every step in the search for the murderer, but it was his interview with the guards who'd been on Eris's door when he was killed that proved the most intriguing. When Jason had believed Neha the murderer, the fact the archangel had said she'd stripped their minds and found nothing hadn't been a surprise.

He hadn't understood she meant that literally.

"I can't remember," the first guard said, a stricken expression in his eyes. "At the time, I had no consciousness of it, but later, when I was asked, I realized I had no memory of several hours of the night."

The second guard told the same story.

Jason knew Venom had the capacity to mesmerize people—the vampire had gained it during his Making by Neha.

"Do you know of anyone else who possesses it?" he asked Mahiya that night.

"It's a family trait," she responded. "My mother was said to share it with Neha, though her abilities were otherwise dissimilar. I didn't inherit it, but Anoushka did. Neha's bloodline is an ancient one—I don't know of any direct descendants with Anoushka dead, but there are some old ones who came before her who do not Sleep."

Jason made a few calls, tracked down those forbearers. "The relationship is distant, and they're all too weak to have killed even Shabnam." The lady-in-waiting had been no power, but like all courtiers, she'd had a certain level of strength.

Mahiya frowned. "I can't think of anyone else who is known to have that ability, but some angels are secretive about their strength."

Yes, Jason thought, especially if the impact of the Cascade was rippling beyond the Cadre. "Did you discover anything?" She'd spent the last hours navigating the maze of afternoon and early evening court functions.

"A sense of unease," she said. "Everyone is scared he or she will be the next target, and a number are making plans to leave the fort, but that's all hot air. Neha will not forgive desertion, and they're too self-obsessed to lose their place in the court." She blew out a breath, rubbing at her forehead with her fingertips. "My head hurts from the inanity of it, and I have not one good piece of information to show for my efforts!"

"Enough," Jason said. "We both need to spread our wings. Come."

He allowed Mahiya to set the pace, to set their direction, shadowing her vibrant wings as she swept across the skies with the ease and grace of someone who knew the vagaries of the winds in the mountains, understood how the land interacted with the sky. She wasn't the most technically accomplished flyer, but there was a lingering happiness to her every movement that was impossible to miss and that made her striking to watch.

"Free," she said to him when they came to a stop on a high hill overlooking the twinkling lights of the city. "In the sky, I have always been free."

Observing the naked pleasure on her face, Jason had to fight the urge to wrap her in his wings, hide her from the sight of those who would turn that joy to despair, using her love of the sky to torture her. "Be careful."

Closing the small distance between them, Mahiya put a

hand to his chest in a gentle feminine invitation he knew he had only to step back to reject. In spite of her vivid emotions, she wasn't a woman who would pursue a man who made it clear he didn't want her . . . or one who knew that in taking her, he might destroy the very brightness of spirit that caught him in delicate chains, agonizingly painful in their hope.

28

"I am," she said, "always careful, but you . . . now I know why you are such a great spymaster."

He didn't understand her meaning, the warmth of her touch seeping through the thin black shirt he wore to linger on his skin. Drinking in the sensation, he ran his fingers down the line of her neck, hot satisfaction in his blood when she shivered. There was a deeper pleasure in this, in knowing what made her sigh, learning the intimacies of her body. Yet it was a pleasure he'd denied himself for hundreds of years.

"Jason?" Wounded eyes, blue and wet. "You're leaving?"

"I told you I couldn't stay." Couldn't give her his heart.

Fist clenching in the sheet she held to her breast, tears rolling down her cheeks. "I thought . . . when you kept returning . . ."

He'd been so young then, very good at his job, but far behind his peers when it came to emotions, to relationships. He'd thought that long-ago lover had understood he spoke the naked truth, never realizing the secret dreams brewing in her heart. A heart he'd broken without meaning to, without even knowing he held the power to do so. It had soon healed for she'd been young, too, and he thought that she might no longer even remember the black-winged angel she'd once pleaded with to stay with her.

But he'd never forgotten the lesson, and he wondered if Mahiya had truly heard what he'd said to her the night before or if she, too, harbored dreams of fixing the broken pieces of him. The truth was, no matter how she compelled him, she would soon realize what was shattered in him was nothing that could be healed, the damage done at such a young age that it had become part of his very psyche.

Yet instead of backing off, he did a selfish thing then. Lowering his head, he claimed the lush intoxication of her kiss, his hands thrusting into her hair to tumble black silk over his skin. She opened for him with a sweet sensual generosity that enticed without design, made him want to caress her every secret pleasure point until her desire was a shimmer across her skin and he knew her like no other man ever would.

"Jason? You're leaving?"

Tugging back her head with the hand fisted in her hair, he forced himself to release lips swollen from his kisses. "Open your eyes." It was a harsh order.

Thick lashes rose to reveal tawny eyes hazy with passion. "I see you, Jason."

"And what do you see?" He stroked his free hand up her side, rubbed his thumb gently back and forth over her nipple through her clothing.

Her breath caught, but she didn't break the eye contact. "A man who is a storm, who belongs to no one and who will never be tamed. To expect otherwise would be to ask for agonizing disappointment."

Open eyes, he thought, she had wide-open eyes. "Some might say you're attempting to seduce me in order to lead me on a leash."

Laughter, warm and startled, spilled over the hilltop. "Only a fool would attempt to contain or direct a storm. I'm far too smart."

He took her lips in an open-mouthed kiss in an attempt to drink of her laughter, steal some of her dazzling warmth of spirit to hoard inside him. Her nails dug into his chest through his shirt, her breast pushed into his hand, and her scent, it tangled around him in an exotic wildness.

The gut-deep sense of connection was an intense shock that made his nerve endings burn. He had never felt more real, more a part of the world.

Breaking the kiss only long enough that she could gasp in air, he slanted his mouth across hers again, licking and tasting and sinking into the carnal pleasure. Her nipple was a hard point beneath the fabric of her tunic, and when he squeezed it between forefinger and thumb, she jerked, pulling away from his touch.

Folding back wings that had become fully unfurled, he watched her attempt to resettle her breathing. "Not here," she said at last, her chest rising and falling in an erratic rhythm. "Will you come to my bed?"

It was such a polite invitation, and yet her lips were wet from his kiss, her cheeks flushed with sexual need. "Yes."

He'd said yes, but Jason left after escorting Mahiya back to the palace, having received a message on his phone he had to follow up on at once. Sensual frustration tearing through her veins, she decided to take care of a task of her own and headed to Vanhi's apartments using busy internal passageways. If she was a target, it'd make it difficult for anyone to cut her from the herd.

Vanhi was reading when she arrived. Mahiya bent down to kiss her smiling cheek before taking a seat in one of the comfortable armchairs in the vampire's living area. "I'm disturbing you."

"You know you are always welcome." Vanhi slid an intricate metal bookmark between the pages and put the book on the coffee table. "It worries me, Mahiya, the look I see in your eyes."

"Vanhi—"

The vampire held up her hand. "I know you too well, my dear. I rocked you when you cried as a babe and when Arav shattered your heart as a young woman." Sighing, she reached out to take one of Mahiya's hands in her own, squeezed. "You've been waiting your whole life to love someone, my sweet girl. I don't want you to squander the power of that beautiful heart on a man who will not value such a gift."

"I understand him, Vanhi." Never would she forget the terrible sorrow she'd tasted in his tale of Nene and her Yavi, until it hurt her to imagine the cause. "I'm not expecting anything but what he can give me."

"You say that, but you're deeply vulnerable to kindness, to any indication of care."

The emotional blow stung. "You make me sound like an abused pet."

Rising to her feet, Vanhi walked over to the dining area to pour two glasses of wine. "I do not begrudge you happiness." Care in every syllable as she retook her seat, having handed Mahiya the second wineglass. "I just don't want you hurt again."

Mahiya gave the other woman a crooked smile. "If the hurt is an honest one, I will survive." Perhaps she *had* spent her life waiting for someone to love, and Jason . . . he needed to be loved, as a wildflower needed sunlight.

Vanhi shook her head. "I bear fault in this—it is to my sorrow that I couldn't be there for you, couldn't give you the love every child should know."

"You did all you could." What Mahiya knew of kindness and affection came from Jessamy and Vanhi. "She is an archangel." *And your loyalty is first to her.* It was a truth Mahiya had accepted long ago.

A bleak sadness in Vanhi's expression. "Tell me why you come to me so late, Mahiya child."

Setting aside her wineglass, Mahiya spoke of the teddy

bear, and the vampire with hair of scarlet and skin of porcelain. Vanhi rubbed at the furrows that had formed between her eyebrows. "Oh, I *know* him." A frustrated sound. "It's flitting at the very corner of my eye, his name, but I cannot quite grasp it."

"Sleep on it." Exhilaration made Mahiya want to push, but Vanhi was thousands of years old, carried a million fragments of memory. "If it comes to you tomorrow morn, send me a message."

Lines still marring her forehead, Vanhi gave a slow nod. "He was not important, I think. But always there, at the edges. That's why he's so hard to remember." A rueful smile. "Truly, I am getting old. So many pieces of a lifetime— sometimes I think they are hidden in secret corners of my mind."

"I only wish my memory were as good as yours."

Vanhi's smile faded. "I wish you could've known your mother, child."

Mahiya's spine went rigid. "She slept with a married man. A man who belonged to her sister."

"Yes." Vanhi gave a solemn nod. "They were ever in competition, Neha and Nivriti." Drinking deep of her wine, the vampire held Mahiya's gaze with eyes of vivid green. "It was Nivriti whom Eris first courted."

The words were a fist punching against her ribs. "*Neha* was the one who committed the initial betrayal?"

"It was never that simple." Vanhi's eyes shut, opened again to display steely resolve. "I never before spoke to you about this, because what good would it have done? The past is gone, buried." Finishing her wine, she played the stem of the glass between her fingers. "Now I see I was wrong. You must know where you came from if you are to take charge of your own destiny. And if I will not share these secrets with you, who will?"

Mahiya's skin felt as if it would burst with all the questions she had inside her, but she kept quiet, intent on listening with every cell in her body.

"Everyone," Vanhi murmured, "always calls Nivriti the younger sister, and she was . . . by five heartbeats."

Her silence shattered. "Twins? How can that be? No one ever mentions it."

"Neha was always stronger, until Nivriti was thrown into the shade. She was also the more innocent of the two, and as the centuries passed, people forgot the truth and just thought of her as younger." Vanhi's voice was grave with age, with history, as she continued. "As children, they didn't fight or compete—Neha used to take great care of Nivriti, and theirs was a bond I thought nothing would break."

Mahiya could barely absorb what Vanhi was telling her. "What changed?"

"Age, time, life." A shake of her head. "Maybe it was jealousy on Nivriti's part, arrogance on Neha's, or maybe it was simple sibling rivalry, but they began to play a game. It started out as a battle of wits and devolved into something so ugly it hurt my heart to stand witness."

Vanhi's eyes shone wet. "First, if Nivriti asked the seamstress to make her a special dress, Neha would steal the design, get an identical one made in a shorter time and wear it prior to Nivriti's big event. Nivriti would retaliate by hiding Neha's gems so her sister would be forced to appear drab, while she glittered. After a while"—a hitching breath—"they began to play the game with people as their chess pieces."

Mahiya's gnawing curiosity twisted into a knot in her stomach.

"If one of them made a friend, the other would either charm that friend away or seed the relationship with vitriol until it curled up and died. It was such a foolish, foolish waste of their talents and gifts."

Mahiya rubbed a fisted hand over her belly, for she knew it was about to get much worse. "I've heard my mother's strongest ability had to do with things that flew?"

"Yes." The shadow of a smile, lush red lips curving in memory. "She assured me the birds spoke to her and that she could see through their eyes. Falcons came to roost on her shoulders without aggression or anger . . . though as her bitterness grew, she no longer took joy in admiring their wild beauty, but began to use them as weapons."

The wet spilled from Vanhi's eye to trickle down to her lips. "I once saw her send a falcon down to claw the eyes out of a vampire's head. He'd been her lover, had taken a position in Neha's new-formed court. When I reached him, his face was a mask of red, his screams of agony piercing me to the bone."

The adult Mahiya had never believed her mother a fairy-tale maiden who'd been wronged . . . but she'd had hopes—that Nivriti had been better than Neha, that Mahiya's birth hadn't been an act of ultimate hate. However, shatter her dreams though they might, she craved the truth, would hear all of it. "So Eris wasn't their first battleground."

"But he was the first they both loved." Vanhi's wineglass cracked under the force of her grip, sending a trickle of blood down her palm. Waving off Mahiya's cry, Vanhi put the broken pieces on the coffee table and dabbed at the wound with a handkerchief. "I am sorry to say Eris was not worth either one of my girls—or of the daughters he helped create."

"Vanhi, let me get a bandage."

"Hush, child. It'll close up soon enough." A smile that took the sting out of the chiding. "But you can pour me another glass of wine."

Mahiya did so, glad to see the vampire had indeed stopped bleeding.

"I've come to believe Eris courted Nivriti first because she was the more accessible," Vanhi said, taking a sip of the crisp white wine. "Neha was already an archangel, but your mother was a power in her own right—I say to this day that she would've become Cadre had she lived. It was just that her development was a slow burn in comparison to Neha's blaze."

"Once Eris had her trust," Mahiya guessed, having no

illusions about the man who had fathered her, "he used that connection to reach Neha."

"I don't know if she knew he belonged to Nivriti at first." Vanhi's words were soft, poignant with love for the girls she'd helped raise. "I think Neha fell so deeply for Eris *because* she was unaware of the truth—had she been driven by the game, she would've made certain to armor her heart so she could discard him once he'd left Nivriti. As for Eris . . . love was an interchangeable token to him."

Mahiya had nothing to say to that—she'd known her father too well.

"At the time," Vanhi said, "Nivriti didn't make any kind of a fuss. My poor child was heartbroken, even left the part of the territory she ruled as a powerful queen, and went away for many years to the lands Favashi now calls her own. I had never seen her so defeated. Neha, too, felt for her sister—I suppose she thought she had won the prize and could be the bigger person. The games stopped."

Anger, clean and bright, bubbled under Mahiya's skin. "My mother obviously decided to change the status quo long after Neha's marriage." Putting in motion events that had led to her daughter growing up motherless and trapped.

But Vanhi shook her head. "No, it was no game. Nivriti never felt about another man as she did about Eris." The vampire put down her glass as if afraid she'd fracture it, too. "It is one of the world's great injustices that *he*, of all men, had the keeping of two such strong women's hearts."

Mahiya's anger shattered into a painful understanding for the mother she'd never known, because behind the ugliness of infidelity was an abiding love. Eris hadn't been worthy of it, but that Mahiya had been conceived in love, at least on one side, it changed the very nature of her history.

"You cry." Vanhi touched her fingers to Mahiya's tears, wiping them away. "Ah, my sweet girl. I didn't mean to make you sad."

"I always wondered if she even cared I was taken from her," Mahiya said, her vision blurred by the tears that kept falling. "Now I think that maybe she would have, that maybe I meant something to her."

Distress bloomed on Vanhi's face.

"You didn't mean something to her. You meant *everything*." Cupping Mahiya's face, she said, "I have kept another secret from you, one I was enjoined by your mother to keep, for I was there at your birth."

29

Mahiya blinked away her tears, her world a kaleidoscope. "I was not ripped from my mother's womb?"

"No, no." Vanhi's distress grew. "I made sure Nivriti's birthing was as easy as it could be for a woman who lay in a cell." Fingers trembling, she brushed back Mahiya's hair. "It was after the birth, when you'd been taken from her that I was alone in the room with your mother for a bare few moments. She whispered to me that she would leave her child a gift, and she made me promise to give you that gift at the right time."

"What is it?" she asked, trembling at the idea of a link to her mother.

Vanhi's laugh was waterlogged. "Mahiya, such a beautiful name, don't you think? One I suggested to Neha."

Mahiya had always taken her name to be a cruel joke on Neha's part, for it meant happiness, joy... and sometimes, beloved. "My mother gave me my name?" It was a gift no one could ever take away from her.

"Yes, but the second part, I had to keep secret for Neha

would not have permitted it." The anguish of a woman who loved the archangel but saw the lack in her.

Mahiya leaned forward, a hundred butterflies in her blood. "What is the second part?"

"Geet," Vanhi whispered. "Your name is Mahiya Geet." *Joyous song... beloved song.*

Her heart shattered from the inside out. Far from being a mockery, her name was a treasure, a last gift from a mother who hadn't, she knew without asking, been allowed to hold her newborn daughter. "Thank you," she whispered to Vanhi through a throat swollen with emotion.

"I thought to tell you earlier . . . but you weren't ready," Vanhi said, taking her into her arms. "Now you are. I think the world will tremble to hear your song, sweet girl."

Beloved song.

Mahiya squeezed the railing of the balcony and turned to look at the man who was the only one other than Vanhi who knew her true name. She'd had to tell someone, and Jason . . . he would keep her secrets.

Close to midnight, the skies were empty aside from the sweep of the outer sentries. Here, within the walls of the fort, it was quiet but for the night insects, the wind still as a glassy pond, the air cool but not cold. The man beside her was a part of the night, his wings near indistinguishable from the shadows.

"It suits you," he said, one of those wings brushing her own as he spread them behind her.

Biting back a responsive shiver, she laughed, the sound soft and intimate in the dark. "I am not the most gifted of singers, but I don't care."

A tug in her hair, Jason's fingers unraveling the neat knot at her nape with exquisite patience, each golden pin put on the railing in order, until they shimmered in the dark and her hair tumbled down her back and over her wings. Mahiya trembled. She had been born in a time when a woman did not put down her hair in front of anyone but her lover, and some part of her was that girl still.

It was an intimacy they shared beneath the starlit sky.

When he slid his hand under her hair to close over her nape from behind, she expected him to tug her back for a kiss, but he just rubbed his thumb over her skin before running his knuckles down the centerline of her back and returning to lean on the balcony on his forearms, his wing lying heavily against her own. "I can sing."

It was the last thing she'd expected to hear from him, this man who threatened to splinter her defenses until she repeated her mother's tale of love unrequited. Yet now that he'd spoken, her mind whispered with half-remembered fragments of conversations overheard.

"A voice more beautiful than Caliane's they say."

". . . made my heart break."

"Purity, that is Jason's voice."

The speakers had all been more than four hundred years old. "I would hear you," she whispered.

"I have not sung for many years."

"Did something happen to still your song?" she asked, unwilling to back away when this was the first time he'd spontaneously offered her a glimpse into the mystery of him.

His reply was slow in coming, but she didn't take his silence for anger, knowing Jason was a man who felt no need to clutter the air with words. Instead, tempted by the way his head was below her own as he leaned down, she reached out to undo the tie that held his hair in its usual queue. It fell like black water around his face, and he didn't stop her when she began to smooth it back to lie over his shoulders. "You have such beautiful hair."

"I prefer yours."

His hand fisted in her hair, his lips on her throat.

Thighs clenching, she ran her fingers over his scalp. "Then we are well matched."

He arched a little into her touch. "The only songs in my

heart were ones that made the Refuge drown in tears. So I stopped."

Having not expected such an unvarnished answer, she was momentarily thrown, her fingers going motionless. She had the panicked feeling of a chance slipping through her fingertips, an opportunity forever lost. "Did it hurt you to stop?" she asked, grabbing at that chance with grim determination.

"Yes," he said at last. "It was akin to cutting off a limb, but such song was not good for me."

Frowning, she parted her lips to ask why, then stopped. Jason was a man draped in shadows—to give voice to the darkness within . . . yes, it would not be good for him to drench himself in it. "If you ever find something worth singing for again," she said, a silent, fierce hope in her heart for his song, "I hope you will invite me to listen."

Jason pushed off the railing to stand at his full height, folding his wings to his back at the same time. Already, she missed the warm weight against her, but then he dipped his head and the warmth turned into a black fire that kissed her bloodstream and spread into every cell of her body.

There would be no forgetting Jason.

He'd led her into the bedroom, but when he stopped at the foot of the bed, she raised her fingers to the buttons of his shirt after undoing the strap of the sword harness across his chest. The way he'd taken control the previous night, she worried he wouldn't accept her desire to discover what pleased him, but he played with her hair as she unbuttoned the shirt to display the beauty of his body.

Each soft tug on her scalp as he twisted a loose, heavy curl around his finger, released it, made her heart skip a beat. But it was the ridges and valleys of his body that had her sighing in feminine pleasure as she pulled the sides of the shirt apart to splay her fingers over his skin. His hand fisted in her hair, but he didn't call a halt to her exploration.

Delighted, she shaped the heated steel of him, caressing the heavy muscle that spoke to his strength and speed. It was a quirk of angelic biology that the incredibly powerful muscles needed to support flight didn't overwhelm the upper body. Instead they lay subtle and fiercely strong beneath the skin.

But Jason's body, it told a different story, that of a warrior who needed to do maneuvers in the sky flight muscles alone wouldn't accommodate. "Can you use your sword in flight?"

"I'd be useless as a fighter otherwise," he murmured, lifting her fingers to the straps on his shoulders that helped hold the sword harness to his back.

Taking the silent instruction, she undid the sleek but strong buckle, repeated the act on the other side, the leather soft from use. "Are you ever without your sword?"

"No." Removing harness and sword, he placed them beside the bed.

Within arm's reach.

"It's my primary weapon."

"Yes, I understand." Pushing aside his shirt, she rubbed her fingers over the light red marks created by the leather. Such a thing would be nothing to an angel of Jason's strength, but she did not like seeing his body abused in even so small a way.

Having kicked off her sandals in the living area, where Jason had left his boots, she rose on bare toes to press her lips to one of the marks. Jason's free arm came around her waist, but he didn't halt her movements when she kissed her way across to the other marks. "I could do this for hours," she said, addicted to the feel of him, the taste of him.

Jason's response was again unexpected. "If that's your wish."

It made her shiver, the idea of having this man in her bed, hers to explore. Dropping down flat on her feet again, she didn't give him time to change his mind and walked around to undo the plain buttons that held the wing slits closed. His shirt fell to the floor seconds later, his wings stunning arcs of heavy black.

She ran her fingers over the shadowy perfection of his feathers, suddenly shy. But he was already unbuckling his belt, the metallic sounds harsh, intimate in the quiet of the bedroom. Breathing ragged, she walked around to take over the task, her fingers brushing his. "I'll do it." It was a whisper, but Jason's hand fell away . . . to rise, undo the buttons on the shoulders of her tunic.

Sliding his belt out of the loops, she dropped it to the floor, cooperated with him to strip away her tunic. Her breasts, small as they were, didn't need support, and she wore only a camisole beneath. It took Jason but a moment to remove that from her body, run the back of his hand over one taut mound. "Beautiful."

A tremor rippling over her skin at the low murmur, she undid the button of his jeans, ran her fingers along his navel. His muscles contracted. It intoxicated her, his response, and she had the craving to know every touch, every caress that made this strong, sensual man shudder in pleasure. Swallowing at the enthralling thought, she brushed her fingers over his zipper and the hard ridge beneath.

Jason's demanding mouth was suddenly on her own, his grip on her hair holding her in place. She didn't know how it happened, but her pants were stripped from her seconds later, and she found herself lying on her back on the bed with Jason between her legs, the heavy denim of his jeans rubbing against her skin as he devoured her mouth.

She hooked one leg around his hip, opened her mouth to the wet seduction of his kiss, licked her tongue against his in molten desire. Groaning, he settled more heavily against her, the cold metal of his zipper pressing into the skin of her abdomen as his wings spread above her in a caress of midnight.

"Later." A husky word against her lips. "You can touch all you wish later."

The rough promise made her melt. "I intend to."

His hand on her breast, squeezing a fraction too softly.

Perhaps it was shameless, but she put her hand over his, increased the pressure. Her reward for such brazenness was piercing pleasure, his lips hot and damp on her neck as he petted her breast, rubbed her nipple. Holding his head to her, she twisted against him, frustrated by the fabric that separated them. "Jason, your jeans."

A sudden chill as he rose to get rid of his remaining clothing. The sight of him in the faint moonlight that entered the room through a high window, formed of fine designs cut into the stone itself, stole her very breath. He was a work of art, every part of him honed to a deadly edge. Raising her arm, she held out her hand, calling him back to bed.

He returned in a primal wave of heat that took her over. Kissing his way down her body, he hooked his fingers into the satin and lace of her panties to tug them off, throw them aside.

A wet, suckling kiss pressed just above her mound before he spread her thighs . . .

Mahiya arched off the bed under the stark intimacy of his next caress, his mouth tasting her most delicate flesh with lush eroticism as his hands held her open for his— *their*—pleasure. Her hands gripped at the sheets, her wings fluttering like creatures trapped, and her breath, it became a sob.

He deepened the kiss, one of his fingers sliding into her sheath.

The sensual intrusion tipped her over, the pleasure so intense, it stole her voice.

Moving up her quivering body with a slow attention to detail that left no inch of her skin untouched, untasted, her nipples hard little berries for him to roll against his tongue, her breasts left slick and wet to rub against the muscled beauty of his chest as he reached her lips at last.

First, he kissed the corners of her eyes, tasting the salt of the pleasure that shimmered over her skin still. But when she turned her lips to his, he accepted the invitation with raw hunger, one of his hands running down her waist to grip her thigh, bring it over his hip, opening her for him.

And then he was pushing into her, slow and insistent. She

gasped, her flesh swollen, but there was no hurt. Only a near-painful need to have him inside her. Wrapping her other leg around his body, she pressed, urging him deeper.

"Mahiya."

Her spymaster's control fractured.

30

In the hours before returning to Mahiya, Jason had flown a considerable distance out from the fort to speak to an angelic couple just returned to the territory after a sojourn in the Refuge. Having received his message, they'd asked him to meet them at the lodge where they rested, as they planned to begin the second leg of their journey at first light—to their home at the other end of Neha's territory.

He'd been lucky to locate the pair; they spent much of their time exploring the world, having earned a respite from their duties after millennia of service. Though the two were unquestionably loyal to their archangel, they also had an unhidden fondness for Raphael.

"We watched him grow from a child into an archangel. He was never too proud to talk to those of us who were weaker, even when his power eclipsed ours while he was but a babe."

That fondness extended to the Seven, and the two had been happy to answer Jason's questions about the vampire with scarlet hair, though he'd made the pattern of questioning such that the most important query was but one among many. He didn't want a careless word to spook their prey. What he'd learned had been . . . interesting, until he could almost taste the answer on his tongue.

A shift against him, Mahiya's fingers flickering on his chest. Her hair slid across his arm and shoulder at the same instant, one of her wings half on, half off his body as he lay on his back, both hands under his head.

"How long did I sleep?" she asked without lifting her head from his shoulder, her voice husky.

He glanced at the moonlight filtering through the high lattice window and said, "Not long. Perhaps an hour." An hour as he listened to her breathe, as he traced quiet patterns on her skin and felt his heartbeat slow, lulled by the rhythm of hers. It had been an unexpected thing, and it had caused a violent response in him, a raw urging to get out, to get free.

But Jason was almost seven hundred years old, understood what drove him—he'd looked into the abyss of his soul, seen the lonely, forgotten boy looking back at him. He knew that boy trusted no one and nothing, knew he looked upon any kind of an emotional bond with suspicion, expected nothing but pain from any such relationship.

That boy, he was so *afraid*.

It was a truth about himself Jason had come to terms with long ago. That scared boy didn't rule his conscious mind, but was so embedded in his subconscious that he often didn't know why he acted as he did until the deed was done and his mind cleared again. Tonight, he'd fought the urge to leave when it hit him, because being in bed with a sleeping Mahiya was a pleasure all its own.

He liked that her scent warmed and seemed to soak into his own skin, liked that he could twine her hair lazily around his fingers and play with it as he thought, liked that she made tiny little noises and burrowed deeper into him every so often—as if she adored being with him. He almost felt real, as if he was a normal man, one capable of loving a woman and holding her close.

It was an illusion, but it was an illusion he was willing to believe in for this night.

"Hmm." Reaching down, Mahiya tugged up the sheet tangled around her thighs to her waist, before placing her hand over his heartbeat again. Her wing rose a fraction as her mouth and jaw moved against his skin in a yawn, and the silver light of the moon kissed the feathers to jewel brightness.

Before she'd fallen asleep, those wings had shimmered in his vision as she spent an hour touching and kissing his body with unhidden pleasure. Drunk on the tactile sensations, he'd had to coax her to straddle him, his shy Mahiya, but once there, she'd used her position to caress him with sweet feminine delight.

Living in the illusion, he moved one hand to run his fingers over the sensitive arch. She shivered, her wing floating down to lie across his body once more. "You could make me agree to commit a great many sins with those fingers, Jason."

"There are no sins in pleasure." It was something Dmitri had once said to him, a sardonic twist to his mouth, the mockery directed inward.

Mahiya's soft laugh changed the words, turned them sensual and playful. "I think I shall make that my motto when I am free, and live the life of an unabashed hedonist."

Images of her clothed in raw silks and exquisite cashmere, her body petted and smoothed with exotic creams, her lips closing over a delicious morsel as she lay on satin sheets flashed through his mind. Sliding a fingertip down her spine, he spread his hand on her lower back, his fingers just brushing the curves below. "I would be happy to massage you with scented oils." Until her skin gleamed and she lay boneless beneath his touch.

Her laugh was startled this time, huskier. Rubbing her cheek against his skin, she said, "Dangerous man—I'm not certain I'd survive the pleasure." Pushing up against his chest, she looked down at him, her hair tumbling over one smooth shoulder, her breasts hidden by the sheet she'd pulled up to hold against her chest. Always so modest, though as a lover, she gainsaid nothing he demanded.

"Vanhi," she said, expression becoming solemn, "said something else important. I forgot to tell you with everything else. She thought she might have seen the vampire with bone-pale skin and scarlet hair once. Long ago."

Jason listened, added that fact to the information he already had.

"So?" she prompted when he didn't respond. "I know you were out doing what you do earlier. What did you learn?" A scowl. "Do not think to keep me in the dark, Jason."

He should've reminded her she held no cards to play, but he knew that would hurt her, and he didn't want to hurt this princess with her heart strong enough to survive three hundred years with an archangel who saw her only as a means to an end. "There is plenty of moonlight."

Making an exasperated sound, she dipped her head to kiss him, sinking her teeth into his lower lip in a bite that didn't so much as sting. "This is not the time for spymaster humor."

Were she another woman, he'd have thought she attempted to use the afterglow of sex to sway him, but this was Mahiya—who had grown up in a hotbed of lies but chose not to use those tactics. Caressing her with the hand he had on her lower back, he said, "I found a couple who remember seeing a vampire who fits the description in Neha's court three to four hundred years ago."

"They can't be more certain?" she asked, a humming kind of tension in her frame.

"At five thousand years old . . ."

Mahiya sighed. "Like Vanhi, their memories are tucked away in secret corners of their minds." A thoughtful pause, before she said, "Just over three hundred years ago, Eris was exiled to his palace, and my mother was executed."

After being kept alive long enough to give birth to the child she carried in her womb.

The words hung unspoken between them.

"They weren't the only ones," Jason said, wondering how much she knew. "Those who had known of the affair and helped Eris and Nivriti were executed; others who were simply loyal to Nivriti were exiled."

Mahiya pushed away from his chest to sit upright, her wing brushing across his body, the warmth of her suddenly gone. "A man on the edge of their circle," she murmured, "would've been considered a hanger-on. Exile, then."

"It's a workable conclusion." To focus only on one possibility when it wasn't yet a certainty was to create blind corners where the enemy could hide. "The question is, why would he expose himself to you?"

"A sense of residual loyalty perhaps." Tawny eyes vivid as a cat's in the darkness met his, the potential locked within her body a luminous brilliance. "But there is another question."

"Which is?" Jason got the same sense of power from Mahiya that he had from a young Illium. It might take her longer than the blue-winged angel to grow into that power—her mother's daughter in that perhaps, but given room to breathe, to develop, Mahiya would become an angel to be reckoned with . . . and he had the sudden, blinding thought that he wanted to witness the change, watch her spread her wings.

"How," she said now, "did he get the box to the temple?"

It was an astute question. "Some vampires can climb like spiders," he said, having seen a grinning Venom scale the Tower one moonless night after he and Illium made a bet, "but the chances of being caught would've been very high." Not only did angelic guards sweep the area, the sentinels who watched over Guardian Fort had a wide field of view.

"He could've used the tunnels—Venom said he didn't see any other footprints along the route he used, but I've heard it's a labyrinth."

"I'll have him check them again." He reached for the cell phone he'd placed on the bedside table after pulling it from his discarded jeans.

"Now?"

"It's the best time." No one would worry overmuch over

a vampire walking about in the night, much less one known to be favored by women.

As it was, he heard a soft female sigh in the background when Venom answered. "No problem," the other man said. "I've just fed, have plenty of energy."

Jason heard the satiation in the vampire's tone, knew he'd fed from the vein—and assuredly from a very willing female. "Watch your back." Sex could cloud even the sharpest mind, and while Neha liked Venom, he remained one of the Seven.

The sound of rustling, as if Venom was getting out of bed. "Don't worry. She's a delicious playmate, but all she wanted to pump was my cock, not my brain."

"Will you be able to check every possible route up to Guardian?"

"I can get it done before dawn."

Hanging up soon afterward, Jason said, "You think the box was flown there," to the woman beside him, her expression pensive.

"Yes." Mahiya took the sheet with her as she got off the bed, the filaments of her feathers a thousand soft kisses across his skin. Disappearing into her dressing room, she returned clothed in a vivid blue robe tied at the waist.

He'd already pulled on his pants, though he'd left off his shirt and sword—the latter within reach, as it always was. Putting his back to the solid wall beside a small window of stained glass, he watched her walk to open that window and look beyond, bathed in the moonlight.

"A teddy bear, it's either a silly romantic gift," she whispered at long last, "or the kind of thing you give to a child."

He thought of the feather of blue green he'd found the night of Arav's murder, of the fact that Nivriti had inherited the ability to mesmerize, and he could not discount the impossibility behind the troubled look on Mahiya's face. "What has Neha told you about your mother's execution?"

"That she began her death screaming and begging for her life." Her fingers tightened so hard on the window ledge that her bones pushed up against skin. " *'I watched my dear sister's organs spill out of the gaping hole that had been her womb and the blood pour off the stubs of her wings, then left her to starve to death.'* That's what Neha said to me when I asked about my mother." She swallowed. "Vanhi says she lied about the manner of my birth, but Vanhi had to leave after I was born. Neha could have done exactly as she said."

Warmth, a hand on her cheek, a thumb on her jaw, the pressure gentle but inexorable. Turning, she found herself the focus of eyes of near obsidian that burned with a dark flame that had her heart skipping a beat.

Jason's thumb moved gently across the dip of her chin. "As we see from Eris, from you, Neha knows how to hold a grudge."

Mahiya sucked in a breath, for she'd expected Jason to argue against the painful hope inside her chest. "But to have kept my mother alive all this time out of spite?" She shook her head. "Why would she do that?"

"The same reason she did it to Eris—love and hate intertwined. You tell me Nivriti was her twin. That is a bond of the soul."

Mahiya thought back to a day she'd come upon Neha and Eris in the courtyard when they'd believed themselves alone. She should've turned, walked away, but she'd been caught by the tableau they made: Neha, her expression young and vulnerable in a way Mahiya had never seen, allowing Eris to tip up her chin with his finger, tease a smile from her lips.

Of course, that moment hadn't lasted, the past too crushing a weight to allow such fragile seeds to sprout, but—"I think if he hadn't died, Neha would have allowed him out. Perhaps even soon." She turned to face Jason, his hand sliding to cup the side of her neck. "Anoushka's death hit her hard. She began to visit Eris more and more."

"There were rumors she was trying to get herself with child."

"I can't give you an answer as to the truth of that, but what I believe is that she needed the comfort of the man who'd fathered her child—and Eris, to his credit, did give her that comfort." How much had been real, and how much a fantasy created in order to get into Neha's good graces, she didn't know. Whatever it had been, it had given Neha some surcease—and who was Mahiya to gainsay the choices of a man who'd spent three centuries locked in pretty chains, even if he had made his own bed?

Releasing his hold on her, Jason shifted to lean one shoulder against the wall. "I'm not certain how long any freedom would've lasted. I've been able to confirm that Audrey was warming his bed." A pause. "If she was the first and he lasted three hundred years before breaking"—Jason's tone made it clear he thought otherwise—"then he may have been a stronger man than we credit."

Mahiya thought again of that vulnerable look on Neha's face and wondered if a woman with so much love in her heart would've eventually been able to forgive every trespass. "It matters little now. Eris is gone, and someone is either playing a sick game with me, or . . ." The words lodged in her throat, too heavy, too *important* to come out.

I hope she lives.

Jason didn't speak the thought aloud, but regardless of how many complications it would create, he hoped that Mahiya got a miracle. He understood what it was to grow up without a mother, but he'd at least had a whisper of time with his own.

"Jason, baby, what in the world are you doing?"

He gave his mother a long-suffering look and paused in his labors. "Planting coconut trees."

A solemn nod. "I see." Going down on her knees, she picked up one of the coconuts he'd collected. "Perhaps you should plant them a little farther up the beach."

He patted the sand over the coconut he'd buried, the sound of the waves lapping at the wet sand a familiar music. "Why?"

"The sea might wash them away otherwise."

Considering that, he decided she was right. "Will you help me carry them?"

Her smile made him feel warm inside in a way nothing else ever did. "I was hoping you'd ask."

Jason could barely remember what that warmth had been like, the echo of his mother's love faded and dull, but he knew it had been something piercingly beautiful to the heart of the boy he'd been, and so he knew such beauty existed. Mahiya didn't even have that. For her sake, he hoped that Neha had found herself unable to execute her twin, as she'd been unable to execute her consort.

"Will you tell Neha?" Mahiya's question was nearly silent. "What we're considering? That. . .my mother might be alive?"

31

"Neha alone knows the truth of our supposition," Jason said, thinking through the matter, "and if we are right, and your mother is already free, telling Neha cannot disadvantage her." The vampire with scarlet hair was unlikely to be the only one of her people Nivriti had found, gathered together. "Neha may also have an idea of where Nivriti might have located her base of—"

Mahiya made a sudden tight sound in her throat. "If it is my mother, I know why she killed Arav."

So did Jason. The man had hurt Mahiya, hurt Nivriti's child, deserved punishment. Jason found he had no argument with that, and the realization made him halt, consider who Mahiya was to him. He had no answer to that, but he suddenly saw one to her earlier question. "I will not speak to Neha about this."

Mahiya shuddered, shook her head. "No. If she murdered Shabnam, I can't protect her."

"This isn't about protecting Nivriti."

Mahiya's eyes searched his face. "What is it?" Closing the distance between them, she placed her hand on his chest.

There was tenderness but nothing proprietary or possessive in the touch, and he knew she spun no moonbeams in the air, expected nothing from him but the man that he was.

Something tense and waiting in him relaxed. He didn't want to end this with Mahiya, but it was a decision he would've been forced to make had she sought to claim him, sought to see in him a future he couldn't build with her. Not in the way Dmitri had with Honor, Raphael with Elena.

"A hostage," he said, his hand on her lower back. "If we give Neha this information, we give her a hostage."

Mahiya's eyes widened in pained understanding, but she shook her head. "You risk breaking the blood vow, Jason." A fierce whisper. "It could mean your death."

"There is time yet." Until he was certain Nivriti lived, this fell under his mandate, his silence no threat to the vow. "And I will not put you in harm's way." He'd made his choice, and it was this woman with her eyes as bright as a creature wild and dangerous for whom he'd raise his sword, not an archangel full of centuries-old hatred.

Mahiya's lower lip quivered. "You must not." Her fingers brushed his jaw, her mouth soft on his own. "Thank you for putting me first. No one else ever has, and I will never forget that you did so." Her voice cracked. "But you yourself said Neha might know where my mother might be hiding. I cannot buy my life with Shabnam's blood screaming for justice. If we are right, then my mother killed her as surely as she killed Arav. But this time, for no reason."

"There was a reason—Shabnam was Neha's favorite."

Mahiya lifted a trembling hand to her mouth. "Akin to a child destroying a sibling's favorite toy out of jealousy or spite."

A scream ripped through the fort on the heels of her horrified words.

No angelic or vampiric body awaited them this time, but there was carnage nonetheless. Thrown across what seemed like every inch of the public audience hall were the limp, mangled bodies of at least twenty of Neha's pet snakes, the columns that held up the structure splattered with blood.

"This took time." Mahiya knelt down beside the thick body of a tree boa whose dry leathery skin continued to gleam a dramatic green. "The snakes aren't tame as such— they come only to Neha's hand. Tracking and patience, this required both."

Hearing the sadness in her tone, Jason met her gaze in wordless question.

"After Guardian," she said with a tight smile, "I can't avoid the fear that curdles my stomach at the sight of Neha's creatures, but I will not allow that fear to rule me." Grim determination. "I try to remember what I've always known— that left alone, these creatures would avoid me as I'd avoid them. They did not deserve to be slaughtered."

A wash of wind, Neha coming to land behind them, the anger on her face shot through with grief. Not saying a word, she stepped to the edge of the audience hall and simply looked, as if taking note of every single snake that had been butchered. And they had been. The boa Mahiya had been crouching beside appeared an exception, but closer examination showed it to be only half of the snake.

After being hacked into pieces, the reptiles had been flung around the audience hall. Such a thing would be impossible to do in daylight, but this particular area would've been all but deserted in the darkest part of night—the early discovery had occurred because of a lover's spat that had sent a male vampire aimlessly wandering the fort.

"Do their bodies tell you anything?" Neha asked with frigid politeness.

Jason shook his head. "Only that the blade used was most probably a butcher's cleaver." A simple, sharp cut. "Is there any pattern to the ones who were harmed?"

Neha's gaze lingered on several of the mutilated snakes. "They were the most docile—older pets who had become used enough to humans that they wouldn't have slithered away at being approached." Her wings held neatly off the blood-streaked floor, she said, "I must care for them."

Reaching back, she took a woven basket from the lady-in-waiting who'd arrived with her.

Not saying a word, Mahiya took a second basket and helped Neha gather up the remains. The silence was acute, Neha's anger a pulse he could almost sense against his skin. But that wasn't what Jason listened for, what he watched for. Because he was almost certain that out there in the shadows, within sight of the audience hall, stood someone who laughed at Neha's distress.

However, not even his eyes, with their extraordinary night vision, could penetrate the thick clouds of black that coalesced inside the arches and doorways he could see from this vantage point. Starting a search for the watcher would be pointless. He or she had the advantage of having planned an escape route, would be long gone by the time Jason reached their hiding place.

Instead, he stood guard, never losing sight of where Mahiya was at any moment, regardless of his focus on the shadows.

"Come." Neha said nothing else as she took flight, basket in hand.

Mahiya rose after her, and Jason followed, rising above them both in order to keep watch. However, Neha didn't go far, landing on a small mountain plateau perhaps five minutes later. In the center of the open space stood a flat gray stone set atop a number of other stones shaped to brick smoothness and slotted in to create a squat pyramid.

Placing both baskets on the flat stone, Neha bent down and whispered something so soft, the wind buffeted her words away before they reached Jason. The first tendril of smoke appeared from below the baskets a second later.

By the time Neha stepped away from the little pyre, flames licked out of the baskets, and he understood the archangel had gained power not just over ice, but over fire. Ice could harm, but fire . . . fire was annihilation and violence on a level beyond. And Neha could now drop the flickering yellow orange death from the sky.

32

Dmitri ensured Honor was comfortable in the four-poster bed she'd made up with sheets of crisp white speckled with tiny blue forget-me-nots. Returning to the country with as much stealth as possible, they'd headed immediately to the house Jason had told Dmitri of on his and Honor's wedding day. The instant Dmitri saw the place, he understood why Jason had been so certain no one would ever come upon them unawares.

It was a fortress created by nature itself.

The mountain had no roads—he and Honor had hiked in up the highly specific path Jason had shared. Any deviation from that path would've sent them to impassable cliffs, dangerous rock faces loose with gravel, hidden traps. Built of stone and wood, the house was a part of the environment, while up above was a dark green canopy that let in stray beams of sunlight while concealing the house from aerial view.

Added to that was a sophisticated security system that would alert Dmitri to anyone in the forest or in the sky.

It was the safe place Jason had promised, a place where

Dmitri's wife embraced her new existence as a near immortal. The toxin that would turn her into a vampire had been introduced into her system three hours earlier, with Raphael having left New York under cover of night to fly here to perform the task—a task the archangel would do twice more several weeks apart.

Dmitri would've trusted no one else with Honor's Making, and Raphael had kept his faith, treating Honor with utmost courtesy. Now, only two neat fang marks on her wrist remained as a memento of a choice that would alter her existence, but Dmitri knew the toxin had already begun to reshape her cells, though she wouldn't feel the burn of the process for another few minutes.

He intended her to be under by then. Everything was ready. From one honey golden arm ran a saline drip he'd set up using medical knowledge he'd accumulated out of curiosity, staving off the boredom of an immortality that had been forced on him. There was another line, one that led to a carefully calculated drip of morphine, intended to offset the pain of the transformation.

"Sleep," he whispered as the haunting midnight green of her eyes began to blur. "I'll be here when you wake." It would take roughly three months for the process to complete this way, but it would be a gentle change, not the agony that had turned him into an animal bound in chains that rubbed his skin raw, his flesh exposed to the filth of the room where he'd been kept. "Dream of me."

"As if," she whispered with a sleepy smile, "I would dream of anyone else." Her lashes fluttered shut, her breathing falling into the even rhythm of deepest sleep.

Caressing fine strands of hair off her cheek, he checked to make sure her vital signs were as they should be. Now came the hardest part—the waiting. Honor would need no nutrients for the first few days, and her body had stopped producing waste the instant the toxin hit her bloodstream, everything burning up in the massive surge of energy needed to begin the transformation.

After those first three or four days, depending on how

fast the change progressed, he'd bring her to a hazy wakefulness so she could drink just a few drops from him. The blood
kiss was a step he'd repeat, until her final feeding would be
a true one. For most Candidates, it was a clinical process,
the blood introduced via a feeding tube, but for Honor, it
would be an intimate journey.

His wife would always wake in his arms, safe and loved.

"Come back to me," he whispered in the language of
their long-ago homeland, part of him deathly afraid now
that he couldn't hear her voice, the husky intimacy of her
laughter silent.

He didn't know how he would bear the quiet, but he'd
find a way, because she would hurt if he initiated a prema-
ture waking. And Honor was never, ever to be hurt. Not so
long as Dmitri lived.

33

Two and a half hours after discovering the mutilated bodies of Neha's pets, Jason called Raphael from a mountaintop touched with the dawn. "One of my people just sent through a report that indicates the possibility of Lijuan making the reborn again is now in the near-certain range."

Jason's man was situated not in Lijuan's home fortress, but at another of the archangel's strongholds. The distance from the origin made every piece of information suspect, but this particular rumor had been gaining momentum for weeks, until the highly intelligent vampire was sure it had been born in truth. The most recent whispers had been dangerously explicit in their detail.

"I cannot believe her a fool." Ice in Raphael's voice. "It was one of her reborn who first attacked her in Beijing."

"It's being whispered that she's no longer choosing candidates from within her court, but from the peasants, those who look upon her as a demigoddess." Lijuan was a good empress in many ways—her people always had enough to eat, and she meted out justice with a fair hand. However, she preferred to keep the majority of her people in a cultural and technological state that had remained unchanged for centuries.

"Why should I create discontent by permitting them to know of things beyond their reach? It is not as if they live long enough for it to matter."

Words she'd spoken to Raphael four hundred years ago while Jason had been in the room, her decision that of an archangel who'd been alive millennia and who considered mortals little more than a disposable workforce. Yet age alone couldn't account for her choice. Caliane was *far*, far older, and from all the reports Jason had had from Naasir, her people were well-learned and within her city lay a sprawling library open to all.

No, the desire Lijuan had to keep so many of her people in ignorance came from within her, as did her power to reanimate the dead to shambling, horrifying life. And it was this archangel who might well be teaching Neha how to handle her destructive new abilities. Jason had to find out the content of those lessons.

If Lijuan had groomed herself an ally to assist her in her malignant games, the earth might yet become a place of endless horror. A place where fire fell from the sky and the dead hunted the living for flesh, warm and blood drenched.

Mahiya was sitting on a bench in the pavilion in the courtyard in front of her palace, her magnificent wings spread on the marble behind her when he returned from speaking to Raphael. She said nothing until he came to stand beside her. "I keep thinking of her."

Jason didn't need her to tell him who she meant. "It's a natural thing. Nivriti was your mother."

Her head lifted, a slight hesitation to her as she said. "Your mother, Aurelani, is she alive?"

"No."

"Wake up, wake up, wake up!"

Hidden from prying eyes by the spread of her wing and the columns of the pavilion, she reached a hand up to close it around his. "I'm sorry. I've made you sad."

"No," he said. "You didn't. It happened an eon ago." His emotions had aged, taken on a hue he couldn't describe.

"Will you tell me about her?" Tawny eyes looked up at him, her lashes casting lacey shadows on her cheeks.

Until Mahiya, he hadn't ever spoken of his mother to anyone, and even then, it had been in the guise of a romantic tale. He didn't know if he could speak of *her*, of the mother the famed Aurelani had been to him, the scar tissue inside him a jagged barrier. "Ask me again another day."

"All right." With that gentle agreement, Mahiya leaned her head against his side. "I asked Vanhi to tell me stories about my mother this morning." Her fingers squeezed his. "She told me many things, including about the lake palace that was her favorite place in all of this land. It's not so very far from here. An hour's flight."

Jason looked down at the black silk of her hair, his mind filling with images of a desolate building covered with moss, its windows and doorways gaping maws. "Abandoned."

"Yes. When my mother was supposedly executed." A quiet exhale. "It was made to last, the palace. Built of marble within the crater of a mountain, the 'lake' is filled by the monsoon rains. I don't know if it still stands—"

"It does." He told her of his previous flight to this territory. "I came in as the sun was setting, and something caught the light. When I turned and circled, I saw only the shimmer of water—it took me a minute to find the building half hidden within the lake." Covered by moss as it was, the water palace merged into the deep dark green of the lake, its camouflage perfect.

"We have the whole day," Mahiya said, her body warm against his own. "Neha is in seclusion—I do not know for whom she mourns, if it is for the people lost or her pets, but I've seen her like this before. She won't reemerge before dark, will not think to ask where we have been."

"Come," he said. "It may take me a few passes to locate the palace."

Mahiya stared down at the building that had become a chameleon over the centuries, hiding in plain sight. Covered not only by a dark green moss that echoed the color of the water, but by fine vines of the same shade, it appeared nothing so much as a floating clump of greenery. Desolate as this place was, few angels would pass over it, and those that did wouldn't be tempted to linger. It was a testament to Jason's curiosity that he'd discovered it.

"I didn't have time to land then," he said, hovering beside her with an ease she envied. "We can't count on its stability."

"It'll hold," she told him. "It was built to withstand water, to endure through centuries." Diving without waiting for him, she headed toward what she guessed had once been a large balcony or courtyard that hung out over the water. A dark blur passed her a second later, and Jason had landed, his wings folded back, before she touched down.

A storm swirled in irises gone a turbulent black. "That wasn't smart, Mahiya."

Fascinated, she stared. Never had she seen him angry, and the leash he kept on his anger even now made her wonder at the depth of his control. "I knew you were faster," she said. "And that you would've stopped me had you glimpsed anything that indicated danger."

The storm crashed, dark and violent. "You shouldn't have such faith in an enemy spymaster."

"I don't. I have it in you." Reaching out to touch his wing, she smiled at this man who was an enigma she would never get the chance to solve and yet who grew deeper into her heart with each breath. "Let's explore."

Jason should've held his ground, forced Mahiya to acknowledge that she'd acted with rash impatience, but he had the thought that unleashing his anger on her at this instant would be akin to smashing the most fragile glass.

He saw the confusion behind the eagerness, saw that she didn't know if she wanted her mother alive or not, for if Nivriti lived, she had a sadistic streak of violence.

"Stay close." Reaching back, he drew his sword from its sheath.

Mahiya raised a hand as if she'd touch the obsidian blade that seemed to roil with black flame, before dropping the blade and falling in step beside him. Deciding against using the vine-shrouded door in front of them, he walked with quiet steps around the side of the palace. They had to be careful of their footing, the moss slippery.

The palace had been designed to sit above the water level, but it was clear the monsoon rains had been strong enough to overwhelm it in years past. The marks of those deluges were waves of brown on the discolored marble of the building. It was probable the lake had some mechanism by which the waters could be bled off to other waterways—he'd seen such in other parts of Neha's land. But this palace and its surrounds had lain fallow for over three hundred years, any blockage in the system untended.

A doorway allowed sunlight to spill into the room beyond.

"Wait." He entered with care, taking in every desolate corner before nodding at Mahiya to enter.

"There's nothing here." Disappointment turned her voice leaden as she took in the debris and moss and the dried remnants of sludge that had come in when the waters rose. While the air wasn't damp, the sunshine probing deep, the layers of dirt created a musty, earthy scent that made it clear this room had seen no other living presence for centuries. "The furniture must've been made of wood, rotted."

"Yes." He stepped to a shadowy doorway leading inward. "If I were hiding within, I would choose the core." Where light would be least likely to escape come night.

Mahiya's wing brushed his as she took her place beside him once more.

The rooms that followed were as bleak as the first. Stripped of furniture, carpet, and paintings, they were hollows broken and echoing, though Mahiya was able to guess at the functions of some from the placement of windows devoid of glass and doors long destroyed.

"It must've been magnificent when alive," she whispered. "Like a jewel on the water at night, the lights reflected in the lak—"

Warned by her sudden silence, he followed her gaze and saw color. *Crimson*. Shiny and sleek, a ribbon that might have come from a woman's dress.

"Lovers," Mahiya murmured, picking up the decadent hue that did not belong in this lonely palace devoid of laughter, "may be using this as a pace for discreet assignations." It was patent she fought hope.

"Perhaps." It was too old and without comfort to tempt most, but he'd known young angels to do startling things.

"It's soft." She rubbed her fingers along the ribbon. "It can't have been here long or the damp would've seeped in, turned the satin rough when it dried." Her voice was near soundless, her wings held tight to her back to give Jason as much room as possible as they moved through the palace.

Two rooms later, he held up a fisted hand.

Mahiya halted.

Not moving a muscle, Jason *listened*. But the wind, it didn't whisper the name of Mahiya's mother, nor did it warn of danger. Still, he'd sensed something, and a second later, he knew what it was.

Sensuality, luxuriant and potent, and a perfume a woman might wear.

The cause of the silent warning identified, he dropped his hand but put his finger to his lips. Nodding, Mahiya held her silence as he reached out to part a doorway of vines . . . to reveal a room as disparate from the others as a ruby was from a hunk of rock. Here, the marble had been cleaned with scrupulous care, until in spite of the permanent staining, the walls gleamed.

Light came in through a skylight devoid of glass and half covered by vines. Rain would easily penetrate the green barrier, but there was little threat of it this time of year.

Certainly, whoever had set up this room was unworried about potential water damage to the rich indigo carpet that lined the floor or the cushions of gold-shot silk scattered over the bed in the center.

A small vanity stood against another wall, hairpins and jewels scattered across the surface. In front of it was a stool on which a woman might sit as she readied herself. "No vampire could've brought this in." Not with the single road up the mountain buried under a landslide old enough to have scraggly trees hugging its jagged slope.

"Jason."

Turning at the shaken whisper, he saw Mahiya's reflection in the mirror above the vanity, her fingers clutching at something.

An envelope.

Written on it was a single word: *Daughter*

Mahiya knew Jason had been right to insist they fly to a safer location before she opened the letter, but by the time they landed in a remote field dotted with a scarcity of trees and surrounded by nothing but balls of dusty foliage rolling across the endless vista, she felt as if her skin would split.

Then they were there and it was time. Back against a spindly tree that nonetheless provided shimmering gray shade, she stared at the red seal of the letter, while the black-winged angel who was no longer her enemy stood a dark sentinel. He said nothing, giving her the time to find her courage, break the seal.

My dearest Mahiya Geet,

I had faith you would find this. You and your dangerous black shadow. I thought to kill him for you at first—

Mahiya swallowed a cry, thrusting her knuckles against her mouth.

*—but I realized upon further reflection that he is
the only thing standing between you and Neha. And
it is deliberate. So, then I must tell you I approve.
You have made a better choice than I.*

Her heart clenched at the pain inherent in that simple
confession.

*I am sorry I cannot be here to greet you, my
beloved child. But this part is done. It was a test of
my strength and skill. A warning, too, but we both
know Neha is far too arrogant to listen, to
understand.*

*This place is for you—stay here, be safe. Your
spymaster will protect you. If he needs must return
to Neha, be assured I will make certain he comes
back to you unharmed after the real game is played
and won. You cannot be in the court at that time.
Neha will slit your throat and rip your beating
heart from your chest, if only to wound me.*

*Your residence in this place will not be for long.
Soon I will hold you as a mother should hold her
child, while Neha bleeds heart's blood and her people scrabble in panic and terror. I have had three
hundred years to plan my vengeance.*

Nivriti

34

Trembling, Mahiya walked to lean her face against Jason's back, his wings strong and sleek and paradoxically soft on either side of her. "I don't know what to think." She passed him the letter without shifting from her position tucked against his back. He didn't force her to move, didn't attempt to turn and take her into his arms—as if he understood she just needed to lean on his strength a little until the world stopped spinning.

"There is a sense of damp to the letter," Jason said after scanning the lines. "But the wax carries a faint impression of her scent still, as did the room."

Her mother hadn't been gone long enough to be erased from the palace. "I think her pride is such that it wouldn't allow her to do what was done to the snakes." But she had no doubt Nivriti had known of the needless cruelty. "She must've departed the lake palace after killing Arav, left some of her people behind to cause further disorder."

Jason returned his gaze to the letter. "She cannot plan a martial attack—regardless of how long she's had to plan, Neha is an archangel with a garrison at her command."

Mahiya knew she should be saying something to that, but she felt lost in a world that had shifted on its axis.

My mother is alive.

A crackle of paper, strong wings shifting under her touch, and Jason was turning around. Startled, afraid that he was pushing her away when she so desperately needed an anchor, needed *him*, she froze . . . until he ran his hand over the back of her head and down to press against her lower back, just enough to let her know that he was there, his strength hers to use.

A sob rocked through her, and then she couldn't stop, her entire body jerking, her bones suddenly brittle.

Strong arms, lips against her temple, wings of midnight opening to curve around her, until Jason surrounded her on every side. His heart beat strong and steady, his hands warm on her head and against her lower back, and his heat, it was a smoldering inferno over her skin.

Black.

That was the color of Jason's power, she knew that without any doubt. It felt as if she was surrounded by a raging storm. The sensation should've been frightening, but the storm didn't so much as lift a hair on her head, the calm within filled with such protective warmth as she'd never before felt.

She didn't know how long they stood in the center of that storm, but after a while, she could breathe again. And every breath carried the scent of black fire. She couldn't describe the intense wildness of the scent in any other way, but to her, it was the essence of Jason. Trying to get even closer to him, she managed to tuck her feet between his boots.

"My mother," Jason said, his voice a low rumble against her, "was my favorite person in all the world. I loved my father, but my mother? She was the one I ran to when I got out of bed in the morning." He stroked his hand down her hair, rubbed his cheek against her temple. "Then one day, she wasn't there anymore. If the world suddenly changed and she stood in front of me, I would run into her arms just like that little boy."

Raising her tearstained face to his, she said, "That's what

I want to do." The visceral reaction had terrified her, speaking of a violent need she'd never acknowledged. "But I never had a mother, never knew her. I shouldn't be responding like this."

Jason moved the hand on her hair to her face, wiping the remnants of her tears away with this thumb, the touch rough, familiar. "You've dreamed about her, thought about her, wondered what she might've been like your whole life. It matters."

"Sometimes," she said past the knot in her throat, "when I was younger, I'd convince myself that she was an awful, hateful person, that she hadn't fought for me hard enough. When I was really angry, I'd tell myself she never wanted me at all, actually gave me up to Neha."

She spread her fingers on his shirt, tried to smooth the wrinkles she'd made when she'd fisted the fabric as she cried. "Then other times, before I grew old enough to understand what she'd done, I'd imagine her as some kind of a goddess, a woman who was lovely and gracious and perfect, and who'd take me away to a place where I didn't ever have to be afraid."

Jason didn't laugh at her. Neither did he attempt to tell her that her dreams had been normal for the lonely child she'd been. All he did was hold her and let her speak, his wings creating a protective cocoon, her body held close to his heat, to his heartbeat, to *him*.

I won't let you go.

It was a vow. No matter what happened, what Jason believed about his inability to form lasting bonds, he was hers, and she'd fight to hold him. They needed each other, her and her angel with his wings meant for the night. He was a power, had far more knowledge of the world, but she had a heart strong enough to care for a man who might never fully open his own to her . . . because even a fragment of Jason's heart, it would be raw, honest, a dazzling joy.

Jason watched Mahiya walk to the lip of the crater within which rippled the lake that housed Nivriti's water palace.

She'd wanted to return here, and given the contents of the letter, he'd seen no reason to stop her. With its use of a name Vanhi alone had known to date, that letter had to be genuine, and so this was meant to be a safe haven for Mahiya. Still, he would take another look at Vanhi, make sure the vampire played no deep game of her own.

Eyes free of the tears that had earlier smudged their wild brightness, Mahiya stood with her wings to him, the peacock blue and vivid green striking in the mountain sunlight. Had he been on his own, he would've chosen a far more concealed position, and even now, he stood in the faint shadow cast by a large tree that had dug in enough roots to nurture itself to a sturdy thickness.

But Mahiya, though she'd been forced to learn to navigate the shadows of an unfriendly court, was a creature of the light. Yet she didn't seem disturbed or repelled by the black flame that was the manifestation of his own power—when he'd held her, she'd tried to burrow closer into him, until he'd felt every soft curve and dip of her body. As he thought of the protective need that had compelled him to hold her tight, she turned to look over her shoulder, those tawny eyes pinpointing him with unerring accuracy.

"There's one thing," she said, walking to join him. "I agree a military assault is unlikely, but we have no idea of how long she's been free—the attack on Eris was merely the start of this 'test.'"

"Thus she may well have gathered far more support than we realize." Jason nodded. "Anoushka's death had a deep impact on Neha, could have caused her to lapse in her oversight of Nivriti's incarceration."

Mahiya looked down at the ground, lines marring her forehead, glanced back up. "Or . . . Neha might have left my mother to rot for years without bothering to check up on her—isolation is a punishment she likes to use."

Darkness roared within him, a violent wave of black fire. "No one will ever again imprison you," he said quietly, aware he was making a promise that might well put him in the firing line of an archangel.

Mahiya's face shone with a radiance that held him captive. "I know." Spreading her wings, she touched her fingers to his cheek, the tenderness in it as powerful as a knife blade, until he had the disorienting sense his world had forever shifted.

"Give me tonight," he said, wrenching calm from chaos. "I may be able to shed more light on the situation." He had contacts and people across this territory—he just hadn't known the right questions to ask until this moment.

Breaking the touch that connected them, Mahiya gave him a funny laughing look. "You're wonderful."

His defenses ignited. "Mahiya, don't see more in me than there is."

She tilted her head a fraction to the side. "Perhaps I am my mother's daughter after all—I have decided on you, Jason. And if that is a foolish choice, it is also one I will never regret."

He clamped his hand over her wrist when she would've turned away, holding her to him. Instead of struggling, she stilled, her eyes glimmering with determination and another emotion far more dangerous.

"I can't give you what you want," he repeated, some unknown thing tearing and ripping inside him at the thought of having to sever his connection to her, when it was the first time in his life he'd trusted even a part of himself to a lover.

A soft smile. "Did I make any demands, hmm?" Lifting her free hand, she ran her fingers along his jaw. "I have so much love inside me, Jason. So *much*. And I have never been allowed to shower it on anyone—no one has wanted it. Let me stretch the wings of my heart with you."

He could feel his fingers tightening on her wrist, forced himself to loosen his hold. "Will it be enough to love and not be loved?" he asked, knowing it was a brutal question. "To give and never receive?"

Her smile grew impossibly more luminous. "You have no idea what you give me."

Jason didn't release her wrist. This could only end in tears—there was no other possibility. But when he would've spoken, she pressed her fingers to his lips. "Do not be arrogant, and I shall not have to be sharp in return." Teasing words but her intent was pure steel. "I am a woman grown," she said. "I know who I am, and I understand the choices I make—if what you can give me isn't enough, I'll walk away. I will not blame you for my choice, so let it be *my* choice."

Jason released her wrist before he did damage to bones so fragile under his strength. Regardless of her eloquent promise, his instincts raged at him to end this, protect her from pain of which he'd be the cause. But the quiet challenge that vibrated in every inch of her body made it crystal clear she wouldn't easily accept his decree. No, this princess who had lived a life that would've broken most, and come out of it believing in hope, in love, was made of far tougher stock.

Mahiya would fight to hold on to him.

A strange violence of emotion crashed inside him . . . and he knew he wouldn't make the rational decision. Not when it came to Mahiya. "I didn't tell you something," he said, wishing the pathways inside him had not been stunted by the lack of light, that he was capable of giving her what a man should give his woman. "Venom did find fresh tracks in some of the other tunnels."

No exultant victory on Mahiya's face at his unspoken decision, just a silent joy that scared him on a level nothing had touched for an eon. "And old as the tunnels are," she said, "some exits and entrances must've been forgotten, left unguarded."

Jason recalled what Venom had said.

"Only reason I even know the ins and outs of the entire labyrinth is that when I was first Made, I was . . . closer to the otherness in me. I can't work out how anyone else would've known some of the oldest parts of the tunnels—but that's where I found the footsteps."

"Twin siblings," he murmured, "one of whom had an affinity for snakes, would've turned those tunnels into their playground." Where Neha might have forgotten the complexities of the underground system, Nivriti had had nothing but time and the driving desire for vengeance to hone her memory. Still—"I don't see Nivriti using them for a large-scale attack. It'd take too long to bring in her people one at a time, leave them vulnerable to extermination if they were spotted." A fire within the tunnels would annihilate.

Mahiya wrapped her arms around herself. "I want my mother alive, but should Neha die, the entire territory will be thrown into chaos, millions of lives at stake."

Jason shook his head. "Only another of the Cadre can kill Neha. Had Nivriti joined their number, the whole world would've stood witness." All ascensions to the Cadre initiated worldwide phenomena that could not be ignored, as if the archangels were locked into the very fabric of the planet.

On the day that Raphael crossed the border, the seas had turned a violent, impossible blue, as had every river and every lake across the world. Even the rain that fell from the sky was a glorious gemstone blue, and when it shattered, it left behind a sparkling residue, faceted diamond dust in the palm.

"We must stop your mother," he said, thinking of the power contained within the bodies of the Cadre. "She'll never survive a confrontation with Neha." The Archangel of India would need but a single strike to end Nivriti's existence forever. "Speak to Vanhi, see what else you can discover."

"I can't tell her that my mother might be alive—Vanhi is loyal to both Neha and Nivriti, and might take it upon herself to attempt to negotiate peace." Her hands fisted, her skin drawn tight over the fine bones of her face. "I just hope I will not have to mourn my mother before I ever meet her."

Jason began to connect with his informants even as they returned to the fort, gathering fragmented pieces of data from across his network. Venom was gone, having left for the Refuge right after calling Jason about the tunnels.

"I stay any longer and Neha will consider me a spy."

However, another one of the Seven arrived an hour before sunset, just as Jason returned from a meeting with a vampire who'd only today come from an area about four hours flight time from the fort.

"Aodhan," he said to the angel who appeared to be made of fractured pieces of light, from the diamond brightness of his hair to wings whose filaments seemed coated in shards of broken mirrors. Only the golden sheen of his skin and the crystalline blue green of his eyes, the irises shattered outward from the pupil, saved him from being a sculpture in ice. "I did not expect you."

"I cannot stay—Neha won't permit another of the Seven here. Venom is an exception."

Jason nodded. "You have something for me?" Aodhan was very, very good at filtering the information that flowed continuously through the Refuge. He would have made an excellent spymaster if not for the fact that there was no place in the world where Aodhan would not stand out.

Instead, the angel had long been Galen's right hand in the Refuge. Now, he went to New York and the Tower, and would take up many of Dmitri's duties while the leader of the Seven helped his wife through her transition. Whether the transfer would work, no one knew. As joint head of Tower operations, Aodhan would have to deal with any number of people, when he was a male who could not handle touch and sought isolation as often as not.

"It is the first time in centuries that Aodhan has indicated a desire to be a part of the world." Raphael's eyes, a blue seen in the wider world only on the day of his becoming Cadre, met Jason's. *"He must have the chance."*

Jason agreed, hoped the angel would make it.

Now, Aodhan said, "I know you can't speak to me about the details of what you're doing here, but I've detected a pattern linked to this region. It may have no relevance to your task, but my instincts say otherwise."

35

Before the other angel could continue, a butterfly, its wings an unabashed red dotted with saffron yellow, alighted on Aodhan's shoulder. Another followed a second later, its markings more modest, its wingspan larger. Aodhan looked at them, and for a fleeting instant, he was a young angel again, woefully embarrassed by his most curious of abilities.

"It's as if they can smell me," he muttered, but didn't brush the delicate creatures away. Instead, he lifted a finger, and a third butterfly appeared out of the sky to alight on it, this one with wings of creamy sunset. "Illium says that perhaps I can use them to flutter someone to death."

Jason watched as Aodhan put the butterfly carefully beside the others, creating a living ornament on his otherwise prosaic T-shirt of deep brown. They weren't the only fragile beings of flight who were drawn to Aodhan—once, long ago, Jason had seen the other angel laughing as he was covered by an array of tiny jewel-hued birds, his attraction greater than the nectar on which they customarily sipped. "As Galen would say," he replied, "Bluebell has the wings of a butterfly himself." He knew Illium had done a great deal to pull Aodhan out of the abyss, that the bond of friendship between the two was fast.

Shaking his head, Aodhan returned to the subject at hand. "A number of older vampires and angels have resigned their posts without fanfare in several courts across different regions over the past six months, then disappeared off the grid. All of them had some tie to Neha's territory in their past."

Six months.

Time enough to set up a well-guarded base. "How strong were these angels and vampires?"

"No one as strong as Dmitri or you, but by no means weak. Together, they'd compromise a battalion powerful enough to withstand a significant and prolonged assault."

If, Jason thought, that assault force didn't include an archangel. "Did they take people with them?" Trusted retainers who could keep their mouths shut.

"Roughly five hundred once you put all the pieces altogether."

Those were the people Aodhan had managed to track. There could well be any number of vampires or angels who pledged service to no court, and thus flew under the radar. Because while Nivriti might not have been an archangel, as an angel of acknowledged power, she'd ruled a vast swath of territory under Neha.

Jason had heard nothing that said her people had not been loyal. Such loyalties died hard, and three hundred years was no eternity in an immortal's life. "Were you able to glean any information about their eventual destination?"

"Just this subcontinent." Aodhan's eyes fractured the reflection of Jason's face into innumerable shards. "It's a secret that's been kept well."

Unsurprising. Nivriti's followers had to know that if Neha discovered the conspiracy, she'd hunt down her sister before Nivriti was ready for battle, and complete the execution she'd begun many mortal lifetimes ago. "One day," he said to the other angel, "I'll be able to tell you what you just gave me."

Aodhan flared out his wings, the air around him busy with pieces of color as the butterflies perched on him took flight. "I will see you in New York."

"Yes. Good journey, Aodhan." As he watched the other angel take flight, a splintered piece of light in the sky, he was already calculating every angle of this problem.

It wasn't until the next morning, the sky still a dark cloud-gray that he found the answer. "It's time to tell Neha of Nivriti's resurrection."

"Yes. Shabnam's blood . . . it screams for justice." Deep grooves around Mahiya's lush mouth. "What is it you've discovered that you choose this moment?"

When he laid it out for her, she sucked in a breath. "You play Russian roulette with an archangel."

He had never feared death, not for himself. But he would not permit Mahiya to be sacrificed on the altar of the bitter war about to take place. It was one born of old vengeance and old pain, twisted and rancid. Nivriti might love Mahiya, but she hated Neha more. Anyone caught in the middle of their conflict would be obliterated.

He thought of Mahiya with her wings broken, her face shattered, her eyes weeping blood, and knew he'd force her hand if need be, earn her hatred, but he *would not* watch her die. Not Mahiya.

"What are you thinking?" she asked softly. "You went away for a second."

He considered obfuscation, decided on truth.

Her response was instant. "I could *never* hate you. I'd sooner love Neha." Kissing his jaw with sweet, hot lips, she said, "All right, Jason. You are more experienced in matters of war—I will take your lead in this."

Jason had planned to approach Neha on his own, but Mahiya folded her arms, shook her head. "I know her in ways you don't, that you can't, especially when it comes to this one thing on which Neha is not rational."

"I want you safe." No one had ever been to him what Mahiya had become. "A single burst of anger from Neha and you will be erased from existence." And he could not imagine walking the world knowing he'd never again see the strange, dangerous hope that lived in those eyes bright as a jungle cat's.

"I take your help because you are the stronger," she said, raw emotion in every word, "but I won't hide behind your wings. This is my battle and I will not act the coward! I won't, Jason."

Before he'd reached this inexplicable equilibrium with Mahiya, before she'd staked a claim on him, he'd have incapacitated her and completed the task before she ever knew it was done. Her anger afterward would've mattered little. Now he understood who Mahiya was, understood what his action would steal from her, knew that to deny her this would be to take something from her that could never be returned.

So it was that she landed beside him in the gardens that overlooked the lake, as sunset lingered on the horizon—Jason having spent the intervening time narrowing down the probable whereabouts of Nivriti's army, with Mahiya assisting by gathering any information she could through subtle questioning of the older servants.

Neha stood alone on the edge where the fort dropped steeply into the water, her gaze on the city beyond.

"I hear Raphael's people now make free in my territory," was her opening statement, her tone limned in frost.

"Aodhan had information that was of help to me in my task."

The folds of the sage green sari Neha wore today flowed around her ankles as she turned, her wings perfect arches at her back. "Must I beg this information from you?"

"I would never expect such," he said, aware of Mahiya's resolute presence and conscious that no matter what he'd instructed, she would not run if this turned deadly. "However, the stakes have changed."

Neha rubbed the skin of the thin golden snake coiled around her upper arm like a living armband. "I see." A dangerous glint in her eye. "You break the blood vow."

He would have done so without compunction if it would've saved Mahiya, but as it was, he no longer had to. "With my action, I protect the best interests of the family." Neha, Nivriti, and Mahiya were the last direct descendants of an ancient bloodline. With Neha and Nivriti about to go to certain war, Mahiya had become the family's only hope for a future.

"You must seek something valuable indeed that you dare play games with me."

"Not valuable . . . but intriguing." He knew Mahiya listened to what he said, and yet he did not sheathe his words, having every faith in her intelligence. "My curiosity is not yet sated."

Neha's gaze went from him to Mahiya, her smile as cold as the blood of the creature around her arm. "You do not need to bargain with me for her, Jason. You're welcome to remain at this court as long as you wish."

"I'm one of Raphael's Seven," he reminded her. "I must soon return, and I ask that you release Mahiya to me."

Neha's eyes were suddenly chips of ice. "Why would I give you my favorite toy?" A flick of her wrist and Mahiya was wrenched up into the air, her neck arched in a way that meant she had to be having trouble breathing.

Rage, black and violent, surged in his veins, but he held it in check. To show even a hint of care toward Mahiya would be to end this negotiation before it began, and unless the Cascade had altered matters, this aspect of Neha's power was very weak. She could not hold Mahiya for long. "Because what I have to tell you will provide you with far more satisfaction."

"I can tear your mind apart like the rice paper of Lijuan's lands."

"No," Jason said. "You can't." He felt it then, her mental touch shoving against his shields, clawing and hard.

Her eyes widened, anger replaced by fascination. "Incredible. It is as if your mind wears an onyx carapace."

Raphael had said something similar to Jason when he'd attempted to reach Jason's mind in order to—ironically enough—teach him how to protect his thoughts from invasion. No one they'd consulted, not even Jessamy or the healer, Keir, had ever seen or heard of its like in an angel so young.

"Perhaps"—Keir's wise eyes in that too-young face—"you created it before you ever knew it to be an impossibility. An instinctive defense."

Jason had always thought Keir had the right of it. Alone and scared when he'd been little more than a babe, he'd had to learn to protect himself from a world too big, too dangerous, too empty. "You can kill me," he said, because that was true, "but in doing so, you lose the information I hold."

"You would make an enemy of me out of a frippery?"

Jason heard Mahiya drop behind him, knew she had to be hurt, but still he didn't turn. "I do not think you'll consider me thus after you hear what I have to say."

Mahiya sucked in pained breaths of air, at least three of her ribs cracked. Pushing up from her crumpled state on the ground into a sitting position, she took as deep a breath as she dared. It felt like knives stabbing into her liver, but the haze cleared from her eyes to bring Jason and Neha into sharp focus. The archangel's face was cold, Jason's a mask, his tattoo dramatic under the sunshine.

All at once, Neha laughed, and it was a true laugh, full of delight. "I knew I had chosen well."

Mahiya's blood went cold, realization a chill rain in her veins.

"I can offer Jason something Raphael will never be able to match."

Jason wouldn't realize, wouldn't understand, but she

knew that look on Neha's face, had seen the calculation in it before, after quarrels with Eris. None of that had ever come to anything, but now *Eris was dead.*

Swallowing the pain that threatened to splinter her thoughts, she tried to reach Jason's mind. She'd never before dared this, for it presumed an intimacy he did not wish to share, but he had to know what he faced.

When her thoughts hit the unyielding glossy black of his shields and ricocheted back, panic beat at her with fluttering wings, but she told herself to be patient, to be calm. If she didn't succeed, Jason could inadvertently insult Neha and in so doing, forfeit his life.

I won't let her kill you, Jason. I won't.

Taking another deep breath, she tried to reach him again, realized with a dash of desperation that she was far too weak to have any impact on a shield so solid it was beyond adamantine. It was unlikely he even noticed her attempts, especially when from what Neha was saying, the archangel, too, was attempting to batter his defenses.

Retreating, she threw every part of her mind into coming up with some other way to either gain his attention or create a diversion.

Are you hurt? A voice, pristine as a bell . . . and inside her head.

The wonder of the fact he'd initiated a link might have paralyzed her had she not been so afraid for him. *No, I'm fine*, she lied, able to taste the gleaming obsidian of his rage. *Jason, listen, there is something you must know.*

Silence, but the connection remained open.

She cares nothing for me except as the toy she called me, but she wants you.

Neha isn't the first archangel to want to poach my skills.

No. She held her breath, released it in a quiet rush as pain stabbed at her chest.

You are hurt.

A few broken ribs won't matter if we both end up dead, so listen. She doesn't want your skills, she wants you—*for her new consort.*

36

Neha's voice broke into their silent exchange. "I did not expect such a weak creature to intrigue you so, but it is undoubtedly a fleeting interest." That quickly, Neha dismissed Mahiya. "What I offer you is far more than you can imagine."

She's mad.

Mahiya blinked at Jason's flat assessment. *No, Neha is sane. Coldly so. She knows you'll be a strong, dangerous, intelligent consort.* Jason was a man any woman would be proud to have by her side. *And you are beautiful. Neha has always been drawn to beauty in a man.* Though Jason was a naked blade to Eris's pretty ornament.

Only madness would make her blind to the fact that it would be a very stupid man who'd accept the offer of a woman who imprisoned her last consort for three hundred years.

Mahiya's mouth threatened to fall open. *Well, when you put it that way . . .*

"I need a consort," Neha said, walking to the edge of the garden once more, her gaze on the lake, its surface a mirror of the blue sky touched with curling edges of red and orange. "I do not want you for a lover, so you may keep Mahiya as a diversion if you wish, but I am offering you power you will never gain in Raphael's court."

Jason was quiet for a long moment. "I did not expect such an offer," he said at last, as if Neha had caught him unawares and he sought time to get his thoughts in order.

Yes, Mahiya thought, watching Neha's face as she turned back to Jason. That was the right tack. To refuse her outright would be an insult the archangel would not forget, never forgive.

"A consort must walk beside an archangel," he added. "I prefer the shadows."

"My last consort was a creature of the light, shining and handsome, and he betrayed me." Brittle words.

Some assistance, Mahiya Geet.

Startled at the tenderness in his mental tone, something she'd never heard in his spoken voice, it took her a second to reply. *She's still in love with Eris, and you're too proud a man to be with a woman who mourns another.*

I am?

Her lips twitched. Jason's laughter was hidden deep within, where the light did not often reach, but it was there. *You are*, she said firmly, taking advantage of Neha's preoccupation with Jason to get to her feet.

"This time," the archangel continued, "a consort who stands in the shadows would suit me well."

Jason bowed deeper than Mahiya had ever seen him bow, his wings spread to their full breathtaking width, the colors of sunset playing over the jet in a display that turned it into a canvas of black flame. When he rose back up, his expression was as inscrutable as always, but his voice gentle. "I am truly flattered."

"But." The edge in Neha's voice was a scythe.

"But though he may have betrayed you, Eris holds your heart."

Neha's sucked-in breath was loud in the silence. "I am not offering you love."

"I know." Jason folded in his wings with neat care. "But I am one of the Seven—I have seen a true archangel-consort match, one bound by the heart, and so I will always know the lack."

Neha's anger whipped her hair back from her face, a faint glow coming off her wings. "Raphael's consort should be dead."

Elena, Mahiya remembered too late, had been critical in Anoushka's execution.

"Yet," Jason said, not missing a beat, "Raphael would take on the Cadre rather than allow her to come to harm. You would not do the same for me."

Neha stared at him, a faint confusion in her expression. "I didn't expect such a romantic heart from you, Jason." Her gaze snapped to Mahiya. "Do you expect to find such a love with *that*?"

Mahiya felt a storm lick against her senses, realized it wasn't her own emotions she was sensing. *Jason*.

"I expect nothing but amusement," Jason said in a tone so calm that had she not been swamped by his rage, she would've never guessed at its existence, "but I want it on my terms, on my turf."

Neha's wings swept over the velvet grass nurtured by the gardeners to luxuriant life, as she turned away. "I will give her into your keeping if the knowledge you hold proves as valuable as you believe."

Mahiya knew that was the best they would get. Neha would take any further attempt to negotiate as an attack on her honor. *We must accept.*

And roll the dice. "The murderer of Eris and the others is not in your court." Jason walked to stand beside Neha, his wings a stark contrast to the indigo-dusted white of hers. "Neither is she any longer in the area, but my sources tell me she returns here in the hours after sunset."

Mahiya's heart ached at the idea of her mother so very close. She knew Jason had been surprised at the discovery of how soon the assault would begin, but it did make a brutal kind of sense—Neha was hurting from Eris's loss, vulnerable.

Now, the archangel's hair flared back in a wind no one else could feel. "One of his whores?"

Mahiya fisted her hands until her nails dug into her palms.

"I do not make judgments." Jason's response was even. "But I am near certain that until his murder, she had not touched him for more than three hundred years."

Neha went so motionless as to be inhuman. It was as if she ceased to exist in the moment, in the now, and went elsewhere. "You bring the dead back to life."

Disturbed by the eerie echo effect in the archangel's voice, Mahiya rubbed at the tiny hairs on her arms, all standing in alarm.

"I do not think so," Jason responded. "I also think this dead woman gathers an army."

Neha's wings snapped out. "Come." With that, she swept off the garden and across the lake before spiraling up and back toward the fort.

Jason followed. *You're hurt. Wait here.*

Mahiya was already in the air. *I can rest later.* Beating her wings put strain on her rib cage, the agony threatening to take her under, but she could not turn back.

Mahiya.

She sensed he was on the edge, that he would bring her down physically if necessary. *I need to know*, she said, laying her heart open, the heart of a girl who'd never known her mother's fate.

A pause. *Then use me.*

Not certain if it was what he meant, she nonetheless clung to the midnight strength she could sense in her mind, and landed at the fortified Guardian Fort only seconds behind Neha and Jason. The archangel didn't even notice her presence, walking with determined steps into a section of the fort that had been closed up as long as Mahiya had been aware of it. She'd tried to explore it once as a child, found her way blocked by fallen debris too heavy to shift.

Now, Neha touched her fingers to the debris in a complicated pattern . . . and that part of the floor just fell in, revealing a staircase on the other side. Mahiya's heart thudded so hard, she was certain the archangel would hear it. Each staccato beat pushed against broken ribs, but that pain was eclipsed by brutal comprehension.

Here, she was here all this time. It was a keen.

She no longer is. Remember.

Wrenching her anguish under vicious control, Mahiya wrapped the essence of Jason around herself as she followed him and Neha down the staircase and into a corridor lit with modern electric bulbs set in wall sconces that threw warm light on the stone walls. Many had burned out, while still others were swathed in cobwebs, a silent indication of how long it had been since anyone walked this passage. A hundred feet down the corridor, Neha revealed another staircase that went even deeper into the earth.

The lights here were naked bulbs, the corridor itself pounded earth . . . and the single room at the end a pit in the earth with crisscrossing bars that hid the shadowed realm beyond. Throwing out a hand, Neha lit up the cell with a blaze of violent power.

It was empty.

Mahiya swayed, would've fallen if Jason hadn't grabbed her hand.

Mahiya.

I'm fine. Air rushed into her lungs as she took in a breath and thought about what she'd seen: the melted metal where manacles might have hung from the walls, the scorch marks around the hole in the bars of the cell. Whoever had rescued her mother had used a blowtorch to cut her free. *Promise.*

He released her before Neha could turn. *How badly are you hurt?*

Already healing. I just . . . this place.

She'd been half afraid they were wrong, that her mother remained trapped in this nightmare place. A creature meant for the skies kept so long in the dark . . . *Her wings would've been wasted. She couldn't have flown out of here.*

It also means she was rescued far longer than six months ago. If I was asked to bet, I would say it was done when

Raphael executed Uram. The world was in chaos, and Neha often had to be away from the fort on Cadre business.

A scream of rage splintered the silence, Neha spinning around in a fury that burned ice along one wall, fire along the other. Mahiya barely escaped being singed by the flames . . . and her step out of its path put her in Neha's direct line of sight. The archangel's eyes pinned her, cold as hell, and Mahiya knew she was dead.

Black shimmered in her vision until Jason's wings were all she could see.

No, Jason, no! In this mood, Neha would execute him regardless of any other consideration.

"The information," he said as she attempted to budge his shoulders, shove him out of danger. "Was it worth the price?"

A chill silence, the ice cracking and breaking to fall at their feet, the fire flickering out to leave the walls scorched, the corridor dimly illuminated by the single bulb that had survived. Neha's laugh this time was inhuman enough to sour Mahiya's stomach, and yet it held a certain amusement.

"Now I understand, Jason. You have a weakness for broken birds, and she would make a pretty hostage." It seemed to please Neha, that justification. "Very well, you have admirably fulfilled the blood vow. Take this broken bird. Keep her, leave her in some protected aerie, it matters nothing. I have no need of a hostage when I can rend my beloved sister limb from limb with my bare hands."

Mahiya's knees almost crumpled, only her grip on Jason keeping her upright. *I'm free . . . and my mother is about to die.*

37

Dmitri handled several pieces of Tower business, clearing as much of the decks as he could from a distance, including a situation that meant sending a senior angel out of state to deal with another angel who thought to create himself a fiefdom free of Tower oversight.

That done, he spoke to Ilium. "Anything else urgent we need to clear?"

"No, Aodhan should have time to settle in."

"Good." Dmitri was conscious the angel would be out of his element, but confident he had the capacity to step into Dmitri's shoes—to a certain extent. Aodhan and Illium were both much younger, had less experience, but together, they were a dangerous force. "You know how to get hold of me if you need me."

"Dmitri." Golden eyes fringed with black lashes tipped in blue met his. "Take care of Honor. I promise I won't burn down the Tower in your absence—I don't know why everyone got so excited about a little smoke."

Aware the blue-winged angel was attempting to lighten his mood, he said, "I'm reassured. Let me just call the fire department." He signed off to Illium's laughter and glanced over his shoulder to check on Honor as he did a thousand times through the day.

He'd moved his desk into the bedroom, was never away from her for longer than a few minutes at most. He didn't ever want her to rouse alone. With the toxin wreaking havoc in her bloodstream, she might panic, be afraid.

"Will you be here when I wake?"

"Always."

Only once he was sure she was safe, her breathing steady, did he force himself to return to his work, the trees beyond the window rustling under the playful caress of the wind. Two more days until he could wake her, until he could hear her voice again. *Two more days.*

38

It took Mahiya only minutes to pack the things she couldn't bear to be without. The bag was pitifully small, but then she'd always known she would one day leave this place. "I haven't taken any jewels except for those that were undisputed personal gifts," she said, and it wasn't a matter of stupid pride but safety. "I can't risk that Neha will brand me a thief, demand my return for punishment."

"You have no need to chance such a thing." Jason nodded in approval at the simple tunic and pants she'd pulled on for the flight out of Neha's territory. "I will lend you what you need to start your new life."

The tension that had knotted up her spine at his first sentence, dissolved with his second. "Thank you." A loan came with an expectation that it would be repaid, did not steal her newfound freedom by making her dependant on him. "Your bag?"

"Nothing I will miss." He withdrew his sword, checked it, slid it back into the sheath. "Give me yours."

"It's not heavy." Designed to be carried on her front, it left her wings unhindered.

He just reached out and took it, carrying it in one hand. "Your ribs haven't yet fully healed, so don't argue."

"I'll carry it by hand as you're doing—at least until we're out of the fort. You need your hands free should you have to fight." Her blade-pins would be useful were they cornered, but a sword wielded by a master would end things before it ever got that far.

You have a tendency to give orders yourself, princess. In spite of the dark words, he returned the bag. "Come, we have to go."

Mahiya stepped out onto the balcony, hesitated. "Vanhi, I can't leave without saying good-bye."

"You can meet her at the Refuge—she visits there at least once a year. And Neha cares too much for her to punish her for continuing to see you."

He stepped off the balcony with those words to come to a graceful landing in the courtyard, wings spread. Surprised, she followed in silence. *What's wrong?*

I don't trust Neha not to shoot us down from the skies.

Mahiya had the same fear—the roof of the fort was spiked with an increasing number of ground-to-air weapons in preparation for Nivriti's return. It would only take a single "accident" to get rid of an inconvenient angel and the spymaster who protected her. *The tunnels*, she said. *Did Venom give you a map?*

Yes. Stay as close to me as you can without entangling my wings.

She discovered the reason for his order a few moments later, when two guards heading in the direction of their palace passed by without so much as a nod, though Mahiya and Jason stood exposed in an alcove just off the path. Guessing they had seen only a smudged pool of darkness, she became Jason's shadow as they made their way through the fort, their pace cautious but steady.

Rather than crossing the courtyards, Jason took an internal path, going down otherwise deserted corridors and through heavy doors until they exited into a small garden lit only by a spare number of tea candles. It was, she remembered, an adjunct to a disused palace. As evidenced by the candles, the garden was utilized by the odd pair seeking privacy, but no one sat on the benches tonight.

Jason halted in the darkness outside the door through which they'd come, and she saw shadows swirl around the candles a moment later, eclipsing even that muted light. *Can you see?*

Not well.

A warm hand gripped hers.

Moving with the feline grace of a man at home in the moonless night, Jason led her to the center of the garden and to the pedestal on which stood a statue of an unnamed angel, her wings spread in readiness for flight. A twist of the statue's right wrist, followed by a hard pull on her opposing wing, and one side of the pedestal slid open. The doorway was narrow, this entrance not meant for a being with wings, but Mahiya bit back her incipient claustrophobia and walked in, Jason's body heat a subtle reassurance as he entered right behind her.

A second later, the door slid shut again.

Stygian, the darkness hissed with ghosts of terror, and she thought she might panic—until a soft, glowing light filled the space, the ball of warmth floating just in front of her. It wasn't something she'd have expected from a man whose power expressed itself in shades of midnight, but she was beyond grateful. *Thank you*, she said, able to breathe again now that she could see the tiny box held no serpents.

His arm came around her. *Stairs into the tunnels will open beneath your feet. Soon as they do, head down.* He pressed something on the wall and half the floor gave away. *Fast as possible, princess.*

Mahiya didn't need him to explain why. Neha might regret it later if she caused them harm, might consider it a stain on her honor, but they'd be just as dead. Using the light that hovered in front of her as a beacon, wings scraping the edges of the narrow staircase, she pushed forward to enter a tunnel as narrow.

It was maybe two minutes later that she finally stumbled into a much wider tunnel.

Turn left. Jason swept around to walk beside her with that instruction, both of them now able to stand fully upright. A single set of footprints preceded theirs in the dust.

Venom?

He says he knows these tunnels like a snake knows its den.

As if he'd called them up, two snakes slid sinuously into their path. Mahiya halted, examined the color of their leathery skin and breathed out a sigh. *They're not poisonous.* Neha didn't tamper with nature except when she had a specific reason.

Jason gave her a searching look. *You're not afraid.*

Not in the light, she answered honestly.

Those weren't the only slithery creatures they saw, but for the most part, the snakes just wanted to be left alone or were curious. Only one acted aggressive, and it died a quick death under the obsidian blade of Jason's sword, its body turned to ash between one breath and the next.

"Is it the sword?" she asked aloud, sensing they were deep enough that sound wouldn't carry. "The black fire?"

"No. However, it's a useful conduit."

His answer was no surprise, not when she'd felt the midnight flame of him more than once.

"The tunnels—"

"I sent Rhys a message just before we left."

"Good." She didn't want to handicap her mother, but as Jason had known about the tunnels' possible tactical use before the blood vow was deemed complete, remaining silent would've blemished his honor and put his life in danger.

"Faster, Mahiya."

Calf muscles straining as the tunnels began to slope steadily upward, she saved her breath and her strength until they exited at last . . . from a trapdoor in the floor of the broken-down temple where she'd found the teddy bear.

"Why didn't Venom use this before?" The exit was cunningly concealed in a dark alcove.

"Chance the door would be stiff with disuse, give him away. He oiled the hinges for us prior to leaving." He went into another alcove, came out with a bag she assumed Venom had stashed. "Weapons, should we need them."

Rubbing at the fine grit on her face, cobwebs no doubt dusted over her hair, she dropped her bag in the corner and entered the open space in the center of the unbroken part of the temple. "I can't leave." The unvarnished words simply spilled out, before she was even aware of making a choice.

"I know."

A terrible ache blossomed in her chest at his simple acceptance.

"If the world suddenly changed and she stood in front of me, I would run into her arms just like that little boy."

It would've been smarter to stay silent, to not push at his boundaries, but a life of walls and secrets was not what she wanted with her spymaster. "Will you tell me?" she said, asking him to share a piece of his history with her, even if he could not share his heart. "How she died?"

Jason leaned against the wall at the back of the ruined temple, his ears cocked to the wind. It brought a single word.

Nivriti.

Not long to wait, he thought, guessing the vengeance-driven angel had a spy in the fort who'd informed her the instant her daughter was out of Neha's reach and no longer at risk of being used as a hostage.

His eyes lingered on the woman who stood with her back to a column that had survived the vagaries of time, her face a study in strength and vulnerability intertwined. Waiting for his answer, waiting for him to tell her of a nightmare he'd shared with no person on this earth. But this princess had nightmares of her own.

It could be that that was why he spoke. Or perhaps it was because of the luminous warmth at the back of his mind that was Mahiya's presence. He should've blocked her out, was certain she didn't realize she'd maintained the connection since he first allowed her through his shields. But he was loathe to cut her off—it felt as if she'd tucked herself into him. Not prying, not in any way aggressive, just curled up against him as she liked to be in bed, her hand on his heart.

"My mother's life," he began, taking strength from that gentle radiance, "was stolen when I was a boy whose wings were yet too big for his body."

Trembling, Jason made himself stop looking at the rust that wasn't rust, and pulled himself out of the hole, closing the trapdoor with careful hands—and averted eyes—so it wouldn't make a noise. And then he stood staring at the wall. He didn't want to turn and see what lay on the other side, what he'd pushed off the top of the trapdoor. But the wall was splattered with the rust that wasn't rust, too. Tiny bits of it had begun to flake off, baked by the hot sun pouring in through the sky-window.

Stomach all twisted and his heart a lump, he looked away from the wall and to the floor, but it was streaked with pale brown, his feet having made small prints on the polished wood. The dirt inside the hole hadn't been wet. Not until after.

After the screams went quiet.

He closed his eyes, but he could still smell the rust that wasn't rust.

And he knew he had to turn around.

Had to see.

She was looking at him from the other side of the room, her pretty dark brown eyes filmed over with a whiteness that was wrong. The stump of her neck was crusted with blood where it sat on the table in the corner, as if placed there for just this purpose.

He didn't scream.

He knew never to scream.

Instead, he looked at the chunk of meat that had been blocking the trapdoor. It wore a silk sheath of brilliant amethyst.

Amethyst. That's what his mother always called her favorite color. Amethyst.

It had taken him a long time to say it right, and she'd always laughed in delight when he used the word, her shining black hair dancing in the sunshine.

The mat crackled under his feet, and he realized he'd moved, realized he was dragging the meat wearing the amethyst top to the other part that matched, that he was adding her arms and legs, the ripped and bloodied feathers of her silvery-white wings, his chest straining with the effort, the pieces too heavy for his small body. But he had to do it.

The sun hadn't dried out the bits in the shade and hidden from direct light, and his hands became slippery with dark red once more. When her head slid out of his hands and thumped on the floor, he bit hard on his lip and picked it up again, stroking back the hair that had gotten in her eyes. "I'm sorry, Mama." He had his mother's hair, her skin, her eyes, she always said so. But today her eyes weren't right, weren't smiling as they always did when they turned his way.

Finally settling her head where it should be on her body, he knelt down on the mat that always made crisscross patterns on his knees and said, "Wake up now."

His mother was an immortal, just like him. Only four hundred and sixty-five years old, but that was old enough.

Angels lived forever.

That's what his mother said the mortals said, but she said angels simply lived a very long time.

He shook her shoulders, her brown skin cold instead of glowing with warmth. "Wake up." He tried not to remember what else his mother had said, but her words whispered into his mind, spoken in the lyrical language of the island where she'd been born and lived until she was taken to school in a place she called the Refuge.

"Angels can die. It is a difficult thing but not impossible. Especially for younger angels."

Now he looked at the chunk of meat wearing the amethyst silk, and he knew what that hole in her chest meant. Her heart was gone, ripped out. Her stomach, too, had a hole. And her head . . . it hadn't been too heavy for him to lift. Because there was a hole in it, too.

All his mother's insides were gone.

An angel of her age and power could not reawaken without her insides, could not reform. Still he shook her, telling her to *"Wake up, wake up, wake up!"* Until he realized he was screaming, when he was supposed to never, ever scream.

Shutting himself up by biting down on his lip again until it bled, he patted his mother's hair back into place and rose, putting one bloody hand on the doorknob to open it. Silence greeted him on the other side. He followed the trail of dried blood, determined to find his mother's insides. If he put them back, she would wake up, he knew she would.

His wings dragged on the ground, streaking dirt and rust red along the shiny wooden floors, and he knew his mother would scold him. He was always supposed to keep them up, so his flight muscles would grow strong, but he was so tired and hungry. *"I'm sorry, Mama,"* he whispered again. *"I promise I'll do better tomorrow."* After she was awake.

Outside, the full might of the sun was blinding, the light reflecting off the white sands on the other side of his mother's lush garden, the water an endless blue horizon. He blinked until the spots faded, and continued on his task. The trail of sun-hardened black brown went around the side of the house and to what had been the small shed where his father had built things, like the instruments their friends took away to sell at the Refuge place and the toys Jason used to love.

Before.

Smoke still rose from the collapsed remnants of his father's work house, but the fire had devoured a good meal and was settling down to sleep, the fallen beams glowing with a final few embers. He knew he wasn't supposed to go near fire, but he went anyway, pushing away still-warm pieces with his hands. When the embers burned his skin, singed his feathers, he shook off the hurt and carried on, kicking aside the ash and the lumps of charcoaled wood until he saw his father's head.

It was rolling around on the floor, all bone, the eye holes empty. His father's body—charred black bones—lay in another part of the small building, and Jason knew then that his father had burned up his mother's insides as well as his own, that he'd cut off his own head using the chopping thing he'd built . . . would have cut off Jason's if Jason had made a sound when his father called out for him after the screams stopped and the blood began to seep through the trapdoor.

39

But maybe his father had made a mistake, he thought suddenly, hope a bright star inside him, and his mother's insides had survived?

He began to dig through the ash again, his skin burning, his face blackened by the dust. He dug, and he searched, and he left a trail of sticky red as his burnt skin peeled and his battered hands began to bleed. It was only when night fell that he realized there was nothing to be found.

His mother's insides had been turned to ash.

"Only a very powerful immortal can rise from the ashes of flame." Brown eyes shining with relief and concern both. "That's why you must never play with fire, Jason. Even I cannot survive a fire should it reach my heart and mind, and you are a babe."

Wings dragging under the half-moon, he walked out to the closest part of their lagoon, washed himself in the warm, shallow water. His mother didn't like it when he came into the house dirty, so he washed and washed until all the blood and the dust was gone from his body, his raw and cut flesh stinging from the salt water. Carrying his dirty clothes, he left them on the porch where she always picked them up to wash. His wings were slick with water, so he opened and shook them off before going inside.

Mama always kissed his cheek and patted his wings dry with a soft cloth, but today, he had to do it himself. It was hard—his wings were bigger than his body, and he couldn't reach every part.

"This way, Bumblebee."

Listening to the memory, he spread the cloth on the floor and lay down on it like Mama and his father had once done, both of them laughing after a swim, their wings glistening in the sunlight as he circled delighted above them like "a big bumblebee." That was a good memory, of the time before his father became a stranger who locked the bedroom door and made his mother make small, hurting sounds that twisted Jason up until he couldn't breathe.

Dry, he put on clean clothes, and even though he wasn't supposed to wear shoes inside the house, he thought it would be all right this time, because the floor was so dirty. Ready, he walked to the back door and out to where his mother kept things with which she worked in her garden. She'd like to be near her big yellow hibiscus flowers, he thought, beginning to dig. They were her favorites—when he brought her one, she always put it behind her ear, where it shone "brilliant as the sunrise against the black silk" of her hair.

His father had said that and kissed her.

Before.

He was only a child. It took him two days to dig the hole. He didn't want to put his mother in the ground, but the flies had started to bother her in spite of the sheets he'd dragged out from the other rooms and spread over her. He knew she wouldn't like that. So after he used a mat to gently pull the pieces of her to the hole he'd dug, he put a hibiscus flower in her hair and covered her up with her favorite amethyst shawl. "I love you, Mama."

Then, he began to put the earth back inside the hole, on top of his mama. His tears ran silent and endless down his cheeks, his body having learned too well never, ever to make a sound. When it was all filled up and he knew none of the small animals that lived in the forest would be able to disturb her, he went to the beach to collect shells over and over, until her entire grave glittered and gleamed with the curves and twists and shine of the sea, the heavy blossoms of the hibiscus hanging overhead.

Then, he put his father's bones in a sack and dragged it into the damp thickness of the trees, the weight too heavy for him to fly. He didn't know how long he walked and dragged. A long time. Sometimes he rested. But finally he reached the small coral-reef encircled lagoon that jutted off the main atoll, like a twin that hadn't quite formed properly.

Unlike their lagoon, he wasn't allowed to play in this one. His father had told him there was a volcano under the surface, its crater deep. That volcano, it did something to the water, made it burn Jason's eyes the one time he'd become curious and come to explore.

Heartbeat pounding against his ribs with the effort, he rose into the air and flew to the center of the bad lagoon and dropped the sack into its dark heart, watching as the sack sank below the surface and into the maw of the hidden volcano. As the lagoon ate up his father, and though Jason wanted to hate him, hate him, hate him, his heart hurt.

He remembered how his father had taught him about coral, about sea creatures, about how to work with wood to build instruments that made haunting music, and his eyes blurred until he couldn't see anymore and he knew he had to get away before he fell into the bad lagoon. Straining his body, he flew up into the air and away, going as far as his tired muscles and heavy wings could take him before he stopped, looked around.

Their atoll was a ring of emerald green that circled a shimmering lagoon. He couldn't fly around it in one day yet, but he planned to when he was bigger. His mother had said she'd go with him, show him all the secret places she'd found, but now she wasn't here.

There was no one else.
He was all alone.

Mahiya's heart had broken a thousand times over as she listened to Jason's story, as she thought of that small boy so alone and scared and sad. Yet she also knew that the man in front of her was not that boy, had not been that boy for hundreds of years. She couldn't wipe away his pain and tell him everything would be all right.

Jason had learned too well that sometimes nothing could fix what was broken.

It wasn't a conscious thought to walk toward him. It just seemed right. Just as it seemed right to slide her arms around his torso and lay her cheek on his chest.

Sometimes, touch could say far more than any words. So she just held him and felt fresh tears prick her eyes as his arms came around her, tucking her close. Her hands were under his wings, his over hers, and it seemed as if this was how they had always gone into an embrace, how they would go into an embrace a thousand years from now.

"My father," Jason murmured, his cheek against her temple, "was a man of incredible talent fueled by a wildly passionate nature. His Nene meant more to him than anything and anyone else in existence."

Black wings came around her, a midnight caress. "Perhaps his passionate attachment to my mother might have been tempered had they been allowed to live in peace in the world, or perhaps the darkness was the price he paid for his talent, but he loved her until it became an obsession, until one by one, he drove off all their friends with his jealousy. Even the women were not welcome—he believed they sought to lure her away with their tales of the Refuge."

Leaving, Mahiya thought, woman and child alone with a man whose love had become a noose. "Your mother—" She cut herself off, realizing too late the question would cause him horrible pain.

But he knew what she had left unspoken. "She went

against her family's wishes in accepting his suit, but it wasn't pride that kept her from taking me and returning to the Refuge. It was love." His arms tightened around her. "Even when his jealousy escalated to the point where he imagined she had a secret lover, one who visited her during the rare times when he flew to a nearby island to harvest fruit. Even when he began to hurt her in ways that left no bruises but the ones in her eyes."

Mahiya wanted to rage against his mother, to shake her. How could she have not protected her son from such horror? Yet, even as she screamed silently at the pain that had forged the man in her arms, she knew emotions were nothing so simple.

Neha's continuing love for Eris was only one example.

"I'm sorry," she said, and the words held all her sorrow, her rage.

Jason's response was a stroke of his hand down her back, his heart beating strong and steady under her cheek, his body a furnace, his strength so inexorable she should've been terrified. But this was Jason, who would never hurt her. She'd known that deep within even before he told her of a past that made her understand why he helped "broken birds."

A lance of pain, but even stronger was her need to bring Jason back from the horror, to remind him that the world was not just a creation of pain and suffering and loss. Pulling back enough that she could look into his eyes, she thought of everything he'd told her, picked out a hidden wonder.

"Do you know how to swim?" she asked into the silence, the night quiet around them but for the clicking sound that announced the presence of an inquisitive little lizard before it flicked its jewel green body and disappeared into a crevice in the temple wall. "You said you played in the lagoon."

The question startled Jason. He'd expected the woman in his arms to ask him for the details of how he'd finally reached the Refuge, but this subject was a welcome diversion from the memories. "Like a fish. I'll teach you if you like." All angels could float, their wings buoyant. However, that buoyancy made athletic swimming, particularly deep dives, difficult. Jason's parents had taught him tricks to negate the effect, at least for short periods of time.

"I'd like that." Mahiya's smile thawed the ice that had formed in his chest as he spoke of the losses that had forever altered the course of his existence.

"There is," he said, tucking her a fraction closer, "as much freedom in the sea as in the sky if you know how to move in it." Alone and with no parents to become alarmed that he'd gone too far, he'd learned to streak through the deep, his wings slicked to his back.

Nivriti.

He released Mahiya at the whisper of wind, folding his wings to his back. "Come." Walking out and around the shadow-shrouded side of the temple, Mahiya silent as she followed, he looked toward the fort, searching for any sign of trouble.

He saw nothing . . . not until he swept his gaze to the right.

The night sky was a sheet of black, the glitter of the stars blotted out by an army of wings. Those wings appeared "wrong" to his vision until he realized they were pure jet. Since no living angel he knew of had wings akin to his own, that meant they had been dyed as camouflage. The vampiric ground guard had to be within minutes of the fort.

This is madness. Mahiya's horrified voice. *Even with this army, my mother cannot hope to take Neha on in combat.*

Jason couldn't disagree. Impressive as Nivriti's forces appeared, they weren't, not in comparison to the garrison that lived in the fort—which represented only a small percentage of the offensive resources at Neha's command. *You should not watch this.*

No . . . I should be a part of it. I may not know Nivriti, but she is my mother, and Neha has done nothing to win my loyalty.

Jason turned to pin her with his gaze. *You put yourself on that field, and you do nothing but distract your mother.*

Neha will use you, make Nivriti watch you bleed. You're too weak to be anything but a liability.

Mahiya flinched. *That was cruel.*

Cruelty is sometimes necessary.

You're strong, she retorted. *You could help my mother— but you're a coward, hiding here.*

He didn't allow her to see what the mental slap did to him. *The instant I step onto that battlefield, I draw Raphael and all his people into a war.* Thousands, millions would die in the aftermath.

Mahiya seemed to wilt, her eyes on the black wings on the horizon. *I'm sorry. I knew that . . . I shouldn't take my anger out on you. Forgive me, Jason.*

He could taste her heartbreak. *It is forgotten.*

Shifting to put her back to the wall, she slid down to sit against it, a desolation in her expression he'd never before seen, that stubborn, beautiful hope close to extinguished. *I've waited so long for her, and now she'll die.*

Jason turned his face toward the skies. *Stay here.* He rose up into the star-studded black before she could question him, blending into the night shadows with an ease that was instinctive. Then he shot straight at the approaching army, their slow, careful pace no match for his speed.

A cry went up only when he wanted to be seen. Raising a hand to halt crossbows being fired, a woman who was unquestionably kin to Neha cut away from the group to head to him. He felt her mental touch, chose not to acknowledge it.

Imperious and haughty, she stopped in front of him, fanning her unpainted wings to hold her position. "Spymaster."

This woman, he thought, might have given Mahiya the delicate angles of her face, the wild blue and green of her feathers, but she was nothing like the child she'd birthed, her eyes touched with a devouring rage. "You should speak to your daughter before you undertake this suicide mission."

Her eyes widened before laughter filled the air, husky

and soft. "Ah, such faith." A twist to her lips. "Lead me to her."

Jason was unsurprised both at her lack of worry about a possible ambush, and her complete disregard of his veiled warning to retreat. Love and hate both had a tendency to blind, to destroy reason. "She is not far."

Guardian Fort was alive with activity by the time he returned to the temple, and it took a combination of fine timing and luck to bring Nivriti down without being detected. Mahiya wasn't where he'd left her—she was standing on the steps to the temple, a crossbow in hand, the bolt notched and in position to fire.

He almost smiled. He knew the dangerous whip of anger in the tawny brightness was for him, for the way he'd left her, but it changed into shock as her gaze alighted on Nivriti.

The dull thud of the crossbow hitting the ground snapped Mahiya out of her stunned motionlessness. Bending reflexively, she picked it up without ever taking her eyes from the woman who walked toward her, dressed in what appeared to be fighting leathers of black, her wings the template from which Mahiya's had been cast.

"Daughter." A whisper-soft word, the woman's fingers alighting on her cheek as her expression overflowed with a depth of emotion that ripped at Mahiya's heart, her soul. "Forever beloved of my heart."

This time, Mahiya didn't worry about the crossbow when it dropped. Tears streaking down her face, she went into her mother's arms and let those arms hold her safe. It didn't matter at that moment that Nivriti was a monster, one who had torn out a man's internal organs and brutalized a woman for no reason but that it would hurt her twin. Nothing mattered but that for the first time in her life, she was being held with love.

40

Nivriti murmured to her, her voice a lilting melody. "She thought to torment me by telling me of how you suffered, but the affirmation my precious child lived was the greatest gift she could've given me."

Cupping Mahiya's face as she drew back, Nivriti pressed her lips to Mahiya's forehead. "I fought to stay alive and to stay sane, even as my wings rotted and my memories threatened to fragment, because of you. I *never forgot you*."

"Neither did I," Mahiya whispered, for no matter what she'd told herself over the centuries about her mother, whether good or bad, the one thing she had not done was forget. "You don't have to go to war with Neha."

Her mother's expression changed, all softness erased. "Yes, I do. Or she will never allow me peace—my dearest sister needs to see I have grown fangs." A smile Mahiya couldn't read. "It is strange what grows in the dark underground, even as other things rot." With that enigmatic statement, she snapped her head toward Jason. "I charged you to get her out of here."

Jason stood unmoved, a dark sentinel. "I serve neither you nor Neha."

Nivriti's response at that plainly worded statement of loyalty was not anger, but a laugh of pure delight. "I see why you are drawn to him," she said to Mahiya. "But remember, he is only a man and not to be trusted." Her eyes glittered hard as diamonds as she spread her wings. "I shall see you soon, daughter."

Mahiya stared up at the sky as her mother rose with flawless grace, her body showing no sign of her long captivity. "My mother has had years of freedom," she said at last. "Her wings would've taken at least a year to regenerate."

"Perhaps." Jason's tone held an unexpected note.

"What have you seen that I have not?" Blinded by emotion as she was, she knew she couldn't trust her own judgment. But Jason's? Always.

"Nivriti is too confident for an angel about to go into battle against one of the Cadre." He looked out over the fort, tracking Nivriti's army. "And she flies with too much strength and skill for someone who suffered centuries of imprisonment below the earth."

"How would the ones who saved her," Mahiya said slowly, "even have known where she was?" She didn't bother to keep her voice low—the noise at Guardian was overwhelming as troops filled the air.

"Not all loyalties are what they seem." Loose strands of Jason's hair blew back softly from his face in the cool night wind. "Were Nivriti smart, she would've seeded at least one of her people in Neha's inner court when that court first formed."

And even archangels, Mahiya thought, touching her fingers to his, could make mistakes of trust.

Jason's hand closed over hers. "Look."

Following his gaze, she saw an angel rise to hover directly above Archangel Fort. From the glow of lethal power that surrounded her form, it could only be Neha. Mahiya twisted her head to the right, hoping that her mother was protected in the mass of fighters, but no, she hovered at the forefront of her troops.

Neha began to fly toward Nivriti as she flew toward Neha, Neha's troops amassing above the fort. Those troops were an insult, a bare squadron. As the twins came to a halt above the city, Mahiya knew the populace below must be gazing upward in wonder and fear both. Because when an archangel glowed, people died.

Neha and Nivriti halted several feet apart, enough that their wings wouldn't touch and yet that they could talk. Mahiya would've given anything to be up there at this moment, to know what it was they said to one another. But whatever it was, it seemed as if her mother threw back her head and laughed before sketching a bow so insincere, Mahiya could sense it from this distance.

Neha's glow intensified . . . and Nivriti dropped the arm she'd raised above her head. Her troops swarmed toward the fort as Neha's own forces flowed to meet them. Both groups avoided the two women in the center of the chaos. Neha and Nivriti continued to hover in front of one another, as steel clashed and crossbow bolts ripped through wings, locked in a battle of wills Mahiya couldn't comprehend. *To kill not only your sister, but your twin . . . I cannot imagine it, Jason.*

They are fools. A harsh summation. *They do not comprehend that what they were given was a gift not to be squandered.*

Understanding sang a nocturne, melancholy and haunting, through her bones. Neha and Nivriti had been born as two halves of a whole. Had they remained locked together in friendship and loyalty as the centuries passed, Neha would have been an archangel with the most trusted of allies beside her. And Nivriti would've been the second to an archangel, the strongest of positions if one was not Cadre. More, they would've both had someone they could trust to tell the truth, no matter the question. Such a trust might well have saved them making the mistakes they had, given them a happier life.

But they had wasted that gift, allowed pride and conceit to tear them apart, until Neha was a woman without consort or child, and about to kill the sister of her blood. Meanwhile, Nivriti was a woman so consumed with rage that she'd rather chance never again seeing her child, than walk away from her quest for vengeance.

The glow around Neha turned white-hot.

"Angelfire," she whispered, naming the deadly force that could kill even an archangel.

Jason shook his head. "Neha cannot create angelfire, but what she can create is just as deadly to the others in the Cadre." Even as he spoke, a whip of green snapped out from Neha's hand, a vicious thing as fast as the serpents that came so easily to the archangel's hand.

Nivriti shut her wings and dropped at almost the same instant the snap left Neha's hand, a move of such speed that Mahiya couldn't follow it with the eye. "What was that?" She wasn't sure if she was asking about Neha or Nivriti.

"The Cadre calls it the poison whip," Jason responded. "A single brush against skin and it releases a deadly toxin into the bloodstream. As with angelfire, an archangel could beat a certain number of glancing blows, but an ordinary angel would die in seconds. A full strike with the whip to the heart or the head equals total death for even the archangels." Jason's eyes tracked the two women as Neha hit out with the whip and Nivriti dodged, her speed unnatural. "Did your mother also have power over snakes?"

"No, birds." Her fingers spasmed on his as the poison whip came within what looked like a hairsbreadth of Nivriti's face.

Suddenly the sky was full of fire. Their wings crisped, angels screamed and fell, crashing onto city roofs. Jason knew that while their bodies might be broken and burned, the majority would survive. So long as the head remained attached to the body and the flames were extinguished before they reached the internal organs, the charred, blackened remains would continue to breathe, continue to suffer.

"Neha's new ability," Mahiya whispered.

The fire winked out as quickly as it had exploded across the sky, but Nivriti's troops had been decimated, though Nivriti herself had been fast enough to avoid the cauldron of flame. Now, she did something with *her* hands and a web of acidic green identical to Neha's poison whip snapped out to wrap around the archangel, wings and all.

Neha fell.

Right when it appeared she'd crash onto the burning city below, she snapped the bonds, halted her descent, but Nivriti did not relent, continuing to entangle her in that clinging green web. It seemed to Mahiya that she heard Neha scream in rage as the archangel broke the bonds again and again before releasing the poison whip once more.

Nivriti dodged, wasn't fast enough this time, and the poison touched the edge of one wing. However, contrary to the known impact of the poison on ordinary angels, she didn't sicken and fall. Instead, she shot higher into the sky.

Neha followed, her wings ablaze with power, her hands wreathed in green. Nivriti turned, dropped a net of green filaments that wrapped around Neha, encasing her entire form. The archangel struggled, a fly caught in a web, and again she fell, but this time, the green turned white and cracked off her in pieces brittle as glass.

Ice.

The second aspect of Neha's new abilities—but like the fire, it appeared limited, for the archangel did not attempt to freeze her opponent out of the sky.

"Jason." Mahiya leaned into him, his wing sliding protectively over her own. "My mother should be dead, shouldn't she?"

"Yes."

Yet Nivriti continued to evade Neha.

A moment later, she did more than that. She threw the sticky web at Neha once more. Clearly confident she could neutralize it, Neha made no effort to dodge the net. But this time, the green strands blazed incandescent, and the archangel's scream was of such agony that every fighter in the sky froze in place.

Mahiya reached out a hand, to whom she didn't know. It just seemed terribly wrong that they should kill one another. Because Neha, flames licking around her body, had broken the trap at the last second—and Mahiya's mother was close enough that she couldn't avoid the strike of the poison whip.

It wasn't a direct hit, but it did damage.

Mahiya stifled her cry of loss, but Neha didn't follow the strike with a deadly second hit, her flight path erratic. "She's badly injured." Impossible—Neha was an archangel. And yet . . .

Fire licked the sky again, fell onto the city to set more of it alight. The sticky green threads her mother flung out in return, one of her wings dragging, missed Neha to alight on that same city. Screams rose up from the ground, eerie and anguished, the city beginning to glow orange as the flames took hold.

Mahiya's blood filled with horror, a ravaging need to do *something* gripping her throat, images of the toymaker's innocent son circling in her mind. Right when she would've spoken, Jason spread his wings. "I must stop this."

"Yes." Between them, Neha and Nivriti would devastate the city and keep going, both too angry and enraged to give up, though it was clear they were injured enough that it might yet be lethal. Ignoring the hows and whys of how her mother could've harmed an archangel, she squeezed Jason's hand. "*We* need to stop this. For now, these are my people and I will not let them burn."

She'd readied herself to fight, but Jason touched her jaw in a fleeting, unexpected caress before giving a curt nod. "Neha's side is in as bad a position as your mother's. Seeing her hurt demoralized them."

"I have value as a hostage again." Mahiya nodded. "I'll stick close to you." It bloodied her to think of Jason hurting in order to protect her, but as he understood her need to do this, she understood he was a man who would never allow his woman to go into danger unaccompanied and unshielded.

Mahiya?

That tenderness again, something she never heard in his physical voice.

Yes?

Do not get hurt.

It was an order, followed by a hard kiss that left her breathless. Intending to pull her weight, Mahiya picked up the crossbow she'd dropped, along with a case of ten spare bolts she hung over her arm. She'd purloined an old crossbow from the guard several decades ago, on the rationale that unlike swordplay or hand-to-hand combat, it was something she could teach herself.

In the intervening years, she'd had to steal replacements, but her plan had worked. She'd managed to sneak in target practice in the mountains at least twice a month until her last crossbow broke five weeks ago. *I'm no expert,* she said to Jason, *but I usually hit my target.*

Good. I'll need you to watch my back.

With that unexpected statement, he led her on a low flight path over the blistering heat of the city, until they were positioned between Neha and Nivriti. She'd assumed he'd fly up to where they fought, somehow attempt to stop the battle, but he drew his sword, pointed it *downward*. A second later, black lightning crackled along his arms and over the hands he had fisted around the hilt of the sword, and she realized he was shoving his midnight power down through the conduit of the blade.

A trickle of sweat poured down his face, his biceps rigid . . . and shadows began to coalesce throughout the city, thick and heavy, snuffing out flame, stopping agony. People screamed at the river of soft black until they saw it sheath burning victims, smother the flames before moving on. Then they tried to direct it to their own homes and shops, but the shadows were driven by the mind of an angel whose body contained a level of power that stunned, and they went where they were most needed.

To people. To animals. To buildings in which living beings were trapped.

When an openly aggressive fighter arrowed toward Jason, she didn't hesitate or bother to wonder to which army he belonged. Lifting the crossbow, she put a bolt through his wing, sending him into an uncontrolled spiral that ended with him crashing into a burned-out roof. Mahiya winced but notched a second bolt into the bow, and when the next aggressor headed their way, she took aim and fired.

Maybe she was no fighter, but she *would not* permit anyone to hurt Jason.

She'd just dispatched the second angel before he could fire his own crossbow, when Jason shuddered and raised his sword. "The worst fires are out," he said, his voice a rasp.

Wonder at his strength, the way he'd used it to save, not harm, had her throat thick with emotion. "You've given them a fighting chance." She could see fire trucks pouring water over the buildings that continued to burn, people racing to the lake to create a chain of buckets.

Jason's face was drawn as he turned to her. "Keep shooting at anyone who comes at you, and wait for my signal." With that, he flew straight upward to hover between the two warring women.

Trusting his skills as a warrior, she didn't argue. *Please be careful.* A single strike from either the poison whip or her mother's acid green web, and he'd crash to his death, but he didn't so much as flinch when the twins hit out at one another, the strikes passing inches from the edges of his wings. As Nivriti recovered to throw another strike at Neha, only for it to veer toward Jason when her arm faltered, he deflected it with a ribbon of black flame that seemed an extension of his sword.

Now, princess, he said and her title sounded like an endearment. *They've exhausted their energy for the time being.*

41

Mahiya pumped her wings upward, making certain to keep to her mother's side of the battle line, so as not to provide Neha with an easy target. Jason gave her an almost imperceptible nod when she reached him, and she knew he was relinquishing the reins, an acknowledgment that she knew the players far better than he did.

"You are destroying the city," she said to Neha. "You are killing your own people."

Wings continuing to glow, Neha looked down, frowned, and waved a hand. A thin layer of ice formed over the places where the noxious green of Nivriti's web had begun to bubble through roofs and walls . . . and people. It froze, then seemed to break off in inert pieces. Neha waved her hand again, but the fires Jason hadn't smothered continued to burn, the archangel's ability to create ice apparently exhausted.

It wasn't only fatigue that marked both women.

Neha's wings and body bore raw wounds from the same acid, her cheek gouged on one side to reveal her jawbone, her left wing sporting a palm-sized hole that would've crippled most angels. Meanwhile, blood of near black seeped from Nivriti's nose and ears, even the corners of her eyes, the poison in her bloodstream attacking her from the inside out.

"Your forces are decimated," she said to her own mother, wanting Nivriti to turn around, to see how many of her people were dead or viciously injured. "And you are fading."

Nivriti swept out a hand, the burst blood vessels in her eyes having turned her gaze crimson. "Get out of the way, child."

"I am not the child here." Mahiya held her position, speaking to them both. "You are at a stalemate, and soon, you'll be wrestling each other on the ground with the mortals watching as they would a circus act."

Frozen silence from both Neha and Nivriti.

Then her mother started to laugh, and it was awash with near-manic delight. "That would certainly not do for your vaunted dignity, sister dearest."

"It would suit you very well" was Neha's cutting response, grooves of pain bracketing her mouth as one of the minor tendons in her left wing appeared to give way. "You have ever wanted to perform."

Nivriti shrugged, wiped her bloody nose on her sleeve. "At least I did not believe a great act for truth and take a man who did not love me as my consort."

"No, you only bore his child and stayed faithful while he rutted like a tomcat."

Mahiya had the strangest feeling of being caught in the middle of a sibling squabble. Except this squabble had already cost hundreds, perhaps thousands of lives. "My father," she said with a deliberation designed to offset their emotion-fueled dialogue, "was a man beautiful enough to enchant a heart of stone, but he was not strong, was not worthy of either one of you."

"My daughter speaks the truth." A great bitterness in Nivriti's expression, an ugly thing that could eat a person up from the inside out. "I did you a favor, sister. He was lifting the skirts of one of his no doubt many whores inside your fort when I came to rescue him. So I returned with a few gifts."

Neha hissed and snapped out the poison whip, but weakened as she was, it didn't go far. "It was not your place to render judgment."

"You dare say that?" Nivriti attempted to spray her with the acid, failed. "After you played judge and jury?"

Jason, you must speak. They won't listen to me, no matter how much sense I make. The fact was, they dismissed her as a child. *Their pride is the weakest point for both.*

Jason stirred. "If you wish to duel to the death," he said in a quiet, steely voice that demanded attention, "we will get out of the way, but in your current condition, you *will* end up wrestling on the ground, amusement for the mortals. I am certain no archangel or angel has died so ignominious a death."

Silence.

Then Nivriti raised an arm and the remainder of her troops formed around her, even as Neha's own troops stood down. The archangel's lips twisted into a cold smile. "Run while you can, little sister. I'll make sure we meet again."

Nivriti's responding smile was as dark as the blood dripping from her eyes. "Be assured I'll be waiting." With that, she swept around, her troops closing behind her in a black guard. *Mahiya.*

Mahiya started at the command from her mother, but that shock was nothing to when she heard Jason's voice in her mind. *Go with her. It is the safest place for you.*

She wanted to argue, wanted to shake him, tell him her place was by his side, but he was already turning toward Neha. Far more, she realized, was in play than the needs and desires of a princess who had never had a kingdom to rule or a man to love, until she gave her heart to an enemy spymaster with wings of midnight.

Even so, he could've taken an instant to reassure her that he would find her.

Agony wrenched through her at the sight of him getting

further away with each wingbeat. Biting her lips, she stilled
the urge to call out after him. She'd already laid her heart
at his feet—she would not beg. Because while she didn't
expect Jason, his scars soul deep, to love her as she loved
him, she understood he must choose to be with her free of
any other consideration.

It wasn't enough, would never be enough, if all he felt
was a responsibility to watch over her because she had no one
else. Now that the latter was no longer true . . . Swallowing,
she reached out one last time with her mind and set him
free. *Take care of yourself, Jason.*

Her mother's squadron parted to allow her into the center,
closing behind her to form an impenetrable wall.

Jason forced himself not to turn and watch after Mahiya.
He knew that at this moment, he was the known, the familiar. If he asked her to come with him, she would. Once she'd
spent time with Nivriti, however. . . .

No, he would not steal the familial relationship she had
the chance to forge, not even if it caused an agonizing hol-
lowness inside him to lose the mental connection with her
as she flew out of range, protected by her mother's people.
He would give her time and space enough to decide if she
wished to walk beside him now that her life had a whole
new dimension.

Having flown escort to Neha while Rhys made certain
of Nivriti's retreat, he kept an eye on the archangel's damaged wing as she brought herself in to land in front of the
Palace of Jewels. When she dipped to the side as she came
in, he deliberately landed too close to her, so that her stumble
would be blamed on his clumsiness rather than taken as a
sign of weakness by the others landing around them.

Pride, as Mahiya had said, was an integral component of
Neha's nature.

Righting herself by pushing off his body, she ignored him
as she entered her private apartments, but he knew that to leave
now would be to undo any good he'd done. So he walked out

to the courtyard to help deal with the injured—just because angels and vampires were hard to kill didn't mean they didn't hurt. A man who knew how to inject morphine and other pain relief medication was always useful in battle conditions.

When Neha's private guard summoned him two hours later, the courtyard was close to cleared, the injured moved into internal rooms. Taking his leave of the healer under whom he'd been working, he entered the palace to find Neha seated on the thronelike chair at the head of the central room. The archangel had bathed and was dressed in fresh clothing, her wounds bandaged.

Those bandages told him both that the wounds were healing at a far slower rate than they should—and that Nivriti was no longer an ordinary angel.

"So, now you are a peacemaker?" Neha's tone was dangerously neutral.

"You are one of the more rational archangels," he said, and in spite of her acts after Anoushka's death, the words were true. "To lose you would create more problems than it would solve."

"Exactly how rational do you believe me to be?" A subtly calculated look.

"Enough to take and use what Lijuan could teach you about accelerating the emergence of your new abilities," he said, "without allowing yourself to fall into her web." It was a wild shot in the dark.

"Finally," Neha said in a sinuous whisper, "we come to it. That was why you were so eager to assist me, was it not?"

"I am a spymaster."

Neha's smile was cold. "And to ask you to act in any other way would be akin to asking an eagle not to eat a rabbit." Picking up a baby eyelash viper that had slithered across the floor to her, she draped it over her shoulders, absently stroking its yellow orange skin. "Yes, Lijuan has been most neighborly of late."

Jason could guess. The trauma of Anoushka's death had left Neha prime pickings for a predator like Lijuan. "I have wondered one thing," he said.

Neha raised an eyebrow.

"Whether Lijuan can somehow siphon power, or is attempting to learn how to do so, from others in the Cadre." It was a theory so nascent, he hadn't even mentioned to Raphael. "Her offer to assist you would then make more sense."

"Well, well, well." Neha rose and walked down the shallow steps below her throne to shake her head. "Such a waste that you will never rule. Yes, the helpful Lijuan thought to play me." A flash of teeth. "But she forgets, I have played this game for millennia, too, and I know how to get what I want."

Jason was near certain there was, in truth, no true secret to accelerating the development of power, that Lijuan had simply taken advantage of the Cascade effect. At least nine thousand years of age, she'd had millennia to mine the Refuge library for such secrets, even had she not come into her power at a time when several Ancients yet sat on the Cadre. They could well have told her of the Cascade.

Such a plan would befit the Archangel of China's intelligent, devious mind, but to bring it up now would be to make Neha look the fool, so he kept his silence and considered his report to Raphael. Though he couldn't speak of the Lijuan–Neha connection, he could now discuss Neha's new abilities—her display over the city had made them public.

"If you wish to keep my favor, Jason," Neha said, sari whispering along the carpet as she walked to the window that looked out over the courtyard garden, "you will discover how Nivriti was able to do what she did, and then you will tell me."

"I do that and I become part of your personal war. Raphael would not be pleased."

"Do you always do what pleases Raphael?"

Jason knew the arch question was meant to prick his pride, but the fact was, he served Raphael out of choice, not compulsion. "I will leave your territory tonight," he said, his tone even.

Neha's wings flared, the indigo filaments catching the

light, before folding neatly to her back as she turned to hold his gaze. "Tell me, when did you gain the ability to use shadows in such a fashion?"

He said nothing, for she could expect no answer. The truth was, what he'd done tonight was only one aspect of his strength—he could use the black lightning in a far more violent way. "Do you wish me to carry a message to Raphael?"

A sigh, a faint smile. "Tell him his spymaster's faultless service has made me rethink our quarrel. I say Raphael is no longer my enemy." She allowed the viper to crawl down her arm, twine itself over her skin. "Safe journey, Jason. I will attempt not to hurt Mahiya too badly when I find her."

"I will attempt not to hurt Mahiya too badly when I find her."
Jason understood Neha's words had been meant to torment him. It wasn't the first time someone had attempted such, but it was the first time they had found their mark. No matter his decision to give Mahiya time with her mother, he knew that was not what he was going to do, even if part of him said he used Neha's taunt as an excuse.

Flying high and fast, he made certain no one tracked him from the fort. Only when he was dead sure he was alone in the skies, did he come down on the dawn-lit grasses of a jagged mountaintop, the biting winds attempting to rip his hair from its tie. Ignoring the chill whip of air, he took out his cell phone and put through a call to Raphael.

Raphael was quicker than Neha, perhaps because he'd been directly impacted by the events of that spring. "The world was in tumult when Caliane rose to wakefulness," he said the instant he heard of Nivriti's ability to harm Neha. "The chaos was put down to the disruption caused by her waking, but what if it was the confluence of two events, the reappearance of an Ancient concealing the emergence of an archangel?"

"I thought the same," Jason said, recalling the violent storms that had hit the world, the sea rising in a fury, the plates of the earth shifting, ice falling when it should've long thawed, "but I didn't sense the same depth of power in Nivriti that I do the Cadre." The prickling consciousness of being in the presence of something *other*.

"And Neha would've known if her sister had become Cadre," Raphael said. "One archangel always recognizes another—but from what you say, it appears she is in the dark about the origin of Nivriti's abilities."

"Yes. It could be that as Neha's twin, Nivriti has a capacity to harm her that no other angel possesses—along with a certain resistance to Neha's own abilities." Twins were beyond rare in the angelic population, and Neha was the first archangel he knew of who had been born with another. "We have no guideline against which to judge the bond that ties them to one another."

A short pause. "Should Nivriti believe herself Cadre, she'll seek to join our number soon enough," Raphael said thoughtfully. "Unlike Neha, the rest of us are not disadvantaged by a blood connection—it'll take but a single meeting to answer the question of her strength. For now, continue to have your people keep a watch on her, on them both."

"Sire." Ending the call, Jason turned his ear to the wind, listening for the fading echoes of a retreating army . . . and the shimmering, stubborn hope of a princess whose presence he missed tucked against his mind.

42

Mahiya didn't know what she'd expected of her mother's base, but it wasn't a fortified palace complex hidden in a mountain valley a bare four hours away on the wing. However, it made perfect sense—Nivriti couldn't have covertly flown a fleet in the dark over a much longer distance. The vampiric ground troops, their journey longer, had traveled to the city in vehicles that wouldn't stand out on the roads and now retreated in the same fashion.

They brought with them the dead and the less critical of Nivriti's injured, Rhys and Nivriti's senior general having negotiated a short window in which the fallen could be retrieved. While Nivriti was constrained to depart the city immediately, she'd sent half her angelic battalion to the ground—supervised by Rhys's men—to rescue and carry home the worst injured, vampires and angels both. That unit was approximately two hours behind them, the ground vehicles almost half a day.

This complex, Nivriti told Mahiya after they landed in the predawn dark under the watchful eye of the small squadron she'd left to stand guard, had once been hers—and was now again. "Neha allowed it to fall into ruin." A pleased statement. "The surrounding village dried up without the palace's custom, and so the area is a barren, forested wasteland."

"A perfect place to hide an army." Entering the palace, Mahiya took in the ancient tapestries, as well as the paintings that had been created using the walls themselves as a canvas—of elephants and horses ridden by sword-wielding vampiric warriors, and angelic maidens shy of smile but with weapons in their hands.

The once brilliant colors were now pale ghosts, the jewels worn by warriors and maidens both dull rocks. It was clear the tapestries and the carpets that covered the stone floor were as old as the paintings, but the surviving pieces had had the dust beaten out of them to reveal works of faded splendor. The walls and floors of the palace itself had also been scrubbed until the beauty of the building, full of intricate carvings and lacework windows, made further adornment an indulgence not a necessity.

"Neha's greatest weakness has always been arrogance," Nivriti said after pouring a glass of water from a nearby pitcher, drinking it down. "She has never believed I could be her equal, and so she left no guards on me or on the places that have always been, and will always be, mine." Words as hard as the stone of her stronghold. "Now she has learned better."

An angel, his left wing dragging as a result of a burn across its upper half, walked in then. "My lady," he said. "I am sorry to interrupt, but we must talk about our defensive plans with so many injured."

Nodding at the male, Nivriti waved Mahiya away. "Go find a place to rest, child." Her eyes dropped to the crossbow still in Mahiya's hand. "You will not need that here, but I'm glad my daughter is not a useless ornament." With that, she was gone.

Mahiya took the chance to explore the palace. What she found was that it was as close to an impregnable fortress as you could get and still be a place that was clearly home for

Nivriti and her people. High perimeter walls, but soft rugs on the floor. Weapons everywhere she looked, but a kitchen that permeated the rooms with mouthwatering smells.

When she made her way to a balcony at the back of the palace, she saw both a working well and healthy fruit and vegetable gardens *inside* the defensive walls. Though the skies were still gray, a vampire had already begun to work the gardens, and he told her the water in the well was sourced from an underground reservoir. "No way for anyone to poison it."

Such precautions wouldn't protect the stronghold against aerial attack, but the mountains around the valley were set up with ground-to-air weaponry Mahiya guessed had been hidden until the assault on Neha, and there was only one road leading in. It was a place meant to hold under a siege, she thought as she walked back inside the palace.

Though no one appeared to be paying attention to her, guards came out of nowhere to redirect her path when she tried to go down a particular corridor. They also took her crossbow, saying they'd get it cleaned for her.

Using her best princess smile, she said, "Of course," and left without argument.

It took an hour of watching and waiting, but the lingering guards were eventually called away on another task, and it took her but ten seconds to make it to the doors and through. The rooms beyond were locked with old-fashioned bolts and padlocks, bars on the small windows cut into the doors.

A sudden chill in her bones, she looked into the first window.

A bloodsoaked and unconscious angel lay within, his wings pinned to the floor by bolts pounded through the feathers, tendons, and muscle. Horror a crushing weight on her chest, she forced herself to walk to the next cell—to find a vampire hanging from his wrists by thick chains, beaten and bloodied, his head slumped forward on his chest. She recognized them both from Archangel Fort. Neither was powerful enough to be immediately missed, but both were old enough to have knowledge of the inner workings of the fort.

"Mahiya."

Having heard the tread of Nivriti's boots, she didn't startle. "You broke these people."

"Neha would do the same to mine." Ice, rigid and brutal. "She did far worse to me."

It was at that instant that Mahiya admitted the thought she'd nurtured in a secret corner of her heart—that the murders of Eris and Audrey, Shabnam and Arav, had been an aberration, that her mother did not harbor the ugliness of cruelty in her bones. "Will you release them now?"

"No." Nivriti reached through the bars to wrap that sticky green web around the vampire's throat.

"Mother, stop." She gripped Nivriti's hand, pulled, but it was too late, the substance already on the prisoner.

As Mahiya watched horrified, his skin and muscle and bone dissolved into bubbling white until the body fell away from the neck. The only mercy was that the male never gained consciousness. "That's . . ."

"More merciful than what Neha would've done to him had he crawled home."

"Your power was to do with birds." It was the plea of a child desperate to save something of her dream of her mother. "With living things." Not this sadistic death.

The smile that touched Nivriti's eyes was tinged acidic green. "The ability died," she said flatly. "But buried in the earth, I found comfort in other creatures." She shifted to the cell that housed the angel. "They sacrificed their lives when I needed sustenance, and shared their strength with me."

"No! Please!" Again, Mahiya attempted to halt Nivriti as her mother—almost desultorily—flicked the deadly green web onto the angel.

But her mother was over three thousand years old, her power vast even in the aftermath of battle. It was an unequal contest, one Mahiya could not win. Trembling, she forced herself to watch, to *remember* this death, as the angel dissolved into nothing. He and the vampire both deserved epitaphs, both deserved not to be simply erased out of existence.

Sighing, Nivriti went to touch Mahiya, shook her head when Mahiya stumbled back. "How did you stay so soft under my sister's loving hand, hmm?"

Because I didn't want to end up like her . . . like you. Her heart broke again, as she realized that some childhood dreams had no hope of ever coming true.

"Never mind. I am here to take care of you now." Nivriti looked over her shoulder. "Escort my daughter to her room. She should rest."

Mahiya allowed herself to be shown to the clean and, by the standards of the palace, luxurious room. It was clear she was being given honor as Nivriti's child.

"I am here to take care of you now."

Sitting down on the four-poster bed, grief a knot in her throat, she wrapped her fingers around one of the carved wooden posts that had been polished until they shone, and then she thought. About who she was, what she wanted to do with the immortal existence that stretched endlessly in front of her.

Regardless of what Nivriti believed, she was no child. She had fought for her freedom from an archangel. Jason had helped her achieve that freedom, and perhaps she wouldn't ever have gained it on her own, but even faced with seemingly insurmountable odds, even after a lifetime with an archangel who wanted to crush her spirit, she'd refused to surrender. And with her spymaster, too, she was the one who'd driven a bargain when she held but a single fragile card.

"You need to give me something in return. I can't surrender the most valuable piece of information I have without gaining something equally valuable in return."

She'd spoken those words, demanded he treat her need for freedom with respect.

But now, once again, she found herself in a prison. There were no locks, no ill will from Nivriti, but her mother had made it patent she saw Mahiya as a babe. Someone who'd be kept safe in this palace, have her wings clipped, and be shut away or ordered into silence when it came time for the adults to talk. Protected from the harsh realities of life.

"Escort my daughter to her room."

Already, Mahiya could feel an oppressive sense of suffocation constricting her rib cage. "It is too late, Mother," she whispered, and it was a decision she'd needed to make before she could carry on with her life. "I have not been a babe for a long time."

Sadness tore through her veins at all they had lost, the time they could never reclaim. But there was also a sweet, sweet relief, the leaden guilt in her stomach at the thought of abandoning Nivriti leavened by the knowledge that to build a relationship with her mother, she'd have to leave her. It was the only way to force Nivriti to see her as a woman grown. A woman who loved a spymaster with wings of black.

Had Jason known? That had she flown away from Nivriti on the battlefield, she'd have forever wondered what her life might've been like with her mother? That her guilt at deserting a woman who had survived a nightmare, and who looked at Mahiya with love in her eyes, would've been a constant pain in her chest?

Her lips curved, because of course he had—Jason thought four steps ahead. Hope bloomed, but fingers tightening on the post, she forced herself to be rational, to remember he'd parted from her without any indication he intended to find her again. Even if he did, he couldn't guess that she'd have come to her decision, be ready to leave only hours after arrival. Loyal as he was to Raphael, he'd most probably already left the subcontinent to make his report.

Which meant Mahiya was on her own.

Drawing in a deep breath, she stood and took stock of herself. She was a little tired from the flight to the palace, but not exhausted, as the army had moved at a slower pace to accommodate their injured brethren. Nevertheless, it would be smart to rest, regain her full strength—except that she wanted to leave now.

Even the most loving restraints were still chains that sought to hobble her.

Departing now did give her one small advantage—the secondary angelic unit, with their injured cargo, had arrived as she was being escorted to her room. Her offer of help had been declined, and from their condescending smiles, she was fairly certain it was because the guards thought she'd faint when she saw the damage, never realizing the things she'd witnessed in Neha's court.

Everyone else who could be spared was tending to the wounded, the palace's defenses the thinnest they would ever be. It was her best chance to slip away—because the fact was, she didn't think her mother would simply let her go. Not when Nivriti believed her a child unable to care for herself. Mahiya's eyes burned, and she wondered if her mother's blindness was willful, if she tried to find the babe who had been stolen from her so very long ago.

Swallowing the wave of raw emotion, Mahiya pushed aside the curtains on the balcony doors, saw that the early morning sunlight was crystalline. She'd be spotlighted against the blue sky . . . but no one had forbidden her from taking flight. Decision made, she walked into the bathroom and washed her face, tidied her hair into a tight braid, then opened the balcony doors and stepped out.

There were any number of angels outside, and one flew toward her at once, his wings a dyed black that told her he'd been part of the assault. "Princess," he said with the curt courtesy of someone who had far more important things on his plate. "How can I serve you?"

"I'd just like to stretch my wings a little before I rest." Widening her eyes, she gave him a hesitant smile. "I assume it's safe to fly in the area above and around the palace?"

As she'd wanted, he focused on the second question and didn't bother to wonder why she'd want to stretch her wings after four hours of flight. "As safe as we can make it." Frowning, he directed a trio of angels with a complex set of hand signals. "However, I'm certain Lady Nivriti would prefer you remain safely in your quarters."

He was a general of some kind, she thought. There was too much authority in his tone for an underling. Instead of obeying as he clearly expected, she straightened her spine and said, "Are *you* ordering *me* to remain in my rooms?"

channeling the dead Anoushka at her spoiled best. "Perhaps you'd like to put me on a leash and lead me around like a pet, too?"

Weariness washed across the general's face, and she had to fight to keep from wincing in sympathy—she wouldn't like to be dealing with this version of herself, either, especially after a battle that had cost him so many of his people. But if she didn't get out now, she could be stuck in this painful purgatory for weeks, even months, smothered by a maternal love blind to the truth of the life Mahiya had survived.

"Please wait," he said, not giving ground in the face of her outrage—which meant he wasn't a general, but probably *the* general. "I will find you an escort." Turning, he flew off to the left.

Well, that was stupid.

Snorting at his assumption that she'd stay where she was put, she stepped off the railingless balcony, swept over the courtyard, and instead of spiraling out in wide circles, went straight up as she'd seen Jason do so many times. If she could get above the fine layer of white cloud before anyone noticed what she was doing, she could confuse and maybe distract any pursuers long enough to get away.

That pursuit came far sooner than she'd expected, a brusque voice ordering her to descend. Older and stronger as he was, she knew the general would catch her in seconds, but she grit her teeth and continued to beat her wings upward, shoulder and back muscles straining until her tendons felt as if they might snap. Let him think her a spoiled brat—it would plant the wrong idea in his mind, perhaps give her another chance later on—

A sweep of black in front of her. *Jason!* She was so startled, she shot past him.

"Ready to leave?" he asked when he came up to join her—as if she had gone for an afternoon visit somewhere. *Are you all right, princess?*

She almost burst into tears at the piercing tenderness of his mental question. "Yes and yes," she said with a shaky smile, wondering if she would ever understand this man she adored. "But I'm afraid I have acquired a problem."

"I see that." *Can you hold the hover?*

Yes. Her body protested the abuse, but she'd handled worse.

Situating himself beside her rather than in front, Jason reached back and withdrew his sword, holding it casually at his side as the general reached them. The angel's eyes snapped from Jason to Mahiya, to the quiet threat of Jason's black sword, and he seemed to decide silence was the best policy. So they all looked politely at one another until her mother winged up to face her.

"Mahiya"—a whip of anger directed at an errant offspring—"I expect my child by my side."

"Mother," Mahiya said with utmost gentleness, not wishing to hurt Nivriti, but knowing she had to force her mother to see the truth if they were to ever build a relationship, "I haven't been a child for centuries. I was never truly allowed to be one. You know that."

In spite of the gentleness, Nivriti flinched. "I will kill her for what she did."

Mahiya held up a hand. "No. Do not think to use me as an excuse in your war with Neha. I want no part of it." Heart twisting, she held that gaze so familiar and so alien. "Three hundred and seven years," she said in a whisper that held a lifetime of lost dreams and shattering pain. "That's how long I survived—I do not want to survive any longer, Mother. I want to fly."

A moment of utter silence before Nivriti's eyes slammed into Jason's. "If you do not care for her, spymaster, I will hunt you to the ends of the earth." With that violent threat, she and her general dropped back down to the palace.

Sliding away the sword, Jason turned to her. *She truly does love you in her own way.*

Enough to set me free.

43

Four days after he'd put her in it, Dmitri brought Honor partway out of her drugged sleep. "Dmitri." It was a sluggish question as he cradled her in his lap, but he heard the panic.

"You're safe," he said. "It's time for the first blood kiss. Do you remember?" He'd told her every step of the process, so she wouldn't be afraid when she woke without full control of her faculties, his Honor who had once been held prisoner by monsters.

Her fingers curled into his chest, fear a slick sheen on her face. "I can't move."

"Honor, baby, I can't bring you fully out." She was ripping him apart. "*Please* remember." He nuzzled and kissed the woman who made eternity worth living, holding her as tight as he dared, for her skin would be sensitive now, easier to bruise. "I would never do anything to hurt you."

A sigh against his neck, the panic subsiding, though her voice remained thick with the drugs. "I love you."

Relieved until he could barely breathe, he allowed himself three precious minutes with her before he used one of his fangs to puncture his wrist and hold it up to her mouth.

"I know it doesn't taste good now"—wouldn't until the transformation had had longer to take hold in her body—"but you only have to take a few drops."

Honor wrinkled her nose but didn't fight.

"Very not sexy," she muttered afterward and made him laugh, the tension leaching out of his body.

"Trust me, it gets sexier." Kissing her, he forced himself to lay her back down. "Ready?"

"I want it done." She cuddled into his body. "Want to be with you."

He reached down to reactivate the drug that would take her under once more. "I'll be here, waiting for you when you wake again." He'd waited near to a thousand years— nothing would induce him to move from her side. "Sleep. I'll keep you safe."

44

Mahiya sat on the roof of the Angel Enclave house that was home to the Archangel Raphael and his consort, scarcely believing it had been but a week since she left her mother's palace. The city of shining metal and sparkling glass she could see across the water fascinated her, almost as much as the angel with hair of near-white who swept toward the roof.

Elena landed beside Mahiya with an open joy that made her smile. "Ten points for certain," she said, having played this game with the other woman earlier in the week

"You're being nice. I had to take an extra step to balance the landing."

"Nine point three, then."

"That, I'll take, even though you're still being nice." Folding those haunting wings of midnight and dawn, Elena took a seat. "Are you waiting for Jason?"

"He's inside, talking to Raphael." Having grown up around an archangel, Mahiya wasn't affected by them as another angel of her age might be, but she never forgot that they were *other* and thus to be treated with caution. "I came to admire your city so busy and bright, and to listen to the water." The river rushed past just beyond the cliff, and not far in the distance, she could see two water vessels about to pass.

Drawing up one knee, Elena hooked her arm around it. "Will you stay?"

Mahiya had considered that, ruled it out—New York was dazzling, a beautiful city, but with jagged edges that overwhelmed. "I think I would like to visit." Taste it in small bites. "But this is not my place."

Elena nodded. "She's not for everyone, my city, but I adore her." Undoing a lightweight crossbow from her outer left thigh, she placed it beside her on the roof.

"Were you on a hunt?" It astonished Mahiya that the consort to an archangel did such a thing, but it also astonished her how Raphael looked at Elena and how Elena looked at the archangel in return. The searing depth of their connection was something she'd never expected, no matter what she had heard of their bonding.

"No, I was running a training session at Guild Academy. My turn on the roster." She lifted her face to the wind, and they sat in companionable silence for almost ten minutes before Elena shifted to look at her. "Jason," she said in a quiet voice, "you will look after him, won't you?"

Startled, Mahiya said, "He isn't a man who needs anyone's protection."

"But," Elena said, eyes of silver-gray incisive, "I think he needs you."

Yes. The question was, would Jason allow her to give him what he needed, or would he shy, as a wild creature might? It wasn't the best of analogies, for Jason knew the ways of sophistication and civilization as well as any court male. Yet, he was not *of* them, part of him still that boy alone in the middle of an ocean. "I feel such things for him," she whispered, "that it terrifies me."

"Good," Elena said with a shoulder nudge. "You'd never fit in our club otherwise."

She blinked at the startling statement. "What?"

"It's for those of us who are insane enough to fall in love with seriously badass men more sensible women would run from screaming. You've now superseded Honor as the newest member." Elena grinned. "I'll teach you the secret handshake."

Mahiya laughed, and it was the laughter one shared with a friend. Elena was consort to an archangel, had access to power beyond imagining. She had no need to cultivate a relationship with Mahiya, and yet Mahiya knew why she did so. Not only because of an inherent kindness that had made her feel welcome from the first, but because Jason was one of "theirs."

Mahiya did not mind being adopted into such a family. There was joy here, loyalty, and best of all, no one wished to use her as a pawn in some political game. Oh, she had no doubts about Raphael's instincts, but she also knew the archangel would treat her with the courtesy due to the lover of one of his Seven.

Except she wasn't certain she was that lover, that her spymaster wasn't simply waiting for her to find her wings. *Don't go, Jason.* Words she'd never say, chains she'd never wrap around him, but oh, it hurt to think of never again feeling the rough heat of his touch, never again seeing that wild black fire in eyes of deepest brown.

Walking out of his study and onto the lawn, Jason by his side, Raphael headed for the edge of the cliff.

Hello, Archangel.

His lips curved. *Hello, hbeebti.* Glancing back over his shoulder, he saw his consort sitting on the roof with the princess Jason had brought home. The women had their faces turned toward one another, Elena's hair a white flame, Mahiya's ebony silk gathered neatly into a knot at the nape of her neck.

If he had ever considered the woman who would get through Jason's shields, it would not have been this elegant princess from Neha's land, with her flawless politeness and a personality that seemed a serene mirror without depth. And yet . . . Jason was his spymaster, skilled at seeing behind shields and beyond defenses. *What do you think of Jason's princess?* he said to his consort.

That she has a will of iron, that she loves Jason with all her heart—and that there is far more to her than either one of us will ever know, she said as he turned his attention back to Jason. *Nothing strange about that. Only you know all the pieces of me.*

As Elena knew him, he thought as he and Jason came to a halt on the cliff above the Hudson. So many discussions he'd had with his spymaster on this very spot—Jason didn't like being confined when he could be under the sky. "The princess," he said, "has sanctuary here as long as she needs it."

"Thank you, Sire, but I think she can safely live in the wider world." Jason settled his wings. "She'll have to be careful, but I am of the belief that threats aside, Neha is too proud to break her word. As for Mahiya's mother, it's a relationship she alone can learn to navigate."

Raphael agreed with Jason about Neha. The archangel wasn't mercurial like Michaela—honor meant a great deal to her, her own something she guarded. "Does the princess have somewhere to go?"

"Yes."

Raphael let the breeze brush his face, weave its fingers through his hair, and waited, knowing Jason had something else to say to him.

"Sire." Jason continued to look outward, toward Manhattan, his tone calm. "I release you from your promise."

Raphael had lived a millennium and a half, had memories strong and weak. He remembered the exact day each of his Seven had sworn fealty—Jason had been *so* young, and yet there had been a contained strength to him that had spoken to Raphael. He had known the boy would become a man of tempered steel. And he had known that steel had a fatal flaw.

"I ask only one promise for my service." Words Jason had said, his skin smooth and bare of the markings that

would begin to appear in another decade. *"I was not . . . formed correctly. Part of me is damaged and may one day shatter. When it does, I ask that you execute me cleanly rather than allow me to erode from the inside out."*

Raphael had never asked Jason about his past, but he had put the pieces together, understood that his spymaster had survived a childhood that would've left many too broken to function, and that he had scars that might never fade. Scars . . . and fractures. So he'd made that promise, and he had hoped never to keep it.

Now, a cool wind kissed his skin, his blood, the weight of the promise lifting from his shoulders. "I am glad of it, Jason."

He continued to look out over the water, and just when Raphael thought Jason might speak again, he gave a near imperceptible shake of his head and kept his silence. Raphael didn't know if Jason had found peace of a kind at last, or whether that peace was only a glimmer on the horizon, but he hoped the black-winged angel would never again have cause to seek such a promise from him.

For even an archangel could mourn.

Mahiya was in Elena's greenhouse, gazing in wonder at the lush yellow flowers of a plant with wide leaves of spring green, when the door opened. She didn't need to turn to know who stood in the doorway—her very skin seemed to sigh at his presence, her need for him a pulse deep within, for he had not touched her since before the battle. "I think this is my favorite place in all of this land I have yet seen." Everything bloomed with life here, and there were no hidden aspects, no subtle politics.

"You can have a garden now if you wish."

Her smile burst out of her. "Yes, I can, can't I?" It was a wonderful thought, and one she'd put into practice as soon as she found a place to call home. *Is your offer of a loan still open?* Though he'd been physically remote, she hadn't lost hope, for never once had he shut her out of his mind since the day he'd allowed her in.

Of course. "I have a house that may suit you until you decide otherwise," he added on the heels of the mental confirmation.

Turning, she leaned her back against the bench that held the pot with the yellow flowers, the plant waiting to be transplanted into the larger pot beside it. Jason stood just inside the doorway, his wings caressed by the curling green of a vine that poured from a hanging basket. He should've looked too hard, too dark for this place, but somehow, he fit.

Wild, she thought, he is as wild a thing as these plants. They were only temporarily tamed by the greenhouse—left on their own, they would sprawl and spread until the glass walls were a sea of green. Jason, too, was only tame when he wished to be, a storm held fiercely in check.

"Is the house vacant?" she asked this compelling mystery of a man who had once sworn a blood vow to her. No . . . wait. "Jason, who releases the blood vow?" His task had been for Neha, but it was Mahiya's blood through which the vow had been made.

He went so motionless, she could almost believe he was not there. "The party to whom it is made."

"Oh, I didn't know. Then I release you." She didn't want him tied to her by a forced bond of any kind. "Is that all I need to say to do so?"

"Yes." His stillness didn't abate. "Caretakers alone live on the property," he said, answering her earlier question. "Trusted vampires recommended to me by Dmitri—they would be glad to see the house come alive again. They prefer to make their home in a separate building, but it's mere seconds away on foot."

"The property, is it nearby?" The gleaming city across from the Enclave wasn't right for her, but she didn't want to be so far from it that she couldn't nurture the fledgling friendships she'd made—with Elena, with a vampire named Miri who worked in the Tower, but who had been at the

Angel Enclave house several times this past week. For a woman who had never been free to have friends, these were cherished gifts.

"Three hours of flight at an average pace, ninety minutes if you push yourself," Jason said. "It's a large estate, enough that no one will be able to come upon you without running afoul of the security system but not so isolated that you need ever be alone should you wish for company."

It sounded perfect, but she had expected no less from the best spymaster in the Cadre, the man who knew people better than they knew themselves. But, did Jason know himself? Lips curving, she crossed the distance to him, put her hands against his chest, unsure of herself and of him in this new place, but unwilling to surrender the claim she'd made.

His arm came around her without hesitation, his fingers splaying on her lower back. "Do you wish to see the house?"

"Yes." It felt so good to be near him again. "I am falling ever further in debt to you."

"This is no debt, Mahiya." His hand moved in a gentle circle on her back. "Not between us."

Her heart kicked, and she wanted to snatch at his words, force him to explain himself, but such demands would never work with this man. "No," she said, "you must allow me to repay you in some way until I have the funds to clear the loan." She pushed off his chest just enough that she could look up into his face. "My home will be yours, so long as you wish it to be."

A flicker in his eyes, but his response was a quiet incline of his head, an acceptance.

The wickedness in her, born of the same will that had kept her personality her own all these years, stretched awake after a lifetime of restraint. "Since I will not have enough money to repay any loan for years, perhaps I'll beg your indulgence with sensual favors."

Darkness shadowing his face, his hand falling away to leave her bereft. "I would not ask such of you."

Laughing, she cupped his face. "Jason, I'm teasing you." She had never initiated a kiss, but encouraged by the way he'd returned her touch, she did so now, sipping and tasting at those firm, beautiful lips until he held her again. "Any sensuality I share with you is freely given, and always will be."

He pressed her closer to his body with the hand he had on her lower back, his free hand rising to angle her chin exactly as he liked, and then he took control of the kiss, stroking his tongue against her own in a caress that made her toes curl, the black fire of him a dark, beautiful thing. *You should not tease me so, Mahiya.*

Someone must. Heart racing at the sinful perfection of him, she tucked her feet between his boots in an effort to get closer and asked a question she felt too shy to do so out loud. *Is the estate isolated enough that we can dance?*

A fine, fine tremor slivered through Jason's powerful frame. *No. But I know a place that is.*

Good. Because she wanted to dance with her spymaster, the sensual erotic dance of angelic lovers that was part courtship, part a test of strength and skill, and—if done right—all pleasure. Never before had she trusted anyone enough to share herself in that way. *I cannot wait to tangle wings with you, Jason.*

Breaking the kiss, a hint of color on his cheekbones, Jason said, "I've created accounts in your name and transferred the funds you'll need to get on your feet." His tone was stripped of tenderness . . . but he continued to press her against him, his wings curved in protective display around her until all she saw was lush black. "The debt isn't due until you feel able to repay it, at an interest rate of zero percent."

"Jason!" Laughing, she fisted her hands against his chest. "That is the most terrible loan I ever heard of—you will lose on every account."

Jason's expression was solemn. "No, I won't. Because so long as you owe me a debt, I will have a home."

Everything in her went quiet, even her pulse, time itself standing still. "Then," she whispered in a voice raw with love, "it is a debt I will never repay."

Before he'd spoken, before she'd understood the depth of his need, she would've insisted on repaying the loan to the last cent as a sign of her independence. Now she knew this wasn't about money or about controlling her. Jason had had centuries to accumulate wealth. It meant little to him beyond the practical.

But a home?

That, he hadn't had since he buried his mother. Neither had she, the fort no safe haven for her. So she grasped what it meant to him to have a home, understood, too, that he needed the unambiguous link created by the debt.

One day, she thought, he wouldn't need that tie any longer, would come to accept he would always be welcome in the place that was *their* home. Then they'd laugh over her long overdue debt, and perhaps she would tease her black-winged angel about having allowed a wet-behind-the-ears princess to tie him to such a terrible deal.

Until then, she would just love him. "Let's go home."

45

The estate Jason took her to was a vast sprawl of greenery broken up by wild bursts of color, the house of gray stone set within a multitude of gardens that had been allowed to run wild, the caretakers having far too much to do to wrangle the plants.

"Oh!" Delighted, she touched her fingers to a dew-kissed amber rose flowering defiantly without regard to season. "This is wonderful!" Already, she could begin to imagine their new life here. "Oh, Jason, the house is perfect." No massive palace or mansion, just a dual-storied building meant to be a home, the stones warm in the lazy late-afternoon sunshine.

The caretakers' residence, created of the same lovely stone, sat at a right angle to the house. "I must see everything!"

Jason didn't smile, not so anyone could've seen it, but she felt his joy in the way he followed quiet and unhurried at her back while she explored the gardens. As yet, she didn't know what she would do with her freedom—though she had a few ideas, excitement bubbling in her veins at the endless possibilities.

Turning to Jason, she admitted a secret. "I always loved the horses Neha kept."

While angels could not comfortably ride horses, they could and did admire the beautiful, strong animals, and kept them not only for the vampires under their command, but as pets and to use in races run against the stables kept by other immortals. Mahiya had studied the subject for many years, because while Neha had taken away the mare she'd called her own, the one thing the archangel had not begrudged her was learning.

"Maybe, once I'm settled, I could set up some stables." She'd start small, become a student again. "When I know more, I could try breeding them, but until then, I could offer to care for the horses of those vampires and angels who have no place for their pets in nearby cities." Immortals could be leery about trusting their horseflesh to mortals, as unfair as that might be. "Do you know of anyone else who offers the same?"

"No."

"Good." Being a custodian of animals would not be considered an exalted position by those of her kind, but what need had she of such a thing? No, she wanted only to live a life full of joy. She squeezed Jason's arm. "It'll be a glorious start to an eternity I can't wait to live." With this man who made her heart beat and the future seem a dazzling promise.

Taking her hand, Jason tugged her around the corner to the back of the house, across the relatively tame herb garden . . . and to the stables beyond. Stables that had been cleaned and repaired until they were ready and waiting for use. Tears burned in her eyes. *I shall have to work very hard to surprise you, spymaster.*

You surprise me every day.

She somehow knew it was her love that surprised him, that he did not expect it, could not quite understand it.

Swallowing her tears, she brought up their clasped hands and rubbed her cheek against the back of his. *Will you stay?*
   Yes.

Though the caretakers, both six-hundred-year-old vampires, were reserved in their joy, their delight at having the house become a home was clear. Jason watched as Mahiya won their loyalty with her quiet warmth and openness of heart, and he knew the dangerous pair—trained in high-level offensive and defensive skills—would watch over her when he had to be away. For a spymaster could not always stay in one place, and he wondered if Mahiya would understand that.

That, however, was a question for another day. Tonight, he dined with a princess who seemed to see no lack in him and who understood the words he didn't, couldn't, speak. Having already given the caretakers the night off, he and Mahiya played in the kitchen like children . . . until he kissed the nape of this woman who looked at him with love so bright, he could almost believe it wouldn't end in pain. She shivered, her body melting into his.

Knowing Mahiya wouldn't be comfortable outside the closed doors of their bedroom—and it was *their* bedroom; she'd made that clear by quietly moving his small bag from another suite—he kissed her again before leading her up the stairs and inside. The caretakers had pulled the curtains before they left, but the stars burned through the skylight.

Shutting the doors behind himself, he stayed in place. *Will you?*

Her skin flushed and she ducked her head, before walking to the vanity and slipping off the bangles of jade green glass leavened with gold he'd bought for her from the same shop where she'd purchased several sets of new clothing, having come to New York with nothing but what she wore. He'd forgotten to pick up her bag from the temple where she'd dropped it, he'd been so desperate to get to her, make sure she was safe.

Bangles clinking onto the vanity, she removed the simple gold hoops in her ears. A slow, deep breath as she shifted away from the mirror, her back to him, and reached up to undo the buttons at the top of her wings that held up a simple tunic of pure black embellished with green and silver embroidery along the mandarin collar. As he watched with a quiet possessiveness that built until it was a primal hunger within, she pushed off the tunic, even as she reached back to undo her hair to create a tumbling curtain of ebony.

Her legs were sleek and graceful when she pulled off the narrow tapered pants of a rich, deep green. Rising to her full height, she gathered her hair over her left shoulder in a move that sent a tide of color over her skin . . . and he saw she'd taken off her last fragile piece of clothing when she removed her pants, the evocative beauty of her wings her only protection.

Breathing jagged and body rigid, he closed the distance between them to run one hand down the centerline of her back and around her hip to splay on her navel. When she whispered his name, he lavished a kiss over the rapid beat in her throat. *Thank you, princess.*

Picking her up in his arms to her soft gasp, he carried her to the bed and laid her on her back, her wings spread in magnificent display. Her eyes slid away, hot red dusting her cheekbones, but though she fisted her hands in the sheets, she didn't attempt to cover herself. And when he began to undo the buttons of his shirt, those eyes returned to watch him with an anticipation that was a caress across his senses.

By the time he covered her body with his own, the need inside him was a craving that pulsed in every inch of his skin. Nudging her thighs apart, he settled between the silken limbs that slid around to lock at his back, a sweet, hot prison he had no desire to escape. He felt her slickness on his cock as she arched toward him, grit his teeth against the urge to surge into her. No matter how much he wanted to seal the bond between them in this new place with an act intimate and honest, he would not hurt her. *Mahiya?*

I'm ready. She opened to his kiss without hesitation. *Come inside me, Jason. I miss you.*

Shuddering with hunger so deep it was painful, he took her at her word and began the slow, exquisite slide into her body. Her spine arched, her pleasure a living current that burned sensation over every inch of him, her hands gripping his arms, her legs keeping him captive.

Oh!

He buried himself to the hilt inside her as her passionate cry reverberated through his bones, his mouth demanding on her own. She gave him everything he asked for, and she made her own demands in turn—subtle, feminine demands a man had to pay careful attention to hear, to sense, and that gave Jason a violent pleasure to fulfill.

Stroking his hand down the curves of her body, he cupped the back of one sleek thigh and rocked against her, pulling out a bare inch before pushing back in. She broke the kiss to suck in a breath, her head twisting on the pillow as her body undulated in perfect rhythm with his own, as if they had always been meant to be lovers.

When he fisted his fingers in her hair and retook her mouth, her hands slid over his nape to close over the sensitive arches of his wings in a caress that made him groan, her tongue dueling with his own. He pulled out a fraction more, rocked in harder, her breasts rubbing against his chest in sweet temptation.

Breaking the kiss, he rose up on an elbow and cupped one of the sensitive mounds. *You are beyond lovely.*

"I happen to think I'm not the pretty one in this bed, wild lover-mine." Husky, breathless words.

He held her cat-bright gaze, rubbed her nipple, once more tasted those lips that shaped such sweet words. Words that entangled, marked him, claimed him. Jason allowed the entangling, the marking, the claiming. For the first time in his life since he'd buried his mother and destroyed what remained of his father, he allowed himself to belong to someone.

Then he loved her.

"I can't create light," Jason said to Mahiya sometime later as he lay on his back with her spread possessively over him, his hand on her lower back. "Only black fire."

Frowning, Mahiya pushed up on the muscled silk of his chest to look at him. "Of course you can—you lit up the tunnels."

A long, steady look.

Her mouth fell open. "Me? That was me?"

"You're very strong, Mahiya Geet, and that strength will only grow. You must work on learning every aspect of your power."

Astonished and pleased, she sat up cross-legged beside him, her hair covering her breasts. "Will you help me?" It was so easy to ask him—she knew he'd never seek to hurt or humiliate her.

"Yes," he said, placing his hand on her lower back again, strong and hot. "And when I'm not here, I will ask the others in the Seven to come by as often as they can, so your development does not suffer. Raphael, too, is apt to take it upon himself to check on your progress."

That, she hadn't expected, but then, Raphael and Jason had a relationship unlike any she'd seen Neha have with her courtiers and advisors. "I suppose I shall have to become used to having the most powerful of visitors." Butterflies in her stomach, born of happiness not worry.

"After I've had time to settle in," she said, "and Dmitri has returned with his wife, we should invite our friends for dinner." She rather thought she would like to do such things, would like to have their home filled with the laughter of friends who were family. "Elena will enjoy the gardens."

Jason moved his hand to play with strands of her hair, his knuckles brushing the tip of her breast with each pass. "We'll have to have two such dinners," he murmured, continuing with the lazy caresses that made indolent pleasure curl through her veins. "They can't all be out of the city at the same time."

"I knew that," she said with a laugh, because they both knew she hadn't considered it. "There's so much I have to learn and explore, Jason." Excitement bubbled like champagne in her blood.

Coming up over her as she dropped back onto the bed, Jason pushed the sheet gently to her waist, his fingers making a swirling design on her hipbone that rippled a shiver over her frame. "If you ever decide," he said quietly, "that you wish to explore other—"

She pressed her fingers to his lips, held that storm-dark gaze. "I may have been stuck in the fort, but I wasn't cut off from the world. Thousands of vampires and angels of all ages and levels of power passed through it in the years of my existence. *Not one* spoke to my heart." Moving her hand, she cupped his face. "I know the man with whom I want to grow, want to explore the world. You. Only you." She would have no misunderstanding on that point. "And I plan to seduce you so thoroughly, you will become my devoted slave."

Jason's lips curved in the most subtle of smiles, and it was a kick to her heart, a treasure beyond price. *Who is to say I am not already your slave, princess?* Tender amusement in her mind. *After all, here I lie, my body ravaged by your passion.*

Laughing softly in delight at the fact that her spymaster was teasing her in return, she reached up to trace the swirling black of a tattoo that spoke of lands of white sand and blue seas, palm fronds waving in a balmy breeze while seagulls fought overhead and jewel-bright fish darted in the shallows. "Will you tell me the story of this one day?" she asked in the intimate murmur between lovers as he settled himself between her thighs once more, his weight braced on his forearms.

"It was to remind me I was alive," he said, the words stark. "I felt so little a part of the world at times that I wasn't certain I wasn't a shadow in truth, a phantom who made no impact, had no place. The pain, and the indelible mark of that pain, told me I lived, that I was a person."

Angry sadness twisted within her, but rather than darkness, she gave him a smile. "Well," she said, rubbing her foot over his calf, "next time you want to feel alive, come home and drag me into a bedroom." She nuzzled at his throat, her skin flushing. *I can't believe I just said that. Truly, I am becoming shameless where you are concerned. It is most disturbing.*

Bending his head, his hair sliding around his face as his body slid into her own, Jason said, *I won't tell,* his quiet laughter more precious to her than a million faceted gemstones.

Epilogue

Mahiya had always known Jason would have to leave—a spymaster could not remain in one place. Though he'd done very well to have information at his fingertips the past two weeks they'd spent entangled with one another as they set up their home.

"Neha and Nivriti appear to be holding their truce for the time being," he'd told her a week ago. "It's impossible to predict what either one will do—theirs is a unique battle."

"Yes." Mahiya had seen the love behind the hate, seen the need to touch behind the need to annihilate. "I wonder if deep down, they didn't want to kill one another, if that's why they both ended up injured but alive."

"Yes."

Now, seven days after that conversation, her lover stood waiting to take his leave, heading to parts unknown for how many days, she did not know.

"I may not be able to contact you every day," he said, the man who had woken her with a kiss this morning buried beneath the obsidian steel of the spymaster. "But I will as often as I can—and should you not be able to get in touch with me, call Raphael or any of the Seven. Or if you're more comfortable speaking to the women, Elena and Jessamy will both be able to get their hands on any relevant information."

This man, she thought as he spoke, would never tell her he loved her, would never give her flowers and pretty romance. He might never even admit either to her or to himself that she mattered to him in a way that was no simple sensual connection but a heart bond that made her chest ache.

But, what did she need of words and flattery? She'd grown up around lies and illusions, whispers and insinuations, the thousand intrigues and romances of a living court. Eris had said he loved Neha over and over, and he'd told Nivriti the same thing.

No, words did not matter to Mahiya, never would.

"I know," she said to Jason's instruction. "I have everyone's numbers." Putting her hands on his shoulders, she rose on tiptoe to claim a kiss to hold her until his return. "I'll miss you while you're gone," she whispered against his lips afterward. "And if you don't take care of yourself, I'll be most displeased."

His fingers spread on her lower back, his head bent over her own. "I'll return home as soon as I can."

Tears clogged her throat at his acceptance that this was his place now, his haven. Stepping back, she twined her fingers through his. "I'll walk you to the edge of my hill." It was a joke, the rolling hillock of land barely deserving of the name, but she'd insisted on calling it that—until she'd woken up two days ago to find a neatly carved wooden sign on it, proclaiming the rise "Mahiya's Hill."

It made her smile and fall impossibly deeper in love with him each time she saw it.

Jason's wing brushed hers as they walked through the gardens, the wild roses scenting the air in sultry perfume, the sunlight warm on her face. Her mother lived and was a lethal creature she didn't wholly understand. Neha might yet plunge her region into war. Lijuan was stirring again, and darkness shadowed the horizon.

And yet this moment, it was perfect.

All too soon, they were at the edge of the silly little hill, and Jason's fingers slipped from her own. Neither of them spoke as he spread his wings and took off, his feathers shimmering jet in the sunlight, his strength magnificent. Instead of rising high up above the cloud layer as he usually did, he did a wide sweep above her . . . and then she heard it.

A voice so pure, it had no match. So clear and exquisite that the birds went silent and the wind sighed, held in thrall. Her heart, it twisted and broke, reformed, the ache so deep, it had no end and no beginning. She didn't know she'd gone to her knees, was crying, until salt water seeped into her mouth.

"The only songs in my heart were ones that made the Refuge drown in tears. So I stopped."

This song was not meant for the Refuge. It was meant for Mahiya. And the tears she shed, they carried no sadness. Because she'd been wrong. Her wild storm had just told her he loved her, the piercing joy of his song branding her as indelibly his.

I'll be home soon, princess.

Author's Note

Archangel Fort and Guardian Fort were inspired by the incredible forts in Rajasthan, India, most particularly the forts known as Amber and Jaigarh. While the Palace of Jewels does not exist (as far as I know!), the Sheesh Mahal, or Mirror Palace, very much does. Part of Amber Fort, the Sheesh Mahal has thousands of tiny mirror fragments worked into its walls. It's said to be a magical vista in candlelight, the light reflected in every fragment. I saw it under sunlight, and it was a stunning sight I'll never forget.

For photos of my trip to Rajasthan, including snapshots of Amber and other forts, please visit my travel diary at www.nalinisingh.com/diary.php.

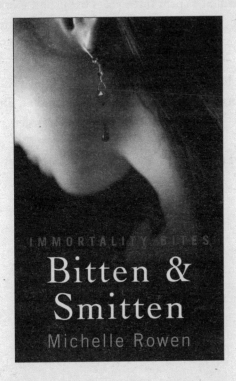

Nalini Singh was born in Fiji and raised in New Zealand. She spent three years living and working in Japan, and travelling around Asia before returning to New Zealand.

She has worked as a lawyer, a librarian, a candy factory general hand, a bank temp and an English teacher, not necessarily in that order.

Learn more about her and her novels at:
www.nalinisingh.com